Round Up
the Usual
Peacocks

ALSO BY DONNA ANDREWS

Round Up the Usual Peacocks

A Meg Langslow Mystery

Donna Andrews

MINOTAUR BOOKS

NEW YORK

First published in the United States by Minotaur Books, an imprint of St. Martin's Publishing Group

www.minotaurbooks.com

Library of Congress Cataloging-in-Publication Data

Names: Andrews, Donna, author.
Title: Round up the usual peacocks / Donna Andrews.
Description: First edition. | New York : Minotaur Books,
    2022. | Series: Meg Langslow Mysteries ; 31 |
Identifiers: LCCN 2022009073 | ISBN 9781250760203 (hardcover) |
    ISBN 9781250760210 (ebook)
Classification: LCC PS3551.N4165 R68 2022 | DDC 813/.6—
    dc23
LC record available at https://lccn.loc.gov/2022009073

Our books may be purchased in bulk for promotional, educational, or business use. Please contact your local bookseller or the Macmillan Corporate and Premium Sales Department at 1-800-221-7945, extension 5442, or by email at MacmillanSpecialMarkets@macmillan.com.

First Edition: 2022

10 9 8 7 6 5 4 3 2 1

Chapter 1

Tuesday, May 10

"We need more peacocks!"

I glanced up from my notebook-that-tells-me-when-to-breathe, as I call my combination to-do list and calendar. Dad was standing just inside the back door. He wore elbow-length white leather gauntlets and a pith helmet with heavy netting thrown back to reveal his face. His beekeeping outfit.

"If you're looking for peacocks in the beehives, that's probably why you're not finding any," I said. "The pair you gave us for Christmas tend to hang out at the far end of Rose Noire's herb field."

"I know," Dad said. "I was tending the hives when I noticed them. They've lost all their feathers."

"It's called molting," I said. "I hear they do it every year."

"Well, I know that." He knocked some mud off his garden boots and clomped over to sit across the kitchen table from me. "I've already called Clarence Rutledge."

I looked down at my notebook. I was up earlier than I liked and had a busy day ahead of me—busier than usual, thanks to all the things Mother had asked me to take care of in preparation for my brother Rob's upcoming wedding to Delaney, his fiancée, now only a few days away. Then I glanced up at the clock. Already eight o'clock. Which said everything about how I expected my day to go. Most mornings I'd have said "only eight o'clock." But if there was something wrong with our peacocks . . .

I took a deep breath, closed my notebook, and gave Dad my full attention.

"I thought molting was a natural process," I said. "Why would they need the services of a vet to deal with it?"

"Because it's much too early!" He began pulling off the gauntlets. "What if it's not normal molting? What if they've developed a skin condition that causes them to shed their feathers prematurely? They could be sickening with something dire!"

"Then Clarence will take care of them," I said. "Relax."

"But the same thing is happening to our flock over at the farm!" he exclaimed. "You realize what that means, don't you?"

"That maybe this is when our peacocks like to molt?" I suggested. "It could be a genetic thing—they're all related, you know. Maybe they're congenital early molters."

"It means we won't have any peacocks for the wedding reception!"

I closed my eyes. I didn't take the time to count to ten—I just took another of the deep, calming yoga breaths my cousin Rose Noire always recommended.

"Actually, we'll have plenty of peacocks available for the reception," I said. "They just won't be very decorative. We can pen them up someplace out of sight that day."

"But your mother will be devastated! She wants peacocks!"

"She'll be disappointed, yes." Why was he getting so agitated about this? Normally if one of our peacocks were ill—or any of the rest of our growing menagerie—he'd have been overjoyed at the chance to work with Clarence on the diagnosis and cure. "I don't think she'll quite be devastated. And frankly, I doubt if Rob and Delaney are all that keen on the peacock idea."

"But they've left the planning to your mother," Dad said. "And she wants peacocks. Strolling around the yard during the reception."

"Adding a note of grace and elegance to the occasion." Did he realize I was quoting what Samantha, Rob's first fiancée, had said so often when we were planning her wedding? The wedding that, thank goodness, had ended with her running off with one of the groomsmen, leaving Rob free to marry Delaney all these years later. I remembered that long-ago failed wedding with a certain fondness, since it had played a major role in bringing Michael and me together. But surely Rob wouldn't want anything at this weekend's happy event to remind him of that narrow escape.

Of course, it was always possible that Rob had forgotten how our family's tradition of owning peacocks began. Or that he'd never known they were Samantha's idea. I didn't plan to bring it up.

"I'm going to go home to look in my files," Dad said. "I need to see if I can locate some peacocks we can borrow. Or even rent, if it comes to that. Clarence will be here shortly to examine yours. If I'm not back by the time he gets here can you—"

"I'll see to it."

"Great!" Dad picked up his gauntlets and dashed out the back door, clearly in a much better frame of mind now that he'd delegated the peacocks' medical needs to me.

I had only just opened up my notebook when my cousin Rose Noire floated in. She was wearing one of her loose, flowered gardening smocks over pastel pink shorts, reminding me that even though it was only eight in the morning, it was already warm outside. The thermometer was supposed to hit ninety by afternoon, which was beastly hot, especially for May.

"What was your dad so upset about?" she asked.

"The peacocks," I said. "Evidently they're molting."

"Yes, poor things." She set her wicker herb basket on the kitchen table. I took a cautious sniff—her herbs weren't always fragrant—then inhaled deeply. Today's crop seemed to be mostly lavender.

Rose Noire was always saying how lavender calmed the mind and stimulated creative thought. It seemed to be working well on me today—I had a sudden inspiration.

"Clarence Rutledge is coming over soon to check out the peacocks," I said. "Can you liaise with him about it? If—"

"Of course." She beamed approval at me, so I decided not to mention that it was Dad who'd called for the vet. "It must be a stressful time for the poor things. If Clarence likes the idea, I can do several things to help them through it. Some essential oils in their coop, and a nice herbal salve for their skin."

I wondered if she had in mind the same nice herbal salve she applied to our llamas when they had minor cuts and scrapes. It seemed to do the trick—the injuries healed rapidly and without any complications. But the salve smelled like rotten eggs cooked in garlic with a dash of eau de skunk. Whenever I caught a whiff, I felt thankful that we'd built the llama pen at the far end of our yard. If she daubed that stuff on the peacocks, they'd be doubly unwelcome at the wedding reception.

Not my problem. And I could absolutely trust her with the health and well-being of the peacocks.

"Great," I said. "I appreciate it. I have rather a lot of wedding tasks to get done today if I want to stay in Mother's good graces."

"I'll go out and wait with the peacocks until Clarence arrives." She rose and floated out—taking the wicker basket with her, to my disappointment. But at least some of the scent remained.

I looked at my notebook and was just starting to plan out my day when—

"Hey, Meg."

I looked up to see my nephew Kevin emerging from his lair in our basement.

"Hey, Kevin," I said. "What's up?"

"You're just the person I was looking for." He leaned against the doorframe. "I could use your help."

"Is this something about the wedding?" I asked. "Because right now I don't have a whole lot of time for anything else."

"Well," he said. "It's not about the wedding."

I looked back down at my notebook.

"But it could affect the wedding," he added. "Big-time."

"And not, I gather, in a good way." I closed my notebook, leaned back, and fixed him with what my twin sons called my visibly patient expression—the one that told them they should just spit out what they were hemming and hawing over.

"It's about the podcast," Kevin said, as if that explained everything. When I didn't react, he frowned and went on. "You knew we started a podcast, right? I mean—do you know what a podcast is?"

"Kind of like a radio show, only it comes to you over the internet instead of through the airwaves," I said. "I know what a podcast is. I've even listened to a few. I didn't know you had one, though. What's it about?" I didn't think I needed to add, "And what does it have to do with the wedding?"

"We're doing true crime," Kevin said.

Odd. I'd never before noticed Kevin to be particularly interested in true crime. Was this another side effect of Dad's obsession with reading mysteries and his enthusiasm for getting involved in real-life murder investigations? Were his interests rubbing off on my nieces and nephews as well as my sons?

"So who's the 'we' you're doing it with?" I asked. "Your grandfather?"

"No." He shook his head. "Although we figured we could probably use Grandpa as a resource sometimes. You know, like helping us understand the medical stuff. We haven't asked him yet, though. It's me and my friend Casey. He's like a total true-crime geek. You want to know about any true crime, whether it's an ancient one like Jack the Ripper or the latest cases, Casey's your guy. He's the subject matter expert, and I do all the tech stuff—although I have to admit, I'm kind of getting into the case stuff."

"Your grandfather will be thrilled." In fact, his grandfather would probably insist on getting involved, whether Kevin and Casey wanted him to or not. "So what's the name of your podcast?"

"*Virginia Crime Time.* We sort of specialize in cases that take place in Virginia, or at least have a strong connection to Virginia. And Casey's particularly interested in cold cases— you know, the cases where it hasn't been solved but there still might be a chance of solving it. Calling the guilty to account—getting justice for the victims."

That was a little reassuring—that they had some socially responsible motive for their podcasting—or had at least thought up one for publicity purposes.

"Sounds interesting," I said. "Send me a link and I'll give it a listen. But why do you need my help? And for what? And what could it possibly have to do with Rob and Delaney's wedding?"

"We have a problem." Kevin frowned and glanced down at the kitchen floor as if gathering his thoughts. Then he looked up, visibly steeled himself, and went on. "We think maybe we've stirred up something. Like maybe someone connected with one of our cases doesn't want us investigating it. I know it sounds crazy, but hear me out."

Actually, it didn't strike me as the least bit crazy. Unless their definition of cold case was a lot different from mine, they were investigating unsolved crimes. Crimes whose perpetrators might still be at large, and willing to do anything necessary to stay that way. And if they were focusing on Virginia cold cases, those unidentified perpetrators might not be all that far away. Hadn't they considered this before starting their podcast?

"Chief Burke thinks it's just an accident," Kevin went on. "But a couple of nights ago, when Casey was walking home from our usual Saturday night Dungeons & Dragons game, this car almost ran over him."

"Caerphilly's full of tourists this time of year," I pointed out. "They do some pretty stupid, careless, even dangerous things."

"No argument there. But they don't tend to be out at two in the morning. And they don't usually lurk in alleys and then gun their engines and try to run someone down. With no headlights. And when they do something dangerous and stupid, they usually drive away—they don't make U-turns in the middle of the street and come back for a second try."

"All good points," I said. "And the chief thinks it's an accident?"

"Casey got the impression the chief thought he was letting his imagination run away with him. Or that he was intoxicated. Which he wasn't. He'd had a couple of beers. Enough that he decided to walk home instead of driving, since it was only half a mile. Not enough to make him hallucinate. And even if the chief does investigate, he seems to think it was some kind of college prank. Or that he'll find out who did it by investigating Casey's enemies, which will be pretty useless, because as far as I know, Casey doesn't have any. He doesn't get out much."

Coming from Kevin, who seldom voluntarily emerged from his computer-filled lair in our basement, that was saying something. Casey must be some kind of hermit.

"So what do you want me to do?" I asked. "Talk the chief into taking a serious look at your theory that someone tried to off Casey because of your podcast?"

"Well, that would be nice, but even if he did, I'm not sure it's his kind of case," Kevin said. "We want you to tackle it. Figure out which of our cases this is connected to."

I looked at my notebook, which was bulging with wedding-related tasks.

"Kevin," I said. "It's not that I don't want to help you. Really. But why do you need *me*? You're the expert at finding information online. Why can't you just do your usual thing and figure this out yourself?"

Kevin looked uncomfortable.

"I've been trying," he said. "I've spent the last few days doing nothing else. I've pretty much exhausted what I can find out online. I think solving this is going to take someone going out and, like, talking to people. In person."

So very much not Kevin's thing.

"Okay," I said. "I get it. But can't it wait a few more days—until the wedding's over?" Or better yet, until the wedding was over and I'd had a few days to recover.

Kevin looked . . . even more uncomfortable? No. More like guilty.

"I'm worried," he said. "I mean what if they come after us here? It's not exactly a big secret that we're podcasting out of your basement. Well, out of someone's basement—we kind of joke about that. We've been careful not to say whose basement, but if someone came to town and asked around, they could figure it out. Plus thanks to the wedding, there are so many more people around, and we don't know a lot of them. What if whoever tried to run over Casey uses all the wedding stuff as cover to make another try at him? Or at me?"

I sighed. He had a point. We were holding the rehearsal dinner at the Caerphilly Inn—someone could easily sneak in as a hotel guest or employee. The wedding itself, at Trinity Episcopal, would be a little more private, but it wouldn't be hard for a would-be attacker to figure out when we were coming and going. And I had no idea how many waitstaff and other temporary helpers Mother had hired for the enormous wedding reception here at the house—where the collateral damage from an attack could include Josh, Jamie, and Michael, to say nothing of several hundred friends and relatives.

"Okay," I said. "I'll do what I can. But you're going to have to give me a lot more information. Do you have any idea which cold case might have provoked this?"

"Not really," he said. "Luckily the podcast's pretty new. We've only done thirteen cases so far."

Only thirteen? I think I uttered an audible groan.

"And at least half of them don't seem all that likely," Kevin went on hurriedly. "There's a couple of murder cases from the fifties, for example. Some of the people involved might still be alive, but I can't see some old geezer prowling around the alleys of Caerphilly trying to mow down pedestrians."

"Don't be so sure," I said. "Remember, 'Old age and treachery will always beat youth and exuberance.'"

"Yeah, right," Kevin said. "Shakespeare pegs it again."

"Actually, David Mamet," I said. "Okay—brief me on these cases. You've got files, right?"

Kevin nodded.

"Bring me your files," I said. "And load up all thirteen of your podcasts into my laptop—don't make me go looking for them."

"Roger. Thanks!" Kevin disappeared into the basement with uncharacteristic speed.

Chapter 2

I glanced down at my notebook. To my surprise, I wasn't dreading this project of Kevin's. Actually, it sounded a lot more interesting than most of the tasks on my agenda. Tasks I could delegate to someone else. Better yet, tasks I could give back to Mother. After all, I wasn't the one organizing this wedding. Mother was doing that, with the able assistance of Delaney's mother. I might be Mother's favorite minion, but she had plenty of others—minions who could take on most of the chores now filling my notebook.

"Here's what I put together for you." Kevin reappeared and set a foot-high stack of file folders on the table, followed by my laptop. "I printed it all out in case you'd rather read it in hard copy, but I put all the files on here, too. And if you want to listen to the podcasts, just click here." He pointed at an icon on the laptop screen. Peering at it, I could see that it was a tiny logo—a magnifying glass, with the words "Virginia Crime Time" appearing in the lens. "Or I could send a link to your phone."

Clearly he'd been expecting me to help him out. Or at least hoping.

"And I put the ones that seem most likely on top," he said, tapping the stack of files. "One here in Caerphilly, one in Clay County, and one down in Albemarle County."

"Let's start with the Clay County one." I held out my hand for the file. As a citizen in good standing of Caerphilly County, I was inclined—in fact, maybe even obligated—to suspect the residents of our benighted neighboring county.

"And it would help if you gave me the highlights of the cases."

"Okay."

Kevin handed me the file, and I flipped it open to meet the eyes of a young blond man staring out at me from a police mug shot. Not a situation in which anyone looks their best—I've seen relatively harmless people whose mug shots made them look like Hannibal Lecter's first cousin. But this guy managed to look reasonably presentable in spite of the circumstances. Lucas Plunkett. Of course—well over half of the Clay County phone book was dedicated to Plunketts, Dingles, Peebleses, and Whickers. But Lucas had made out better in the genetic lottery than most of his cousins. His features were regular, almost handsome. He looked like an ordinary clean-cut kid of eighteen or so.

"A lot more presentable than most of the dudes from Clay County," Kevin said. Was he reading my thoughts, or maybe my face? I made a mental note to check my bias against residents of Clay County. They weren't all bad. In fact, I'd met a few really nice people from Clay County. Unfortunately, none of them in positions of power. I focused back on Lucas Plunkett.

"What's he supposed to have done?" I asked.

"Robbed the filling station."

"*The* filling station?"

"There's only ever been one in Clay County," Kevin said. "So yeah, even most of the court documents just say *the* filling station. I don't know what brand it was. Probably one of those cheap off-brands, or they'd have mentioned it. Anyway, after emptying the register it occurred to him that the cashier might recognize him, since he was probably his third cousin once removed or something. So he pumped a couple of bullets into the guy and killed him and got ten years in the slammer."

I shook my head slightly. Lucas Plunkett certainly didn't fit my mental image of an armed robber and casual killer.

"When did this take place?" I asked.

"About five and a half years ago."

"So he's still in prison?" I groaned inwardly at the thought of having to interview a convict.

"No, it was a first offense, and he kept his nose clean and got out in a little over five years. He's back home in Clayville."

"Isn't five years a pretty short time to serve for murder?" I asked.

"His lawyer bargained it down to voluntary manslaughter," Kevin said. "And I gather for that, ten years is kind of a lot, especially for a first offense."

"Still seems short to me. For a human death."

Kevin shrugged, and I decided to save that question for someone who might know more. Chief Burke. Or maybe one of his officers, if I decided not to advertise my snooping to the chief.

"As a crime, this seems pretty ordinary," I said. "And over and done with. What made it worth a podcast? I thought you guys mostly focused on cold cases and wrongful convictions and stuff like that."

"We were having a hard time coming up with a case that week," Kevin admitted. "Casey had exams, and with Delaney going to be away on the honeymoon for two weeks, everyone at work has been slammed."

I nodded. Kevin, like Delaney, worked at Mutant Wizards, Rob's computer game and software company. I had no idea precisely what either of them did, but I knew they sometimes worked killer hours.

"Anyway, we were kind of reaching for something easy, and Casey had heard this rumor that Plunkett took the fall for someone else. A friend or relative who already had a bunch of convictions and wouldn't have gotten out as fast. Or might even have gotten the death penalty—Virginia still had that back then."

"Virginia still had it until 2021," I pointed out. "So your theory was that he took the fall for someone?"

"Yeah, or maybe was set up. He's not exactly hardcore Clay County. His mother was from someplace else and growing up he spent most of his time with her. If they were looking for a fall guy, he'd be someone they'd pick. So basically we just made a lot of noise about how inbred and backward the county was, and managed to give the impression that the local law enforcement was pretty stupid and corrupt without actually coming out and saying it."

"And you're surprised that maybe they came after you?"

"Well, yeah." He looked sheepish. "Maybe not the smartest move we've ever made. But still, the attack on Casey didn't really feel like something Clay County guys would do. It wasn't a truck—when was the last time you saw a bunch of good old boys from Clayville riding around in a Japanese compact? And they didn't take any shots at him, either."

"Good points," I said. "I'll look into the case."

Actually, I probably wouldn't do that much looking into it myself. Mother had nothing on me when it came to delegating.

"What else?" I reached for the second file. "You said you had a case in Caerphilly."

"Cheating scandal at the college," he said. "Twenty-six years ago."

"Before my time here, or Michael's," I said. "But I'm surprised I haven't heard about it."

"They did their best to hush it up. They expelled the students involved, and the professor who was helping them hung himself, so they didn't have much trouble keeping it quiet."

"Which department?" I was half expecting—and maybe even hoping—Kevin would say the English Department, whose feud with the Drama Department went back at least twenty years. Maybe it was petty of me, but as the wife of a tenured professor in the Drama Department I always felt a sneaking satisfaction when the English Department got into hot water.

"The business school," Kevin said.

"No wonder I haven't heard of it," I said. "They kind of stick to themselves. Which is fine with most of the rest of the college—I mean, who wants to hang out with a bunch of people who have zero interest in art, music, theater, literature, history, or science?"

"Why don't you tell me what you really think?" Kevin chuckled. "So the business school's almost as much hostile territory as Clay County?"

"I'll manage." The business school might not be friendly turf, but I'd been dealing with Caerphilly College academic politics for over a decade. I was pretty good at it. Michael was even better. "Were you just going over what was already known about the case, or did you invent a new angle, the way you did with the Clay County case?"

"We kind of raised the idea that maybe the professor who offed himself got framed," Kevin said. "Young idealistic guy who made a lot of waves. The kind of guy the old fogeys would be happy to get rid of."

"Please tell me you didn't try to blame the business school for his suicide," I said.

"Well, conspiracy theory goes down well with our listeners," Kevin said. "We kind of hinted that no one really knew."

"Lovely." Of course, the faculty of the business school were probably even less likely suspects for committing a hit-and-run than a bunch of good old boys from Clay County. Especially since whoever had been in charge then was probably long since retired. Still, Kevin and Casey clearly hadn't anticipated the possible danger of one of their subjects coming after them. Had they also ignored the risk of being sued for defamation if someone involved in a case didn't like how they covered it? I grabbed my notebook and jotted down "Check with Festus re podcasts." My cousin Festus Hollingsworth was a brilliant attorney, and it was usually to him we turned when any of the family got into trouble that involved bail or lawyers. And he was always delighted when anyone was proactive enough to ask for his advice before doing something stupid. I turned back to Kevin. "Any other promising cases?"

Kevin shuffled through his files for a minute, then pulled one out and handed it to me.

"The disappearance of Madeleine duPlaine."

The name sounded familiar—so familiar that I suppressed the impulse to ask who she was. Kevin obviously assumed I knew, or ought to, and I hated giving him any opportunities to say gotcha. So I flipped open the folder and nodded when I saw the top item—a photocopied flyer with the heading *Have you seen her?* over a large black-and-white photo of a young woman. The photo wasn't all that clear—it had obviously been blown up from a much smaller snapshot—but it still had power. You noticed the eyes first—enormous dark eyes. Then the narrow face, with its high cheekbones and thin, slightly aquiline nose. The long, straight black hair.

I'd seen that poster before, my first year at the University of Virginia. Seen copies of it all over Charlottesville—stapled to telephone poles, tacked up on bulletin boards in the dorms and academic buildings. Of course the outdoor posters were starting to fade by the time I'd seen them, and the indoor ones were being buried under newer flyers. I'd forgotten her name, but not the face.

"You know who she is, of course?" Kevin asked.

"Of course." My eyes were still fixed on the picture. "Up-and-coming young singer from Charlottesville. Disappeared the year before I went up to UVa. Did they ever figure out what happened to her?"

"No." He shook his head. "Case went totally cold. Still technically open, though, which meant we couldn't get much out of the Charlottesville cops. Local opinion's divided between the people who think she was killed by some crazy fan and the people who think she got cold feet about signing a record deal and ran off to hide in a convent or a Buddhist temple or something. Before your time, then? I was hoping you might actually know something about her. We drew a blank—couldn't find any recordings of her, just a bunch of people who said she was as good as Joan Baez or

Judy Collins or Cher or Whitney Houston or Mary Chapin Carpenter or whoever they thought was really great. They're probably just exaggerating."

No, they weren't exaggerating. I'd heard her sing once. The spring of my junior year of high school I'd gone up to check out UVa, staying with a cousin who studied there. The cousin had taken me to see duPlaine and her band at a local coffeehouse. "You can say you saw them before they were big," she'd said. After hearing them—hearing her—I hadn't doubted that they would be big. But by the time I got to Charlottesville, there was nothing left except for those flyers, gradually disappearing.

"You don't ask much," I said. "People have been trying to find her for years now. Her or proof that she's dead."

"You don't need to find her, alive or dead," he said. "You just need to check out whether there's any possibility that she—or someone who knew her—hated our podcast enough to come here and go after Casey."

I nodded. This case looked even less promising than the first two. But I felt a sudden surge of nostalgia. I'd have to go down to Charlottesville to check this one out. Maybe it wouldn't be bad, taking a trip down memory lane and seeing what I could learn.

"I'll see what I can do," I said. "But don't expect miracles."

"Don't sell yourself short." Kevin shot me a surprisingly broad smile. Then he frowned slightly as he saw me reach into my tote and pull out my headphones.

"I could give you a set of earbuds if you like," he said. "Unless you're deliberately going retro on account these being vintage cases."

"I'm deliberately going retro, as you call it, because earbuds hurt my ears." My tone sounded a little sharp, probably because I considered my brand-new wireless Bluetooth headphones the height of modernity. "Not to mention the fact that the minute I take out earbuds and put them down I lose the wretched little things."

"Cool, then. Whatever floats your boat." He turned and vanished into the basement.

I was about to plug my headphones into the computer when it occurred to me that if I just sat here in the kitchen listening to the podcasts, I'd look as if I was doing nothing. Not a good look, this close to the wedding to end all weddings. And for that matter, I'd probably get restless pretty soon. So I picked up my phone and called Mother.

Chapter 3

"Good morning, dear," Mother said. "I'm so glad you called."

"Morning," I said, cutting off what I was sure would be a request to take on a project. "Do you have any small errands that need running?"

"Well, yes, dear," she said. "But I'm sure I can find someone else to do them. I have more important things you could do if you have the time."

"I don't," I said. "In fact, I might need to hand back a few of the things you already asked me to do. But I can run errands. I'm doing something for Kevin that means I have to listen to a bunch of his podcasts—but I can run errands while I'm listening."

"Doing something for Kevin?" The slight brittleness in her tone suggested that while Kevin might be a beloved grandson, she was in no mood to tolerate his interference in something as profoundly important as the wedding preparations.

"Something that needs doing ASAP, to avoid problems that could affect the wedding arrangements." After mollifying her with that explanation I gave her a concise summary of the reaction the *Virginia Crime Time* podcast seemed to have stirred up, downplaying the idea that there was any real danger but stressing how concerned Kevin was to avoid any disruption to the wedding.

"A pity Kevin didn't wait until after the wedding to start this podcast thing of his," Mother said with a slight sniff.

"I'm sure if he'd realized it would cause problems, he would have." Which wasn't exactly the truth—Kevin was far more concerned about his and Casey's necks than the wedding. But it had the effect of calming Mother.

"Well, I suppose there's no help for it now." She sighed deeply. "And I suppose you're the best person to deal with it. But I really have a lot of work for the other volunteers to do today, so if you can squeeze in a few errands . . ." She began to rattle off a list of important but uncomplicated errands, and I scribbled the list into my notebook. I cut her off after half a dozen—they should give me plenty of time to listen to the three podcasts Kevin thought were most likely to have stirred up Casey's attacker. And after making me promise to check in with her for more as soon as my schedule allowed, she released me from wedding duty.

I forwarded the relevant podcasts to my phone and took my laptop and all of Kevin's papers out to the barn so I could lock them up in my office. I waved to Clarence, who had arrived and was hovering over the peacocks. Then I grabbed my Bluetooth headphones and took off. I listened to the Clay County murder and robbery podcast while fetching a box of place cards from the calligrapher, who lived at the far end of Caerphilly. I took in the podcast about the college cheating scandal while making a visit to the seamstress to drop off some bridesmaids' dresses requiring last-minute alterations and picking up more glue gun sticks at the craft store. Then I discovered that the third file I'd forwarded was the wrong one—instead of the melancholy tale of the missing singer I'd gotten Kevin and Casey's podcast on the 1980s' Colonial Parkway Murders. Well, if I struck out on the first three cases, I might end up poking into that one. And listening to it whiled away the time it took to fetch Dad's truck, round up our peacocks—who, though bedraggled, had received a clean bill of health—and ferry them over to Mother and Dad's farm so they'd be out of sight during the reception.

Actually, I turned off the podcast while rounding up the peacocks, since that proved to be a lot more work than

I expected. On top of being half-naked, they were both sopping wet, which always seemed to make their normally cranky temperaments even worse.

"It's your own fault, you know," I told the peahen when I finally got her to dash up the ramp and into the cage. "The door to your coop was open, and you could have gone inside to stay dry, instead of standing around in the yard all morning complaining."

Like most of my conversations with the peafowl, this discussion was rather one-sided.

Once I'd captured them both and gotten underway, I was relieved to find the Colonial Parkway podcast fact-filled and straightforward. By now I had gathered the general structure of their shows—Casey provided the facts, in a pleasant if slightly breathless voice, while Kevin contributed mostly by asking leading questions and providing snarky but amusing comments in his slower, deeper voice. The first two podcasts, on the filling station murder and the college cheating scandal, contained very few facts and a whole lot more Kevin, providing local color along with the snark. I'd be willing to bet that they'd run out of time to research those cases but covered them anyway, because they didn't have any other case anywhere near ready for prime time.

I was sitting in the truck in Mother and Dad's driveway, listening to the last few minutes of the podcast, when Dad showed up and tapped on the window.

"Great," I said. "You can help me unload the peacocks."

"Is something wrong?" His face was creased with concern. "You were just sitting there."

"Listening to something." I pointed to the headphones. "And frankly, I was bracing myself to deal with the peacocks. They're in a foul mood."

"Poor things," he said. "It's normal for them to be moody, even cranky, when they're molting. I know it's a natural process, but they look so unhappy. Still, there's good news!" His face lit up. "One of my peacock-raising friends is willing to lend us half a dozen birds—magnificent ones that are in no danger of molting by the weekend." He frowned and looked anxious. "But someone's going to have to fetch them—we can't expect a working farmer to make deliveries. And your mother has all sorts of things for me to do."

I suspected most of those things were busywork, designed to keep him miles away from anything Mother considered important, but you never knew.

"And just how far away are these magnificent peacocks?" I asked.

"Not that far," he said. "And you can use our farm truck. They're in Crozet. It's—"

"Near Charlottesville," I said. "I know. Actually, I think I can manage a trip to Crozet. I could do it tomorrow, as long as he's okay with having them picked up near the end of the day." I didn't fancy the idea of sleuthing while saddled with a truckload of peafowl.

Dad was jubilant, and offered to bring his truck over to our house tonight, so I wouldn't have to waste time picking it up in the morning. Or to let me keep it until tomorrow—an offer I declined. I much preferred driving the Twinmobile, as we called the SUV we'd acquired to haul around the boys and their many friends.

I reclaimed the Twinmobile with relief. If I was going to make a trip over to Charlottesville tomorrow, I had a lot to do today. For starters, I could go home and transfer the duPlaine podcast to my phone and listen to it. Maybe that would give me some vague idea of what I could look for in Charlottesville.

Then inspiration struck. I could consult Faulk, my old friend and blacksmithing teacher. He'd also attended UVa, but a couple of years ahead of me, which meant his time there had overlapped with Madeleine duPlaine's. And he'd lived in or near Charlottesville until he and his husband moved to Caerphilly a few years ago. He'd have heard whatever rumors went around town after her disappearance. Maybe I should plan to talk to him after I'd listened to the podcast. I pulled out my phone.

"Got time today for me to pick your brain about something?" I texted him.

I didn't expect an answer right away—Faulk didn't live on his cell phone like some people. So I pulled out my notebook and had been jotting down possible sleuthing angles on the other cases for several minutes when his reply came.

"If you can talk while I work," he said. "Out at Ragnar's all day today."

"See you this afternoon," I texted back. I decided that in addition to picking up the third podcast I should also drop by the police station before beginning my snooping. Kevin seemed convinced either that Chief Burke wasn't investigating the attempted attack on Casey at all, or that he wasn't taking the podcast seriously as a motive. I knew the chief didn't always show his cards. What if he was taking both the attack and the podcast connection very seriously and had already started investigating the same cold cases Kevin had steered me to? Probably a good idea to let him know what I was doing—and let him warn me off if I'd be stepping on his toes.

Back at the house, I found Mother in the front yard talking to a young woman whose loose tunic and faded jeans were both liberally daubed with smears and flecks of paint in every color imaginable. Was this some new fashion trend I hadn't heard about, or was she an artist of some kind? Both she and Mother were staring intently at the concrete walkway that led from the street to our porch. Mother glanced up when I drew near.

"Meg, dear." Mother grazed my cheek with a brief kiss. "This is Demetria, the pavement artist."

Demetria nodded briskly, her eyes still on the walkway.

"She's going to decorate your front walk," Mother said. "And the porch and—well, all the outdoor surfaces. For the wedding," she added, as if there could be any number of other occasions for which we might be decorating. "So the rain won't wash it away?" she asked, turning back to Demetria. "They're predicting more rain this afternoon."

"No." The artist shook her head. "It's completely permanent until I apply the removal formula. And completely
environmentally friendly," she added, glancing up at me as
if I'd made some objection—which I hadn't. I'd probably
frowned, but that was because I thought the idea of painting the sidewalk was pretty silly, not that I was worried about
its ecological consequences. "This is all regular paint," she
added, gesturing at her clothes. "I do all kinds of painting.
The paint I use on the pavement is completely removable."

"Of course," I said. "Carry on. I just hadn't heard that we
were decorating the sidewalks," I added, turning to Mother.
"And the grass should look a bit greener after tomorrow's
rain, so we don't have to worry about spray-painting it."

"No, probably not." Mother took her eyes from the walkway and was studying the grass with a slight, thoughtful
frown. I'd been joking about spray-painting the grass. Had
she been seriously considering it? Or had I just given her
another beautification idea?

I decided not to worry about it. My phone's weather app
showed the chances of rain later today at almost 100 percent. The grass would be fine.

"We could do both roses and lilies." Demetria pulled out a
small sketchbook and began drawing in it. Mother watched
intently, nodding slightly.

I watched with a feeling of unease. It wasn't that I had
anything against the sidewalk painting. But this was the first
I'd heard of it. And since the wedding preparations had increasingly dominated Mother's conversation for the last six
months, surely I would have heard of it if they'd been planning it for a while. The wedding seemed to be escalating
with every passing day. That worried me.

But since there wasn't much I could do about it, I left
them to it and went into the house.

Michael was standing with the hall closet door open, staring inside.

Chapter 4

"Looking for something?" I was wiping my feet, which were still wet from chasing the peafowl back and forth over the lawn.

"My bicycle helmet."

"It's on the top shelf on the left," I said, finally deciding to shed my damp shoes.

"That's where it's supposed to be," he said. "It's not there. Nothing's there."

I tucked my shoes under the coatrack and went over to look into the closet. He was right. It was completely empty.

"Maybe Mother's planning to paint the inside of the closet?" I mused. Surely Demetria didn't also do closets.

"This close to the wedding?" Michael asked.

Rose Noire bustled in.

"Oh, if you're looking for anything from the closet, I took everything up to people's own closets," she said. "And anything that didn't belong to anyone in particular I boxed up and took to the basement. Your mother wanted the closet empty, so there's plenty of room for the wedding guests' things."

With that she dashed out again. Michael sighed, and closed the closet door.

"It'll all be over in less than a week," I said.

"Have I remembered to thank you today?" Michael turned and headed upstairs. "For agreeing to elope instead of letting your mother plan a wedding?"

"You have." I followed him up the stairs. "But you can repeat it as often as you like. I'm not sure it would have been quite this bad. You're seeing two decades of pent-up unful-filled bridal planning."

"No, it would have been worse." He ambled into our bed-room and headed for the closet. "My mother would have been just as gung-ho as Delaney's mother is."

"But at least Delaney's mother is perfectly happy playing second fiddle to Mother," I said as I grabbed a pair of dry sneakers.

"Exactly," Michael said. "Whereas Mom would have tried to take charge. She'd have butted heads with your mother. And on top of working you to death, they'd have tried to get you to take sides."

"You'll be happy to know that I've found a way to weasel out of helping with the wedding preparations today," I said. "Kevin's started a podcast—had you heard?"

"No," Michael said. "About tech stuff?"

"True crime," I said. "And the friend he's doing it with almost got run over Saturday night, so now they're both con-vinced one of their cold cases isn't so cold after all. He wants me to help him investigate whether anyone connected to one of the cases is still alive and spry enough to come after them."

"Just don't let him talk you into anything dangerous," he said.

"Two of the cases are over twenty years old," I said. "I plan to start by talking to the chief and letting him discourage me if he thinks there's any real danger. And you can help me out—what do you know about the Caerphilly College Business School?"

"As little as I can get away with knowing," Michael said. "They're basically philistines. Don't quote me on that, of course."

"That's what I figured," I said. "And yes, probably not very diplomatic to let the outside world know what a low opinion you have of business schools."

"Not business schools in general," he said. "There are some very fine business schools out there—places I'd be happy to see Jamie or Josh go to if they decide their talents lie in that direction. But the Caerphilly College Business School isn't one of them."

"Really?" I was puzzled. Michael was usually pretty loyal to the college. "They're fairly highly rated, aren't they? Not one of the top twenty business schools in the country, last time I looked, but not that far out of it."

"Yes, and that has always puzzled me." Having found his bicycle helmet, Michael was now ransacking the sock drawer. "Are the ratings really that unreliable or has our B-school faculty just figured out exactly how to pull the wool over the eyes of whoever does the ratings? They're very good at what they do—it's what they don't even try to do that's the problem. They're all about profit and loss, with no eye to all the other things that a business has to think about. The welfare of its employees. The ethics of how it operates. What contribution it makes to society. They don't seem to consider any of that a part of business."

"'Mankind was my business,'" I intoned. "'The common welfare was my business; charity, mercy, forbearance, and benevolence, were all my business. The dealings of my trade were but a drop of water in the comprehensive ocean of my business!'" Michael's annual one-man dramatic readings of *A Christmas Carol* had given me the ability to quote lines from Dickens at the drop of a hat.

"Exactly," he said. "The unreformed Ebenezer Scrooge would fit right in at the Caerphilly College B-school. The new, improved, enlightened Scrooge would be a fish out of water. And it's bad enough that we have them over there in Pruitt Hall, turning out anachronistic little replicas of the old nineteenth-century robber barons. On top of that, they're always trying to rewrite college policy to their liking and making unreasonable demands of other departments. They've been battling for years to exempt their students from taking any of the required courses, which never flies, so they're constantly trying to get all the other departments to develop special 'business' versions of our courses."

"By which I bet they mean watered-down versions that even the most clueless students can pass," I said.

"Yup. They're sending students out into a global economy, and they want to exempt them from languages. Their students might want jobs in complex technical industries, but heaven forbid that we make them take any science or engineering or math. Or any psychology to help them manage their staff and work with clients. Or any history, so they can learn what not to repeat. And if they think art, music, literature, and theater have nothing to teach them—well, as I said, philistines. Why are we even talking about the B-school? Just thinking about them makes me cranky." He sat down on the bed and began changing into a pair of old, ratty socks so unprepossessing that my fingers itched to throw them out. Unfortunately, they were Michael's favorite comfortable biking socks, so pitching them wasn't an option. I averted my eyes instead.

"Do you know anything about the cheating scandal they had in the B-school?" I asked.

"Cheating scandal?" Michael looked up with an eager expression. "Seriously?"

"Don't get all that excited," I said. "It was twenty-six years ago. I gather everyone had pretty much forgotten about it until Kevin and his friend dug it up and did a podcast about it."

"Maybe it deserves to be unforgotten," he said. "Spill."

So I filled him in on what little I knew about the long-ago scandal. He looked thoughtful when I'd finished.

"Seems a little far-fetched," he said. "Not the cheating itself, of course—we all have to be vigilant to spot that when it happens. And not the part about them hushing it up, which totally sounds like the way the B-school would handle it. But the idea that anyone would try to kill Casey over it so many years later." He frowned slightly and shook his head. "Seems a little far-fetched. Especially if the professor who killed himself admitted his involvement and took the fall for it."

"There were also two unfortunate students who got expelled," I said. "Not all that dramatic a scandal if there were only two students involved. Although maybe they were the only two who got caught. But you're right—after so many years, who would care enough to kill about something like that?"

"Exactly," Michael said. "If the culprits turned into the kind of successful, laissez-faire, conscience-free businesspeople the B-school tries to produce, are they really going to be that damaged by revelations of a youthful peccadillo?"

"No," I said. "More likely some of them would even boast about how clever they were to pull it off. So Kevin's probably off base on this one."

"Maybe not." Michael had a thoughtful expression. "Someone who's still in academia would care. They'd care a lot. It could be a career ender if Kevin and Casey managed to prove some professor had done something like that in his student days."

"I'm not sure Kevin and Casey had any intention of trying to dig that deep," I said. "I think they just enjoyed stirring up a little local scandal. Embarrassing the stuffed shirts at the college."

"But if one of the cheaters heard their podcast—one of the ones who got away with it—how would they know that?" Michael asked. "I seem to recall that a lot of true-crime podcasts ask listeners to send in tips, and promise updates if they learn any more about the case."

"Yes, Kevin and Casey do that," I said.

"So for all the cheaters know, Kevin and Casey could be busy digging up the dirt on them."

"True," I said. "So if I want to figure out who is most likely to be upset about the podcast, I'll need to get a list of all the students who were taking B-school classes the year of the scandal and figure out which of them are teaching somewhere."

"Check out the faculty, too," Michael said. "I know it was twenty-five years ago, but some of them could still be teaching somewhere. Including here at Caerphilly. They have an awful lot of fossils on the B-school faculty. Guys so behind the times they refuse to acknowledge the existence of emails."

"Arg." I shook my head and winced.

"But don't worry," Michael said. "Getting your lists won't be a problem. Ask Charlie."

"I should have thought of him immediately," I said.

Michael's friend Charles Gardner had been steadily moving up in the ranks of the college administration and was now assistant dean of something or other. Ordinarily that would have made me suspicious of him, but he was a thoroughly nice guy—and an avid and very talented amateur actor, who had appeared in several productions Michael had directed. And he and Michael shared a jaundiced view of academic bureaucracy. This wouldn't be the first time one of us had called on Charlie to guide us through its tangles.

"I'll text him before I set off," Michael said. "Let him know you need some info, and have him let you know when he'll be in his office."

"Dad! What's taking so long?" Our son Josh appeared in the doorway. Peering over his shoulder were Jamie, his twin, and their friend Adam, Chief Burke's grandson. The three were already clad in their biking clothes, including helmets.

"I had to find where Rose Noire hid my helmet," Michael said.

"Let's go, quick," Jamie said. "Before Grandma finds some more work for us to do."

"She got really excited when she found out the school was giving us back our unused snow days this week," Josh explained.

"So I came up with the fiction that they're supposed to spend them doing something improving," Michael added. "We're going out to the zoo."

"We're going to help Great," Josh said, using the boys' nickname for their great-grandfather. "And learn valuable lessons about the environment."

"Actually, we're just going to watch the meerkat cubs and the baby rhino," Jamie said. "But if Grandma asks—"

"I'll tell her your presence is urgently needed at the zoo," I said.

They grinned, and vanished. Michael gave me a quick kiss and followed them.

I headed downstairs. On the way I greeted a brace of cousins who had arrived to stay with us and were headed up to change into work clothes. When I went out to the barn to snag the third podcast, I found a volunteer crew giving it a fresh coat of paint. And Mother and Demetria, her artist, were gazing at the barn and frowning. Had the painters chosen a shade that would clash with the pavement art? Or did Demetria also do vertical surfaces? I wasn't sure I wanted our barn painted with lilies and roses. But I was in no mood to argue with Mother, and besides, hadn't Demetria assured me that her work was removable?

I got in my car and fled toward town.

The sky was overcast, with occasional small showers of rain. Once I'd parked at the police station, I pulled out my phone to check the weather app. Rain today, then clear skies for the next week. Which meant I'd have good weather for the drive down to Charlottesville, and Mother wouldn't panic and start to put up the dozen or so large party tents she'd acquired, just in case.

As I was pulling into the parking lot at the police station, I got a text from Charlie Gardner telling me that apart from a meeting between one and three he'd be in his office all day. I texted back that I would drop by soon.

When I strolled into the police department, I found my good friend Aida Butler leaning against the front desk, talking to George, the civilian employee who usually staffed it.

"Look who's here!" she called out when she saw me. "You look pretty sane for someone who's organizing a wedding."

"That's because I'm not organizing one," I said. "Mother and Holly McKenna are doing all that. I just take care of whatever they delegate to me."

"And don't tell me they haven't been delegating up a storm," Aida said. "Please don't tell me you came over here to rope me into something else. I still have blisters on my fingers from helping braid all those ribbon garlands for your mama."

"Then I should tell her you're pulling extra patrol duty if she tries to recruit you to stick a few million flowers into the garlands?" I asked. "I think that's happening tomorrow."

Aida rolled her eyes and nodded vigorously.

"Relax," I said. "I'm taking a break from wedding duty today—and before you ask, I'm not going AWOL, I've got an official reprieve from Mother. I dropped by to see if I could talk to the chief for a few minutes. If he's free." I glanced over at George, who punched a button on his intercom.

"Meg Langslow is here and would like to see you," he said.

"Send her back." The chief's voice was calm and welcoming—a good sign.

"I'll fill you in later," I said to Aida, who nodded and turned to head for the front door.

"Looking forward to seeing Kayla singing at the ceremony this weekend," she called over her shoulder. "She's been rehearsing like crazy."

I sighed. Mother had hired the New Life Baptist Church's justly famous gospel choir to sing at the wedding, and evidently Aida's daughter would be one of the soloists.

"Did they finally settle on what songs they're doing?" I kept my face and voice nonchalant.

"Oh, no!" Aida shook a finger at me. "You know very well that's supposed to be a surprise. My lips are sealed." With that, she sailed out the front door of the station.

Not that it mattered. If Rob and Delaney wanted to keep it a secret, I could wait for Saturday. Especially since I knew that Minerva Burke, who directed the choir, would veto anything really weird or inappropriate. Even the weird and inappropriate things the bride and groom kept suggesting, like the Rolling Stones' "(I Can't Get No) Satisfaction" as the recessional.

I headed down the short hallway to Chief Burke's office. I found him talking with Vern Shiffley, the department's senior deputy.

"I bet I know why you're here," the chief said. "Your nephew Kevin thinks we aren't taking his friend's report seriously."

Chapter 5

I wasn't sure whether to be pleased or concerned that he'd guessed my mission so easily.

"Exactly," I said. "He's afraid you're treating it as an accident, instead of an attempted hit-and-run."

"Well, we have a witness who confirms the story, so we know darn well it wasn't an accident," the chief said. "But there's no such thing as attempted hit-and-run. The charge would be attempted felonious assault. We take that very seriously."

"Ooh," I said. "Attempted felonious assault—I like the sound of that. But why not attempted murder?"

"Attempted felonious assault carries a heavier penalty, for some reason," the chief said.

I could tell that Vern, who was known to have memorized large portions of the Virginia Code, was aching to tell me in what class of felony attempted murder and attempted felonious assault fell and what penalties they carried. Maybe I'd gladden his heart by asking later. For now, it was enough to know that the chief was taking the attack on Casey seriously.

"What I'm having a hard time with is the idea that the attack is related to one of those cold cases Kevin wants us to investigate," the chief went on. "The warmest of those cases is a good five years old, and we're looking into that. But the other two happened more than twenty years ago. So while I'm not ignoring his theory, I think I should check out more recent possible motives first."

"Makes sense to me," I said. "But unless you're going to

warn me off, I'd like to do a little digging into those older cases. For one thing, it will make Kevin happier—and reduce the chances that he'll spread panic to all the rest of the people who are starting to arrive for the wedding."

"For one thing," the chief echoed. "Do you have any other reasons?"

"Well," I said. "If he thinks I'm investigating the cold cases, maybe he won't badger you to do it."

"That would be a blessing," the chief said. "Kevin has been rather . . . importunate."

"Importunate?" Vern echoed. "Is that a two-dollar word for a damned nuisance?"

"And then there's the fact that I seem to have convinced Mother that if Kevin's right, there's a real risk of fallout for the wedding," I said. "So checking out the cold cases lets me duck a whole lot of wedding-related work."

The chief and Vern both chuckled.

"A valid reason if ever I heard one," the chief said. "And as I said, we are going to look into the most recent case."

"Since the perpetrator only got out of prison a couple of weeks ago," Vern said.

"Yes," the chief said. "But perhaps more relevantly, since the hit-and-run attempt happened only two days after the podcast on the Clay County case. They release their new shows every Thursday, and Casey was attacked Saturday night."

"Seems logical." I wondered why Kevin hadn't mentioned the timing—it would have strengthened his case for having me investigate.

"For starters, the chief's having me check out Lucas Plunkett," Vern said. "We already got hold of a transcript of his trial. Wanted to see if our new citizen was apt to be much of a headache."

"Our new citizen?" I repeated. "I thought he came from Clay County."

"He did," Vern said. "But when he got out on parole he

found a job here in Caerphilly. And a place to live—an apartment over at the College Arms."

I nodded and winced. The College Arms—locally nicknamed the Armpits—was a small, seedy, run-down low-rise garden apartment complex on a street near the bus station, located in an area that was the closest Caerphilly came to having a bad neighborhood. People tended not to stay at the College Arms for long unless they were really down on their luck and couldn't afford anyplace else. Lucas might not even be the only parolee there. I felt almost sorry for him.

Then again, the few people I knew of from Caerphilly who'd gone to jail or prison wouldn't have needed the Armpits. They'd had families eagerly awaiting them—to help them make a new start, or at least do what they could to keep them from straying again. Lucas almost certainly had family in Clay County. What did it say about him—or them—that he was striking out for himself here in Caerphilly?

"If you're interested, I can have George make you a copy of the trial transcript," the chief said. "Unless your nephew already gave you a copy. After all, it is a matter of public record, although Clay County doesn't have a very good grasp of that fact."

"If Kevin has it, he didn't share," I said. "And I kind of think he would have."

"It's not long," Vern said. "After the three eyewitnesses identified Plunkett as the guy who emptied the service station's till and shot the attendant, his lawyer went into a huddle with the prosecutor and they arranged a plea bargain. After that it was pretty pro forma."

"I'd still appreciate it," I said. "Getting a copy, I mean."

"I'll tell George to have it ready this afternoon," the chief said.

"And after I talk to Plunkett's parole officer, I'm going over to check out the man himself," Vern said. "I'll let you know what I think," he said, turning back to the chief.

I opened my mouth, about to ask if I could come along

when Vern went to see Plunkett, then shut it again. The chief noticed and frowned. Then he sighed.

"If I let you tag along with Vern, will you promise not to go interrogating Mr. Plunkett yourself?" he asked.

"Absolutely," I said.

"Make sure you've got your credentials with you," he said. "That ID badge that shows you're the special assistant to the mayor. Officially, you'll be doing a few hours of ride-along for some civic purpose or other. And then you can add your take to Vern's on whether this Plunkett fellow's a menace to public safety or someone trying to make a clean start. I want as much perspective on that issue as possible. Frankly, I'd like to talk to him myself, but I don't want to spook him, or appear to be persecuting him."

"Our theory is that his moving here could be a good sign," Vern said.

"Yes," the chief said. "It could indicate that he wants to avoid going back into whatever situation led him to committing his crime."

"But it also could mean he knows he wouldn't be all that welcome back in Clay County," Vern said. "And if Clay County doesn't want him back—that would worry me."

"Maybe he's afraid the family of the guy he shot will retaliate," I suggested.

"If he's afraid of that, he should have moved a lot farther away," Vern said. "Clay County folks manage to find their way across the county line pretty easily when they want to."

"It's a waste of time speculating about all this before you even meet him," the chief said.

Vern nodded.

"About those other two cases," I said.

The chief looked thoughtful.

"I have a hard time imagining either of them has anything to do with the attack on Kevin's friend," he said. "Which means it shouldn't be particularly dangerous to have you studying them."

"Do you mean dangerous to me?" I asked. "Or dangerous

because I could screw up any investigation you might later want to make?

"Well, both," he said. "But I assume that if you find anything that seems to connect either of those old cases with the attack, you'll have enough common sense to back away and bring me whatever you've found."

I nodded.

"And frankly, even Lucas Plunkett doesn't look all that plausible a suspect," he said. "I think the attack will turn out to be racially motivated. We don't get much of that here in Caerphilly, thank goodness, but we're not immune to it, especially with Clay County so close by, and lately we have had an uptick—"

"Wait," I said. "Racially motivated? Casey's Black?"

"Asian, actually," the chief said. "You hadn't noticed?"

"I've never actually seen him," I said. "Kevin says he doesn't get out much."

"Ah." The chief was suppressing a smile. "Understandable." He glanced down at something on his desk. "Casey Murakami," he said, pronouncing the last name with careful precision and just a note of uncertainty. "A graduate history student at the college."

"And Kevin knows you're pursuing this theory of the case?" I asked.

"Not *only* this theory of the case," the chief said. "But it's pretty high on my list of possibilities, and yes, I told your nephew so."

I nodded. Maybe Kevin didn't agree about the likelihood of a racially motivated attack. Or maybe he acknowledged its possibility or even likelihood, trusted the chief to pursue that angle, but wanted me checking out the cold cases for insurance.

"Sadly, it seems all too possible to me," I said. "But just in case Kevin's right, I'll see what I can find out about the cold cases. And will share everything I find with you."

"And it will give you reason to duck some of the less amusing pre-wedding chores," he said. "Although I have to say, my grandson had a lot of fun helping Josh and Jamie with the poop and feather collection."

"The what?

"You hadn't heard about that?" The chief grinned. "Apparently this weekend your mother hired a small army of middle-grade boys to pick up every bit of trash in your backyard, since you're holding the reception there. Mostly a lot of chicken feathers and sheep droppings. Also quite a few pebbles and bits of broken glass."

"Good grief," I said. "No, I missed that. It must have been the day I went all the way up to Washington to collect the special ribbon they wanted to make the flower garlands."

"Adam didn't mind," the chief said. "He found a dollar and a half in spare change on top of what your mother paid him, so he's feeling like a billionaire at the moment. He had me drop him off at your house again this morning—does your mother have more wedding work for the boys?"

"No, they're biking over to the zoo with Michael," I said. "Officially, they're helping Grandfather and learning important lessons about the environment. Doing something useful with the no-snow days."

"Good plan," the chief said.

"Well, I'm off to track down Meredith." Vern didn't sound happy about the idea.

"Who is—wait, do you mean Meredith Flugleman?" I asked.

"Yes," the chief said. "Ms. Flugleman is Mr. Plunkett's parole officer."

"That sounds like an unfortunate combination to me," I said.

"I agree," the chief said. "But unfortunately Ms. Flugleman is currently the county's only parole officer."

"Bet you're not going to beg to go along on that interview," Vern said with a sly smile.

No, I wasn't. Meredith Flugleman was one of the most kindhearted and well-meaning people in the county—and one of the most annoying. She was tirelessly upbeat, mind-numbingly literal, and incapable of letting go of a detail or changing a schedule. She didn't strike me as an optimal fit for the job of parole officer. Of course, she hadn't been an optimal fit as the county's social services officer, either.

"Does that mean she's no longer working for the county?" I tried not to sound quite so pleased. My part-time job as special assistant to Mayor Randall Shiffley brought me into contact with Meredith all too often—but I couldn't recall ever having to deal with whoever had been her predecessor as parole officer.

"Alas, no," the chief said. "When the county job went part-time, she managed to get on part time with the Virginia Department of Corrections."

"Which means we see even more of her than before," Vern said. "Cheer up, Chief—maybe she'll decide she loves parole work and move someplace where she can do it full-time."

The chief pursed his lips as if finding it a trial to follow the old adage about not saying anything if you can't say something nice.

"I'll shoot you a text when I'm finished talking to Meredith," Vern said, turning to me.

"Thanks," I said.

As I strolled out to my car, I pondered what to do next. Probably a good idea to hold off on heading out to Ragnar's farm. Vern struck me as a "rip the bandage off" kind of guy. He'd be looking to get his dreaded interview with Meredith over as soon as possible so he could move on to the much more amusing job of vetting Lucas Plunkett. So maybe I should stay nearby.

The college campus was only a few blocks away. I decided to head over there and talk to Charlie.

Chapter 6

I parked the Twinmobile in one of the lots where Michael's faculty sticker would save me from towing and hiked across the street to the Admin building. Serious students of architecture generally referred to it as a Gothic monstrosity, but I rather liked gargoyles, carved stone, and pointed arches.

I wondered, not for the first time, what it said about Caerphilly College that its senior administrators stubbornly insisted on occupying a building that looked as if it had time traveled from the Middle Ages. Only today did it occur to me that the B-school occupied a very similar building, separated from the Admin building only by the Quadrangle, a stretch of flawless green lawn bordered by lush rose gardens. Was there any significance to this proximity? I hoped not. But I suspected there was more than a little significance to the fact everyone still called the B-school building Pruitt Hall. The Pruitts were a family of robber barons who arrived in the town of Caerphilly as carpetbaggers and ruled it with an iron hand for over a hundred years until they finally bankrupted it and were driven out by the outraged citizens. Almost every other street, building, or park once named after them had been rechristened. But since after five years the B-school hadn't yet chosen a new name, the old one clung.

Charlie's latest office was on the second floor of the Admin building and boasted a large window looking out over the Quadrangle. He was definitely coming up in the world. He looked up when I knocked on his doorframe and greeted me warmly.

"Michael says you want to enlist my expertise," he said. "But he didn't say how. Dare I hope I can help you strike another blow for the forces of progress and academic freedom?" Charlie was one of the few people—at least I hoped it was still few—who knew about the backstage role I'd played in helping the Drama Department secede from the English Department.

"Well, that's not on the agenda today," I said. "Today I'm focused on either saving my nephew's life or being able to tell him his life isn't in danger. But if it turns out doing that requires overthrowing the patriarchy, I'm game."

I gave him what I hoped was a succinct but accurate account of Kevin's new podcasting project and the possible attack on Casey. And for dramatic effect, I saved my mention of the podcast about the cheating scandal at the B-school for last. It had the desired effect.

"Ooh," Charlie said. "A scandal in the B-school! You just made my day. Please tell me that protecting your nephew will involve embarrassing the B-school as publicly as possible."

"Not your favorite neighbors, then." I couldn't help glancing out Charlie's window, which showed a glimpse of Pruitt Hall across the Quadrangle. Why did its gargoyles and turrets suddenly look so sinister, like the castle of the Wicked Witch of the West?

"The most annoying neighbors imaginable." He sighed. "I think they cause me more trouble than any three other departments combined. We're currently doing battle with them again over who gets to decide what they do with their endowment funds. Right now they have complete control, and frankly they've made some rather dodgy decisions."

"Bad investments?" I guessed.

"Oh, their investments are usually profitable, I'll give them that," he said. "It's the ethical side of the equation they don't seem to pay much attention to. All those corporations your grandfather's always going after for polluting the environment, for example. If they're profitable polluters, you can almost bet the B-school owns some of their stock."

He glared out the window at the building opposite.

"So you think they'd be embarrassed at having the cheating scandal raked up?" I asked.

"Probably," he said. "But I can't see them trying to run over your nephew's friend. A menacing phone call from a high-powered attorney is more their style. Cease and desist or we'll sue you for defamation and take every penny you'll earn for the rest of your lifetime."

I nodded.

"Or maybe just a dignified silence, since they know saying anything would fan the flames. And managing to imply that by bringing it all up you've somehow committed a tragic error in taste and judgment. Still—any chance you can share that podcast?"

"I can send you a copy," I said. "Better yet—they have a website for the podcast. The link will be there." Something I'd realized only after making a trip home to retrieve the podcast I'd missed. I pulled out my phone, typed in the URL Kevin had given me, and sure enough, there was a page with links to all of the podcasts. I texted the URL to Charlie, who had pulled out his phone and nodded when the text arrived.

"Awesome," he said. "I'll listen to it later and let you know if I can think of anything useful."

"Great," I said. "But actually there already is something useful that Michael thinks you could help with. Is there any way to get a list of all the students and faculty members who could have been involved in the scandal? Everyone who taught or took a B-school class that year?"

"That'll be a big list," he said. "You don't have anything more concrete? Like, was the cheating associated with any particular class?"

"At the moment, that's all I know," I said. "The podcast was long on insinuation and short on details. Didn't even mention the names of the people involved. I can give you those, of course, from Kevin's files. A professor and two students—but, those were just the ones who were caught."

"There are a lot of ways to cheat," Charlie said. "Do you

have any notion exactly what they did? If it was connected with one of the guilty professor's classes, for example, we could get a list of the students who took it. Or—"

"Not a clue," I said. "So I think we need the broadest possible list"

"And the bigger the list, the harder it's going to be for you to check them all out. It'll be a couple of hundred people— you can't possibly be planning to track down all of them."

"No way," I said. "But if we can get a list, Kevin can probably find what most if not all of them are doing today, and then I can interview the likely ones."

"What constitutes likely?" Charlie sounded dubious. "Ones who are still local?"

"Michael and I figure most people would laugh off their involvement in the cheating as a youthful folly," I explained. "Unless they were in a profession where that kind of unethical behavior wouldn't be tolerated."

"Like maybe they went into the ministry?" Charlie chuckled. "B-school to seminary? Stranger things have happened."

"Or, more likely, they went into teaching, either here or at some other business school," I said. "So we give Kevin the suspect list and let him figure out which of them are professors someplace."

"I might even be able to help with that," Charlie said. "First we get that list of suspects—B-school faculty members who were here when the cheating scandal broke, plus anyone who took a graduate or undergraduate B-school class that year."

"Damn," I said. "I was thinking it would be only business majors. If it's anyone who took a class—"

"Don't worry," he said. "Very few people take courses at the B-school unless they're majoring in business, or planning to. B-school classes aren't most people's cup of tea. Word gets around."

"That's good," I said. "It'll keep the list small."

"In theory it should also be good because the B-school does an impressive job of keeping track of their alumni,"

Charlie said. "Probably because alumni make up a huge portion of their donors. They keep good track of all the donors, too—that's how they've built that huge endowment fund. Quite a thorn in my side, since part of my job is to try to steer those donors into giving to the college as a whole, instead of the already well-endowed B-school. Anyway, I bet they know exactly where each and every one of those alumni and ex-faculty members are, so if we could access their records, we could find out really quickly which ones were teaching. Or preaching," he added, with another chuckle.

"In theory," I repeated. "Then I gather you don't have computer access to alumni files."

"To the main college alumni files, yes," he said. "But not to those much more detailed B-school files. And believe me, I've been trying to get a look at them for ten years now. They're completely unconnected to the main computer system. If you could get hold of them, you'd have no trouble finding those alumni."

"Let's worry about the list of students and faculty for now." I suspected that if he had their names, Kevin could find them, even without any help from the B-school's records. But I kept that to myself, in case it sounded as if I were scorning Charlie's suggestions. "How hard is it going to be to get such a list?"

"If you were asking me at this time last year, I'd lead you to a dusty file room and say you're on your own," he said. "But I got a student intern this past fall. Double major, computer science and statistics. The kid's a marvel. She's managed to get decades' worth of paper records into a database—along with electronic data from half a dozen old systems that either don't work anymore or don't talk to each other. And she's set up an interface that even I can use. Do you prefer a printout or a data file?"

"If I were planning to do anything with it myself, I'd say a printout," I said. "But since I hope to sic Kevin on hunting them down, I'd say a data file."

"You never know," he said. "I'll give you both."

He tapped away on his keyboard for a few minutes. He was frowning slightly, but it was the sort of frown you see when someone's concentrating. He was also humming, and the movements of his arms and fingers were more like those of a virtuoso playing a piano than a bureaucrat struggling to wrest information from his computer. Finally he sat back with a smile, and his printer erupted into motion.

"You have no idea how happy this new system makes me," he said. "Some days I deliberately try to think of something to use it for, just for the pleasure of making the data do somersaults. I'll email you the file. You can send it on to Kevin and take the printout with you."

"You're a wonder," I said.

"My intern's the wonder. Although I do take a little credit for figuring out how to make use of her talents."

"If she's that good, tell Rob and Delaney about her," I suggested. "They're always looking for new talent."

"I'll do that." He jotted a few words on a yellow legal pad on his desk. "And meanwhile—" He glanced at the clock, and I fully expected him to apologize that he had to run off to a meeting, But instead he put on his reading glasses.

"Let's take a quick look at the printout and see if I know anything about any of these people." He took the papers from the printer tray, picked up a pencil, and began running his eyes down the list, using the pencil as a pointer.

I sat back and waited.

"Aha!" He made a tick mark on the paper. "J. Morton Fairweather, alumnus. Still here. Not faculty, though. Administration. Pencil pusher in Facilities. And Claude Vansittart, alumnus—on the B-school faculty." Another tick mark. "One of the worst stuffed shirts in the department. Got tenure in record time—rumor has it less for his academic brilliance than for his skill in multiplying the endowment. That's it for students, but on the faculty list there's Professor Wyndham—Old Windy. He's still around, although God knows why. He was an old fart back then—must be nearly a hundred now. No other professors from that era still around. And only one staff member—Ingrid Bjorn-strom."

He lifted his eyes from the paper. His face held a thoughtful expression.

"Ingrid's okay," he said. "Can't think why she stays in the B-school. She's too nice by half to fit in there, and plenty of other departments would be glad to have her. But she's loyal. Too loyal for her own good. Of course, she has been known to drop a hint now and again when there's something going on in the B-school that the administration might want to know about. Something that would hurt the B-school in the long run if we didn't know—like when they tried to hush up the fact that one of their faculty was harassing women students. It's possible she stays on because she sees herself as the hidden conscience of the department. She never actually tells me anything, of course. Just drops hints. And I always make sure to figure out a way to make it look as if I stumbled on the information myself."

"You think she might know something?" I asked. "About the cheating scandal?"

"She was very junior back then," Charlie said. "So maybe not. And if she did know, she'd probably consider it an embarrassment for the department. Something to keep quiet. Unless . . ."

"Unless she thought keeping quiet was putting someone in danger?" I said.

"Yeah, but I think you'll need a little more than a theory to convince her of that. Still—it might be worth talking to her. If we can think of a way to approach her."

"How about if I come right out and tell her about the podcast?" I suggested. "And maybe imply that I'm concerned about the embarrassment Kevin's causing for the college, and want to find out what really happened so I can straighten him out."

"That might work," he said. "Worth a try, anyway. Do you have time for a visit to the Grill?"

"The Grill?" The sudden change in subject startled me. I

glanced at the clock—not quite eleven. "It's a little early for lunch for me."

"And for me, too," he said. "But we could have tea, and one of those lovely pastries the Grill bakes. And as it happens, Ingrid usually eats lunch early. Usually at the Grill."

"Let's go."

The Grill was one of the college dining areas—and the nearest one to Charlie's office. While it wasn't restricted to staff and faculty only, it served a slightly fancier and more conservative menu, at slightly higher prices, which kept the number of students using it to a minimum. Well, that and the fact that its location, in the basement of one of the old buildings around the Quadrangle, was so difficult to find that many students didn't stumble across it for the first year or two they were on campus.

"So how are the wedding preparations going?" Charlie asked as we strolled toward the Grill. "Rob getting nervous?"

"So far he's fine," I said. "But every time I turn around Mother is adding something new to the plans—which is making me a little nervous."

I wasn't sure if he'd actually spotted one or more B-school professors within earshot or was just being cautious, but we kept up bright chatter about the wedding as we went through the nearly empty serving line, acquiring cups of tea and pastries.

When we'd paid for our snack, I followed Charlie. There were plenty of empty tables, but he seemed intent on trekking to the far corner of the café until—

"What luck!" he exclaimed. "Meg, have you met Ingrid Bjornstrom? Come on—I'll introduce you."

He led the way to a table where an older woman with a worn but pleasant face was sitting. She had half a sandwich on her plate and her nose was glued to a book.

"Mind if we join you?" he asked.

Ingrid looked up and smiled.

"Be my guest."

She closed her book and tucked it into the oversized

purse at her feet—though not before I noticed she was reading *Sense and Sensibility*.

Charlie noticed, too.

"Reading literature again," he said in a tone of mock chiding. "They'll kick you out if they catch you doing that across the way."

"Oh, they don't mind me." Ingrid had a lovely voice, soft but resonant. And rather familiar-sounding, which probably meant that she sounded like an actress I'd seen perform recently. Possibly in one of the noir classics Michael and I had been watching lately.

"You know, Meg, you might want to ask Ingrid about what you were telling me," Charlie said. "She's been at the college for quite a long time—over at the business school. She might be able to help."

Ingrid turned her eyes to me with an expression of polite helpfulness.

"I'm not sure I should," I said. "Maybe the less said the better—but then again, it could have the potential to embarrass the college, so maybe I should."

Ingrid nodded slightly and looked a little more interested. As I hoped, the idea of embarrassing the college seemed to pique her interest.

"One of my nephews has started this thing called a podcast," I said. "Which I gather is like a radio show, only instead of being broadcast it's distributed over the internet. His podcast is all about true crimes, specifically ones that happened in Virginia."

"I wouldn't have thought Virginia was a hot spot for true crime," Ingrid said with amusement in her voice.

"Maybe that's the problem," I said. "Maybe he was running out of real crimes. Anyway, he did this one episode all about something that happened here at the college. I'd never heard of it before, and I'm not even sure it technically counts as a crime. Supposedly there was a scandal twenty-some years ago when several students were caught cheating, and they were expelled and a professor who'd been helping them committed suicide—"

To my horror, Ingrid's face crumpled in obvious pain. She leaped out of her chair and ran away, leaving her purse and the remains of her lunch behind, and disappeared into the ladies' room.

Chapter 7

Charlie and I sat frozen for a moment, watching Ingrid's flight.

"Oh, dear," Charlie said. "I had no idea she'd react that way."

"Clearly I hit a nerve," I said. "I think one of us should go after her."

"And given where she went, I rather think it has to be you."

"Yeah." Charlie knew her better, but I couldn't see him barging into a ladies' room. I reached over and picked up her purse. "I'll take her this—she'll probably want it. And she might kick me out the second I hand it to her but . . ."

Charlie nodded. He watched with wide, anxious eyes as I crossed the room. I pushed the ladies' room door open about a foot.

"Ingrid?" I could hear sobbing. "I'm very sorry. I didn't mean to upset you. I brought your purse—I thought you might want it."

The sobbing died down a bit and was replaced by sniffling.

"Come in," she said finally. I pushed the door open. Ingrid was in the outer part of the ladies' room, where a wide wooden shelf formed a sort of dressing table, topped by a tall mirror and outfitted with two old but sturdy wooden chairs. Beyond her the door to the inner room was open, giving a glimpse of a vintage toilet and a pedestal sink. Ingrid was sitting in the farther of the two chairs, head on hands, tears streaming down her cheeks. I set the purse on the shelf at her elbow.

"I'm so sorry," I said. "If I'd known—"

"Not your fault," she said through sniffles. "How could you have known?"

I nodded. Technically I still didn't know why the mere mention of the cheating scandal upset her so much. Not something I could ask, so I settled for yanking a couple of tissues out of a box that was at my end of the dressing table and handing them to her.

"Thanks." She blotted her eyes and scrubbed her cheeks. "I'm sorry. It's silly, I know. It was so long ago. But you took me by surprise."

"I'm the one who should be sorry." I offered more tissues.

"I knew him, you see," she said. "Professor Bradshaw."

I nodded as if I understood completely. Presumably Professor Bradshaw was the one who'd been implicated in the scandal—the one who'd committed suicide when it was exposed. His name hadn't stuck in my mind, because Kevin and Casey hadn't actually mentioned it in the podcast—they'd referred to him only as "a young professor." Sometimes "a popular young professor" or "a young professor from a prominent Virginia family." I wasn't sure whether they were aiming for discretion and avoiding embarrassment to the survivors, or whether they'd been smart enough to get legal advice on what to avoid saying, in case the professor's family turned out to be not only prominent but also litigious.

"We were both newcomers that year," she said. "Of course, he was a professor, and said to be on a fast track toward tenure, and I was only a junior secretary. Still, it was something of a bond, that we were both learning our way around at the same time. And both . . . well, both a little impatient with how old-fashioned everything was in the business school."

She fell silent. Nodding and proffering tissues seemed to have worked well so far, so I plucked a few more sheets from the box and handed them over.

"I never believed he did it!" She spat that out with sudden fierceness—almost venom. "Never! They framed him—I know they did."

"Who?"

She shook her head and hunched her shoulders slightly. Did that mean she didn't know? Or that she knew but wasn't going to tell?

"If I'd known, maybe I could have done something." Her voice was quiet again, but not calm. Rigidly controlled. "But I didn't. I just knew it couldn't be him. I was really too junior to know much about what was happening. I suppose it could have been the students—the two who were . . . *expelled*."

She said the last word in a half whisper, as if it were almost an obscenity. Perhaps it was to someone who'd spent the past twenty-five years toiling here at the college. *Expelled.* Cast into the outer darkness. Not just obscenity—heresy.

"And they drove him to kill himself," she said. "He thought his career was over—his life. Which wasn't true. There were other colleges. Other careers. I didn't understand it." She blew her nose. "I still don't."

"If it's any consolation, they don't actually mention his name in the podcast," I said.

"Well, that's something," she said. "Although I'm not sure why it matters. He's past caring now. And as for his family— *hmph!*" She looked fierce again. "Very snooty. FFV, or claimed to be. That's First Families of Virginia, you know."

I nodded.

"They didn't stand by him," she said. "They abandoned him. It would serve them right if someone showed how horrible they were to him. Can you imagine the despair he must have felt?"

I nodded and handed over more tissues. And I decided maybe I could be more open with Ingrid.

"Charlie actually brought me over here because he knew you'd been in the department back when—when all that happened," I said. "Of course, he had no idea you would be so upset by the topic."

"Not his fault," she said, dabbing at her eyes. "Not sure why it hit me so hard. After all, it was all such a long time ago."

I wondered, just for a moment, if there had been something more than friendship between her and Professor Bradshaw.

"I'm actually trying to figure out if that podcast hit a nerve with someone else as well," I said. "Shortly after it came out, someone tried to run over my nephew's friend, the one who does the podcast with him."

Ingrid looked up, an expression of alarm on her face.

"Someone tried to . . . to kill him?"

"To kill him or to scare the dickens out of him," I said. "Of course we don't know that it has anything to do with the podcast. And this wasn't the only case the podcast covered— although it was the only one in Caerphilly."

She nodded slowly and blew her nose.

"I can't imagine the Bradshaws would care, as long as their precious name wasn't mentioned," she said. "They didn't even come to the memorial service. And the idea of someone from the business school trying to run someone over is . . ."

"Pretty far-fetched, I admit," I said, and she nodded.

"But maybe one of the students," she suggested. "One of the ones who got expelled. They could be angry that someone's raking it up all over again."

"Of course, they weren't mentioned by name, either," I said. "So I'm not sure why they'd be that upset. But what if there was someone who was involved and didn't get expelled?"

She blinked, as if this was a new and rather unwelcome idea.

"Other students who cheated?" she said finally. "And managed to cover up their involvement?"

"Do you think that's possible?" I asked. "That they didn't catch all the culprits?"

She stared into space for a bit, sniffing occasionally. Then she looked up.

"Not just possible. Probable." Her tears had dried up, and she was clearly getting into the idea. "In fact, highly probable. I don't know why it didn't occur to me at the time. The two students they kicked out were both scholarship students. Academically a great deal more gifted than most of our student body. I remember feeling puzzled about why they would need to cheat, but I put it down to their feeling rather like fish out of water. But of course if you were looking for scapegoats, they were perfect."

"Especially if kicking them out saved the college the cost of their scholarships," I suggested.

"Yes, it would have." Ingrid's nose wrinkled as if she had suddenly detected a bad smell. "Oh, that's a horrible idea. I would never have imagined it back then. But now—"

She broke off, and squeezed her eyes shut for a moment, as if trying to avoid seeing something that was right in front of her.

"Anyway," I said. "I'm going to do a little digging to see what else I can find out about the whole thing. Maybe it has nothing to do with the attempted hit-and-run on my nephew's friend."

"Or maybe it does," she said. "They drove him to it, you know. Professor Bradshaw, that is."

"They?" I echoed.

"Whoever was behind the cheating. They're responsible for his death, as surely as if they'd tied the rope around his neck."

"Any information you have about that time would be helpful," I said.

"I'm not sure if I know anything," she said. "It was so long ago. And they didn't . . . we weren't encouraged to gossip about the whole thing. And I was so new I didn't really know all that much about how things worked."

I nodded.

"But I'll go home and . . . I keep a journal. Always have. I'll dig out the notebook for that year and reread some of the entries. Maybe it will jog my memory. I could always ask around, you know. Talk to some of the old-timers."

"Why don't you hold off on talking to anyone else?" I suggested. "If someone really is upset enough about the podcast to try to run over someone—"

"That's true," she said. "I'll keep quiet for now. But you should talk to someone."

She stopped and sat looking down at the floor, frowning.

These days if you told another person "you should talk to someone" it generally meant you considered them in need of therapy. That didn't seem to be Ingrid's meaning.

"Professor Forstner," she said finally. "Giles Forstner. In the History Department. He was Professor Bradshaw's friend. His best friend. Maybe he could help."

Just then we heard a gentle tapping on the door.

"Meg? Ingrid?" It was Charlie. "Everything okay?"

"Fine," I called, loudly enough for Charlie to hear. "Out soon!"

"Poor Charlie," Ingrid said. "I'm sure I've worried him. Why don't you go out and reassure him while I rinse my eyes and make myself presentable? I should be heading back to my desk anyway."

"Good idea," I said. "Only— Well, there is one other thing you might be able to do." I had been about to say "to help me with," and stopped myself. She might not be all that interested in helping *me.* "Something that might help reveal what really happened," I said instead.

She nodded.

"According to Charlie, the business school does an admirably thorough job of tracking its donors and alumni."

"It does," she said. "Although I'm sure the thoroughness is the only thing he admires about the process. They don't share with the rest of the college, you know. I'm sure Charlie finds that galling."

"I gather he does." I was about to go on when something suddenly struck me. Ingrid had used "they" in talking about the business school. Not "we." I felt a sudden surge of warmth toward her. And optimism. "Do you have any idea how far the records go back?"

"Forever," she said. "Well, not literally, of course, but as far back as the school itself. There's a whole file cabinet full of archived cards going back to the late eighteen hundreds."

"Cards?" I echoed. "The records aren't computerized?"

"No, they're on index cards," she said. "Hand printed."

No wonder Charlie hadn't been able to get access.

"So if there's anyone of interest we can't track down, you might be able to find their contact information in those index cards."

Ingrid didn't answer immediately.

"You know what else you could find out from those cards," she said. "Who gave money to the B-school that year. Logically speaking, there ought to be reports, of course, listing all the donors for each fiscal year. But if they exist, I've never seen them."

"Probably only distributed on a need-to-know basis," I said. The whole system sounded completely unbusinesslike to me.

But then, it wasn't about business, was it? It was about money.

And power.

"The cards would show you a donor's pattern of giving," Ingrid went on. "How much they gave each year. That might be a way to figure out who else was cheating. See whose parents made a larger than usual donation the year of the scandal."

"You think some of them bought their way out of it?" I asked.

"It wouldn't have occurred to me back then," she said. "But now—yes. Of course, someone could have made a large donation that year for reasons unconnected with the scandal. They could have had a windfall. An inheritance, for example. Or they could have had an unusually profitable year and decided to share some of it with the alma mater that had helped them achieve their success. It wouldn't have to be . . . you know."

"A bribe," I suggested. "For overlooking the fact that the donor's son or daughter got caught cheating."

She pursed her lips and nodded.

"Do you want me to find a way to look at the cards?" Her voice quavered slightly. "I'm not really authorized to access them."

"Then no," I said. "You could get in trouble. Lose your job."

"That's true." A note of relief.

"But can you help me figure out how I can look at the cards?" I asked. "Without them being able to trace it back to you?"

Another silence.

"They're kept locked up in the dean's office," she said. "And they're very protective of the office keys."

"They still have office keys?" I asked.

"Oh, yes," she said. "You should have seen the fuss when the college tried to install those fancy new electronic card readers. The dean and all the powers-that-be thought they were an eyesore. They couldn't keep the college from installing them on the exterior doors, of course, but they blocked having them on the inside. A pity—I bet if they had put card readers inside you could probably get Charlie to give you a card that would work on the dean's office."

"And maybe it's a good thing they don't have the card readers, because I wouldn't want to get Charlie in trouble, either. If we did this, we'd want to go low-tech. Could you manage to leave a ground floor window open someplace in the building? And tell me where it is?"

"Yes," she said. "Getting you into the building's no problem. But the dean's office . . ." She shook her head.

I nodded. Evidently looking at those files wasn't going to be easy. If Ingrid, after twenty-six years in the department, couldn't get to them—not to mention Charlie, who was one of the most resourceful people I knew—I didn't think much of my chances. A pity there wasn't a real crime connected to the donor files, or Chief Burke could get a search warrant for them.

"Maybe I can figure out another way to find out the information," I said. "I'll see what I can figure out. And if worse comes to worst, if you could get me into the building that way, I could probably finagle those old-fashioned locks."

"Do you really think so?" she asked. "Is lockpicking one of those skills you learn as a blacksmith?"

"No," I said. "It's one of those skills you learn as the daughter of an avid mystery fan. Dad loves Donald Westlake's Dortmunder character. And Lawrence Block's Bernie Rhodenbarr. One summer Dad decided that any self-respecting amateur sleuth should know how to pick locks, so he got a bunch of manuals and talked my brother and me into learning it with him."

"A family skill, then."

"Not really," I said. "I'm the only one who ever made any progress. I'm no expert, but I think there's a decent chance I could pick those antique locks in the B-school building. What about the cabinets where the cards are kept? Do they have fancy modern locks?"

"The cabinets? They're not even locked," she said. "When the library did away with its card catalog system, the B-school commandeered all those lovely old oak card cabinets. And since they're always locked up in the dean's office, I suppose they didn't think they needed to retrofit locks to them. If you can get into his office, you can get to them just fine."

"And there's a window you think you can leave open?"

"I think the ground floor ladies' room window would be the best." I got the impression that she'd already been pondering this question. "And it would be perfectly natural for me to go in there—my desk is on the ground floor, so that's the one I use all the time. And it's just an ordinary window—not one of those small, high windows you see so often in restrooms. They put in frosted glass, but some of the ladies still felt the lack of privacy, so they planted several large holly bushes outside as a buffer. And that was years ago—the bushes must be ten feet high now, and they cast so much shade that they rather defeat the purpose of even having a window. But they'd make it much less likely that you'd be spotted when you go in. Although you'll have to be careful—they're rather prickly."

"Perfect," I said. "I'd wear long sleeves. And gloves." Probably a good idea to wear gloves anyway—I jotted a reminder in my notebook.

"And it's on the Quadrangle side of the building," she added. "You could still be seen if anyone's working late and happens to look out their window, but still, there's much less chance of being seen than if you were on the street side. I'll see if I can email you a little map showing where the room is. And once you know the general area, you can just look for the bushes and the frosted glass. But once you get in, do you know how to find the dean's office? Should I draw you a map?"

"A map would help," I said.

"Of course, it would be even better if you could actually scout it out in person," she said. "But I suppose that would look suspicious."

"Yes," I said. "Unless I could think of a valid reason to be there. Do people other than B-school students and faculty ever visit for any reason?"

"Occasionally one of the architecture professors will bring one of his classes over to scoff at the building." I could tell from her tone that she resented the scoffing. "Oh, and we get the occasional young Goth coming in to wax enthusiastic about the gargoyles and carvings."

"Perfect!" I said. "I'll drop in sometime this afternoon. I'll spend some time taking pictures in the Admin building first, and then come across to your building. If anyone asks why I'm suddenly so interested in gargoyles and carvings, I can explain to them that I'm working on some new gargoyle-themed ironwork for Ragnarsholm. That's—"

"I know," she said. "The estate where that rather Goth

musician lives. The architecture classes scoff at that, too. Shall I admit to knowing you?"

"Better not," I said. "In fact, it might help if you were to follow me around as if trying to discourage me, and warn me away from the places you think I might need to know about."

"I can do that. And— Oh. Tonight won't be a very good night for burgling. The dean is having a meeting today for some of his biggest donors. Technically, it's a meeting of the committee that awards one of our more prestigious scholarships, but they've already decided whose nephew is getting it this year, so it's mainly a big junket. After the meeting they'll go off to play golf, and then come back for a sherry party in the dean's conference room. They sometimes go on till past midnight. You'd have to come very late."

"And I have to get up early tomorrow," I said. "And besides, we don't want to rush into this. We have a plan for how we could do this if it's necessary, but we should hold off for now. I might be able to find out the information some other way."

"Tomorrow night would be better anyway," she said.

She didn't sound very optimistic about my chances of finding out the information. Of course, she didn't know Kevin. Then again, she did know the B-school.

"If you think of anything else, call me," I added to Ingrid. I rummaged in my tote until I found one of my business cards—the blacksmithing ones, not the special assistant to the mayor variety. It had my cell phone and email on it. I handed it to her.

"Thank you," she said as she tucked it into her purse. "I could give you my number, in case you come up with more questions. Do you have something to write it down with?"

She nodded with obvious approval when I pulled out my notebook, with its attached pencil, and rattled off both her office and home numbers.

"I can't really talk freely about this at the office, of course," she said. "If you call me there, I'll sound cross and pretend you're someone else, and then call you back as soon as I can from someplace more private. Now go put poor Charlie out of his misery." She smiled, and I decided she was going to be okay. I nodded and slipped out of the bathroom.

Chapter 8

Charlie was sitting at the nearest table, pretending to be nonchalant and failing miserably.

"Is she—"

"Fine," I said. "I'll fill you in outside."

We tried to keep a normal pace until we were outside in the Quadrangle. Then I stopped and looked around as if appreciating its beauty.

"So the bad news is that she knew the professor who committed suicide," I said. "Knew and liked him."

"Oh, my goodness." He shot a quick glance back over his shoulder.

"The good news is that after her initial shock she has decided she agrees with the podcast's suggestion that he was driven to it," I went on. "And she's willing to help."

"Help how?" Charlie asked. "We don't want her going out on a limb, if there could be danger."

"No, I warned her about that," I reassured him. "For starters, she's only going to search her diaries from that year for useful bits of information. And she's going to see if she can get us in to look at those alumni records—"

"We should only ask her to do that if we can think of a way that can't possibly get her in trouble," Charlie said.

"Agreed," I said. And then I had to smile. The "we" suggested that Charlie had promoted himself from information source to fellow sleuth. "And a way that won't get you in trouble, either. Oh, and she recommended I talk to a professor in the History Department who was a friend of the professor who committed suicide. Professor Forstner—do you know him?"

"Yes," Charlie said. "Not well—I'm not sure anyone knows him well, apart from a few of his colleagues in the History Department. Rather a frosty character—terrifies the students. At least the newer ones—the majors and the grad students seem to worship him from afar. Very distinguished scholar. And while he mostly stays out of academic politics, when push comes to shove, he shows up on the side of the angels, if you ask me."

"Glad you added that last bit," I said. "Maybe I won't chicken out of talking to him. Do you know where to find him?"

"He lives a few blocks from the town square," Charlie said. "I can look up his address when we get back to the office."

Just then my phone buzzed.

"Can you text it to me?" I said as I glanced at my phone and saw a text from Vern. "Something just came up."

"Off to interrogate another possible witness?" Charlie asked.

"Even better," I said. "Off to watch the police interrogate an actual suspect. I'll fill you in later."

Back at the police station, Vern was in the parking lot, leaning against the driver's side of his police cruiser, sipping a Diet Dr Pepper and doing something on his phone. I parked as close to him as I could and raced over.

"No need to rush," Vern called out as I drew near. "Plenty of time. We're having a slow day. Even the felons must be hunkered down waiting till all these rain squalls blow over."

"Then if we're not in a terrible hurry, can we go by an address on our way to the College Arms?" I asked. "Just to take a look at the place. It's supposedly not far from the town square so I don't think it can be too much of a detour."

"No problem," he said as he slid into the driver's seat. "Let me guess—corner of West and Bland Streets?"

"No," I said. "What's so special about that?"

"Intersection where young Casey was attacked," he said. "Thought maybe you might be curious to see it."

"Actually, I am," I said. "But right now I'm even more curious to see 513 Rochambeau Street." I read the address from Charlie's text.

"I know where that is," he said. "Something to do with one of those podcasts?"

"Yes," I said. "With the cheating scandal at the college. Professor Forstner, who lives there, was supposedly a good friend of the professor who killed himself."

He nodded, and I decided it wouldn't hurt—and might even be useful—to give him a brief rundown on my conversations with Charlie and Ingrid. Well, minus my discussions with them about burglary.

"So you're going to try to talk to this professor," Vern said when I'd finished.

I nodded.

"Smart to scope out the terrain first," he said. "That's his house coming up, third on the left—what you can see of it behind the shrubbery. I'll take it slow."

We were, as Charlie had said, only a few blocks off the town square—but this was one of the quiet, tree-lined streets that seemed half a world away from the tourist-infested center of town. In fact, it was one of the streets Michael and I had often driven along, back when we were house hunting, coveting nearly every house on every block while knowing the odds that any of them would go on the market were almost nonexistent, given Caerphilly's legendarily tight housing market. And while I didn't specifically remember his house, I knew we'd have coveted it. What I could see of it seemed to be in the charming, vaguely Tudor style that had been so popular in Caerphilly's more affluent neighborhoods a century ago. Michael and I had been particularly fond of that style. A freshly painted white picket fence enclosed the yard, and the house itself was almost hidden behind the azaleas and dogwoods. An old but well-maintained brick walk led up to the front door.

"Driveway's empty," I said.

"He could still be home," Vern said. "Parks his car in the garage. Which is smart, since he has one of those fancy new Volvo hybrids—I've seen him come and go in it a few times. You want me to pull over so you can study the layout a bit?"

"No," I said. "I just wanted to catch a glimpse of it."

He nodded and continued at the same sedate pace until the end of the block. I craned my neck to stare at Professor Forstner's house as long as I could. When Vern turned the corner and sped up slightly, I texted Charlie to thank him for the address and ask if he happened to know Forstner's class schedule.

The neighborhood gradually changed, the houses and yards growing smaller and the trees less plentiful. Businesses replaced houses—the less glamorous businesses that didn't cater to the tourist trade, like the feed store and the dry-cleaning plant. Then we spotted the bus station, and beyond it, the College Arms.

Vern frowned when we pulled up in front of the half dozen shabby, two- or three-story buildings that made up the apartment complex. Did his disapproval arise from the buildings themselves, which had been cheaply built and badly maintained? At least half of his male relatives—and these days a rapidly growing number of the female ones—worked in some branch of the building trades, so I could well imagine that he knew enough of the business to despise an eyesore like the one in front of us. Or was he remembering the many times he'd had to visit this block in his professional capacity? In a typical week the police blotter column in the *Caerphilly Clarion* was made up mostly—if not entirely—of goings-on at the Arms.

"Could have been a nice little set of apartments if they'd built it honest," he said as he parked in a vacant space in the building's courtyard parking lot. "And just once I'd like to go a whole week without having to visit this dump. I'm trying not to hold that against this Lucas Plunkett fellow. Probably the only place he could find."

"Or afford," I said. "What did Meredith Flugleman have to say about him?"

"He's been keeping his nose clean so far." Vern pulled out his phone and punched a few keys. "Does everything she tells him to. Not only makes all his appointments with her, he shows up early. I gather that's made a particularly good impression on her. So she's optimistic about his chances of rehabilitating himself, but worried that he might get pulled back into a life of crime by evil associates."

"He has evil associates?" I asked.

"Well, he has friends and relatives in Clay County." Vern chuckled. "Pretty much the same thing to Meredith. Clay County makes her nervous. She's pretty much ordered him not to set a foot across the county line. I'm not altogether sure she has the authority to do that, but maybe it's not such a bad idea. And so far he's following orders. Hang on—I've got the apartment number in here somewhere." He frowned at his phone for a few seconds. "Aha. Apartment two."

We got out and Vern led the way to the nearest open stairwell. Apartment 2 appeared to be a half-basement apartment—we took the stairs down to a landing whose corners were filled with last fall's dead leaves and a few thousand cigarette butts. Vern knocked on a door with a faded spot in the paint where the metal door number had fallen off.

We waited briefly. I didn't hear anything inside, but the stairwell was dark enough that we could easily see when the tiny bit of light coming from the peephole was blocked, presumably by an eye. Vern was the one who could be seen from inside, and I could tell he was deliberately keeping his expression calm and neutral.

The door opened halfway.

Chapter 9

"What can I do for you, Officer?" Lucas didn't sound confrontational, but you couldn't exactly call his tone warm or welcoming. He looked different from the mug shot. He was five years older of course, but it wasn't that. His face was leaner. Harder, maybe.

"Mind if we come in?" Vern said. "Just for a couple of minutes. We won't make you late for work, I promise."

I suspected Lucas did mind, but he wasn't about to say so. He stepped back and opened the door all the way. I followed him into the apartment's main room, which clearly served as both living room and kitchen. Lucas didn't have much furniture, which was probably a good thing, because the apartment wasn't big enough for much more than he had—a card table and two folding metal chairs in the kitchen end, and in the other a battered couch, and a TV set so old it actually had a picture tube. A short hallway by the kitchen probably led to the tiny bedroom and bathroom. The only natural light was from the sliding glass doors that led from the living room out onto a small sunken patio. And since the patio was surrounded on three sides by the yard-high brick walls that held back the earth and roofed by the concrete bottom of the balcony above, the apartment would have been pretty dim even on the sunniest of days.

I felt bad about staring at Lucas's rather sad living space, but he was so focused on Vern he hardly noticed me. For that matter, Vern was eyeing Lucas pretty closely. It was like watching two hounds trying to decide whether honor required them to fight or whether they could knock it off and go chase a squirrel together.

"I'm Vern Shiffley," Vern said. He didn't hold out a hand to shake, but he gave a quick nod.

"The mayor's cousin," Lucas said.

"Yup," Vern said. "Of course, I've been a deputy longer than he's been mayor. And this is Meg Langslow. Special assistant to the mayor—doing a ride-along with me today."

"Mayor Randall want something from me?" Lucas asked.

"No, the chief asked us to drop by," Vern said. "To kind of give you a heads-up about something. Mind if we sit?"

Lucas nodded toward the couch. Vern and I sat there, and Lucas turned one of the folding chairs around and sat in that.

"A heads-up," he said. "About what?"

Vern glanced at me before answering.

"Someone did a podcast about your case," Vern said. "Trying to cast doubt on whether you were really guilty."

"Wasn't me," Lucas said quickly.

"We know," Vern said.

"It was my nephew," I added. "Along with one of his friends."

Lucas really looked at me for the first time, with a puzzled expression on his face.

"And someone tried to run over the friend the other night," Vern said.

"That wasn't me, either." Lucas was starting to look angry.

"Yeah, I know," Vern said. "I checked it out. Your boss alibied you. But the chief figures maybe you might know something that could help us figure out who did do it."

"You think I got one of my friends to do it?" Lucas said. "I didn't, but there's no way I can prove it."

"According to your parole officer, you haven't had much to do with any of your old friends from back home," Vern said.

"Yeah." Lucas's face softened a little. It made him look a bit more like the kid he was in his mug shot. "I want to make a clean break. A new start."

"And do what?" I asked. The second the words came out of my mouth I wondered if Vern would find my interruption annoying, but if he minded, he didn't show it.

Lucas opened his mouth as if to answer then shut it and looked at Vern. Vern didn't say anything, so Lucas turned back to me.

"You'll probably think this is crazy," he said. "I mean, people in Clayville thought I was crazy for wanting to go to college. They'd ask what I was doing it for, and I didn't know myself. I just knew whatever I did, I didn't want to do it in Clay County."

I nodded.

"But while I was inside I . . . I fell in love with the law." Lucas laughed softly. "I guess that sounds pretty strange coming from someone who was doing five to ten in the slammer, but it's true. When I first got in I planned to focus on taking any kind of courses that would count toward getting a degree. But pretty soon I started helping other inmates with stuff. Like writing letters. Specially letters to their lawyers."

"That was a kindly thing to do," Vern said.

"Maybe it was kindly," Lucas said. "Bit of an ego trip, too. I mean, I'm no genius, and I only finished a year of community college before I went in, but I was like Einstein compared to a lot of those guys. And pretty soon I figured out a lot of them also seriously needed help figuring out what their lawyers were saying. Like the time I read this one guy a letter from his lawyer. It said something like 'I have found some evidence that could very well lead to your exoneration.' And the guy started cursing the lawyer and making all kinds of threats about what he'd do to the guy if he ever got his hands on him. Turned out he thought exoneration was another word for execution."

"Poor guy," I said.

"Yeah." Lucas leaned forward, and you could see that this excited him. "And he wasn't the only one who needed help translating letters from their lawyers, or dealing with their lawyers in other ways. Or finding a lawyer in the first place, and then there's trying to work the system when you can't afford a lawyer. Before long, I got to be pretty good at helping them. And I liked doing it. I'd like to keep doing it."

"So you became a jailhouse lawyer," Vern said.

Lucas frowned, until he saw that Vern's expression was approving rather than mocking.

"Pretty much," he said.

"Were you hoping to get exonerated yourself?" Vern asked. "From what I heard, when you were arrested you maintained that you were nowhere near the filling station that night, and the witnesses against you were mistaken."

"Yup," Lucas said. "Actually, I maintained that they were lying through their teeth. But I couldn't prove I was somewhere else. That's the problem with being innocent—you don't have an ironclad alibi, because you don't expect to need one and you didn't set one up. Anyone who actually pulls something like that filling station job is going to have a dozen people ready to swear on the Bible that he was at home watching television with them when it happened."

"So you were set up?" I asked.

He seemed to stiffen slightly, and took a few seconds before answering.

"You hear a lot of guys in prison saying they were set up," he said. "And it does happen. But a lot of guys jump to the conclusion that they were set up when what went wrong was bad eyewitness testimony, lazy police work, and maybe a bunch of dumb jurors who figure you wouldn't be on trial if you didn't do something bad. You don't need to be set up to be unjustly convicted. Sometimes it just takes a few bad breaks."

I noticed that he didn't actually answer the question of whether *he* had been set up.

"So if you're innocent, wouldn't it be a good thing, this podcast?" Vern asked. "You get exonerated, you won't have to serve another five years of parole."

"With Meredith Flugleman looking over your shoulder every minute," I added.

That got a flicker of a smile from Lucas, but his face grew serious again.

"Could mess with my parole if they think I'm trying to overturn my conviction," he said. "Parole board wants you repentant, not protesting your innocence. I thought of talking to them—the guys who did the podcast—to try to make them see that. Decided it was a bad idea. I should just steer clear. But you know them—do you know what they thought they were doing? Did they have some kind of evidence that would exonerate me? And if they did, why didn't they spill it? Because if they actually found anything, I'd sure like to hear it. And if they didn't have anything, what was the whole point of the damned podcast? If it was all rumors and guesses, why rake up the whole case? If I keep my nose clean for the rest of my five years, I'll be home free. But doing that's going to be a whole lot harder if Sheriff Dingle thinks I've been complaining about him and his department to some podcaster. Even here in Caerphilly they could find ways to make my life harder."

Vern nodded and said nothing. Lucas was looking at me.

"This whole podcasting thing is pretty new to me," I said. "But from what I've heard, I don't think they necessarily have to find new evidence to make it worth covering a case. In fact, I get the idea sometimes they're hoping to generate new evidence. Jog people's memories of things they might have forgotten. Make them realize they have information that hasn't yet been reported. Guilt-trip them into coming forward and telling the truth."

"Yeah, I figured out that was one thing they were trying to do," Lucas said. "Do you know if they've heard anything?"

"I think Kevin would have mentioned it if they had," I said.

I couldn't tell from Lucas's face if he was relieved or disappointed. Maybe a little of both.

"Friend of mine works cold cases down in Richmond,"

Vern said. "He's told me a lot about the methods and weapons they use. You could still have the biggest one on your side."

"If you're talking DNA, forget about it," Lucas said. "Sheriff's department didn't collect anything you could run a DNA test on. Even if they had, I wouldn't trust them to keep it uncontaminated."

"DNA's useful," Vern said. "But the biggest weapon is time. People change. They fall out with the friends who alibied them. Divorce the wives who covered for them. They get religion and want to confess. They join AA and want to make amends. They get drunk and brag about getting away with something. Stuff comes to light."

"If this was a cold case, I'd find that encouraging," Lucas said. "But it's over and done with, except for a few more years of parole. I just want to put it behind me."

"So you never talked to Kevin or Casey?" I asked. "For their podcast, I mean."

Lucas shook his head.

"Would it help if they made that point clear on their website?" I asked. "If they put up a disclaimer. 'We reached out to Lucas Plunkett, who was convicted of this crime, and he declined to speak with us.' Something like that?"

"I don't know." Lucas shrugged. "Couldn't hurt. But I'm not sure it'll help all that much. If Sheriff Dingell has got it into his head that I'm trying to cause trouble, it could take more than a disclaimer to calm him down."

"It would be a start, at least," I said.

"I'll see if I can find a chance to talk to Dingell," Vern said. "Convey to him that we've been keeping an eye on you, to make sure you keep your nose clean and your head down. Suggest that you were blindsided by the podcast and not too happy about it."

"Yeah." Lucas nodded. "Wouldn't be a lie, either."

"Maybe you could talk with Kevin and Casey, too," I suggested to Vern. "So by the time you talk to Sheriff Dingell you can say that you've had a word with the people responsible, and read them the riot act about casting aspersions on the criminal justice system, and you don't expect to hear any more about it."

"Might work." Vern chuckled softly at the idea. "I'll do that."

"As long as it doesn't put your nephew and his friend in any more danger," Lucas said. "After all, they didn't set out to cause me trouble."

"Good point," Vern said. "I can make it clear that it's a couple of kids trying to make a big noise when all they have to work with is a few newspaper articles."

"A few newspaper articles and a big dose of the sort of inter-county hostility that both sides have been working so hard to eliminate," I added.

"Truth," Vern said. "I can work with that."

Lucas nodded.

"But if they do hear anything—" Lucas began, then stopped short and stared down at the ground.

"Anything that would prove your innocence, you mean," I said.

"Yeah." He looked up. "You don't have to believe me, but I am innocent. I kept telling them—Sheriff Dingle and the prosecutor and even my own damned lawyer—and all I got back was an offer to reduce the charges to voluntary man-slaughter if I'd plead guilty and save them the hassle of a trial. They told me I'd be out in five years. After a while, didn't seem much use even trying to fight it, you know? So I gave in."

I glanced over to see how Vern reacted. He was frowning. Was that because he thought Lucas was guilty after all? Because he didn't like Lucas's implied criticism of the justice system? Or because he agreed that no matter how weak the case, Clay County could manage to convict Lucas if they wanted to?

"But back then I had no idea what I wanted to do with my life," Lucas went on. "Now I do. I want to be a lawyer. And being a convicted felon could kill that. It'll make it harder to get into law school. And even if I do manage to go to law school and pass the bar exam, they might not let me practice. They say you have to prove by clear and convincing evidence that you possess the requisite good character and fitness to qualify for admission to the bar."

He sounded as if he was quoting some official document that he'd reread countless times, looking for a loophole.

"I think that applies to all applicants," I said. "I remember when my brother was studying for his bar exam he spent a lot of time figuring out who he knew who could write him a good recommendation."

"Yeah, it applies to everyone," Lucas said. "But I'm pretty sure they set the bar a little higher when you've got a felony conviction on your record. Hell, my backup plan if I couldn't get into law school was to work as a paralegal, and it might even keep me from doing that."

"So you'd welcome the kind of evidence that would over-turn your conviction," Vern said. "But unless it's absolutely solid, you don't want to rock the boat."

"Not just don't want to," Lucas said. "Don't dare. I need to keep my head down and my nose clean for another five years."

Vern nodded.

Something occurred to me. I turned it over in my mind for a minute or so, then decided just to come out with it.

"You can tell me this is none of my business," I said. "But I saw the trial transcript."

Lucas nodded.

"You said they offered you the manslaughter deal to save the trouble of a trial," I continued. "But the case did go to trial—part of one, anyway. They called three eyewitnesses to identify you as the one who robbed the service station and shot Floyd Peebles."

He nodded again.

"And then your attorney called for a recess, and when the trial started up again, you changed your plea to guilty. Why? Because you saw how bad the case against you was? And how come they still gave you the deal, even though they had to have part of the trial?"

He stared at me for a little bit with an absolutely expressionless face. I wondered if that flat, deadpan expression came naturally or if it was something he'd developed in prison.

"Yeah," he said. "They said if I went to trial, they'd charge me with first-degree murder, and go for the death penalty. I said no, I'm innocent, so let's have a trial. Pretty stupid really. I should have realized if they wanted to convict me, they'd manage it. That got very real after that first morning of the trial. So I asked my lawyer to see if the deal was still open, and it was, and we agreed to it. Didn't seem much use even trying to fight it, you know? But it wasn't for nothing, that bit of a trial."

"What do you mean?" Vern asked.

"I didn't want to believe they'd do it," Lucas said. "The witnesses. I thought when it actually came to putting their hand on the Bible and swearing, they'd back down. Tell the truth. But they didn't. They lied through their teeth. Said whatever they thought it would take to convict me. And it's on the record, in black and white."

"Which could get them charged with perjury if you ever got enough evidence to overturn your conviction," I said.

"Not much chance of that," Lucas said. "I realize that now. But yeah. That's what I was thinking. Pretty stupid of me, I guess. I knew even back then it was a million-to-one shot. But I kept hoping. Because telling the sheriff a bunch of malarkey is one thing. Swearing to it in court is another. They're sworn perjurers. They helped convict an innocent man and let a killer go free. They know it, I know it, and the man upstairs knows it. It's enough." His face fell. "Well, maybe not enough. But better than nothing."

I nodded.

"You have any idea who set you up?" Vern asked.

Lucas shook his head. But he dropped his eyes. He was lying; I'd bet anything on that.

"That's a pity," Vern said. "Because if you ask me, the most likely suspects for that hit-and-run attempt would be who-ever set you up. Maybe they're afraid about what could hap-pen to them if the podcast turns up new evidence."

"I wish I could help," Lucas said.

"You think of anything, you let us know," Vern said. "And we should be running along so you can get to work."

"Thanks."

Lucas saw us out. I know it was only my imagination, but I could almost hear relief in the sound the door made when Lucas locked and chained it behind us.

Chapter 10

Vern and I walked to the car in silence.

"That was interesting," he said when we were back in the car.

"Hope it wasn't a problem, me butting into the conversation," I said.

"No, actually that worked out just the way the chief and I hoped it would," Vern said with a chuckle as he started the car. "We thought there was a better chance he'd open up to you. The man probably has good reason to be wary of anyone in uniform, but a civilian—and a woman to boot, and one who's worried about her family—we figured he'd open up more with you around."

"Glad I could be of service."

"Okay," Vern said as he pulled out of the parking lot. "This is going to sound pretty weird coming from me—but what if our friend Lucas there really did get a bad rap?"

"I'm listening," I said.

"You go up to any of the state prisons, and to hear the inmates tell it they've all been unjustly convicted, so normally I take something like that with a truckload of salt. But I checked out that podcast of your nephew's, and like I said to Lucas, anyone who was paying attention could tell that there really wasn't much to it. Nothing worth running someone over about. Just stuff anyone could come up with from reading the news reports on the case and knowing how Clay County works."

"I gather it was exam time," I said. "They had to pull together a podcast in a hurry."

"And did a good job, considering what little they had to work with, but there's just not much there. Bunch of vague hints that maybe Lucas either took the heat for someone else or got set up by the Clay County sheriff's office. Either of which is pretty plausible. Now that I've met him I can see Lucas doing the whole chivalrous, self-sacrificing thing if someone he cared about was mixed up in the robbery. And I definitely wouldn't put it past Sheriff Dingle to set someone up—either to protect one of his buddies, or just to improve their closure rate."

"Lucas sacrificing himself seems more plausible," I said. "After all, if Clay County set him up, why wouldn't he be trying to prove his innocence?"

"Maybe 'cause he likes breathing," Vern said.

After that, we rode on in silence for a minute or so.

"Okay, maybe that was a little melodramatic," Vern said. "But even if he's not worried about his physical safety, he could be worried about being sent back to prison."

"By revoking his parole."

"They'd have a hard time doing that unless they convince Meredith Flugleman that he's a bad egg," Vern said. "But they could also charge him with something else."

"Not as long as he stays out of Clay County."

"Something else from back when he was living there," Vern said. "They only convicted him of manslaughter back then. They could file armed robbery. Twenty years to life."

"Damn," I said. "And the robbery was only five years ago—I assume the statute of limitations on armed robbery is longer than that."

"Virginia has no statute of limitations on felonies," he said.

We drove in silence for a few more minutes while I digested that.

"Anyway," Vern said eventually. "Like I said, I'm starting to think maybe Lucas really wasn't guilty. Whether he did it to himself to protect someone else or whether they set him up, the podcast has got his hopes up. Made him think maybe some evidence will turn up to clear him."

"Or—playing devil's advocate here—maybe he is guilty," I said. "And thus afraid Kevin and Casey will unearth some evidence to prove it, thus making law school and being admitted to the bar even more unlikely."

"You really think he's guilty?" Vern asked.

"No," I said. "But I've been fooled before. And we don't really know for certain whether he has a motive for running down Casey or a motive for keeping him and Kevin alive and well and continuing to poke into the case."

"Even if he does have a motive for going after Casey, he's no dope," Vern said. "I don't think he'd do that without first finding out what Casey knows and who else knows it."

"Makes sense," I said. "So you don't think the hit-and-run is connected with the Clay County podcast."

"I didn't say that." Vern shook his head firmly. "I'm putting Lucas near the bottom of my own personal suspect list. But remember, they got internet over in Clay County, you know. Could be people besides Lucas who heard that podcast and want to find out what Kevin and Casey know. Or who think they can take care of the problem by getting rid of them."

I nodded.

"Some professor at the college had her car stolen Saturday night," Vern said.

"A Japanese compact?" I asked. "According to Kevin, that's what kind of car tried to run over Casey."

"Silver Toyota Corolla," he said. "And we found it in a ditch just this side of the Clay County line. Could have nothing to do with the hit-and-run. Kids joyriding."

"Or it could be some people from Clay County who wanted to shut Casey up, or at least scare him," I said. "And stole a car to make sure no one recognized their own vehicle."

"Could be," Vern agreed. "Chief's keeping an open mind. You don't need to tell him I told you that."

"Understood." It made me feel a little better to get confirmation that the chief wasn't totally disregarding Casey's story.

"Point is, I'm starting to believe Lucas," Vern said. "Maybe Clarence has the right idea after all."

"Clarence Rutledge?" I wasn't sure what our local veterinarian had to do with Lucas Plunkett.

"He's the one who gave Lucas a job when he got out," Vern said. "Not sure what his title is, but Lucas is the one walking the dogs and cleaning out the kitty litter boxes and staying up all night to bottle-feed orphaned puppies. And watching the shelter when Clarence takes off to rescue another load of critters from some out-of-state kill shelter. And Clarence can give him an alibi for the time of the attack on Casey Murakami."

"That's good," I said. "And—wait. Why was Clarence up at two a.m.?"

"Maudie Morton's beagle escaped again, and got hit by a passing tourist," Vern said. "He'll be fine—the tourist did the right thing and brought him over to the veterinary clinic, and Lucas called Clarence, and then helped him with the surgery. And either the tourist or Clarence or both of them can alibi Lucas from quarter past eleven until three in the morning."

"Good," I said. "And you know, if Clarence trusts him to take care of animals . . ."

"Pretty good vote of confidence in my book." Vern chuckled. "I remember I was pretty dubious when I heard Clarence was hiring an ex-con—and one from Clay County to boot. But he's a good judge of character, Clarence is. I shouldn't have doubted him."

"So Lucas moves to the bottom of our suspect list," I said.

"To the bottom," Vern said softly. "But not off it."

"Check," I said. "But now we need to figure out if anyone else from Clay County is up in arms about the podcast."

"Correction—*I* need to figure it out," Vern said. "Not a good idea for you to go poking your nose in there asking questions about Lucas Plunkett's case. I can find reasons to be hanging around there. Reasons to bring up the subject. You'd stick out like a sore thumb."

"If I did go there—"

"If they're worked up about the podcast, they'll have figured out that Kevin's your nephew and lives in your basement," he said. "So they'd be suspicious of you no matter what. You should probably steer completely clear of Clay County for the time being."

I didn't like it. Maybe because he was probably right. Vern's brand of good old boy charm would probably work on the denizens of Clay County. And even if it didn't, he was a lot better able to defend himself. Because if someone there really had tried to run over Casey . . .

"Keep me posted, then," I said.

"I will," he said. "If only to keep you on the right side of the Clay County border."

Just then we arrived back at the police station. Vern parked his car beside mine, and after we wished each other a good day he loped inside. Going to brief the chief, no doubt.

I got into my car and pulled out my notebook so I could jot down a few tasks—like asking Kevin if he had, or could find, any information on Lucas Plunkett's family and friends. Strategizing a way to run into Meredith Flugleman so I could drag the conversation around to Lucas Plunkett and see what she knew about him. Trying to decide how to approach Professor Forstner. Charlie had texted me Forstner's contact information and class schedule—should I call? Email? Just drop by?

Okay, I had to admit it—I was loitering here in the parking lot, just for a little while, in case the chief wanted to debrief me as well as Vern about our meeting with Lucas Plunkett. But after ten minutes of scribbling down notes—well, five minutes of scribbling and another five of trying to think of something else worth scribbling—I put my notebook away.

And then, before I could chicken out, I opened up my phone and composed a quick email to Professor Forstner, asking if he would be willing to talk with me briefly.

And then I bogged down. How to explain why I wanted to talk to him? Maybe I should wait until later. And do this at my computer, where it would be easier to compose the kind of long, complicated, nuanced email I'd need both to explain why I wanted to talk to him and to maximize the odds that he would agree.

I sat there for a while, mentally composing long paragraphs of explanation and then mentally tossing them into the trash. I finally added, "Ingrid Bjornstrom steered me to you" and pasted in a link to the podcast about the cheating scandal.

Then, muttering "just rip the bandage off," I pressed SEND and felt an immediate surge of relief.

Since neither the chief nor Vern had called on me to join whatever discussion they were having about Lucas Plunkett, I decided to head out. Drop by the B-school for my gargoyle photography session, and after that, out to Ragnar's to talk to Faulk. I seemed to be making progress on the Clay County case and the college cheating scandal. Maybe Faulk's expert knowledge of Charlottesville would help me come up with a way to tackle the Maddy duPlaine mystery.

Chapter 11

I started out in the Admin Services building, which felt like friendly territory—at least when compared to the B-school. Luckily I had my pocket-sized digital camera in my tote. I didn't use it as much as I once had; the pictures I took with my phone seemed just as good—in fact, as far as I could tell, the phone photos were probably better—and the phone had the additional benefit of being almost always in my pocket. But the little camera still sometimes proved useful—for example, when I'd taken Mother to a bridal show and realized that the camera would protect me from running down my phone's battery and filling its entire memory with pictures of centerpieces, cake toppers, finger bowls, ring pillows, lacy garters, and other expensive accoutrements that contributed to the wedding services industry being a fifty-billion-dollar-a-year business.

And running around with the camera in hand had another benefit. Having an actual camera, however small and cheap, seemed to place me firmly in the ranks of photographers, either of the journalistic or the artistic species, instead of the less palatable one of mere nosy snoops. It even helped me get completely into character as I roamed the halls of the Admin building. I squealed with delight when I spotted a particularly ornate bit of bas-relief. I borrowed a stepping stool from one of the custodial staff to get a better close-up of a hallway gargoyle. I used my phone's flashlight feature to better illuminate an intricate bit of carving that happened to be hidden in a dark corner. In fact, I actually began to make a mental plan for a bit of gargoyle-themed ironwork that would be inspired by the Admin building's baroque woodwork. I'd do a sketch later. Ragnar would love it.

When I'd taken a hundred or so photos and explained my mission to half a dozen bemused Admin Services employees, I decided it was time to venture across the Quadrangle to Pruitt Hall.

And luck was with me. Well, luck and a little strategic planning. Before leaving the Admin Services building, I managed to borrow a copy of the college directory for a few minutes. It included both phone numbers and office numbers for all staff and faculty along with almost unreadably tiny maps that showed where all the various offices and classrooms were located. I figured out which door would bring me into Pruitt Hall as close as possible to Ingrid's desk.

And my calculations were correct. I'd snapped only half a dozen shots of carvings and gargoyles when I heard her voice ring out, in a much less friendly tone than she'd used in our bathroom conversation.

"I beg your pardon, miss—were you looking for someone?"

I turned to find Ingrid standing in the hallway behind me. A smile quirked the corners of her lip before she controlled it and returned to her stern gatekeeper's look.

"Only for gargoyles," I said. "I'm working on a design for a set of wrought iron gates, and the customer wants gargoyles. They have some over in the Admin building, but they told me the business school has a greater selection, since it's done a much better job of preserving the design integrity of its building."

"I believe you're correct on that score." She did a good job of pretending to thaw after my praise of the B-school's preservation efforts. "Have you—"

"What's going on here?" A balding, beak-nosed man in a pin-striped suit darted out of a door on my left and glared at me and Ingrid in turns.

"Good afternoon, Professor Vansittart," Ingrid said. "This

young lady is taking pictures of gargoyles for a design project. The Admin Services Department suggested that she come over here, since our commitment to maintaining the integrity of our building's architecture means we have a vastly superior collection of them."

I thought she might be laying it on a bit thick, but Vansittart seemed to buy it. I was doing all I could to hide my reaction to his name, but I'd definitely lucked out. Vansittart—one of the other three people who'd been at the B-school at the time of the cheating scandal. I studied his face, all while smiling as if delighted to see him.

"I see." Vansittart gazed up at the nearest gargoyle, with the satisfied look of someone who discovers that a recent purchase was an even better bargain than he imagined.

I had to suppress my laughter when I realized that the gargoyle was thumbing its nose at him.

"Yes." Vansittart's voice was nasal, as if he might be recovering from a head cold. "I think we can safely say that we do a better job of maintaining the value of our property than most departments. Gratifying to know that Administrative Services is aware of this. But the dean is meeting with the Renfrew Committee this afternoon. To discuss the scholarship selections. We can't have random people wandering the halls while that's going on."

Left to my own devices I'd probably have spoiled my chances of continuing my tour by asking what right he had to keep people out of a college building. How did he know I wasn't a student? Did he realize that I was, in fact, a faculty wife? Luckily Ingrid appeared to be expert at managing her department's temperamental faculty.

"Of course not," Ingrid said. "I will accompany her to ensure that she doesn't disturb the dean, or interfere with any other department activities." She turned back to me. "This way, if you please."

Evidently Vansittart had no objections to my presence as long as I was under proper supervision. He nodded his approval and went back into his office. In the few moments before he shut the door, I got the impression of a really large space filled with brass and mahogany.

For the next half hour, Ingrid and I made our way decorously up and down the corridors of Pruitt Hall, stopping to take pictures of every gargoyle we passed. She did a great job of helping me get a sense of the building layout, mainly by telling me, in a stage whisper, why we had to keep our voices down in a corridor, to avoid disturbing a class in session or a faculty member hard at work on his or her research. In a few cases, she pointedly explained why a corridor was off-limits entirely.

"I'm afraid I can't permit you in that corridor," she said at one point on the second floor. "The dean's office is down that way—his office and his conference room. He's got a very important meeting going on at the moment."

I took particular note of that corridor, peering down it with a show of sighing at the lost opportunity to immortalize its gargoyle population, before following her on to the next point of interest.

We ended up back on the ground floor again, near Vansittart's office.

"I hope you got enough photos for your project," she said in that tone of institutional courtesy that suggested she'd used up all the time she had to spare for me. Only the occasional twitch of her lips into a fleeting smile reassured me that she was enjoying this.

"You've been a great help," I said. "Thank you."

"You're welcome," she said. "Oh, and I think you suggested you'd like to use the ladies' room before you left—it's down that way." She pointed to a small side corridor.

"Great," I said, and trotted obediently in the direction she indicated.

The ladies' room was unoccupied. It was old-fashioned, but in a stately vintage way. The decor probably dated from the 1940s, though I could tell some of the sinks and toilets had been replaced with newer fixtures in the same style. The walls were made of pale aqua ceramic tile with borders of black tiles at the top and bottom and pristine white plaster from the top of the tile to the twelve-foot ceilings. The floors were made of inch-square black and white tiles laid in a diagonal pattern. A small crystal bowl held a bouquet of lush silk peonies. At first glance I thought they were real, actually, and they might even have earned Mother's approval. She generally disapproved of using silk flowers unless real ones were unavailable or impractical, but she'd have forgiven the deception here since the faux petals were absolutely dust-free.

Having appreciated the decor, I turned my attention to more practical matters. The window was, indeed, a suitable one for burglary. It was an old-fashioned sash window of enormous size—three feet wide and at least eight tall, with panes of frosted glass. I could see why the ladies hadn't thought the frosted glass enough, though. I tried to imagine how light and airy the bath would be if the windows weren't totally blocked by holly. And the bottom sill was only a foot off the bathroom floor, which meant I'd have no problem getting out again. But how far down was the ground outside? And had Ingrid ever actually opened this huge window? If it was painted shut, or if the sash was old and hard to raise, we'd have to find another plan. And maybe finding a plan that didn't involve burglary was the smartest thing anyway.

But as long as I was here, I should check the window. I glanced around, and paused to listen for footsteps outside. I didn't hear anything. And this bathroom probably wasn't that heavily used, given the male-to-female ratio here in the B-school—I pegged it as about ten to one, both in the students I saw when I glanced into classrooms and the staff and faculty I encountered in the halls.

I strode over to the window, reached up to unlock it, and then gave the lower sash a tentative push. It floated up as smooth as silk. And the ground outside—what I could see of it under the thick layer of spiny holly leaves—was only an inch or two lower than the bathroom floor.

I was about to shut the window again when I heard a voice.

"I still say they're up to something."

Chapter 12

I started, and looked around, but I saw only holly leaves. And I realized the voice wasn't coming from here in the bathroom. It was coming from another open window—probably one in the room next door.

"What could they possibly be up to?" Another voice, but a very similar one. Both were rather thin and nasal, as if their owners had shared a cold and were both slightly congested.

"They're trying to dig up dirt. They're dangerous, I tell you."

"I suppose that's why you came down for the Renfrew Committee," the first voice said. "You don't usually bother."

I finally recognized the first voice—Professor Vansittart. That made sense—he'd come out of an office near here.

"Someone had to look after the family reputation," the second voice said.

Family reputation? Could there be more than one Vansittart?

"You always panic unnecessarily," Professor Vansittart said. "If you'd just relax and leave it to me—"

"Oh, don't play the condescending big brother with me," the other voice said. "I think I have a much better idea what constitutes real danger. I'm the one who made it on the outside, remember, in the rough-and-tumble of the corporate world, while you hide away here in your cushy little academic nest. Those who can, do, you know."

Professor Vansittart didn't reply immediately. I could imagine him bristling with resentment at the familiar insult. And just for a moment, I felt sorry for him.

"Am I putting you up this time?" he said finally.

"No, I've checked into the Inn," his brother said. "Since the college is paying. I'm sure you'll be happier without having to host me. And I can pretend I'm staying on to play some golf."

"Staying on?" The professor's voice sounded sharp. "After the meeting?"

"As long as it takes to settle this," his brother said. "To find out if we have a problem. And take care of it if we do."

"Take care of it how?" Professor Vansittart asked.

I'd have loved to hear the answer, but just then I heard footsteps approaching the ladies' room. I eased the sash down as quickly as possible and managed to be back at one of the sinks, fussing with my hair, when the door opened and an angular middle-aged woman with a stern face strode in with brisk steps. She looked surprised to see me—surprised, and not entirely pleased.

"Afternoon," I said over my shoulder.

She nodded in reply and disappeared into one of the stalls. I fiddled with my hair for another few seconds, then made a faint grimace as if to suggest I'd done as much as I could with it. Maybe it was overkill, but the lady in the stall looked like the nosy kind who'd peek through the crack in the door to catch me not playing my part. I picked up my tote, left the ladies' room, and made my escape from Pruitt Hall.

When I got back to my car, I picked up my phone to text Kevin. Then I decided this warranted a call.

"I assume this is important," he said instead of hello. I made a mental note to work on reforming his telephone etiquette when I had more time.

"I think I've found a good suspect," I said. "In fact, two of them."

I related everything I could remember about the conversation I'd overheard—jotting the highlights down in my notebook as I talked.

"Sounds suspicious to me," Kevin said. "But kind of vague. I mean they *could* be talking about Casey."

"Or they could be talking about something entirely unrelated," I said. "It's not like they're going to come out and say something like 'Now that our first attempt to run over Casey Murakami has failed, let's discuss how we're going to assassinate him and his friend Kevin.' That only happens in the movies."

"So what am I supposed to do?" he asked. "Look up their pictures so I'll have a clue if they come after me?"

"For a start, yes," I said. "Then find out everything you can about them. Professor Claude Vansittart and his younger brother. I don't know the brother's first name, but it can't be that hard to track down someone with a name like that."

"Yeah, should be a lot easier than Smith," Kevin said. "I'm on it."

After hanging up, I took several of the calming breaths Rose Noire was always recommending. Breathe in for four counts, hold your breath for four counts, then breathe out for four counts. And I reminded myself that if the Vansittarts were the ones who had tried to run down Casey, we were onto them. We could sic the chief on them.

In fact, should I do that now? I glanced down at my page of notes. It all sounded so vague. And then there was having to explain what I'd been doing skulking around the B-school, eavesdropping on faculty conversations.

I'd send him an email tonight, after I'd had time to digest the conversation.

And maybe after Kevin had found a little more scoop on the Vansittarts.

Then it occurred to me—was there more than one Vansittart on the list Charlie had given me? I still had it in my tote. I pulled it out and flipped through it until I got to the *V*s. There they were. Two Vansittarts, Claude W. and Vincent R. Charlie hadn't ticked off Vincent's name, because he wasn't still here but out "in the rough-and-tumble of the business world."

I texted Kevin the name. Not that he wouldn't find it himself eventually, but I liked to show I did manage to find out information myself on occasion.

I was in a good mood as I threaded my way through the tourist traffic at the center of Caerphilly, and an even better one once I left the town behind and was cruising along the road toward Ragnar's farm. Partly because it felt as if I was making progress in my quest to find out more about the cases Kevin and Casey had featured in their podcasts. I'd already located two possible information sources about the cheating scandal and I'd as good as delegated the filling station murder to Vern and the chief. With luck, Faulk would help me figure out a strategy for investigating Madeleine duPlaine's disappearance. And for the first time in weeks, I hadn't spent most of my day enmeshed in the minutiae of the looming wedding.

Or maybe I was just in a good mood because I was headed out to Ragnar's.

Ragnar Ragnarsen was a retired heavy metal drummer who'd bought a farm near Caerphilly. Actually, most people called it an estate. Ragnar was slowly redoing the house and grounds to suit his own aesthetic vision, which was a sort of mishmash of high Goth, renaissance faire grandeur, and the set of a Hammer Films horror flick. Yards of black velvet, occasionally relieved by touches of blood red. Lots of carved dragons and gargoyles. And enough wrought iron to build a steampunk battleship. Under several previous owners, Ragnarsholm, as he'd dubbed it, had once been a staple of local Garden Week tours, but even though Ragnar would have been perfectly willing to open his gates for the occasion—had even offered it several times—the mere thought of subjecting unsuspecting visitors to its new decor caused Mother and the other garden club ladies to retire to their couches with cold compresses on their aching foreheads.

And since so many of his projects involved custom-made wrought iron, he kept Faulk and me busy. I was still his favorite blacksmith, but once he understood that Faulk had taught me everything I knew, he would reluctantly agree to settle for Faulk if I wasn't available. Faulk, bless his heart, took this philosophically.

I arrived at the wrought iron front gates, which were all my creation. I stopped outside them, at the stone pillar that held the security keypad, and took a moment to appreciate what I'd done—the intricately wrought, slightly twisted bars, graced with black metal roses, bony claws, and delicate iron spiderwebs. Faulk might be better at certain kinds of blacksmithing—much more skilled at sword-making, for example. But thanks to Ragnar, I'd become a past master at the kind of Gothic fantasy ironwork he loved. Candelabra shaped like skeletal hands. Lamp finials in the form of miniature buzzards. Fences that looked like something Sauron would commission to defend the borders of Mordor. There was a lot of it, none of it easy, and none of it cheap. Ragnar never counted the cost.

And for that matter, adaptations of things I'd done for Ragnar sold pretty well at craft shows, and especially at renaissance faires. I didn't have as much time for my forge as I liked these days, but thanks to the inflated prices my work earned both from Ragnar and other like-minded buyers, I was still making a decent living at it. Now that Michael had received tenure, his job was relatively secure—but it was still reassuring to know that, in a pinch, I could probably support the family rather well with my blacksmithing.

No time for daydreaming, I reminded myself. I punched in the security code and went in.

I drove slowly. Ragnar had a lot of animals, many of whom strayed onto the driveway with alarming frequency. He raised several breeds of heritage cattle, including shaggy black-coated Scottish Highland cattle with enormous curved horns; Ancient White Park cattle, ghostly white with horns that were almost as impressive; and two kinds of what Jamie and Josh called Oreo cows—black cows with white belts around their middle. He'd inherited the Belted Galloways from the previous owner of the house, but realized, to his dismay, that they were naturally polled—which was cow-speak for born without horns.

"I thought someone lopped them off," he'd said. "And I was not going to do such a cruel thing to the new little baby cows. But it turns out they were bred to have no horns. The poor defenseless creatures!"

As a result, he'd acquired some rare Lakenvelders—Dutch belted cows that he considered much more satisfactory, since they came with horns of a respectable length. I hadn't figured out whether he was simply planning to gradually phase out the Galloways or whether he thought he could restore their horns through crossbreeding with the Lakenvelders, but in either case he was vastly proud of them all.

He also had flocks of black sheep and goats, but I had a hard time keeping track of them all. Or of the various black chickens, ducks, turkeys, geese, and swans that freely roamed his pastures.

Given the fact that even the best-maintained fences weren't very successful at keeping the goats confined, he limited his gardening efforts to two spots protected by ornate twelve-foot black wrought iron fences that Faulk and I had crafted. One, right below the terrace, was a moon garden, featuring only pale flowers that bloomed or released their scent at night, and the other included every species of black or nearly black plant or flower he could find.

Ragnar was nothing if not persistent in pursuing his landscaping and architectural visions. And well able to afford it, thanks to his several decades of drumming for bands that must have been highly successful in spite of my never having heard of them, since heavy metal had never been one of my favorite musical genres.

As I drew near the house I saw that his latest construction project was going well. Over the last few years he'd gradually had the exterior redone so it looked less like an ordinary (if enormous) stone mansion and more like a working medieval castle. Now he was halfway through the project of erecting towers at the various corners of the building. Two towers were complete, and the third looked almost ready for occupancy.

When I reached the house I took a sharp right turn and followed a side lane to the brink of the moat. After I entered my code into the keypad on another of the little stone pillars, the drawbridge slowly creaked down, and I was able to drive over the moat, through a menacing iron portcullis—Faulk's design—and into the guest parking lot, which was roofed over with wrought iron trellises thickly covered with flowering datura vines, so that from above, our internal-combustion anachronisms wouldn't offend the sight of any newcomer who was looking for the full medieval experience.

I spotted Faulk's truck, but didn't recognize any of the other half dozen vehicles occupying the lot. And half a dozen suggested it was a slow season for Ragnar as a host. Ragnar always had guests. A lot were visiting musicians who wanted to jam with him, spin yarns together about their wild days on the road, or talk him into doing a guest appearance on one of their recordings. But he also played patron to any number of what he called "starving artists"—writers, painters, sculptors, actors, stand-up comedians, mad genius inventors, and of course musicians. Some had been in residence for years, and had gradually been given jobs suited to their abilities. The shepherd who tended the sheep and goats was a prize-winning poet. The head landscaper was an elderly former actor who'd been blacklisted in the McCarthy era and had lived in genteel poverty until Ragnar invited him to stay. And Ragnar had lucked out a few years ago when he'd given refuge to a friend of a friend who reputedly needed a place to recover from a toxic work situation. It turned out that Alice, the refugee, was a recent graduate of the Culinary Institute of America and the toxic work situation was a prestigious restaurant with a Michelin star or two, run by a misogynistic tyrant of a chef. Ragnar had hired Alice at a generous salary and rebuilt the kitchen to her specifications. These days even the people who were appalled by his decor rarely turned down his dinner invitations.

I punched my security code into yet another keypad while smiling up at the security camera I knew was concealed above it. Inside I followed a stone-lined corridor complete with leering gargoyles until I reached the elevator. I wanted to keep following the corridor to the workshop where Faulk would be, but I knew I should pay my respects to my host first. So I smiled and waved at yet another invisible security camera, stepped inside the elevator, and hit the button for the main floor.

I emerged in the entry hall, a large octagonal room decorated in black, red, and silver. A black-and-red rug softened the black marble floor. Dark tapestries hung on the nearly black stone walls. At regular intervals along the walls, skeletal black wrought iron hands appeared to thrust out of the stone, holding torches so cleverly made you had to look very close to realize the flames weren't real. Suits of black armor stood at intervals around the periphery, and the walls were festooned with black-hilted swords and brooding black gargoyles.

"Meg! Is that you?" Ragnar ran out into the entry hall to give me a bear hug.

Chapter 13

At six foot eight Ragnar was several inches taller than Michael, and a great deal burlier, so being hugged by him was always slightly nerve-racking—would this be the time his enthusiasm for seeing me caused him to forget that I was a mere mortal whose bones were not made of iron?

"Of course it's me," I said. "Or weren't you watching me arrive in your surveillance cameras?"

"Come and meet my guests!" Ragnar exclaimed, pulling me into the great hall, which performed much the same function as the rooms we mere mortals called our living rooms. It was decorated for comfort rather than grandeur, so even though the black, red, and silver theme continued, the whole room had a much more relaxed feel. The black velvet couches and red velvet chairs were sinfully comfortable and all the dark—almost black—wooden side tables and coffee tables were already decorated with enough rings, slashes, and stains to make it perfectly clear that no, you didn't need a coaster.

"Everyone—this is Meg, my blacksmith!" he exclaimed.

"Along with Faulk," I said.

"My main blacksmith," he corrected. "The blacksmith of my heart. This is Ben." He indicated a shaven-headed man of about fifty who was sitting on one of the comfy couches, dressed in a black t-shirt, black jeans, and black Doc Martens, which meant that he blended into the upholstery. Probably one of Ragnar's musician friends, or possibly a former bandmate—they tended to look like this. His eyes were closed and he was frowning slightly, as if annoyed by something.

At Ragnar's words Ben opened his eyes, nodded at me, and closed them again.

"And that is Lars at the piano."

Lars was a moody-looking twenty-something, rail-thin with a blond mohawk. He was also dressed in black, although his black clothes were tighter, cut along a more medieval line, and decorated with bits of silver and strategic rips. He was draped over the keyboard like a swooning vulture and appeared totally absorbed in playing and replaying six or seven notes. Doubtless this was meant to convey the impression that he was enmeshed in the throes of musical creation. It might have worked better if the notes he was playing didn't sound so much like the opening of the theme from *The Godfather*. Perhaps Lars was the source of Ben's annoyance.

"And *this* is *Cassie*," Ragnar's tone clearly showed that he had been saving the best for last. "She is making me a new guitar. Acoustic," he added.

"Nice to meet you." Cassie had a soft, husky voice and a pleasant smile. She rather stood out among Ragnar's guests, mainly because she looked perfectly normal. She was wearing faded jeans and a loose gray t-shirt. Her mostly gray hair was pulled back into a casual ponytail and she wore large glasses with slightly tinted lenses. She looked vaguely familiar. If she was a guitar maker—and one good enough to earn Ragnar's approval—we might have met at some craft event. Possibly at one of the high-end American Craft Council shows, which were all about craft as art, with prices to match. I hit one of those occasionally, although I felt more comfortable at the shows that focused more on craft as making beautiful stuff you can actually afford to buy and don't feel guilty using in your day-to-day life.

From the way Cassie was looking at me I suspected I also looked vaguely familiar to her, and we were probably about to have one of those conversations in which we tried to figure out where we'd met before and which crafter friends we had in common. But instead she stood and turned to Ragnar.

"I should get back to my workshop," she said, and disappeared.

Not in the direction I'd be heading, though. Ragnar had set up a lovely workshop in the ground floor of one wing of the house—I almost said castle. The workshop had plenty of room for me and Faulk and several other people to work at the same time.

Ragnar saw my face and guessed what I was thinking.

"I set up a workshop for her in one of the towers," he said. "Her work requires great quiet and serenity. She must get the acoustics of each instrument just right."

"I can certainly understand that," I said. Even people whose work didn't require that much quiet and serenity might not want to share working space with a blacksmith or two. "This isn't Cassie's first visit, is it?" I added. "I think I've met her before."

"Not here." He frowned as if puzzled. "This is her very first visit." Then his face cleared. "But of course! You recognize her from seeing her onstage! Which is very clever of you—between the Viking costumes and painting our faces to look like skulls, I have a hard time telling which one I am in the photos from those old days. Still, except for her hair, which was blond then, she has changed less than any of us. She would probably still fit into her costume. I would need two costumes now." He sighed, and patted his stomach, which showed definite signs that Alice's cooking was having its way with him.

I nodded. Although Ragnar knew heavy metal wasn't my favorite genre, I'd managed to avoid confessing that I'd never heard him play until his arrival in Caerphilly. But now I knew where I'd seen Cassie. The next time Ragnar invited me to his well-equipped home recording studio, I'd study the framed posters that decorated the walls and figure out which of his old bands she'd been in. Avoid embarrassing myself if that particular band came up in conversation.

"I should be going to the workshop myself," I said. "I just

stopped in to say hello before I talk to Faulk about something."

"You should stay for dinner," he said. "We are having a Norwegian feast to make Lars feel at home."

Over at the piano, Lars rolled his eyes in a manner that suggested he'd much prefer takeout from the local burger joint.

"We are having *lapskaus!*" Ragnar exclaimed. "*Kjøttkaker! Rømmegrøt! Raspeballer! Brunost! Vafler! Kanelboller! Lefse! Tilslørte bondepiker! Medisterkaker! Sodd! Fårikål!* And *trollkrem!* Alice has outdone herself."

From over by the piano I heard a heavy sigh. Lars was probably a new arrival. Even people with no appreciation for haute cuisine or ethnic feasts usually enjoyed Alice's meals.

"I have no idea what any of that is," I said. "But I'd stay and give it a try if I wasn't expected home to play hostess to the hordes of relatives arriving for the wedding. Rain check?"

"I will save you some," he said. "Except for the trollkrem— you have to eat that as soon as it's made. But I will invite you and Michael and the boys out soon to enjoy it all."

"It's a deal," I said. And I meant it.

I returned to the entry hall and pressed the button for the elevator. As I was waiting, one of the guests spoke. Probably Ben, since Lars's monotonous plunking continued uninterrupted.

"You know, Ragnar, that's one thing I really like about staying 'ere." He had a definite cockney accent. "Everyone treats you just like an average bloke. It's a nice change from 'aving to fight off the birds all the time."

From which I deduced that Ben probably was—or at least had been—a person of note in the world of heavy metal.

Then the elevator arrived and I didn't catch what, if anything, Ragnar said in reply. It would have been something tactful.

Back on the ground floor I took a series of stone-lined passages that snaked and twisted through a perfect maze of rooms—storerooms, mechanical rooms, workrooms, and for all I knew, replica dungeons for visitors who liked that sort of thing. Strange to remember how many times I'd gotten lost when I first began coming to Ragnar's. Now my feet followed the familiar route almost mechanically.

I eventually arrived at a heavy wooden door with impressive iron hinges. I flipped up a faux stone cover to reveal the hidden keypad, typed in my code, and entered the workroom.

Faulk was at his anvil, hammering on an iron bar. He was working thoughtfully rather than briskly, which suggested he was experimenting with something—probably working out a new design. He knew I was there—we both made a habit of rattling the door loudly before we entered, because sneaking up on a blacksmith is never a good thing. I watched, admiring his technique. Okay, admiring Faulk as well. He was almost as tall as Michael, with blond, blue-eyed good looks and the kind of muscular body you'd expect from a blacksmith.

After a few more sharp raps he plunged the iron into the waiting water trough and turned to greet me.

"Consider yourself hugged." He reached for the towel he kept near his forge and scrubbed his face and hair dry. "But you might want to skip the real thing. Not only have I been sweating here at the forge for two hours, but the goats got loose this morning, and I had to help wrangle them back into their pasture. Have some krumkaker before I eat them all."

He gestured toward his worktable, where I spotted a plate piled high with cookies—flaky little tubular cookies dusted with powdered sugar.

"*Krumkaker,*" I repeated as I reached for one. "More of Alice's Norwegian goodies?"

"It's insidious," he said. "Ragnar keeps dropping by with goodies today. I have no idea what any of it is, but it's all delicious, and I've probably gained ten pounds. At least I can take the krumkaker home and feed them to Tad, who can eat his weight in pastry and not gain an ounce."

"I don't want to eat all of Tad's cookies." The krumkake was delicious, and I'd been on the point of reaching for another.

"Don't worry—if you clean that plate, Ragnar will insist on giving me more to take home. In fact, I'll see if I can bring some for Josh and Jamie when we come over tomorrow for the rehearsal."

"Another rehearsal?" Faulk and his husband, Tad, were among the groomsmen for the wedding. Mother seemed to have recruited half the county to the wedding party—would there be anyone left to fill the pews and watch us process into the church? "She didn't tell me."

"One o'clock tomorrow," Faulk said. "She probably assumes you'll figure it out, given your superior powers of intuition and deduction."

"She'll have to get a stand-in for me," I said. "I'm going down to Charlottesville tomorrow. Partly on wedding business, and partly on a sleuthing mission."

"A sleuthing mission—has your dad sucked you into another one of his projects?" Faulk sounded a little wistful, as if he wouldn't mind helping Dad with a project.

"Actually, it was my nephew Kevin," I said. "Did you hear that he and his friend Casey have started a podcast?"

"I've actually listened to a couple of episodes," he said. "And while I can see that they'd be better off if they had someone who actually did a little real boots-on-the-ground research, I'm surprised they've suckered you into doing it."

"Actually, I'm only trying to find out which one of their cases almost got Casey killed." I related what I knew about the hit-and-run attack. "Kevin's convinced whoever did it is connected to one of their cases," I added. "And just in case he's right, I'm seeing what I can find out about the most likely ones."

"I bet the Clay County case is one of them." Evidently Faulk really had listened to some of the podcasts. "I remember thinking at the time that it wasn't exactly a brilliant idea, making fun of Sheriff Dingle and his merry band."

"The chief's taking an interest in that one," I said. "So I can focus on the other two leading candidates. The cheating scandal at the Caerphilly College Business School—"

"And the disappearance of Madeleine duPlaine," he finished. "I assume that's why you're going down to Charlottesville."

"You really have been listening," I said. "I have no idea exactly what I'm looking for—or what I can possibly find that the Charlottesville police haven't dug up in the last twenty years. But you know the town better than I do—and you were there around the time she disappeared. I thought I'd see if you had any ideas."

He nodded. He was holding the iron bar he'd been hammering on, twisting it slowly in his hands.

"I actually knew Maddy, you know," he said. "Not well. We sort of dated for a few months."

Chapter 14

"Sort of dated?" I echoed. Faulk hadn't come out as gay until a year or so after I met him, but he'd known his own mind, as he put it, since high school, and I didn't recall him dating any women.

"Protective camouflage for both of us," Faulk said. "Seeing me squiring around an attractive woman kept my family from disowning me until I'd graduated. They didn't approve of her, of course. Complained that she was a hippie."

"A hippie?" I said. "Wouldn't that term have been just a little out-of-date, even back then?"

"Yeah, but that's my family. Hippie was pretty up-to-date for them. Still, they were pleased, although I could tell they were hoping I'd ditch her for someone more suitable. And Maddy was looking for protection. She had this crazy stalker who wouldn't leave her alone. She thought having someone around with my size and strength would keep him at bay."

"And did it?"

"Seemed to, for a while," he said. "He stopped bothering her. Eventually he disappeared. Just packed up all his stuff and left town. When we were sure he was gone, Maddy and I faked the sort of friendly breakup that would make it easy to pick up the masquerade again if he came back, but he never did. And a few months later, she disappeared."

"According to what Kevin told me, the police never did figure out if it was murder or kidnapping or if she disappeared voluntarily," I said. "What was your take?"

"I don't know." He shook his head. "First I heard of it was

when the police showed up at my door to see if I'd done her in."

"Yikes!" I felt a twinge of stress, even though I knew it must have ended okay, since he was here telling me about it and not sitting in a prison cell.

"Her two bandmates covered up her disappearance for as long as they could." Faulk grimaced slightly. "They were on the verge of signing a contract with a big record company, and worried that if their lead singer looked like an unreliable flake it would ruin the deal. So they ran around looking for her for a couple of weeks, which made things a lot harder when someone else reported her missing."

"Harder for them or for the police?" I asked. "The trail would have been pretty cold by then."

"Ice cold." His mouth tightened briefly as if holding back a condemnation of the bandmates. "Plus the rumor got out that they were only pretending to look for her, to cover up the fact that one or the other had lost his temper and killed her."

"Why would they do that?" I asked. "I got the idea that she was the main reason a record company was even interested in them."

"That's kind of the point. The story was that they'd found out the record company didn't want to sign the whole band, just her. The police seemed to think that was a plausible motive for murder. So when the police started putting pressure on the bandmates, they tried to throw me under the bus."

"Damn."

"Didn't get them far," he said. "When my family found out, they hired a top defense attorney. And I sicced the cops on the stalker. Who, as I said, had also completely disappeared. Kind of focused their suspicions on him instead of me."

"Did they ever find him?"

"If they did, I never heard about it."

"Okay, am I allowed to say that this is a really weird coincidence?" I asked. "I knew there was a chance you'd have a little more information about Madeleine duPlaine than I did, since you moved to Charlottesville three years earlier. But that you actually knew her? Sort of dated her? I'm not sure I buy a coincidence quite that weird."

"That's because it's not a coincidence." He chuckled, raised the iron rod he'd been toying with, and shoved it back into the fire. "I told your nephew Kevin about the case. I ran into him at the diner and told him I'd listened to the first few podcasts. He started complaining about how they didn't have a good case for their next podcast. And I thought of Maddy. Something had happened recently to remind me of her."

"Anything in particular?" I asked. "Not that I'm trying to be nosy, but—"

"But now you're interested in anything about her." He pulled the iron rod out of the forge, but instead of hammering it, he set it down on his anvil and studied me for a few seconds. Then he smiled.

"I know you're good at keeping secrets when you're asked to," he said. "So . . ."

He let the word linger as he walked over to the workbench and picked up something. His phone.

"This is what reminded me," he said.

He pressed something on the phone, and guitar chords emerged from a small Bluetooth speaker someplace else on the bench. No, not chords—a series of arpeggios that made up the familiar introduction to "The House of the Rising Sun." One of the first songs a beginning guitar student would learn, at least back in my college days. I could almost feel my fingers forming the chords: A minor, C, D, F.

Then came the voice. Maddy's voice, a contralto that managed to be bell-clear and yet throbbing with emotion. I felt the hairs on the back of my neck rise as I listened. I closed my eyes so I could listen without distractions.

When the music ended I opened my eyes again to see Faulk standing, phone in hand, with a bemused expression on his face.

"Just her and her guitar," he said. "And the sound quality's not great."

"You don't notice that when she's singing," I said. "Where did you get it? Kevin said he and Casey couldn't find any recordings of her."

"A couple of weeks ago I walked in on Ragnar listening to it in his library," he said. "From an old cassette tape he got hold of someplace—he wouldn't say where, which probably means it's a bootleg. Though why that would matter after so many years I have no idea. Anyway, I'd been listening to my digital version when I ran into Kevin."

"And didn't play it for him?" That didn't sound like Faulk.

"Wasn't safe to do that—Ragnar doesn't know I have it." Faulk looked shamefaced. "I snuck back into the library and stole the cassette. Not permanently—just long enough for Tad to make a digital copy of it. Then I slipped it back where Ragnar was hiding it. Don't tell him."

"I won't," I said. "As long as you make me a copy. Don't worry—I won't share it with Kevin, either."

He laughed.

"I'll get Tad to send it to you," he said. "You know I'm all thumbs when it comes to electronics. He's now officially as besotted with her voice as I am, and he's doing a deep dive into all the places that sell bootleg recordings, trying to see if he can find any more of her music. So far no luck. But you can see why she was on my mind when I ran into Kevin. All that glorious talent, and not a trace of it left except for one cassette tape that was already starting to disintegrate."

I nodded.

"So what do you hope to find in Charlottesville?" he asked.

"I have no idea," I said. "Some sign that anyone there even noticed the podcast, I guess. It's not really about finding her so much as figuring out if the podcast ticked off anyone connected with her case."

"Talk to Amanda," Faulk suggested, referring to an African American weaver we both knew from the craft fair circuit. "She's been in Charlottesville for a while now, and I think her husband was actually born there."

"And he's also a musician," I said. "Why didn't I think of that?"

"Because she was living in Richmond when you first met her, and since you only see her at craft fairs, you haven't had to update your mental map."

"Yeah." I pulled out my phone and checked my contact list. I had a Charlottesville address for Amanda, which meant the odds were good that the phone number I had was current. And while I had the phone out, I shot a quick text to her: "If I find myself in Charlottesville tomorrow, will you be around?"

"No time like the present, is there?" Faulk was grinning at me.

"The life I save may be my nephew's," I said. "Besides, I have to go down there in the next day or two anyway to pick up some peacocks for the wedding."

"More peacocks?"

"More decorative ones. Ours have all molted. So what happened to Maddy's bandmates? Did they ever make it big?"

"They never made it out of Charlottesville," Faulk said. "The bass player OD'd a year or two after Maddy disappeared. The drummer was still there when I left. I'd run into him occasionally if I went someplace where they liked to have live music but didn't want pay a lot of money for a decent band. He always pretended not to remember me, and I was happy to return the favor."

"Do you remember his name?" I flipped my notebook open, just in case.

"Tony something." Faulk closed his eyes as if eliminating visual distraction would improve his memory. "Antonelli. Tony Antonelli."

I nodded and jotted it down. I wondered if his parents had actually given him a name like Anthony or Antonio that was almost a clone of his last name or if the nickname came from the last name. I could sic Kevin on that question.

"Let me know if you find out anything about Maddy." Faulk was glancing over at his anvil. Probably a hint that he wanted to get back to work.

"Seems unlikely," I said. "I'll probably start by finding out where the luckless Tony was Saturday night."

"Kevin and Casey did rather bash the bandmates, didn't they?"

I nodded. I was remembering the show I'd seen during my high school visit to Charlottesville. I didn't remember any bandmates—just Maddy herself, singing in a spotlight on the tiny stage of the basement coffeehouse. Was she performing solo that night? Or did she just overshadow the rest of the group that much? Either way, maybe the bandmates were right to worry that she was going to ditch them.

But did that add up to a motive for murder?

Just then Ragnar dashed in.

"Meg! Faulk! You must taste this!"

He was carrying two small dishes filled with what looked like pink whipped cream flecked with reddish spots. He handed one to each of us, along with a spoon.

"If this keeps up, you'll have to roll me out of here in a wheelbarrow," Faulk said. But I noticed that he didn't hesitate to pick up the spoon and sample the dessert.

I followed suit and scooped up a spoonful. The texture was lighter than whipped cream—more like beaten egg white. Almost like cotton candy. But instead of being sticky-sweet it was tart and fruity.

"*Trollkrem!*" Ragnar said triumphantly.

"Delicious," I said.

Talk of Madeleine duPlaine gave way to exclamations of delight over the trollkrem, along with discussions of when I could bring Michael and the boys out for a Scandinavian feast. Ragnar had also brought a tin full of krumkaker for me to take to the boys, and insisted on helping me carrying it to my car.

It wasn't until I was waiting for the drawbridge to lower so I could leave that I noticed I had a reply from Amanda.

"Tomorrow's great. Arriving when?"

I stopped long enough to reply that I'd give her an ETA when I saw how early I managed to make my start. I added "And this is what I'm looking into," and shot her a link to Kevin and Casey's podcast about Madeleine duPlaine. Then I headed for home in a happier frame of mind.

I managed to limit myself to eating only three krumkaker on the way home.

Chapter 15

There were a lot more cars parked up and down the road when I got home. The clan was already gathering for the wedding. Although actually anyone here this early had arrived not just to attend the wedding but to help make a reality out of Mother and Holly McKenna's vision of it. But at least someone had put up a sawhorse to save my usual parking spot.

As I got out of my car I noticed that rather a lot of the visiting relatives were using wheelbarrows to haul large potted plants into the backyard—roses, azaleas, camellias, gardenias, hydrangeas, and several other kinds of flowering bushes. Other cousins were rearranging the pots under orders from Mother and Holly McKenna. Who seemed to have two different ideas about where the various plants should go. I watched one poor cousin move the same rose back and forth four times before sitting down, crossing his arms, and refusing to touch it again. Mother and Holly both came over to chastise him, and after a short discussion, they both laughed, and Holly turned her diagram upside down from the way she'd been holding it. The cousin didn't seem as easily amused by her mistake, and waited until both Mother and Holly were pointing in the same direction before picking up his shrubbery again.

I walked around to the front door and found Rob standing just outside the opening in the hedge, a bemused expression on his face as he stared down at the front walk, which was now ornately decorated with lilies and roses. And roped off with clothesline from which a WET PAINT sign hung.

"Hey, Meg," he said.

"I gather we should go in the back way," I said.

"What do you suppose they would say if we told them . . . you know what."

Rob was referring to the fact that he and Delaney had secretly gotten married over the Christmas season, with only me and Michael as witnesses—making the elaborate extravaganza Mother and Holly were organizing technically an astoundingly elaborate renewal of their vows.

"They'd kill you," I said. "And repurpose this weekend's festivities into an over-the-top funeral. Seriously, don't even think of it."

"Oh, I'm not," he said quickly. "Just wondering. And starting to feel the pressure a little."

Uh-oh. From what I could see, the one indisputable benefit of the fact that he and Delaney had already tied the knot was that neither of them appeared to be suffering from pre-wedding jitters. Of course, maybe it might be more believable if one or both of them showed some signs of jitters. I'd suggest that to Delaney, who was a better actor than Rob.

"Have a krumkake," I said, opening the tin and holding it out. "It'll make you feel better."

I helped myself to one while the tin was open, and we began making the detour to the backyard, munching happily.

"Oh, before I forget—here." Rob handed me a key ring. I could tell it was Dad's by the small plastic skeleton dangling from it. "Dad insisted that I help him ferry his truck over here. It's in the driveway, all ready for you, with that big cage strapped in the truck bed. What do you need it for anyway?"

"Fetching some peacocks," I said. "I'll be gone most of the day tomorrow."

"All day? Where in the world are the peacocks?" Rob asked. "California?"

"Charlottesville," I said. "But I have a couple of other errands there."

"Dad couldn't find any more-convenient peacocks?" he

asked. "And why do you need to fetch any peacocks in the first place? Don't we have enough already? Mother and Dad must have nearly a dozen over at their farm if your two aren't enough."

"We can't use any of the family peacocks," I said. "Haven't you noticed? They're all molting. Which means they're losing all their beautiful feathers and will soon look like large, naked chickens."

"So instead of being decorative they're totally gross," he said. "Cool! I've got to see this."

"You'll have to go over to Mother and Dad's to see them," I said. "They're in exile there until after the wedding."

"But they can't miss the wedding," Rob said. "They're family members, too, aren't they? I mean, Cousin Frank showed up with a killer case of poison ivy—his whole face is covered with oozing blisters. You're not going to banish him, are you?"

"Mother might already have banished him," I said. "The calamine lotion he's wearing totally clashes with the bridesmaids' dresses. And I'll banish him myself if the poison ivy makes him as cranky as the peacocks are."

"The peacocks are always cranky."

"Not like this."

"Oh, you're no fun." Rob shook his head as if saddened by my attitude. "I think we should find a place for them in the ceremony. I think we should find a place for *all* the animals in the ceremony. Tinkerbell can be dog of honor, with Spike as the best dog. And all the Pomeranians can be bridespuppies. We let the flower girls lead the llamas. The chickens will love cleaning up all the birdseed people will throw at us instead of rice. And—"

"Sounds fabulous," I said. "Why don't you talk to Mother about it?"

"Just because it's an important occasion doesn't mean it can't be fun." Rob sounded almost sulky.

"I agree," I said. "If I were in charge, I'd say no problem.

Let the llamas *be* the flower girls—they're more predictable than toddler cousins. Have the wedding in the barn—it's freshly painted. Just don't ask me to talk Mother into any of it."

"You know, that gives me an idea," Rob said. "A really interesting idea." He wandered off with an absent-minded look on his face. Normally that look would mean that he'd thought of a good idea for another game. And according to the statistics maintained by the Mutant Wizards' Vice President in Charge of Useless But Interesting Stuff—a real title—Rob's thoughtful looks translated into successful electronic games nearly 80 percent of the time, which gave him a better batting average than Ty Cobb and Rogers Hornsby combined.

Should I warn Mother that Rob might be plotting something?

No. Rob was always plotting something. And Mother knew it.

If coming up with some ridiculous suggestion for the wedding and trying to convince Mother he was serious was his way of dealing with his pre-wedding jitters, maybe it was a good thing.

I pulled out my phone to check the time. I had a solid two hours before dinner. Now seemed like a perfect time to spend some quality time with all those files Kevin had given me.

Assuming I could avoid getting sucked into any of the work that was happening around me. In the backyard, a posse of relatives were grooming the llamas and braiding bells and ribbons into their shaggy coats. Not, I hoped, for the reception—no one who knew llamas would expect them to stay clean and decorated for the next several days. More likely the official wedding photographer was coming over to take more advance photographs. Or maybe they were experimenting with different ways of decorating the llamas. I decided not to ask, lest I get roped into helping.

Another nine or ten people—a mixture of family plant enthusiasts and members of the local gardening club—

were pruning the bushes—though not the kind of whole-sale pruning in which you lopped off big branches and changed the whole shape of the plant. They were giving each shrub the kind of careful, delicate attention that bon-sai masters give to their charges. Much stepping back and scrutinizing the plant in question from all sides before tip-toeing forward to snip off nearly invisible bits of foliage. I steered clear of that group, too.

I could tell by the sounds coming from the kitchen that a crew was hard at work there, preparing for the evening meal. Definitely not something I wanted to get drafted for. I hurried across the yard before they could spot me.

Still another crew was obviously readying more parts of the barn for painting—scrubbing any dirt off the sides and taping the glass in the windows. I managed to slip inside without being recruited, and retreated to my office. I texted the boys that I had goodies for them in the barn. Then I sat down at my desk, propped my feet up, and began digging through the files Kevin had given me.

Interesting. Of the thirteen files, ten were fairly fat, and three were remarkably slender—the three he'd flagged for me as top priority. Had he sicced me on these cases because they were the most likely to have triggered an attack on Casey, or mainly because he hadn't been able to find out much information about them?

I put on my headphones and began sampling some of the other podcasts while I perused the matching case files, just to get an idea of what they were like.

It was obvious why Kevin hadn't asked me to look into the case of the Three Sisters in Black, who'd run a girls' board-ing school in Christiansburg, Virginia, and had been respon-sible for the untimely deaths of several well-insured family members. A picturesque story, especially the bit about the three of them dressing all in black and never going out with-out heavy mourning veils—but it had all happened around 1910, so the odds were that anyone even remotely connected with the case was long gone. Maybe they'd included it in an effort at equity, since it seemed to be a rare example of a female serial killer—or killers.

They had a fat file on the Colonial Parkway murders, in which at least four couples had disappeared or been killed in the late '80s near my hometown of Yorktown. Some of the people connected to these cases were still around—surviving family members or law enforcement officers who'd worked the cases. Kevin and Casey had actually interviewed a few of them. But so had countless other people. The file wasn't fat with new evidence but with copies of existing coverage of the case. Articles from the Newport News *Daily Press* and the Norfolk *Virginian-Pilot*. Printouts from Michelle McNamara's *True Crime Diary* blog. Transcripts of shows from the Investigation Discovery Channel and from the local CBS affiliate. Kevin and Casey had done a good job of summing up the case. Casey gave an impressively logical analysis of which canonical and related cases he believed were connected and which were done by different perpetrators. And I had to admit that Kevin, who had seen the Parkway hundreds of times while visiting his grandparents in Yorktown, knocked it out of the park on atmosphere and local color. During the day, driving twenty-three miles of highway with no commercial development or houses, just trees, was pleasant. Relaxing—even inspiring. But Kevin captured how downright spooky and isolated it felt at night. All in all, a creditable show on the case. But I couldn't imagine that anything in it had struck fear in the heart of an aging serial killer who'd evaded detection for more than thirty years.

It was the same with all of the ten fat files—a lot of information, but nothing that looked like a breakthrough. Sometimes they seemed to use the cases more as platforms for a topic. Their show on the Martinsville Seven, a group of Black men executed in 1951—on little or no evidence—for attacking a white woman, for example, was more about the still timely topic of racial bias in the justice system. Until I listened to their podcast about Richmond's Southside Strangler, I hadn't known that this case from the '80s marked the first time DNA had been used to solve a capital murder case, and the show was less about that one case than about the evolution of using DNA in crime solving. Someone—probably Casey—had clearly spent a lot of time thinking about crime and justice.

But while all of the ten fat-file shows were informative, entertaining, and well researched, they clearly hadn't done the kind of probing, in-person sleuthing you'd probably need to do to uncover exciting new evidence. Then again, I gathered the whole point was to crowdsource the investigation—to reach people who either liked doing that kind of digging or who already had pieces of information that for whatever reason they hadn't previously shared with either the press or the police.

Of course, crowdsourcing an investigation would work a lot better if the podcast was actually reaching a large number of people. But was it?

I flipped through the papers Kevin had given me. Somewhere—yes, here it was. A printout showing how many people were listening to the podcasts.

"Now this is interesting," I muttered, sitting up straight in my chair. According to Kevin's graph, their audience had been pretty minimal . . . up until last Friday. One day after the podcast about the Clay County case . . . and the day before the attack on Casey.

I was reaching for my phone to text Kevin when I heard the familiar tones of the family dinner bell. Even better—I could ask him in person.

I tucked the printout into my tote and left my office.

The buffet dinner was laid out in the backyard on two of our collection of picnic tables, and the rest of the tables were quickly filling up with diners. But Kevin wasn't among them. I went up to where my cousin Horace was waiting in line.

"End of the line is back there!" a couple of teenaged cousins chorused, pointing to the other side of the lawn.

I turned to give them a withering glare and saw that Mother had beaten me to it.

"Meg *is* your hostess, you know," she said. "And a key part of the wedding planning team. If she has something more important to do than wait in line—"

"And I don't," I put in. "I just wanted to talk to Horace." I refrained from actually saying "so there" and sticking out my tongue at the young cousins, but they could probably hear it in my voice. I turned back to Horace.

"Have you seen Kevin?" Horace tended to see more of Kevin than most people, largely because when he was on duty he often brought his Pomeranian puppy over to play with Kevin's.

"Not since I got here," he said. "But his car's here, so I assume he's down in the basement with his computers."

I nodded and went inside. I dodged the dozen or so frantic members of the kitchen crew, breathing a sigh of relief when I could close the basement door and take the stairs down into the cool, dark quiet of the basement.

Well, relative quiet. If you stopped and listened you could hear the humming of at least a dozen computers. Occasionally one of them would beep, or a printer would erupt into action. And often you'd hear Widget, Kevin's puppy, barking joyously as he ripped yet another squeaky toy to shreds. Not today, though.

I expected to find Kevin either staring moodily at one of his computer monitors or typing at lightning speed on one of the keyboards. Instead, he was pacing up and down beside the broad wooden counter on which most of his computers lived. As I watched, he went up to a keyboard, apparently at random, typed in something, then swore and went back to pacing. Widget, his Pomeranian, was sitting on the counter and watching him with a worried expression.

"What's up?" I asked. I took a seat in one of his many ergonomic desk chairs. Widget walked closer, hopped from the counter into my lap, and curled up as if in need of comfort.

"We're screwed." He looked ashen.

Chapter 16

"What's wrong?" I asked. "Who's screwed, and why?"

"Casey and me. We don't have anything."

"Don't have anything for what?" I asked.

"For this week's podcast, of course." He rolled his eyes slightly. "I was so busy trying to figure out which of our past cases might have made someone try to bump off Casey that I didn't have time to research any of the new cases on our list. I figured it wouldn't be a big deal—Casey would have something. But he was so shook up that he couldn't concentrate, and he figured I'd come up with something. We're supposed to record tonight, and we've got nothing."

"Can't you just skip a week?"

"That would be a big mistake," he said. "We're trying to get advertisers, and maybe place the podcast on one of the premium podcast providers. To do that, you need the numbers, and you need to prove you can deliver on schedule. And at the stage we're at, reliability's even more important than a big audience. Hell, reliability's one of the ways you *build* a big audience—people know they can tune in every week for fresh content."

And here I thought the podcast was merely a labor of love.

"We're totally screwed," Kevin moaned.

"No you're not," I said. "This week you're introducing a special new feature—an interview with a medical examiner."

"A medical examiner? But where would— Oh! You mean Grandpa?"

"Of course." I had already pulled out my phone and started a text to Dad. "When do you need to start recording?"

"Casey will be here at eight," he said. "But what are we supposed to interview Grandpa about? We can't ask him about a case if we don't have one prepped."

"Good heavens," I said. "You're the true-crime experts. Hang on a sec." I finished the text to Dad, asking him to come to the basement ASAP because Kevin needed his help. Then I turned back to Kevin. "You know your grandpa. When is it ever hard to get him talking about any of his favorite subjects? And so many of his subjects are about crime. Just ask him a leading question and turn on the microphone."

Kevin nodded slightly, but his face still showed doubt.

"Ask him why it's important to have a medical examiner system instead of elected coroners," I suggested. "Or about times when he or other doctors he knows of have detected murders that might otherwise have gone undetected. Or what crime shows and novels get wrong about the medical side of crime. You could even do a follow-up from the ME's perspective on one of your existing cases."

"You're right," Kevin looked a little less gloomy. "He certainly can talk. And he's usually pretty entertaining."

"You might want to be careful if he gets into autopsies," I said. "He can get a little graphic sometimes."

"That's okay." Kevin was grinning now. "We tape the shows, so we can edit out anything we don't want. And besides, it's a true-crime audience. They can take graphic. And just in case, we can slap a content warning on at the beginning."

"And if Dad goes over well, you might consider interviewing other special guests," I suggested. "Horace can be fascinating if you get him started about forensic stuff. Get Chief Burke to tell a few war stories from his days as a homicide detective in Baltimore. Interview Festus Hollingsworth about some of his most memorable court cases. And I bet your great-grandfather could spin a few yarns about environmental crimes. The show could take on a whole new direction."

"It just might work," Kevin said. "Do you have any idea where Grandpa is?"

I glanced down at my phone.

"He'll be here in about fifteen minutes," I said. "He's in the backyard, filling his plate at the buffet."

"Awesome!"

"You want me to have someone bring a plate down for you?"

"Maybe later." He shook his head. "I'm too wired to eat right now."

"Can you answer a few questions?"

"Okay." He sat in another of the chairs, wearing the expression you'd expect from someone about to undergo a hostile interrogation.

"Chill," I said. "You're freaking out poor Widget." I handed him the Pomeranian, since I knew from experience that it was hard to stay stressed while scratching a small furry dog behind the ears. "These statistics about how many people listen to the podcast." I brandished the printout.

"Yeah," he said. "You see why it's important not to skip a week. We don't want to lose our momentum."

"This doesn't look like momentum to me," I said. "It looks like something suddenly happened a few days ago to bring in a whole lot more listeners. Do you have any idea what?"

"Yeah." Kevin looked calmer now that he was holding Widget—or maybe now that he knew rescue for his podcasting problem, in the form of his loquacious grandfather, was on the way. "Two things, actually. That Friday the *Caerphilly Clarion* did an article about the podcast. A really positive article. That morning, as soon as the article went online, we started seeing two or three times as many hits."

I nodded, and refrained from pointing out how unimpressive their statistics must have been to start with, if coverage in our weekly community newsletter tripled them.

"And then Friday evening Casey shared a link to the *Clarion* article in a couple of true-crime discussion forums," Kevin went on. "And our hits went through the roof. A lot of sites would have been overwhelmed by that much volume, but we did just fine, because I planned for it and had the server capacity ready to handle it. Although I didn't really expect it to rev up quite that quickly."

"That's useful to know," I said. "About the *Clarion* and the forums, I mean. At first, I thought the Clay County case was the most suspicious of the cases—not only because it was the newest but also because the hit-and-run attempt happened only two days after it went live. But it's not like network TV or live radio, is it? You put out the Charlottesville case three weeks ago and the college cheating scandal one seven weeks ago, but not many listeners even heard them until a few days ago."

"Yeah." He waved a hand at the spreadsheet I was holding. "Only about one percent of our listeners heard those episodes the week they went up. The other ninety-nine percent listened in the last few days. So that means the older cases are just as likely to have upset someone, right?"

"I still think the Clay County case is more likely to be connected with the attack on Casey," I said. "But it does mean the other two are still in the running. By the way, I have a data file for you. Check your email."

I pulled out my phone, opened up my email, and forwarded the email from Charlie. Kevin hitched himself closer to one of the computers and typed in a few keystrokes.

"Who are all these guys?" he asked a few seconds later.

"Are they all guys?" I reached into my tote to pull out my copy of the printout. I knew the business school wasn't particularly progressive, but surely they did let in some women.

"Okay, I stand corrected," he said. "Maybe one in eight or so is a woman. So who are all these mostly guys?"

"Everyone who took or taught a class in the business school the year of the cheating scandal. Start looking for them."

"All of them?"

"Well, technically they're all suspects," I said. "But I'm particularly interested in finding out if any of them are on the faculty of other business schools." I explained Michael's and my theory that people still working in the academic world would care a lot more than most people about being revealed as a college cheat.

"Cool." His fingers flew over the keyboard for nearly a minute, and then he nodded with satisfaction. "Consider it done. Anything else?"

I assumed that meant he had set in motion some kind of program that would start hunting down possible mentions of the people on the list. Probably better not to ask, because his explanation was unlikely to enlighten me. Was there anything else? I thought for a moment.

"You're recording your podcast tonight," I said. "Are you free tomorrow night?"

"I can be. What for?"

"We might need to burgle the business school."

He didn't look nearly as excited by this idea as some other family members would. Michael would have exclaimed "What fun!" Dad or Rob would have been over the moon.

"Don't we already have their suspect list?" He waved at the monitor, on which bits of text flashed and disappeared at random intervals.

"We need to get access to their donor list." I explained the theory that the donor list might show if some students—or their parents—had bribed the school to overlook their involvement in the cheating scandal.

"Well, that makes sense," he said. "But why don't I just see if I can access it? I mean, not that I go around poking into college files that aren't any of my business—"

"Sure you don't."

"But I could if I needed to," he said. "If it was justified, and I think catching whoever went after Casey would be pretty good justification. If you have any idea where the data is stored, let me take a crack at accessing it."

"I know exactly where the data is stored," I said. "On a set of three-by-five index cards in an oak card file that's locked in the B-school dean's office."

Kevin blinked for a few seconds as if he had trouble taking in the concept.

"Wow," he said. "I thought maybe you were going to say that they stored their data in a computer with no internet connection. But index cards? They must be really paranoid."

"It's possible," I said. "But I think it's more a case that they're just really, really behind the times."

"So what do you need me for?" he said. "It's not as if I have any burgling skills."

"No, I have the burgling skills," I said. "But I want backup in case something happens. And at first I thought I'd ask Michael to help, but I don't want to get him in the kind of trouble that would happen if a faculty member got caught burgling another department. And Rob's too busy with the wedding. And Dad would have a blast, but he'd tell everyone about it afterward and get us in trouble. So you're elected. Besides, it's your case. And if contrary to my expectations our mission does happen to involve computers or any other post-medieval technology, you'll be there to cope with it."

"Okay," he said. "I'm going to do a little snooping in their systems tonight or tomorrow, though. You never know—maybe they back up the index cards with some kind of modern system."

"I hope they do," I said. "Because if they don't, we might have to burgle the B-school to get the information."

Just then Dad came bouncing down the stairs. He was carrying his bag—which in spite of looking just like an old-fashioned doctor's black bag was actually a remarkably complete modern emergency medical kit.

"What the problem?" he called out.

"Sorry," I said. "I should have mentioned that it wasn't a medical problem."

"And Kevin knows I'd be no help on a computer problem." Dad chuckled.

Kevin winced as if remembering past times when he'd had to untangle computer problems for Dad.

"He needs your brain," I said. "Did you know Kevin and a friend of his have started a true-crime podcast?"

Dad's eyes grew wide. His jaw dropped. It took him several seconds to speak.

"A true-crime podcast? How wonderful! What do you need me to help with?"

I left them to it.

Upstairs, I almost ran into Rose Noire, who was about to descend into the basement with a tray. Presumably for Kevin, although there seemed to be enough food on it for a dozen people.

And when I went outside, I ran into Chief Burke. He was eyeing the chow line with surprise.

"Horace and Rose Noire both insisted that I drop by for dinner," he said, as if he felt the need to explain his presence. "I thought they were kidding when they said no one would notice me in the crowd."

"The line should ease soon," I said. "And while we're waiting for that to happen, could I have a word?"

Chapter 17

We strolled away from the line and found a place where we weren't likely to be overheard—leaning against the fence near the far end of the llama pen.

"I gather you've spent the day investigating Kevin's cases," he said.

"Not the Clay County one," I said. "I totally understand the wisdom of leaving that to the professionals. So if anyone told you they saw me sneaking across the county line, they're pulling your leg."

"Glad to hear it."

"I'm concentrating on the two older cases," I said. I filled him in on the four people who had been in the B-school at the time of the cheating scandal and were still around today—although I didn't name Charlie as my source of information. I managed to imply that Kevin had gotten the information. "And when I went over there to see if I could talk to one of them, I overheard a scrap of conversation that struck me as rather . . . creepy."

I related what I could remember of the conversation between the two Vansittarts.

The chief listened in silence. Then he pulled out his notebook and asked me to repeat what I'd told him.

I wasn't sure whether to be pleased that he was taking an interest in the Vansittarts or worried that he thought he needed to.

"I'll check them out," he said when I'd finished.

"Check them out how?"

"Well, for starters," he said, "I can probably find out if

Vincent Vansittart was in town when Casey Murakami was attacked—without alerting him to the fact that I'm looking at him."

"But asking Professor Vansittart for an alibi would be reaching," I said.

He nodded.

Over by the picnic tables a cheer went up, and we turned to see that Rob and Delaney had arrived and were instantly surrounded by well-wishers. The chief's face relaxed into a smile at the sight. Then he turned back to me.

"I agree, the conversation sounds creepy," he said. "Especially since we know about the attack on Mr. Murakami. Although I think I'd find it creepy even if we didn't know about that. Or the connection between Professor Vansittart and the cheating scandal. But it's still rather vague."

"And I could be jumping to conclusions," I said. "I know that."

"And I agree that it is possible that they were talking about the cheating scandal," he went on. "The bits about 'family disgrace' and 'digging up dirt'—those certainly seem to fit. And yes, since we know about the attack on Mr. Murakami, 'dealing with it' does have a rather ominous ring. But let's assume that they are talking about the cheating scandal. That one or both of them was involved. It doesn't follow that their method of dealing with it would be to run down one of those responsible. Especially since that would do nothing to clean up the problem—the podcast would still be there."

"True," I said. "And it's not as if either Kevin or Casey got a sinister threat, the whole 'we know where you live—take down the podcast or we won't miss next time.'"

"Exactly. Sinister threats, or maybe just a cease and desist letter from their attorney."

"That was my idea, too," I said.

"Anti-Asian prejudice and ruffians from Clay County are still my top two theories on the case. But we'll do what we can to check out the Vansittarts."

"You know," I said, "the attack on Casey didn't happen

that far from the campus. From the old part of campus where the B-school is."

"True." He looked thoughtful. "Of course, we're reasonably sure we've identified the car used in the attack."

"The stolen one abandoned near the Clay County line?"

"Yes," he said. "But we haven't made that public yet. It would be perfectly natural for us to do a little canvassing of people who live or work in the area."

"Asking where they were at the time of the attack, and whether they saw or heard anything."

"Well, since the attack took place at two in the morning, I expect most of them will have seen nothing and heard only snores."

"Ah, but what if you suspect the car to have been stolen much earlier," I said. "Or what if it was a part of a rash of stolen cars that night? Or over several nights, so you'd be asking their whereabouts on several other days, thus concealing exactly which day you're asking about lulling their suspicions. Or—"

"I'm going to assign Vern and Aida to canvass the buildings around the Quadrangle tomorrow." I was relieved to see that he appeared amused rather than annoyed. "I'll tell them that if they have any trouble constructing a plausible cover story, they should consult you."

"I was sounding a little like Dad, wasn't I?" I said. "I'm sure neither of them needs my help. I'm just relieved that they'll be looking into this. Want to rejoin the chow line? It's gotten a lot shorter."

"Good idea."

Of course we still had a short wait before we reached the food, so while the chief chatted with a couple of my uncles, I pulled out my phone to check my email.

I had a reply from Professor Forstner.

"Ingrid Bjornstrom believes you are seeking the truth about what happened twenty-six years ago," it read. "If that is correct, I would be willing to talk to you. I will be home this evening between seven and nine o'clock." He followed it with his address, which I had already, of course.

It was six fifteen. I had enough time to eat and drive into town. I might even make it by seven on the dot if the buffet line moved at a reasonable speed.

So I sent a reply that I'd try to be there by seven, and spent the next few minutes glaring at anyone ahead of me who seemed to be dawdling at the buffet.

Glaring worked. By twenty minutes to seven I was fueled up and on my way into town.

Michael was still out with the boys, or I'd have asked what he knew about this Professor Forstner. And told him where I was going. It occurred to me that it would be a good idea to make sure someone knew where I was going. In fact, several someones.

So when I got to within three blocks of Forstner's house with five minutes to spare, I pulled to the side of the road to kill a few minutes, in case the professor was persnickety about people showing up early. And I used the time to text a couple of people. Michael. Kevin. And Aida. She was the only one who texted me back right away.

"I'm on duty," she said. "You want me to do some extra patrols on his street? And maybe a welfare check if you're in there too long?"

I hesitated for a moment. Charlie seemed to think Forstner was okay. And Ingrid had steered me to him.

But I didn't know him.

"Yes, please," I texted back. "Why don't you check with me by text in an hour. And if I don't answer . . ."

"Roger."

By then it was time to cover the last few blocks. At 7:00 P.M. I had parked my car on the street in front of Forstner's house and was striding up the brick walkway to his front door.

I felt a brief twinge of anxiety. I wasn't sure why. I wasn't doing any of the silly things Dad complained about when the heroines of his beloved mystery books did them. Like traipsing down to the cellar with a flickering candle to check the fuse box. Several people knew that I was calling on a perfectly respectable Caerphilly College faculty member. And Charlie Gardner thought Forstner was on the side of the angels. He was a good judge of character, wasn't he?

I rang the doorbell.

Chapter 18

Forstner answered the door after a reasonably short time—I think it would have unnerved me if he'd answered too quickly, as if he was poised to pounce.

"Ms. Langslow, I presume." He stepped back and opened the door all the way. "Come in."

I tried to be discreet about giving him a good, long look as I walked in. He was younger than I'd expected—probably still in his fifties. Tall, lean, and handsome in an elegant, unstudied way. His face was thin, with high cheekbones. His close-cropped beard was grizzled with gray. His gray-streaked hair was well cut, but he hadn't tortured any of it to cover up where a thin patch would probably soon give way to a small bald spot. He was dressed in khaki slacks and a pale blue dress shirt with the collar open, giving the impression that when he got home from his last class, he hadn't changed out of his work clothes, just shed his tie.

"This way," he said, and walked ahead of me, presumably to lead me out of the rather long entry hall into the living room. I was so busy trying to figure out just how I should approach him that I didn't pay much attention to my surroundings until suddenly I stepped out into—

"How wonderful!" I exclaimed.

Books. Hundreds of them. No, thousands. Three of the living room's soaring twelve-foot walls were covered with them. And not the kind of gold-embossed, leather-bound junk so beloved by a certain pretentious school of decorating. This was clearly a well-organized working library. Hardbacks and paperbacks intermixed, faded vintage tomes side

by side with bright new dustjackets. The shelves were interrupted only by the occasional door or window and by a brick
fireplace.

And the fourth wall was all glass and looked out onto a
brick patio and a lush garden with wide beds of shrubs and
flowers enclosing a small but perfect patch of grass. I could
see dogwoods, azaleas, rhododendrons, roses, astilbes, peonies, irises, and dozens of other plants that I'd need Dad to
identify.

Only the fact that I was here on a mission kept me from
darting over to either a shelf or the window, to take a closer
look at the books or the flowers. Well, that and the notion
that it was probably rude to give one's host the idea that his
library and garden were more interesting than he was.

But my obvious delight seemed to warm Forstner a little.

"I've been here fifteen years," he said. "Plenty of time to
get the house and garden in reasonable shape. Please, sit."
He waved me to an overstuffed sofa. "I was about to have a
sherry—will you join me? I could make tea, if you prefer."

"Sherry would be lovely." I wondered if he always offered
sherry to his guests, or if I was being rewarded for my obvious appreciation of the books and garden. "More than I
deserve for barging in on you like this."

He gave a dry chuckle and disappeared through a doorway. I used his absence to peer at the book titles on the
nearest shelf. American history, with a focus on Virginia.
Although on another shelf, a little farther away, I was pretty
sure I could detect the same battered one-volume complete
Sherlock Holmes that graced our shelves at home, and there
was definitely a decent collection of contemporary fiction a
little beyond that.

He returned after a minute or so carrying a tray with a
bottle of sherry and two sleek crystal glasses. He set the tray
down on the coffee table, poured out two glasses, and sat
down, leaving me to select my own glass. I picked the one
closest to me, figuring that if he was planning to poison
me, he'd expect me to be suspicious and choose the farther

glass. Not that I could think of any reason for him to poison me, and between the library and the garden I'd pretty much decided he wasn't a complete ogre. But I was sure if I'd read as many mysteries as Dad had, I'd have come across more than one pleasant and distinguished-looking serial killer with a huge library, a beautiful garden, and excellent taste in sherry.

He had seated himself in a Victorian armchair—the least padded, most upright chair in the room. Did he usually choose that instead of the sofa or one of the two overstuffed easy chairs? Or did his choice reflect his attitude toward our conversation? He sat upright, with his back barely touching the upholstery.

"Langslow," he said. "Are you related to Dr. James Langslow?"

"My father," I said.

"He patched me up last year when I had an unfortunate encounter with a Weedwacker," he said. "And I think I've seen you at the odd faculty gathering."

"My husband is in the Drama Department," I said. "Michael Waterston."

"Ah." He nodded. "I always enjoy the shows he directs." Then he broke into a soft laugh. "Sorry," he said. "I'm putting you through the usual drill we all so hate at cocktail parties. Interrogating you to find out exactly where you fit in the college hierarchy. And assessing you in terms of the men in your life. What do *you* do?"

"I'm a blacksmith," I said. "I also work part-time for Mayor Shiffley, helping organize special projects like Christmas in Caerphilly and the fair. And when one of my large family gets into some kind of trouble, I'm usually the one they turn to for help."

"Which is what you're doing now?"

"Yes." I decided to be straightforward with him. "My nephew, Kevin McReady, is worried. Someone tried to run over a friend of his, and he thinks it's because of a podcast the two of them did. And that they're still in danger."

"I've listened to your nephew's podcast," he said. "To several episodes, including the one about what happened in the business school in 1996."

"Thank goodness," I said. "You have no idea how tired I am of explaining what a podcast is."

"And you've already answered one of the questions I had for you." He sipped his sherry. "Namely, why you're doing research on the case after the podcast, instead of before."

"Because the B-school podcast wasn't long on information, was it?"

"Not long on new information." He smiled. "Actually, I was surprised at how much information they had. The business school would have done their best to make sure it was all forgotten. Do you know how they found out about the case in the first place?"

"No," I said. "I could kick myself for not knowing. But I'll find out."

I pulled out my notebook and jotted down a reminder.

"Good." Forstner nodded approvingly. "So you have no idea why your nephew and his colleague decided to dig into the cheating scandal."

"No idea how they found out about it," I said. "But once they did, I can make a good guess about why they decided to do the podcast, even if they didn't have that much information. They're young. Iconoclastic. Not at all reluctant to embarrass what they consider the stuffed shirts at the college. Disinclined to accept the official story."

"It isn't always wise to accept the official story." He was nodding slightly. "Especially on something that everyone's been trying to sweep under the rug for so long. Just what is the official story nowadays?"

A rather strange thing to ask. Surely he already knew. From the podcast if not from any other source.

"That Professor David Bradshaw was involved in a cheating scandal at the B-school," I said. "And someone found out. Versions differ about whether they were blackmailing him about it or just planning to turn him in. But both versions say he killed himself because he knew this would mean the end of his career."

"Yes," he said. "That's what I'd expect they'd all be saying. It isn't true, you know."

He fell silent for so long that I wasn't sure he intended to say anything else. But I stifled the urge to ask questions. Somehow I suspected he'd clam up if I did. I sipped my sherry and tried to be patient.

"He wasn't involved in the cheating scandal," he said at last. "But they set him up. Made it look as if he was. And when he wouldn't roll over—when he told them he'd fight, and prove his innocence—they threatened him."

He stared moodily into his sherry.

"Threatened him how?" I asked finally.

"They made it clear that if he didn't take the fall for the cheating scandal, they'd out him. Reveal to the administration that he was gay. Back then, that would have ruined his career—in the business school, at least." He made a short, sharp sound that was probably meant to be an ironic chuckle. "For that matter, even today it wouldn't do his career much good in a lot of places, including over there in the B-school. Back then, he'd have lost his job. And not just his job—his family, too. They were very . . . old school. They'd have disowned him. Of course, they would probably also have disowned him if the college fired him for helping students cheat. I don't think he could see any way out."

I nodded and tried to think of something to say. Clearly he was reliving all the pain of losing his friend. His friend—or perhaps his lover? I wasn't going to ask. It would be prying.

Clearly I wasn't really cut out for the job of true-crime investigator.

"So he took the only way out he could think of," Forstner went on. "But if you heard that he left a note confessing that he'd been involved in the cheating scandal, it's a lie. I know—I was one of the ones who found him."

"I'm sorry," I said.

"And I wasn't the only witness," he went on. "A young

secretary from the business school was worried because he hadn't shown up for any of his classes."

"Ingrid Bjornstrom," I said.

"Yes. She and I talked his landlady into letting us in, and the three of us found him."

No wonder Ingrid had reacted so strongly to my mention of Bradshaw's suicide.

"David was just hanging there," Forstner went on. "There was no confession. No note of any kind. They just put that story around to help hush things up. They never came right out and accused him of being the culprit, mind. Just kicked out a few of their least favorite students, issued a solemn memo expressing their sympathy to Dr. Bradshaw's bereaved family, and then declared their investigation into the cheating scandal closed. People got the message."

He shifted his glance to the fireplace and stared at the hearth, which would have seemed like a perfectly ordinary thing to do if there had been a fire burning in it. The dried flower arrangement currently occupying it didn't really merit that much study.

"I wanted to do something," he said eventually. "But I didn't dare. They'd have come after me. The History Department was a great deal more progressive than the business school, even back then, but still—I didn't come out to anyone until I had tenure."

I nodded.

"I'm sorry." He didn't appear to be apologizing to me. He was looking at the mantel.

No, not at the mantel—at a polished oak box sitting on one end of the mantel.

"That's him," he said when he saw where I was looking. "I got in touch with his parents to express my sympathy and ask if there was anything I could do to help them. They told me to make arrangements to have him cremated. Send them the bill. A few months later the funeral home called me to ask what they should do with him. The family—well, they didn't want him. So I went by and brought him home with me. I've always intended to find a place to bury him—a place that wouldn't kick up a fuss if they knew he was a suicide. Somehow I've never gotten around to it. I probably should while I'm still here."

"Talk to Robyn Smith, the rector of Trinity Episcopal," I said. "I can't imagine she'd mind. Or anyone in the congregation, for that matter."

"I'll take that under consideration. Anyway. I'm not sure how poor David's story could have anything to do with the attack on your nephew's friend. I'm not sure anyone remembers it, apart from Ingrid and me. I'm sure she was upset to be reminded of it. For my part, curiously enough, I got a certain melancholy pleasure out of listening to the podcast. Knowing that David hasn't been entirely forgotten."

"I gather you believe in his innocence," I said. "So what if whoever really was guilty got upset at the idea that someone might be digging up the case and investigating it again? You said 'they set him up'—who were they?"

"I don't know." Forstner frowned and shook his head. "He knew, or thought he did, but he was too . . . too paranoid to even say. And I was too paranoid to try to find out. I'm not sure it would be possible to find out after all this time."

"It might," I said. "If whoever set up your friend is worried enough about being exposed that they'd come after my nephew."

His eyes widened and he nodded slightly.

"Yes," he said softly. "It's come alive again, hasn't it?"

Chapter 19

"If by come alive again, you mean that someone's remembering it and talking about it, then yes," I said.

"And the podcast did suggest that they were doing more than just talking about it." Forstner looked eager. "It sounded as if they were actively looking for clues that would justify reopening the case. I can see how that might make the actual cheaters nervous."

"Everyone talks about the cheating scandal," I said. "Do you know exactly who was cheating on what, and how they were doing it?"

"More or less." He set his sherry glass on the coffee table and sat up straighter, as if buckling down to some task. "In those days, all the business school faculty turned in their grades to the dean's administrative assistant, who in due course would enter them into the college computer system."

"The professors couldn't figure out how to do this themselves?" I asked.

"They were still in the phase of resisting having anything to do with computers," he said. "Keyboard work was menial work. Woman's work—their opinion, not mine."

"I'm familiar with the sentiment," I said. "It's why I deliberately almost failed typing in high school."

"How do you manage to fail typing?" Forstner looked genuinely puzzled. "Okay, you said almost fail, but still."

"The teacher had us do a speed test every Friday morning," I explained. "And the class textbook included the text for all the Friday tests. People who weren't doing so well used the textbook to practice the speed test, so they could pass.

I used it to type out a version that, when you added up the words and subtracted all the errors, would just barely miss passing. And I'd hand that in when we finished the speed test. I'll never forget how every week the teacher would try to hide her disappointment in me and say, "Never mind—you're almost there. I'm sure you'll manage next week."

"And in the final week you turned in your real work and passed?"

"Bingo," I said. "But a reputation for nearly flunking typing was a useful thing back then. No one tried to pigeon-hole me into doing volunteer jobs that involved typing."

"I still know a few women in the department who profess to be bad at typing, so no one tries to dump a committee's paperwork on them," Forstner said with a note of amusement in his voice. "Or who claim to have such bad handwriting that it would be unwise to ask them to take the notes of a meeting. Of course, that's mainly women my age or older. The younger women just come right out and say they have better things to do than perform unpaid secretarial work for their male colleagues."

"I'm with them," I said. "But I can see that twenty-six years ago, no self-respecting male chauvinist pig would be caught dead entering data into a computer."

"I suspect there may have been a more strategic reason for having it all come to the dean's admin." Forstner looked thoughtful. "Only the B-school had that rule—in other departments the onus was rather on the faculty member either to enter the grades or find someone to do it for them. But in the B-school even the younger professors who were not computer-phobic were required to submit their grades through the admin. Because if just anyone were allowed to enter their class's grades directly into the computer, the dean would have had no opportunity to massage the grades of the students whose parents were substantial donors to the department's endowment fund."

"You think that happened?"

"I know it happened." Forstner's jaw tightened. "At the

end of his first semester here, David found out quite by accident that they'd changed some of the grades he submitted. When he protested, the dean's admin apologized and said it was her error. That she'd deciphered his handwriting incorrectly. Which was nonsense. His handwriting was exceptionally legible. Almost like calligraphy. Anyway, he put up a fuss and had the grades corrected. At least they said they were corrected. They didn't make it easy for him to check. Student privacy, you see."

He fell silent for a moment. I wonder if he was thinking the same thing I was—that if they changed the grades once, they could change them again. Especially with Professor Bradshaw no longer around to notice.

I was also thinking that he shared Ingrid's suspicion that the B-school would do anything for large donations. Change students' grades . . . or cover up their cheating.

"That's what the cheating scandal was about," he said after a bit. "It happened at the end of that year. Someone went in and changed the grades for a bunch of students who were flunking some of their courses. Unfortunately whoever did it didn't limit their edits to business school courses. They also improved the students' grades in several other departments."

"I'm surprised the system let them change grades from another department," I said.

"It wouldn't now," he said. "And even back then Admin Services realized that the system was too loose. So while they worked with the IT department on the enhancements needed to tighten security, they assigned someone to review all the changes that went in. And their watchdog caught some suspicious ones made through the business school login."

"How did Professor Bradshaw get blamed?"

"Whoever did it used David's computer." Forstner scowled at the memory. "The computer in his office, which would have been locked at night, when it happened. And at a time when anyone who had studied his habits could have predicted that he would be both out of his office and yet unlikely to have an alibi."

"How come?"

"He was in the habit of going to the college gym quite regularly," Forstner said. "Late in the evening. I don't know if they still do it, but back then, they let staff and faculty have a key card that would let them into the gym after hours, so they wouldn't have to fight all the students for the equipment. He'd go at midnight, even one a.m. Loved it because most of the time he had the place all to himself. But that meant he didn't have an alibi for the time when someone used his computer to change the grades."

"If the business school is like every other department here at the college, they've probably got dozens of spare keys floating around for most of the rooms," I said. "Anyone could have gotten into his office, even if it was locked. And if his gym visits were that regular, plenty of people would have known enough about them to frame him. In a reasonable world he could have pointed all this out to the police or the college authorities or whoever. Of course, from what I've been hearing, the B-school wasn't operating under reasonable world rules. But still, what possible motive could they have invented for him to change grades?"

"A bribe," Forstner said. "Someone deposited nine thousand dollars in his bank account the day after the grades were changed. That didn't come out until after his death, when the police did their investigation. So you can imagine how it looked."

"That he took a bribe to change the grades, and when he got caught, committed suicide to escape the consequences."

Forstner nodded.

"Ingrid says the two students who were expelled were scholarship students," I said. "And such good students that she was surprised that they would resort to cheating. And she doesn't think it impossible that there were others who didn't get caught."

"Or at least others who were not expelled." Forstner said. "But I'm not sure how you could prove that they'd cheated."

"That might not be possible," I admitted. "But I'm working

on some angles." Probably not a good idea to mention Ingrid's suggestion about the B-school donation records. I was starting to think Forstner was on the side of the angels, as Charlie had said, but it was probably a good idea not to make my interest in those records widely known, in case I ended up having to burgle the B-school.

Forstner nodded, a bit absently. He seemed to be thinking about something.

"It's remotely possible that Admin Services might still be able to identify the students whose grades were changed," he said finally. "There must have been memos or emails. From whoever found the unauthorized changes to his or her supervisor. Then up the food chain from the supervisor to whoever in Admin Services was senior enough to confront the business school. And then either a memo or an email to the dean of the business school."

"I suspect it was a pretty sensitive issue," I said. "Is it possible that they handled it orally—with a meeting or a phone call?"

"I'm sure the B-school would have liked to handle it that way," he said. "Not Admin Services. They'd have had a paper trail on something like that, and they're not good at letting go of paper. Of course, I have no idea how one could convince them to provide that information—Admin Services tends to be somewhat protective of the college's reputation. They'd comply with a search warrant, of course. But however convincing I may find the notion that someone who doesn't want their past sins revealed might want to silence your nephew and his colleague, I don't see that it adds up to something that would convince a judge to issue a search warrant."

"And I can't see the chief even requesting one on what the judge might consider a wild theory," I said. "But I'll keep my eyes open for something that would make him take an interest in the B-school files."

Forstner nodded. He seemed to be thinking again. I wondered whether I should take my leave. Or maybe . . .

"Do you know anyone named Vansittart?" I asked.

"Quite a few, actually," he said.

I fought down a surge of excitement.

"Such as?"

"Well, there was Peter Vansittart, a wealthy Dutch merchant who emigrated to England in the sixteen hundreds and was an early director of the East India Company." Forstner appeared to have fallen into class lecture mode. "His grandson Henry, governor of Bengal in the seventeen hundreds, and a member of the infamous Hellfire Club. A more recent member of the family would be Sir Robert Vansittart, quite an influential British diplomat before and during World War Two. Very involved in foreign affairs, and he had Hitler's number right from the start. If the British government had paid more attention to his arguments against appeasing the Nazis—but of course these aren't the Vansittarts you're looking for."

I had to smile. Was that a deliberate *Star Wars* reference?

"No, they're not," I said.

"You're thinking of Claude Vansittart, who's a professor at the business school." From his expression I gathered he knew Professor Vansittart. Knew him and didn't like him.

"That's him," I said. "He also has a younger brother whose name I don't remember."

"Nor do I," Forstner said. "I haven't met the brother, and if he's anything like Claude, I'd as soon keep it that way. Incidentally, if they're related to any of the many distinguished British Vansittarts it's only quite distantly. I got curious once and did some genealogical research on them. They were mere Smiths until their grandfather's time."

I nodded.

"Claude Vansittart was a business school student back then," he said. "No idea if he was graduate or undergraduate. I wouldn't have known him from Adam except that the day I went in to pack up David's office, he was the only other person who showed up, ostensibly to help."

"Ostensibly?"

"I soon figured out what he was there for—gossip and

loot. He kept trying to read every bit of paper he picked up. And whenever any of the office's contents caught his eye, like a set of nice bookends or a pricey reference book, he'd pick it up and ask, 'Do you suppose this is his? Or does it belong to the department?'"

I had to laugh.

"You've got his nasal whine down perfectly," I said.

"It was a memorable day," he said. "And Claude was memorably annoying. On top of everything else, he kept looking at the door as if expecting someone. He finally asked if the family would be coming to collect David's possessions or if I was going to deliver them, because he'd be happy to help in either case."

"He wanted to meet the family," I said.

"Yes." Forstner closed his eyes and shook his head slightly. "The wealthy, influential Bradshaw family. So I told him that I was doing the packing because David's family had disowned him and wanted nothing to do with him or his possessions. That I was going to take the boxes home and see what, if anything, they wanted me to do with them. After that, it wasn't long before he found a reason to leave. Are they your prime suspects? The Vansittarts?"

"I suppose you could call them that," I said. "Since so far they're the only suspects we've got."

"What have you got on them?"

"Claude Vansittart is still here, all these years, as a professor," I said. "And it's our theory—Michael's and mine, anyway—that former students who had gone out into the business world wouldn't be all that worried about the podcast revealing their involvement in a twenty-six-year-old cheating scandal."

"However, it would be a career ender for Vansittart," Forstner said. "I can see that. But I'm afraid I have a hard time seeing him having the gumption to attack anyone. He gets flustered if you interrupt him with a point of order during a faculty meeting."

"Maybe he got his brother to do it," I said. "The brother

who left the cushy academic nest for the rough-and-tumble of the business world. That's a quote, by the way. Something I overheard the brother say to Professor Vansittart when I was over in the B-school visiting Ingrid."

"Cushy academic nest," Forstner repeated. "Clearly the man has never seen the viper pit we call a faculty meeting."

Michael had the same jaundiced view about such meetings. He'd probably like Forstner. Hell, I liked him.

Just then my phone dinged to announce the arrival of a message.

"I should check this," I said. "I know that's rude, and it's probably nothing important, but we have twin sons who like to announce their misadventures in texts."

It was Aida. I typed "Leaving soon" and put the phone back in my pocket.

"Nothing urgent," I said. "But I've probably taken up enough of your time. If you happen to think of anything that would cast more light on the cheating case—"

"Or any of the other cold cases *Virginia Crime Time* has covered." He smiled. "I'll let you know. I hope this won't discourage them. All things considered, they're not doing a bad job on their podcast."

"I'm glad to hear that," I said. "They had a little bit of a hiccup this week—they're supposed to be recording tonight, and just found out that they were both too busy investigating the attack on Casey to research a new case. And of course they each assumed the other was doing it."

"So I should expect this week's podcast to be late?" Forstner said. "Or missing altogether?"

"On time, but different," I said. "They're interviewing my dad. Not sure about what, but between what he's seen as a medical examiner and his fascination with any crime that happens in his vicinity, he's a font of knowledge."

"I'll look forward to it."

"If you're a regular listener, don't be surprised if the cases are colder than usual for a while," I said. "I've suggested that maybe until we figure out who has it in for them they should

avoid any case that has a whole lot of living persons of interest who might resent being mentioned."

"Probably wise," Forstner said. "Casey Murakami's a graduate student in the History Department, you know. I'm not
his adviser, but I've had him in a class or two. An excellent
scholar. I might give him a suggestion of a case he could
cover."

"If you do, make sure it's an old one."

"About as old as you can get here in Virginia," he said.
"Did you know that archaeologists may have discovered a
murder that happened in Jamestown in 1624?"

"Definitely old enough to be a safe topic," I said. "I like it."

"Archaeologists at Jamestown dug up a skeleton in
1998—young, well-nourished male, with a lead bullet and
a bunch of buckshot still lodged in his knee and lower leg.
That was a common kind of ammunition in those days—
buck and ball. A round bullet backed with buckshot. Broke
the tibia and fibula, and would almost certainly have rup-
tured the popliteal artery. He'd have bled out in minutes,
which explains why they didn't try to remove the bullet."

"Dad is going to love the medical details," I said. "But how
do they know it was murder? I mean, do they even know who
he is?"

"Well, it took a few years, and they may never be positive,"
he said. "But in all likelihood it was a man named George
Harrison, who fought a duel with a Jamestown merchant
named Richard Stephens in 1624. In a pistol duel you usually stood sideways, dominant leg forward, to give your op-
ponent the smallest target possible—which corresponds
perfectly with where the bullet hit—the right side of his
right knee."

"They never tried Stephens?"

"Dueling wasn't illegal back then," he said. "So at the
time, it wouldn't have been murder. They might still have
tried to do something to him, but he was powerful—a member of the House of Burgesses—and Harrison wasn't noted
for anything in particular. Of course, some sources say Har-

rison didn't die of the wound, but two weeks later of something else, although if that's so, what about the bullet? Two weeks would have been plenty of time to remove it, even back then. So for my money, Stephens killed Harrison, and by modern definition, it was murder."

"May I suggest to Casey that he talk to you about this?" I asked. "Because, yeah, they could do an informative podcast about it. Especially if they rope in Dad for all the medical stuff."

"I'd be glad to brief him on it."

I drank the last sip of my sherry and rose to take my leave. He escorted me to the door. He paused before opening it.

"If you find out anything new about David's death, I would be very grateful if you shared it with me," he said. "Someone drove him to it. I know that. I have no evidence to back up that belief—only my own knowledge of his character. And it's not as if anything could be done after all these years. I'm not even sure that kind of pressure would be illegal."

"I bet it would," I said. "Blackmail, I should think."

"They didn't ask him for money."

"They were doing it for pecuniary gain," I said. "I think that counts."

"But could the police do anything after so many years?"

"Blackmail's a felony," I said, remembering my earlier conversation with Vern. "And Virginia has no statute of limitations on felonies."

"Really? I had no idea. Perhaps there's hope." His face took on a fierce expression, just for a fleeting second, and I decided that if I did find out who'd driven Professor Bradshaw to suicide, I should make sure Chief Burke found him before Professor Forstner did.

"Let me know if there's anything else I can do." His voice held just a slight note of eagerness.

"Thanks. I will," I said. "Good night."

He stood on his front step and watched until I was safely in my car. Then he waved, and disappeared inside.

Chapter 20

I backed out of Forstner's driveway and set out for home. But almost immediately I spotted a Caerphilly police cruiser behind me. When I reached the stop sign at the end of the block, it pulled up beside me. Aida. She rolled down her passenger-side window and I rolled down my window.

"Visit go okay?" she asked.

"Fine," I said. "Pretty sure Professor Forstner's harmless."

"Smart not to assume that, though. Did you tell anyone else you were coming here?"

"Yes," I said. "Michael and Kevin."

"That's all?"

"Well, I got Forstner's address from Charles Gardner in the college Administrative Services department, so he knows I was going to try to visit the guy. He wouldn't know when, though."

"But you didn't notify anyone who'd be tooling around in a late-model gray Ford F-150 pickup with a Clay County sticker?"

I shook my head.

"Didn't think so," she said. "Spotted it parked on the professor's street. Would have been just out of sight from the house, and there were two guys sitting in it. Activated my Spidey-sense, so I circled around and did another drive-by about ten minutes later. Seemed to convince them that they'd worn out their welcome in the neighborhood. They skedaddled. So if you didn't ask any of your buddies from Clay County to babysit you, I think I'll just call in the plate and see who they are."

"I don't know a whole lot of people in Clay County," I said. "I'd be curious myself to find out who they are."

"Why don't I just see you on your way," she said. "Slow night. If I don't get any other calls, I'll follow you home and see if I can score a doggie bag of leftovers from whatever family feast y'all had tonight."

"If the family locusts ate up all the leftovers, I'll cook you something myself," I said. "Thanks."

So Aida and I caravanned back to the house. At first I thought Aida was being overly cautious—did she think I wasn't able to look after myself? But then a few blocks into our journey I stopped at an intersection, looked up at the street signs, and realized I was at the corner of Bland and West Streets. The place where Casey had been attacked. It was a quiet intersection now—Aida and I were the only vehicles, and only half a dozen pedestrians were in sight. Bland Street marked the border between the town and the campus, and most of the pedestrians were headed to or from the college. Students, returning to their dorms, most likely, as whatever restaurant or business they'd been visiting closed for the night.

If the corner of Bland and West was quiet now, at eight o'clock, it would have been deserted at two in the morning, when Casey was attacked.

Aida tapped her horn lightly, as if asking what was up. I waved and set my car in motion again. I made a mental note to ask Casey for a few more details about the hit-and-run attempt. And instead of feeling annoyed, I was grateful for the presence of my friend in her cruiser, a visible guarantee of safety every time I checked my rearview mirror on the way home.

"All quiet now," she said as we strolled toward the house. "But maybe you should lie low a bit until we get more of a handle on this hit-and-run thing."

"I'm going out of town tomorrow," I said. "Down to Charlottesville."

"Good," she said. "And if you spot a gray pickup following

you, call the local cops. And if they don't take you seriously, tell them to talk to the chief. I'll brief him."

"Will do."

The house was quieter than it had been earlier. When we went inside, we found Rose Noire standing at the foot of the stairs. She looked exhausted, and I felt a twinge of guilt. I suspected a lot of the things Mother would normally have delegated to me had fallen to Rose Noire in my absence.

"Michael took a bunch of the kids into town, to the movies," she said. "Your mother and Holly McKenna went back to the farmhouse. And everyone else is enjoying having the night off."

I'd already seen cousins around a campfire in the backyard, singing and making s'mores. And through the archway that separated the front hall from the living room I could see bridge games and conversations. But still, considering how many people had come to town for the wedding, a light crowd.

"Is Kevin running his usual Dungeons & Dragons game in the library?" I asked.

"No, he's working on something down in his real-life dungeon," she said. "But a bunch of the die-hards are playing Risk and Settlers of Catan if you're interested."

"Not tonight. I plan on going to bed as soon as I find Aida some food and have a quick word with Kevin."

"Of course—there's plenty left." The prospect of feeding someone seemed to re-energize Rose Noire, and she led the way to the kitchen.

"Don't go to a whole lot of trouble for me," Aida was protesting.

When we reached the kitchen I left them to it and went downstairs to the basement.

Kevin and a young Asian man I assumed to be Casey were both sitting at the long counter that held all the various computers, each staring at a monitor. The number of dirty plates and empty soda cans littered among the keyboards suggested that they'd been at it for a while. Widget wagged his tail and barked when I arrived, and ran over to be petted.

The barking roused Kevin and Casey from their concentration, and they both swung their chairs around and looked at me as if hoping for some kind of rescue.

"You've met Casey," Kevin said.

"Actually, no." I held out my hand and, after a brief hesitation, Casey reached out and shook it. He was lanky and tall—probably not far from Michael's six foot four—but stooped as if trying to minimize his height or disappear altogether. He wore his hair in a shaggy mop reminiscent of the early Beatles, but I suspected it was less a style decision than a form of camouflage. The way he peered over his wire-rimmed glasses and through his long bangs made me think of a shy forest creature peeking out from a thicket.

"You find out anything interesting?" Kevin asked.

"Possibly," I said. "But before I brief you, let me ask you guys a question—how did you first hear about the cheating scandal in the business school?"

Kevin shrugged and looked at Casey.

"My uncle knew about it," Casey said. "He was here then. At the college, I mean. He started out planning to be a business major. Figured out the B-school was a total snake pit, and he was trying to decide whether to change his major, or transfer, or suck it up and bull through. Then the cheating scandal broke, and his favorite professor—the only one in the B-school that he could stand—killed himself over it. And Uncle Barney didn't believe he'd done anything wrong. Still doesn't."

"Did your uncle stay in the B-school?" I asked.

"No." Casey shook his head vigorously. "He was only going to do business because he thought it was a nice practical major for someone who was good at math. After seeing what the B-school here was like, he decided, if he was good at math, he should just major in that. Went on to get his PhD at MIT. Teaches there now. Specializes in partial differential equations. Don't ask me what that is—there's a reason I went into history. Anyway, when I was home over the winter break I was telling my family about our plans for the podcast, and Uncle Barney just erupted. Told me everything he knew about the cheating scandal. Which wasn't much, but he also shared all the rumors. Like that the B-school had his favorite professor killed for embarrassing them, which he didn't actually believe. And also that there were so many students implicated in the cheating that they wouldn't have had enough to keep the department going if they kicked them all out, so they only got rid of the worst cases. He didn't think that was quite so impossible."

I nodded. The idea that kicking out all the cheaters would cripple the B-school sounded a little far-fetched. But the notion that there were guilty students who'd escaped punishment was sounding more plausible all the time. Although maybe I'd have found the idea fairly implausible myself if not for the fact that Ingrid and Professor Forstner believed in it so readily.

"Did he name any names?" I asked.

"No." Casey shook his head. "Of course, I wasn't really asking for names. I figured if we actually named anyone, that would make us a lot more likely to get sued."

"Probably wise," I said. "But can you call your uncle and see if he does remember any names? Not for the podcast, but it would be nice to figure out who might be aiming Toyotas at you."

"Okay." Casey looked pale. Pale but determined.

"Kevin, shoot him that list of names I gave you," I said. "Names of people who took business courses that year," I added to Casey. "It might refresh your uncle's memory. But don't show it to him immediately. See what names he can remember first."

"Done," Kevin said. "Might help if your uncle could see the faces. The library's got yearbooks going back to the Stone Age—we could scan in all the B-school students' pictures."

"Do they let you check old yearbooks out?" I asked.

"Probably not," Kevin said. "Which is why I'd take my hand scanner over there."

"I shouldn't have doubted you," I said.

"I'll go over there tomorrow morning," he said. "Shouldn't take long. So does this mean you found some more dirt about the cheating scandal?"

I realized that while I'd talked to Kevin a time or two during the day, it had been mostly to give him names that needed tracking. So I settled down on his lumpy sofa with Widget in my lap and gave the two of them the highlights of my day. It still took a while.

"Wow," Casey said when I'd finished. "You found out all that in one day? We could really use you on the podcast."

"So you're going to let the chief work the Clay County case while you focus on the cheating case and the missing singer," Kevin said. "Smart."

"The chief will look into the cheating case, too, if we can convince him it might have something to do with the attack on Casey," I said. "Like if one of those guys in that data file I sent you suddenly turned up here in Caerphilly and doesn't have an alibi for two a.m. last Sunday morning."

"Kind of a long shot," Casey said.

"Start whittling down the list," I said. "Eliminate anyone who died. Or anyone who's in prison—given how that department operates, I bet there are a few. And focus on people who would have the most to lose if their involvement in the cheating scandal became public knowledge."

Casey nodded and turned back to his computer.

"And you figure it would also help if we knew whose parents had shelled out big bucks to the B-school," Kevin said.

"Definitely," I said. "And if you can't find that out in cyberspace—"

"I know," he said. "We're working on it."

I put Widget back in his usual bed on the computer counter and went back upstairs.

Aida and Rose Noire were gone, and the kitchen was dark. I poured myself a glass of lemonade and headed for the stairs.

In the front hall I found Delaney. She appeared to be annoyed about something.

"Do come out of there," she said to the door of the coat closet. "It's only Meg."

The door opened and Rob popped out.

"Meg," he said. "The one person even more invisible than us."

"Not so loud," I said. "The mothers probably have spies here somewhere. If they find out we're here, they'll draft us for something."

"That's why we're leaving," Delaney said. "Going over to my place."

"We've been spending a lot of time there," Rob said. "And they try to guilt-trip us, and I always remind them that we said they could plan anything they wanted as long as we didn't have to do a damned thing except show up."

"In retrospect, maybe we should have tried to keep a little more control over things," Delaney said. "Water under the bridge now."

"By the way," Rob said to me, "you know the one thing our mothers haven't planned?"

"Well, they probably haven't yet set up a college fund for the grandkids they're expecting you to provide," I said. "But apart from that, they seem to have covered everything else."

"The bachelor party!" Rob exclaimed.

"Technically, I think your best man's supposed to organize that," I said.

"Then it's Michael falling down on the job." Rob shook his head as if gravely disappointed in his brother-in-law.

"Yeah," Delaney said. "The way you, as my matron of honor, should have been planning my hen party."

"We asked you about that months ago," I said. "Multiple times. And every time, you ordered us not to plan anything. You said you were being driven crazy by all the stuff the mothers were planning and you didn't want to add anything else."

"I know, but we've changed our minds," Rob said. "But

don't worry, you're both off the hook. Ragnar's taking care of it all."

"Ragnar's planning both events?"

"He's planning a combined bachelor and hen party," Rob said. "It'll be family friendly. Lots of music. Dancing."

"Including, but not limited to, Norwegian folk dancing," Delaney said.

"And pony rides for the kids," Rob went on. "And Xtreme croquet in the pastures. And goat yoga. And trollkrem for everyone. Whatever that is. If Alice is cooking, it will be great."

"Be there or be square," Delaney said, giving me a fist bump.

"Sounds great," I said. "Count me in."

"We're off," Rob said. "See you later."

They opened the front door, looked furtively in both directions as if expecting to be ambushed, then slunk down the front walk to Delaney's car and took off.

I grabbed my tote, in which I'd stuffed most of the files Kevin had given me, and went upstairs.

Chapter 21

It had been a long day. I took a leisurely hot bath with some of Rose Noire's best rose-and-lavender-scented bath oil and then put on my most comfortable nightgown and slipped into bed, with a huge stack of Kevin's files on my nightstand. But I didn't immediately open any of them. Instead I closed my eyes and began to think over my day. And plan tomorrow. And yes, I probably came close to dozing.

A little while later I heard Michael come in. Evidently he thought I was asleep, and was trying to be quiet. Curious how whenever he or the boys did this they always ended up making more noise than if they'd just behaved normally.

"I'm not asleep, you know," I said with my eyes still closed. "I'm just pondering. How was your day?"

"Relaxing," he said. "And yours?"

"Well, I spent the whole day running around, poking into those cases Kevin thinks might have provoked the attack on his friend," I said. "But since I spent almost no time at all working on or even thinking about the wedding, my day was also curiously relaxing."

"Good," he said. "Be glad you weren't downstairs after dinner. It would have undone all of your relaxation."

"Why?" I opened my eyes and sat up. "What happened?"

"Your mother had everyone sorting confetti."

"Sorting confetti?"

"Apparently they ordered mixed pink and lavender confetti," he said. "What arrived also had green and blue. They can live with the blue, but the green's the wrong green. So everybody was sitting around with flat boxes of confetti, sorting out the green bits."

"Oh, good grief," I said. "Is that why you took the boys to the movies?"

"Curiously, they both seemed to be allergic to the confetti," he said with a perfectly straight face. "Amazing amount of sneezing. No idea if anyone else tried to pull the same thing after we left."

"It'll be a wonder if anyone sticks around for the actual wedding."

"Don't worry," he said. "Either everyone is taking it in their stride or your mother's entire family are better actors than anyone in my department. But I've figured out a way to make myself scarce tomorrow while appearing to be making an important contribution to the wedding."

"And that is?"

"I'm taking the kids over to Ragnar's for the day. Not just our crew—all the family kids, so no one has to watch them or entertain them and all the grownups can focus on wedding prep. We will learn about farm animals and watch Faulk work."

"You're doing this solo?"

"Rob and Delaney are coming along."

"The other two people who will do anything to avoid getting sucked into the wedding prep," I said.

"They seem to view it as a dress rehearsal for a big party Ragnar is going to throw Thursday night to take the place of the hen party and bachelor party that we failed to organize. I could have sworn they told us not to do that."

"They did," I said. "They changed their minds."

"We might also recruit a few more people who are getting jaundiced about the whole thing," he said. "Ragnar is going to give drumming lessons and let anyone who doesn't want to learn drumming play with a whole bunch of his other musical instruments. And then we'll have a feast in his dining hall. Alice is supposedly working wonders, as usual."

"It will be a Scandinavian feast," I said. "Make sure you get some of the trollkrem. It's divine."

"I will probably have trouble getting some of the kids to leave at the end of the day," he said. "And for that matter, a few of the grownups might desert us and move in with Ragnar."

"He'd be fine with that."

"You can come, too, if you're not tied up with Kevin's problem."

"It's tempting, but I got so much done today that I'm fired up to keep working on it tomorrow," I said.

"You mean you actually found out something about those ancient cases?" he asked.

So I filled him in. I started by describing my talk with the chief, my visit with Vern to Lucas Plunkett, and our conviction that he was in the clear for the attack on Casey.

"That's good, right?" Michael said. "One less case for you to worry about."

"We still need to worry about the case," I said. "Just not Lucas Plunkett. There's a very real possibility that the podcast upset someone in Clay County. Fortunately Vern and the chief agree, so I can leave investigating that theory of the crime to them."

"Good," he said. "Maybe I'm giving way to the old stereotypes about the denizens of Clay County, but the idea of you trying to investigate anything there would worry me. It could be dangerous."

"And it would be pretty pointless," I said. "I can't imagine anyone from Clay County opening up to me, but Vern just might get them talking. So I spent a lot more time working on the college cheating case."

"Was Charlie helpful?"

"Even more than I expected." I filled him in on my meeting with Charlie, our encounter with Ingrid, and this evening's visit to Professor Forstner.

"Forstner," Michael said. "I know what he looks like. Can't say that I've ever gotten to know the man."

"He's reclusive," I said. And then realized it didn't ring true. "Actually, I don't think he's reclusive so much as painfully shy. And quite possibly a little lonely. When this is all over—and by this, I mean both the wedding and what I'm doing to help Kevin—let's plan to invite him to supper. To thank him for helping me."

"If you say so." Michael looked dubious at the idea.

"We invite Dad and they can talk books and gardens," I said.

"And maybe Ms. Ellie," Michael said. "No one can talk books like a librarian."

"Exactly." The idea was growing on me. "If he turns down the invitation, or comes and has a terrible time, at least we tried."

"Just don't be upset if it turns out he's just a misanthrope and likes being by himself," Michael said. "I'm sure he's not quite the ogre the undergrads seem to think he is—"

"Did I mention that he appreciates your directing skills?" I said.

"Oh, well, then he can't possibly be an ogre." Michael's tone was facetious, but I could tell he was pleased. "He just does a very good job of pretending to be one."

"He's intelligent and articulate and has a fabulous house with an impressive library and a really cool garden. I think you'll like him, and if you don't, we don't have to have him back."

"I'm willing to give him a try on your recommendation," he said. "So what are you going to work on tomorrow?"

"The Madeline duPlaine case. Hang on a sec."

I pulled out my phone and checked my email. Yes! Tad had sent me the file of Madeleine duPlaine doing "The House of the Rising Sun." I pulled my wireless headphones out of the tote and handed them to Michael. "You need to hear this."

He listened in silence, but I could tell from his face that he was impressed. Maybe even moved. When the song ended, he pulled the headphones off.

"Wow," he said. "I can see why people still remember her. But why haven't I ever heard that before? You'd think Kevin and Casey would have used it in their podcast. Or was there a rights issue?"

"Kevin and Casey don't know this exists," I said. "No one does except Ragnar, Faulk, Tad, and us. And Ragnar's not supposed to know the rest of us have it. Kevin and Casey and now Tad have been looking all over to find some of her music, without any luck. So tomorrow I'm going down to Charlottesville to see what I can find out."

"Here's hoping you find her, and she's been making a whole lot more tracks just like that," he said.

While Michael was doing his bedtime toothbrushing and face washing, I listened to the song again. And then I reminded myself that I wasn't going down to Charlottesville to find Maddy duPlaine or solve the mystery of her disappearance. I was going to see if I could find anyone in Charlottesville who had it in for Kevin and Casey.

Wouldn't it be nice if that led to solving the bigger mystery?

I reminded myself not to be silly, and drifted off to sleep.

Chapter 22

"Damn."

I woke up to find Michael squinting against the sunbeams that were streaming in through the open blinds.

"Sorry!" I said. "Looks as if we forgot to close the blinds last night. I'll take care of it."

Actually, opening and closing the blinds was normally Michael's thing. I didn't need the sunlight the way he did in the morning, to make him feel as if his day had properly started. And if the sun was up before I wanted to be, I didn't need the blackout blinds—I could go back to sleep just as easily by throwing an arm over my face. So most of the time I left fiddling with the blinds to him.

"I'll get it in a sec," he mumbled. Although he wasn't stirring.

"No need." I slid out of bed and went over to the offending window. "I'm awake."

"Glad someone is."

"Maybe it's because I went to bed at such a disgustingly early hour," I said as I closed the blinds and darkness fell over the room. He sighed with contentment. "Maybe I'd feel this way every morning if I reformed my night owl ways and went to bed with the chickens."

"You'd find their coop pretty uncomfortable."

"Get some more sleep," I said. "I'll see you later."

Actually, I decided, as I quietly threw on my clothes, I was probably cheerful mainly because I had spent most of yesterday without working on or even thinking much about the wedding. And because today held more of the same.

And it was a beautiful sunny day—though I wouldn't be saying that to anyone else. Far too many of my family were gardeners—even farmers, in a few cases—which meant that what we ordinary folk called a beautiful sunny day was only acceptable to them if their plants and crops had recently received an optimal amount of rainfall.

But a sunny day suited my plans perfectly. And it was only a little past seven. I could grab a quick breakfast—the odors of bacon and coffee were already floating up from downstairs. Then I could throw all the podcast material Kevin had given me into the truck, make sure the enormous cage intended for the peacocks was properly lashed down, and take off. I could easily make it to Charlottesville by ten. And if Mother came up with any more additions to the wedding plans, I wouldn't be around to worry about them.

The ride there was peaceful. I listened to several more of Kevin and Casey's podcasts along the way. They really didn't do a bad job when they had a reasonable amount of factual material to work with. Would it seem bossy if I told them they needed to do more research? Probably. But if I dropped a hint about how good the well-researched episodes were . . . ?

Better yet, maybe I could encourage Professor Forstner to do it. Let Casey know the eyes of the History Department were on him. Or at least the ears. Maybe Casey could recruit a few history undergrads to help with the research. If he struck out there, I knew a couple of professors in the Criminal Justice Department who could probably help.

And then I told myself to stop trying to organize Kevin and Casey from afar and enjoy the drive.

Amanda and Jared, her husband, didn't live in Charlottesville proper but on ten acres out in the country, a good twenty miles from the center of town. So long before I was close enough to see any traffic, my GPS app steered me off the highway and down a series of increasingly smaller and more scenic country roads that I hoped would lead me to their farm. Although they always protested when I called it that, saying it was more like a large yard with occasional livestock. In my book, any place with even one sheep was a farm, and Amanda had a growing flock to provide wool for her craft.

"We bought an old wreck," Amanda told me once. "But with plenty of room for my looms, his music stuff, and of course the kids. And Jared and I are both pretty handy, so fixing things up isn't a big deal."

Luckily I'd be arriving after their two kids had gone off to school. They'd probably used up their snow days here at the foot of the Blue Ridge—or maybe they hadn't adopted Caerphilly's popular plan of giving back the unused ones. It wasn't that I didn't want to see the kids, but I knew from experience how little it took to throw a wrench into a family's weekday morning routine. It was 10:20 when I pulled up in front of their house.

Either their definition of a wreck differed greatly from mine or they were very handy indeed. An architect might not approve of their house, which had obviously been added onto multiple times and sprawled across the landscape in a relaxed and unpretentious fashion. But I could see nothing wrong with its condition. Siding and trim were both in good repair and freshly painted. A picket fence enclosed a small front yard with herbs and flowers planted so closely on either side of a concrete walkway that it left no room for a lawn that would need mowing. To one side of the house, a driveway led into a gravel-covered parking area—obviously designed to accommodate the cars bringing musicians to Jared's small recording studio and aspiring weavers to Amanda's classes. I turned in there.

Amanda dashed out the back door while I was still parking, and greeted me with a fierce hug.

"About time we got you down here," she said. "Of course, I was hoping you'd bring the twins and that devilishly handsome husband of yours. But maybe now that you know the way, you'll bring them next time."

We didn't see each other as often as we once had, since neither of us did as many craft shows as we used to. So we talked nonstop as she gave me a tour of the house, ending up in the kitchen, where Jared was fixing an immense lunch. Their huge oak kitchen table was set for three and laden with a platter of ham and dishes of oven potatoes, green beans, broccoli, and tossed salad.

"We knew you'd probably have to head home before dinnertime." He gave me a quick hug on his way to the oven, where he pulled out a pan of golden-brown biscuits. "So we decided to make lunch our big meal."

While we ate I filled them in on the mission Kevin had tasked me with and what I'd done about it yesterday.

"So you're down here to get the scoop on Maddy duPlaine," Jared said when I'd finished.

"It was smart of you to let us know why you were coming," Amanda said. "Although I have to tell you, if you're hoping to solve the mystery of what happened to her, a lot of people have been working on that for years."

"And given it up because it's pretty much impossible," Jared said.

"Then it's a good thing I'm not trying to solve it," I said. "Not that I'd turn up my nose if the solution fell into my lap—but my mission is to figure out if there's anyone down here so worked up about the podcast that they'd go after Kevin and Casey."

"That's probably a lot more doable," Amanda said. "And we're the perfect people to help you with that. Jared's pretty plugged in to the local music scene these days, thanks to his studio. And he's got a surprise for you."

"Two surprises, actually," Jared said. "But they can wait till we're finished with lunch. More ham?" He held out the platter.

"Don't tempt me," I said. "I'm stuffed."

"But do you like it?" Amanda asked. They both looked anxious.

"It's great." I meant it. It was an old-fashioned country

ham, the kind some people would turn up their noses at, saying it was too salty, or maybe muttering direly about having to cut back on sodium. I'd had three helpings, washed down with at least that many glasses of lightly sweetened iced tea.

"Do you think your mother will like it?" Jared asked.

"I'm sure she would if she were here." I glanced involuntarily over my shoulder. "Are we expecting her?"

"When she found out you were coming down to Charlottesville, she called me," Amanda said. "Remember how I sent you a ham like this last Christmas?"

"Yes," I said. "It was a real hit at her dinner. She wants another?"

"She wants half a dozen," Amanda said. "For the wedding feast. She asked me if I could pick them up and give them to you before you headed back."

"She didn't." I closed my eyes and shook my head.

"And before you start worrying about it, she's not trying to cadge free food," Amanda added. "She told me to send her the total."

"It was no trouble," Jared said. "They come from an organic pig farmer just down the road. He was tickled pink to hear your mother wanted nothing but his hams for the feast."

"And it was a great excuse to get a couple for ourselves." Amanda speared another smallish slice of ham as she spoke.

"It's just that the wedding feast keeps escalating," I said with a sigh. "Like everything else about the wedding. Mother worries there won't be enough food, or there won't be enough variety, so she adds a few more dishes. Then she worries that there will be too much food, and invites another batch of people."

"So we shouldn't feel bad about taking her up on the invitation to the feast?" Amanda said. "It's not as if we're close friends of either bride or groom, but it does sound like a lot of fun."

"She'll be hurt if you don't accept the invitation," I said. "And don't think she won't notice."

"Then we'll definitely see you this weekend," Amanda said. "Should we have dessert now or save it?"

"Save it," I said. "I'll have more room later."

"Yes, we should get out to the studio," Jared said.

So after a quick post-meal cleanup—which didn't take long with all three of us working—Jared led the way out the back door and across the gravel parking lot to a small, rustic but charming building at the far side of it. The building had probably started life as an old-fashioned detached double garage. A dramatic sweep of glass took the place where the garage doors had been.

Inside it was a thoroughly modern music studio. The back wall and the back half of the two side walls were covered with equipment. A short stairway led up to a raised, glass-enclosed area filled with more electronics—presumably the control booth. Along one side wall—the one opposite the entry door—were a shapeless but comfortable-looking couch, a coffee table, and a half-height refrigerator. And at the end that was mostly glass was a small stage, not quite a foot high, that held several microphone stands, many snaking cables, and a drum set.

"Some guys, especially the old-timers, are a lot more comfortable with a stage, even if it's kind of a token one," Jared said, waving his hand at it.

"And sometimes, in the summer, we slide open the glass doors and have concerts in the yard," Amanda said.

"The studio started out as a sideline gig, mostly doing demo tapes," Jared said. "For people who wanted something a little better than what they could do in their basement."

"A little better?" Amanda snorted. "He's a wizard with all that electronic stuff. He could make *me* sound like Tina Turner or Aretha Franklin if he wanted to."

"Now, I pretty much make a living out of the studio," he said. "Between the recording sessions and the post-production work."

"And he's starting to get his own music out there, too," Amanda said. "Anyway—play it for her."

"No time." Jared glanced at his watch. "They could be arriving any time now."

"Ah," she said. "The other treat you arranged."

"Yeah." Jared grimaced. "The things I do for my friends."

"We figured maybe you'd like a chance to scope out Tony," Amanda said, turning to me.

"Tony Antonelli?" I asked. "The guy who was duPlaine's drummer?"

"Exactly." Jared looked solemn. "But we figured maybe you wouldn't want to let him know at first who you are or why you're interested. Since he is a suspect and all. You could check him out first. See how much you want to tell him. He's kind of . . . um."

"He drinks," Amanda said. "And when he's drunk he talks. You don't want to tell him anything you don't want the whole town to hear."

"Nice to know," I said. "So what's the plan for meeting him?"

"He's playing with a band," Amanda said.

"If you can call it that," Jared said. "Random agglomeration of amazingly unmusical wannabes, if you ask me."

"Well, they call themselves a band," Amanda said. "And Willie's all right. Anyway, they've been trying to talk Jared into letting them rent his studio to do some tracks."

"Which I have been resisting," Jared said.

"Even though we can always use the dough," Amanda put in.

"Because life is too short to have to listen to these clowns. But last night I bit the bullet and told them I had a last-minute cancellation, and if they could get here by noon, I'd let them have a couple of hours. So with luck, you'll get to check out Tony. Always a possibility they've found a better drummer—they keep threatening to. But I can't imagine anyone else wanting to play with them."

"And when there's some downtime, I can also drag the conversation around to your nephew's podcast," Amanda said. "See if Tony says anything useful. About Maddy duPlaine's disappearance, I mean," she added, cutting off what I suspected would be a sarcastic comment from Jared about the likelihood of Tony saying anything useful.

"That's good," I said. "But remember—it's more important to drag the conversation around to what Tony was doing this past Saturday night. As I said, finding out what happened to Maddy duPlaine would be cool, but it's a long shot after all these years. I'm more focused on who went after Kevin's podcasting partner."

"So we find out if he has an alibi," Amanda said. "Check. Jessica Fletcher has nothing on me."

Just then we heard car tires crunching on the gravel.

"That could be them," Amanda said.

Jared loped over to stare out the glass doors. I turned to look and saw a mud-spattered blue pickup truck parking outside.

"Yup," he said. "Some of them, anyway. Okay, just in case they get all shy or something about having a spectator, we're going to pretend you're doing something useful." Jared ambled back to the electronics end of the studio, picked up a set of headphones, plugged them into one of the bits of equipment, and handed them to me. "Put these on and sit there." He pointed to a chair at the far end of the row of electronics. "We're going to pretend you're my trainee. Don't say anything—just keep looking at all the dials in front of you, and nod occasionally, as if everything's going fine."

"And if they ask me any questions?" I took the chair and headphones, but I was a little worried.

"Just look over at me. Or say, 'You should ask Jared.' Don't worry—these guys are so untechnical they can barely plug in their guitars. They won't ask anything you can't answer."

I hoped he was right.

Chapter 23

Just then the door opened, and two men came in. One was short and pudgy, with a cheerful, open face and a short but disheveled mop of straw-colored hair. He looked to be in his late thirties, or maybe forties, and carried a guitar case so battered that it could have been older than he was. He was dressed in faded, baggy jeans and a rusty black t-shirt that appeared to be promoting a band—though not one I'd ever heard of.

"Hey, Jared," he said. "Hey, Amanda. Hey there." The last was in my direction, and he gave a cheerful nod to go with it, as if to suggest that he didn't know my name yet, but he was really glad to see me, whoever I was, and positive we were about to become best friends. He made a beeline for the small stage, set down his case, and took out what I recognized as an electric bass guitar. I had the vague feeling I'd met him before. Of course, I'd been having that feeling a lot lately.

"Hey, Willie," Jared said. "Good to see you." He sounded as if he meant it.

The other man paused in the doorway and swept his gaze around the room. He didn't say anything for several seconds—just stood there, eyes hidden behind oversized sunglasses. He was dressed all in black—black jeans, black cowboy boots, black t-shirt, and a black leather vest. His black hair was pulled back into a short ponytail. The vest was oddly long—I suspected he'd had it custom made to camouflage the fact that he was starting to get a bit of a pot belly. And without the four-inch heels on his boots he'd probably be eye-to-eye with me at five ten. Hard to tell his age, given the size of his shades. Thirty-something, maybe.

"Hey, Rock." Jared's welcome sounded a little less warm. "Come on in."

Rock paused for a few more seconds, and I found myself thinking of how, in the movies, the vampire always has to wait for an invitation to enter someone else's territory. And also of a recent debate I'd had with Michael over whether you could call a man a drama queen.

"In or out, Rock," Amanda called. "Enough posing."

Rock stepped in and strutted over to the stage. He was also carrying a guitar case. He took off his sunglasses, and I revised my estimate of his age upward. Forties. Maybe fifties. He lifted his wrist to look at a large watch with a heavy black leather strap.

"We should have gone by to pick up Tony," he said. His voice surprised me. It wasn't so much high as thin. Reedy. No depth or resonance. Presumably one of the other band members was the vocalist.

"It's okay." Willie was tuning his bass. "He'll be here. I dropped Bob off at his house earlier. Bob can get him here."

"We need a better drummer," Rock said. "Jared, do you know anyone who's looking for a good gig?"

"Not offhand," Jared said. "But I'll keep my ears open. Ask around. Let you know."

Rock nodded, and the expression on his face suggested that by merely asking Jared to find them a drummer he had conferred upon him a favor of inestimable value.

"Here they are," Willie said. I suddenly realized who he reminded me of—Sam Gamgee, in the Peter Jackson movie of *The Lord of the Rings*. Sam, or any of the cheerful, feasting hobbits. But a Sam from an alternate Middle-earth, where Sauron had never been a threat, a Sam grown older without ever having to worry about anything but eating and drinking.

And making music. He'd finished tuning and was playing little improvised scraps of music and rhythm, smiling happily.

Meanwhile more sounds of tires on gravel announced the arrival of another truck—this time a battered white truck with the right front fender painted in gray primer paint.

The door opened and two more men strolled in—a thin, anxious-looking young man in his twenties—if that—and a disheveled man in his fifties. Both wore faded jeans and ratty t-shirts.

"See, Tony," the younger man said. "Like I told you—Jared has some drums you can use." He spoke in the overly loud, careful tone people use when they have to speak to a child and have no idea how to do it.

Tony shambled over toward the drums.

"Did he pawn them again?" Rock asked, sotto voce.

"No, but he hadn't even started packing them up." The younger newcomer—presumably Bob—didn't really lower his voice.

"How bad is he?" Rock asked.

"I've seen him worse." Bob strolled over to the stage, carrying both a guitar case and a larger case that turned out to contain an electric keyboard.

Rock sighed heavily and stared over at Tony with a disapproving frown. I could see why—Tony had a sweaty, rumpled look that made me suspect he was hungover.

"Let's get started," Rock said. "Jared, why don't we run through our first song so you can get an idea of the sound level."

"Roger." Jared retreated to his glass booth.

It actually took them half an hour of fiddling with cords and instruments and microphones to get started, and as soon as they did I couldn't wait for them to stop. Thank goodness for the headphones, which shut out a lot of the volume. But the headphones didn't disguise how wretched the band was.

Well, except for Willie, who actually seemed to be a capable bass player. Not that I was an expert, but I could find nothing wrong with anything he did—except for the fact that he was playing with a look of undisguised happiness on his face, as if he'd achieved his life's ambition and was playing in the band of his dreams.

Bob played both rhythm guitar and keyboards badly. Rock played lead guitar, and he was reasonably good at it. But someone should long ago have talked him out of singing. Amplification didn't improve his voice and while he wasn't exactly tone-deaf, he was a lot closer to that than to having perfect pitch.

And they seemed to be playing what I thought of as arena rock, straight out of the '80s. Their first song sounded vaguely familiar—had they actually had a minor hit that I'd heard on the radio? But no—if it had been on the radio, they wouldn't need to record it, would they? And it certainly wasn't a song worth covering. I finally figured out that the song, though ostensibly original, was actually an unholy alliance between Led Zeppelin's "Whole Lotta Love" and Def Leppard's "Pour Some Sugar on Me." After five or six renditions of this, I was overjoyed when they decided to move on to another number. Alas, the second song so closely resembled Aerosmith's "Rag Doll" that it was clearly a plagiarism suit waiting to happen and seemed to require almost continuous simultaneous screeching from Rock and Bob.

I glanced up occasionally to see Jared staring down from his booth with a fixed smile on his face. He needn't have bothered. Rock and Bob were completely into their performances, posturing and leaping as if playing to an audience of thousands. Willie played on steadily, his face fixed in the sort of seraphic smile I often saw on Rose Noire's face while she meditated or did yoga.

The only member of the band who didn't seem to be enjoying himself was Tony. Maybe it was just the sheer volume of sound—playing in a rock band had to be some kind of torture for someone suffering from a hangover. Although it was also possible that Tony was the only one really listening to the noises they were producing. Rock and Bob seemed to pay little attention to what their performances sounded like and Willie clearly went to his happy place the instant he picked up his bass. But Tony looked as if he were trapped in a nightmare.

And maybe the others were too involved in the music to notice, but I'd spotted Tony pulling a flask out of his pocket and taking a sip. At least he started with a sip, a couple of times during the first number. When Rock announced the title of the second number, Tony scowled, muttered something, and took what appeared to be a sizable slug.

I was relieved when, after the first run through of the ersatz Aerosmith number, Bob announced that he had to hit the head and disappeared into a door under the control booth. Rock nodded, set down his guitar, and slouched over to the sofa. Willie returned to his happy noodling on the bass.

Amanda came bustling in, bearing a plate of brownies and pitchers of cold milk and lemonade. Rock ignored the treats on offer and rooted in the mini-fridge until he found a beer. Willie accepted several brownies and glasses of both lemonade and milk. Tony scowled first, then went for a lemonade, though he stopped Amanda before she completely filled the glass, and I suspected he was going to spike it with the contents of the flask so he could tipple more openly.

"Hey, people are talking about your old bandmate," Amanda said to Tony. She'd probably kill me if I told her this, but she sounded amazingly perky. "Have you heard that new podcast about Maddy duPlaine's disappearance?"

Tony just looked at her for a couple of seconds. Then he stood up and ran for the door, dropping the lemonade glass along the way. It shattered on the hard studio floor. Bob was just emerging from the bathroom, and Tony careened into him and knocked him sprawling.

"What the hell?" Bob spluttered.

"Damn the man," Amanda said. "Watch out, there's broken glass all over."

We heard an engine start up.

"Man, he should *not* be driving," Bob said.

"Go after him," Rock said. Although I noticed he didn't move himself.

Willie got up and began carefully putting his bass in its case. Jared bounded down the steps from his control booth, and he and I raced outside. Willie appeared almost immediately and joined Jared and me in looking up and down the road. The truck Tony and Bob had arrived in was not only missing from the parking lot, it was out of sight.

"Amanda can hold down the fort," Jared said. "Let's try to follow him. Meg, you go that way." He pointed to the right. "Willie, let's go the other direction—we can each take one way when we get to the fork."

I ran to the truck and took off in the direction Jared had pointed to—which would be heading back toward town. I went at a reasonably fast speed, but it was a winding road, with a lot of SLOW CURVE signs, and whenever I reached a driveway or a crossroad I slowed down to see if I could spot him.

I had gone fifteen miles and was getting near the outskirts of town when I spotted Tony's white pickup, half on and half off the road. He'd crashed into one of the white brick pillars that marked the entrance to a lane that disappeared into some woods and probably led to a farm or a fancy house. At least he'd hit it with the fender that hadn't yet been repainted. And he seemed fine. He was sitting on the truck's tailgate, drinking from his flask.

I parked behind him and opened my window.

"You okay?" I called.

He nodded.

I pulled out my phone and called Jared.

"Found him," I said.

"Where?"

I described the white brick pillars. If there was a number, it was on the pillar Tony had demolished, but Jared said he knew the place.

"Shall I call 911?" I asked.

Jared was silent for a few seconds.

"We probably should," he said. "But if we do, he'll probably get another DUI. And maybe end up in jail. And yes, he probably deserves it. But maybe we can talk him into doing a program. Cleaning himself up. Stay there—I'll get there as soon as possible."

We hung up. I got out of the truck and walked over to where Tony was sitting. He said he was fine. But maybe I should take a closer look. And if he showed any signs of injury or trauma, I was calling 911, no matter what Jared said.

"You sure you're fine?" I asked.

"What does it matter?" he groaned. "What does any of it matter?"

He wasn't bleeding. Testing him for concussion would probably be a smart thing to do, but most of the warning signs of concussion—such as dizziness, lack of balance and coordination, disorientation, and slurred speech—could also be caused by intoxication. His pupils seemed normal. I was trying to recall what else Dad would have done when he spoke again.

"I did it, you know."

"Did what?"

"Killed him."

Chapter 24

I decided checking Tony out for concussion could wait for a few minutes.

"Killed who?" I asked.

"That dude who was bothering her."

"What dude?"

"I don't remember his name. Not sure I ever knew it."

"Okay," I said. "Who was he bothering?"

"Maddy."

"Maddy duPlaine?"

He nodded.

I didn't try to stop him when he lifted the flask, though I was relieved when he discovered it was empty.

"What happened?"

"He was following her. So I followed him. She went out to Beaver Creek Lake. It was one of her favorite places. We shot our first PR photos there. And he followed her down one of the trails. I wasn't sure what to do—I mean, I figured she didn't want to talk to him, but she was also mad at me. We'd been arguing over stuff. She didn't want to sign the record deal, and she wouldn't tell us why. So I just followed, and then I saw it."

"Saw what."

"He killed her." Tony looked stricken. "Just hauled off and hit her on the head with a rock. And then he threw her in the lake. I lost it."

He just sat there, staring at the empty flask, for what seemed like forever.

"What did you do?" I asked finally.

"I killed him."

More silence.

"Killed him how?"

"Hit him over the head. With a rock. The same rock he used to kill her. And then I threw him in the lake."

"And you didn't tell the police?"

"I couldn't," he said. "I killed him."

I could think of a lot of things I wanted to say to him. I wanted to ask why he didn't think of pleading self-defense— who could ever tell that the stalker hadn't been killed in a struggle? Or diminished capacity of some sort. I wanted to point out that he didn't even know for sure either of them was dead. Why didn't he at least try to pull out his friend's body? But just then Jared's car pulled up. He and Willie got out.

"Is he okay?" Willie asked.

"As far as I can tell," I said.

"He did a number on their brickwork," Jared said.

"Yeah." Willie grimaced. "Got some paper? I'll leave a note in their mailbox. Should we call a tow truck?"

"The car might be drivable," Jared said. "I'll check while you write."

I tore out a page from my notebook and gave it to Willie, along with my pen. While he wrote a note to the owner of the brick pillar, Jared started the car and eased it away from the pillar. The dent in the truck's fender wasn't even that bad.

"I could drive him home," Willie said.

"How about if we take him to the ER, just in case?" Jared countered.

We eventually decided that Jared would drive Tony to the ER. Willie would drive Tony's truck to his place, with me following behind to give him a ride to the hospital.

I noticed that no one suggested drafting Rock or Bob into the proceedings.

"And we can meet back at the farm when I'm finished," Jared said in an aside to me. "I still have something interesting for you."

We helped Tony into the passenger side of Jared's truck and they took off. While Willie was getting behind the wheel of Tony's truck and adjusting the seat, I took a picture of the license plate, and then one of the truck itself. I figured it might be helpful if Chief Burke decided to check out Tony.

Willie was a considerate caravanner, always putting on his turn signals far in advance and never running a yellow and leaving me stuck behind the red. And a good navigator, once we'd dropped Tony's truck off and he joined me—conscientious at giving advance warning about turns and lane changes. But as a source of information on the Charlottesville music scene, past or present, he was a dud.

Well, except for one tidbit he provided as I was pulling up to drop him off in front of the ER.

"Thanks for the ride," he said. And then he paused with his hand on the door handle. "I hope Amanda isn't too upset," he said. "Tell her it's not her fault, okay? That Tony got upset. She couldn't have known how he'd react."

"I'll do that," I said. "But help me out—is the whole Maddy duPlaine thing a sensitive issue generally here in town? I mean, with people who knew her. Should I tell her to avoid the subject entirely?"

He thought about that for a few seconds.

"Pretty much just Tony, I guess," he said finally. "I doubt there's anyone else around who really knew her. I mean, I was around back then, but I can't really claim to have known her, you know. And it was twenty years ago. Nobody much thinks about it anymore except when some true-crime blog does a feature on it, and then it's like why are they even bringing it up after so long? But it sure does upset Tony."

I wondered, just for a moment, what he'd say if I told him about Tony's confession. Then I decided it was probably a bad idea.

"I'll tell Amanda," I said. "Thanks."

"No problem," he said, and hopped out of the car.

I went to the far end of the hospital's parking lot and

paused for a moment. Should I head back to Amanda and Jared's? It could be a while before Jared got back, if he was going to battle the bureaucracy of medicine on Tony's behalf, but Amanda and I could have a nice visit in the meantime.

But shouldn't I report Tony's confession?

Okay, I should definitely tell the chief about it. But since the crime had happened in or around Charlottesville, and I was already here . . .

I grabbed my phone, looked up the address for the police station, and headed there. It wasn't all that far away. I texted Amanda that I was going to run an errand in town while I was here and took off.

The police station was downtown—a section of Charlottesville that held little nostalgia for me, partly because it had undergone an immense amount of renovation since my college days and partly because I hadn't spent that much time there. I hadn't had a car, and downtown was a mile and a half from the campus and sometimes more from whatever dorm or apartment I was living in. Which meant it was walkable, if you weren't in a hurry, but there were plenty of shops and restaurants much closer and more convenient. In fact, almost the only things that lured me downtown were the several used bookstores, like Daedalus and Read It Again, Sam— and I could usually talk Dad into taking me to those when he and Mother came for a visit. That thought did bring back a twinge of nostalgia—the lazy weekend afternoons Dad and I spent rummaging through dusty bookshelves while Mother browsed the nearby antique shops. Followed by a dinner together—at the Boar's Head Inn or the steak house, if Mother had her way, or at one of the cheaper and noisier student hangouts if Dad prevailed.

But most of the bookstores were on or just off the pedestrian mall, which was probably a good thing. Waxing nostalgic over the bookstores had almost made me miss a couple of turns. I parked in a huge public garage next to the police station, gathered my nerve, and walked in.

The officer staffing the desk gave me a funny look when I asked to speak to the detective in charge of the Madeleine duPlaine case, but she just told me to have a seat. Eventually an officer in plainclothes showed up. He looked at least my age, and probably older, which I decided was a good thing. He might even be old enough to have been on the force when Madeleine duPlaine had disappeared. Probably too young to have been in charge of the case back then, but he might know more than a newer officer.

We introduced ourselves, and then Detective Smith led me back to what I thought of as an interrogation room, although I suspected he'd have said interview room.

"You said you wanted to talk to the detective in charge of the Madeleine duPlaine case," he said. "That would be me. But I should warn you, if you're from the media, I can't tell you anything we haven't said a million times before."

"I'm not from the media," I said. "But it's possible I might have new information about the case."

"I'm all ears."

He didn't look impatient so much as deliberately, almost ostentatiously patient. I decided to skip a long explanation about the podcast and the hit-and-run attempt and Tony's drunken flight from the recording session at Jared's and cut to the important part.

"A guy just confessed to me that he witnessed duPlaine's murder," I said.

"Do you know this guy's name?"

"Tony Antonelli," I said. "Who used to be the drummer in her band."

He nodded slightly.

"Tony also said that he killed the person who killed her," I went on. "And dumped his body in Beaver Creek Lake. Which was also where the killer had dumped her body. He didn't tell me the name of her killer, but it was probably the same person you probably already have in the file as her stalker."

Detective Smith sat there expressionless for a few seconds, then frowned a little.

"Beaver Creek Lake?" he asked. "That's odd. Tony usually tells people the bodies are in the reservoir. Or sometimes Chris Greene Lake."

My jaw fell open, and I could only stare at him for a few moments. His deadpan expression gave way to one of mild amusement.

"So you already know about this?" I asked.

"We do." His mouth quirked into a slight, sardonic smile. "And just so's you know, we've searched Beaver Creek Lake, and the reservoir, and all the other places he's claimed the bodies were in over the years. Dragged them, drained them where possible, sent divers down. I'm not saying he's a liar. But we haven't found any bodies in the lakes. And a lot of other things about his story don't check out. The timing, for example. When Ms. duPlaine disappeared, Antonelli was in the middle of a three-month stay at Western State."

"The psychiatric hospital?"

"Yeah. Not sure if he was just there to dry out or if he had other problems. But he was definitely there. Was he sober when he told you this?"

I shook my head.

"Well, there you go," he said. "A pity. Been a while since he's done that—confessing, I mean. I was hoping he'd given it up."

"I feel like an idiot."

"Don't," he said. "Tony's plausible, I'll give him that. He really did know her. No idea if he was just telling a tall tale to begin with or if he hallucinated it. But if you ask me, I think by now he's told that story so much he believes it himself. Of course, it's always possible he did do it, and telling fifteen different impossible versions of how it happened is his brilliant way of keeping anyone from seriously suspecting him. I don't really think he's that smart, but what do I know? And even if it's true, it would be pretty impossible to prove."

"I'm sorry I wasted your time."

"Not your fault. Folks trying to solve the duPlaine case usually run into Tony sooner or later."

"Actually, I wasn't really trying to solve the duPlaine case," I said. "And I didn't just run into Tony—I arranged to meet him. I wanted to see if he tried to run over a friend of mine."

Chapter 25

That got his attention. In fact, he suddenly looked wide awake for the first time in our conversation.

"You want to tell me a little more about that?" he asked. "Wasn't here in Charlottesville, was it?"

"No, in Caerphilly, where I live." I explained about the podcast, the attack on Casey, and Kevin's suspicion that someone connected to one of their cases had done it.

"Your local police know about this?" he asked.

"Yes," I said. "Chief Burke knows about it."

"Henry Burke?" the detective asked.

I nodded.

"I know him, a little."

"He doesn't think the duPlaine case has anything to do with the attack," I said. "So he had no objections to my doing a little research on it, although I'm under orders to back away and bring it to him if I find anything that would change his mind. If I hadn't already been almost on your doorstep, I probably would have just gone home and told Chief Burke what Tony said. Good thing I didn't. He'd have loved that, finding out he was calling you only to finger someone you'd already cleared."

"Well, he's not totally cleared," the detective said. "We just haven't been able to prove or disprove his story over the last couple of decades. So call him one of our usual suspects. Henry and I would have had a chuckle over it. Still might. So you weren't trying to solve the duPlaine case—but what about your hit-and-run? Do you still suspect Tony?"

"He doesn't seem like a prime suspect to me," I said. "I have a hard time imagining he could get all the way to Caerphilly, hunt down his target, and manage not to get caught after he missed. But I was hoping for something a little more concrete. Like an alibi for him."

Smith nodded and took out his notebook.

"When did the attack happen?" he asked.

"This past Saturday night," I said. "Well, technically Sunday morning, around two a.m."

"The seventh?"

I nodded.

"Then he's alibied," the detective said. "By me, actually. The band he's in plays at a dive bar that's not too far from where I live."

"And you went in to catch their act?" I asked.

"Oh, hell no," he said. "Have you heard them?"

"Unfortunately."

"Two a.m.'s closing time," he said. "And that particular bar tends to be a little careless about watching the clock. Not to mention the fact that their patrons don't always take last call very well. So most Saturday nights I drop by, do what I can to see that closing time goes smoothly. Keep the drunks off the roads. I happen to know Tony was there this past Saturday. He was visibly impaired, so I took away his keys myself, and made sure one of his bandmates drove him home."

"Willie?" I guessed.

"Willie," he confirmed. "He's okay. Anyway, if Tony was still drumming along with 'Born to Be Wild' and 'Whole Lotta Love' at two a.m. here, no way he could be running down pedestrians in Caerphilly. Over an hour away, right?"

"Yeah," I said. "Closer to two. So Tony's out. Of course, there could be other people in town who got upset by the podcast. If you hear any rumors about that—"

He was frowning—probably thinking I was about to ask him to do my snooping for me.

"Chief Burke would probably appreciate hearing them," I went on. "Would you like his cell phone number?"

"Please."

I rattled off the number, and he jotted it down in his note-book. And scribbled in it for a little longer than it would take to write a ten-digit phone number, so maybe he was planning to look into the case.

"Anyone other than Tony you were suspicious of?"

"He was the only person connected with the case that I knew about," I said. "Apart from the stalker, if Tony didn't actually do him in, but I don't know his name. I was hoping to get Tony or someone talking so I could find out if there was anyone else from her circle still around."

"We've probably got a reasonably complete rundown on her associates in the case files," the detective said.

Was he actually about to offer some information?

"I'll take a walk down memory lane," he said. "See if any of them are still around. Give Henry Burke a call if I come up with any likely prospects."

"That would be great," I said. "Thanks very much for your time."

He led me back to the exit. He thanked me, we shook hands, and I headed back for my car.

So much for having the solution to a twenty-year-old cold case fall into my lap. I should head back to Amanda and Jared's.

But since I was in town anyway, I decided to do a short detour and cruise by the Prism, the coffeehouse where I'd heard Madeleine duPlaine play. It was back in what I thought of as the college end of town—just off campus, near the Rotunda, the frat houses, and the several run-down places I'd lived after my first year.

And it was still there, the two-story white frame building on its tree-shaded lot. And still a coffeehouse, apparently, though under a different name, and now offering Wi-Fi rather than live music. I pulled into the parking lot of the substantial red brick Presbyterian church next door. I re-called that the church had owned the building and started the Prism as an alternative to the bar and frat scene. I half closed my eyes and tried to recall what it had looked like back then. The coffeehouse was in the basement, I was pretty sure, and you went into a side entrance. Or was it in the back? I caught a vague memory of small tables and chairs under a lowish ceiling, the buzz of conversation, air hot and a little stuffy, since there was no air-conditioning—

And then a shout startled me and I opened my eyes to see that a game of Frisbee had started up in the front yard of the coffeehouse. Three young men threw the bright red disk back and forth while a golden retriever joyously chased the Frisbee's shadow from one to another.

"This isn't getting me anywhere," I said aloud as I started the truck. What was I expecting? Some modern-day Phantom of the Opera, haunting the coffeehouse from which he'd abducted the object of his obsession twenty years before? Maybe if I stayed until evening I'd have better luck recalling my visit there on that long-ago May night—but nostalgia wasn't going to solve either Maddy duPlaine's disappearance or the attack on Casey.

I set my phone's GPS app to guide me back to Amanda and Jared's and pulled out of the church parking lot.

Evidently Jared had arrived just before I did, and was out in the parking lot telling Amanda about his visit to the ER when I pulled in. The other truck was nowhere to be seen.

"So they probably won't do more than keep him overnight for a psych evaluation," Jared said as he led the way back into the studio. "Which is a pity, because he really needs to be in a program, but what can you do? I gather Rock and Bob took off."

"They said they'd call you later to reschedule." Amanda turned to me. "Sorry! But you can't say I didn't try to get you some information."

"Actually, your question turned out to be useful," I said. "While I was waiting for Jared and Willie to show up, Tony confessed that he witnessed Maddy's murder and killed the guy who did it."

"Whoa," Jared said.

"Awesome!" Amanda held up her hand for a high five. "You solved it! A decades-old cold case!"

"No, I didn't." I passed up the high five. "According to the Charlottesville police, he's either telling a tall tale or hallucinating."

Amanda and I settled on the sofa in the studio, and while Jared did things with his equipment, I told them all about Tony's confession and my visit with the detective.

"Ah well," Amanda said. "After all, you did say you weren't really trying to solve her disappearance."

Yes, I'd said that. But it was a heady feeling, thinking I'd cracked a case that had stumped everyone else for two decades. Of course, even if I had, it wouldn't be through any brilliant sleuthing, but because I'd just happened to be there when Tony felt like confessing. Still, I'd be lying if I didn't admit, at least to myself, that I was feeling a bit disappointed.

"Okay," Jared said. "Ready for your other surprise?" He was standing in front of his banks of electronics with his finger hovering over a button. Clearly he was about to play me something.

"Sure." I said. "As long as you're not about to make me listen to a replay of—what do they call themselves?"

"They're between names at the moment," Jared said. "They were calling themselves Rock and the Rollers, but they got a cease and desist order from another, better-known band with almost exactly the same name, so they're going back to the drawing board."

"Tell me what they pick when you hear," I said. "So I can make a point of avoiding anywhere they're playing."

"It'll have Rock in it, whatever they pick," Jared said. "Because it's all about Rock. Now listen to this. Of course, you need to overlook the sound quality, because it's obviously not a studio recording, and I haven't had the time yet to clean up the file, but—"

"Just play it, sugar," Amanda said. "She probably doesn't care about that sound engineer kind of stuff nearly as much as you do."

"Okay. Listen to this." He pushed a button on one of the consoles. Faint sounds emerged from the speakers—a couple of taps, along with the kind of faint hissing that you'd get if you amplified an imperfect recording. A guitar being gently strummed. Then the voice. I was pretty sure it was Madeleine duPlaine, but I glanced up at Jared, who nodded an answer to my silent question.

Then I stopped thinking and just listened. It was a quiet, meditative song, with the singer imagining herself first a bird, then a cloud, and finally a beam of light, and then each time realizing it was only a dream. Maybe the words were profound, or maybe they just seemed that way because of the beauty of her voice and the poignant simplicity of her performance.

When the song ended with a few plaintive chords Jared turned off the system.

"Play it again, Sam," Amanda said with a sigh. "Not really my kind of music, but the voice just sucks you in."

"Is that the only song of hers you have?" I asked.

"I've got two more," he said. "But this is the important one. You realize why, right?"

"No." I shook my head. "It sounds familiar—I know I've heard the song before. But not that version."

"You've probably heard it before because Mary Chapin Carpenter wrote it," Jared said. "Called 'I Was a Bird.' She performed it on her *Age of Miracles* album."

"Of course." Carpenter was one of my favorite performers, and I might even own that album—although that kind of thing was getting harder to remember now that most of my music listening was done via electronic files on one or another of my devices, rather than physical media. I felt a brief pang of nostalgia for the excitement I used to feel when I'd bought a new CD by one of my favorites and unwrapped it as soon as I got to the car, so I could start listening to it in my car's stereo on the way home. I made a mental note to set aside some me time to listen to Carpenter's last few albums when I got home. Carpenter and some of my other favorites. And then I focused back on the present.

"And that's significant because . . . ?" I asked.

"*The Age of Miracles*," Jared repeated. "Her eleventh album."

"I'm impressed that you knew that," I said.

"He looked it up," Amanda said.

"I'm impressed that he knew how to look it up," I countered.

"The important thing is that *The Age of Miracles* was released in 2010," Jared said. "And Carpenter wrote the song, and maybe she wrote it a year or two before that album came out, but not ten years. You see what that means, right?"

"Madeleine duPlaine was still alive in 2010."

Chapter 26

"Where did this recording come from?" I asked.

"I have no idea," Jared said.

"A bootleg recording of Maddy duPlaine just appears in your studio like magic?" I asked.

"In my email, actually," he said. "And I have no idea who sent it."

"Start at the beginning, sugar," Amanda said. "Don't drive her crazy telling it all backward."

"Right." Jared drew himself up and assumed an air of wounded dignity. "Some weeks ago word went around the local music scene that someone was doing another story on the mysterious disappearance of Maddy duPlaine. Got some discussion on social media. And as usual, the reaction was about evenly split between people who were saying maybe this time they'll finally figure out what happened to her and people who are all 'Why don't they stop obsessing about her and pay attention to performers who are still around?'"

"And if you ask me, that second group are mostly just pea green with jealousy," Amanda said. "Given that duPlaine probably had more talent in her left pinkie than they have in their whole bodies."

"And somebody said they'd talked to Tony and that he claimed the podcast people tracked him down," Jared went on.

"Now that's interesting," I said. "Maybe the podcast had triggered more than just Tony's fictitious confession."

"Could be. From what I heard, he said he just ignored all

their calls and emails because for all he knew maybe they were from this guy who'd been stalking Maddy back in the day. So I chimed in to say that I knew someone who could vouch for the podcast guys, and they'd probably have been in kindergarten when Maddy disappeared, so it wasn't very likely they were connected with the stalker."

"I figured out your nephew was one of the podcasters," Amanda put in.

"You're one up on me," I said. "I didn't even know he was a podcaster until yesterday."

"And then late that night I got an email," Jared said. "I didn't recognize the email address, and the subject line said "Listen to this." No message other than that, and what looked like three MP3 files attached. At first I was just going to delete them—I mean, you get attachments from someone you don't know, you figure it'll be a virus or something, right?"

"Smart," I said.

"And even if it wasn't some kind of virus or Trojan horse, I get a lot of people sending me unsolicited music files, and I always delete them. I don't want the hassle of having someone claim he sent me his demo and I stole his ideas, you know? So I deleted the email, and then for some reason I fished it out of my trash folder. And I sent it to my friend Duane, who does cybersecurity for the university. Asked him to check it out. Warned him that I had no idea who sent it and it could be boobytrapped. I didn't open the files until he got back to me the next morning to say they were clean, and who the heck was the singer."

"Guy's got good taste in music," Amanda said.

"I told him the story, and said if he wanted more of Maddy's music, he could help me track down who sent me those files. Last time I heard, he's still working on it. The email it came from was a Gmail account, created that same day on a computer in the Hopewell branch of the Appomattox Regional Library."

"That's down near Richmond," Amanda added.

"And the email hasn't been used since," Jared said. "Duane's been monitoring it."

"The email equivalent of the burner cell phone," I said. "Do you think maybe you could put your friend Duane in touch with Kevin?"

"You think Kevin can find something when my friend can't?" Jared asked. "Duane's good."

"Maybe hearing what your guy's been doing might make Kevin feel better about how little he found," I said. "And they could do the whole techie bonding thing. More importantly, Kevin and Casey haven't yet found any recordings of Maddy's music. They'd be over the moon if you let them hear yours."

"That's easy enough," he said. "And before you ask, I'll send you copies. Not till I clean up the quality a bit, though."

"Send them anyway," I said. "I want to hear them now. And then you can send the cleaned-up versions later and I can marvel at how much better they are."

"Sounds good," he said.

"Is one of them her version of 'The House of the Rising Sun,' by any chance?" I asked.

"No," Jared said. "Does such a thing exist?"

"And I have a copy," I said. "Trade you."

"Deal."

Just then we heard more gravel crunching outside. I was a little apprehensive—what if Rock had located a replacement drummer and was returning to finish the studio session? But Amanda and Jared both looked so pleased that I decided this was unlikely to be the case. In fact, it was the carpool dropping off their two kids. Cold case discussions gave way to happy chatter and a hearty after-school snack. Ordinarily I'd have accepted Amanda's invitation to stay for dinner and bunk down in their spare bedroom, but I still had picking up the replacement peacocks on my agenda.

Well, that and possibly burgling the business school later in the evening, but I figured the less said about that, the better.

So we loaded the hams into the truck—on the floor in the passenger side of the cab, actually, since the peacock cage filled the bed. I insisted on giving Jared a check for them, although having bought good country ham before, I suspected he'd quoted me a lower price than he'd paid. I made them promise to accept the invitation to the wedding reception, and they extracted a promise that I'd come back soon with Michael and the boys in tow, and then, after many hugs, I set out on my peacock chauffeuring mission.

The farm belonging to Mr. Fremont, Dad's fellow peacock-fancier, turned out to be not in Crozet but out in the country, somewhere north of the scenic road between Crozet and Charlottesville and west of Amanda and Jared's farm. And considerably deeper into the country. My journey there was made livelier by the way my phone's GPS app kept repeatedly losing signal and urging me to make a U-turn, and then changing its mind a minute or two later. I'd become so used to this that I initially missed the turn into the Fremont farm and finally had to make a U-turn for real nearly a mile past the driveway.

A faded but elegant sign to the right of the driveway informed me that Mr. Fremont raised Charolais cattle. A newer but much less formal sign announced, FOR SALE: LOCAL HONEY. BROWN EGGS AND GOOSE EGGS. PASTURE RAISED.

In the field to the right of the driveway I spotted the Charolais cows, bunched together in the shade by a small stream. They were all gleaming white—I'd never seen cows that clean outside of the State Fair. Many of them had calves standing beside them. And nearly all of them were standing in the same pose—head toward the distant barn. Rump toward the stream. Wide, white face turned toward me with an expression of mild curiosity. Tail twitching rhythmically to fend off flies. The field to the left of the driveway appeared empty. Perhaps it was normally occupied by the pasture-raised hens and geese—they might have gone to bed early.

I hoped I wasn't arriving after the peacocks' bedtime. Our peacocks always resented being awakened. Of course, since Mr. Fremont's peacocks weren't molting, presumably they wouldn't be as cranky as ours. Still—they were peacocks. Cranky was their default mode.

As I drew near the house, I spotted them—and heard them. Two large males were strutting up and down in the front yard, displaying their plumage and shrieking at each other. The rest of the flock—ten or twelve peahens and a much smaller peacock—were sitting on the roof, where they could have a good view of the competition. Although most of them didn't seem to be watching—they were all either preening their feathers or deliberately gazing in some other direction.

And then they spotted me.

"Dad's right," I muttered as I watched them swing into action. "They're excellent guard animals."

The two alpha males stopped shrieking and displaying at each other and began to strut, side by side, down the driveway toward me, shrieking even louder. The rest of the flock quickly fluttered down from the roof. Peacocks are not skilled or graceful fliers. Several of these landed so awkwardly that I began to worry—what if one of them broke its silly neck in its haste to challenge me? I wasn't sure whether to be relieved or concerned that all of them seemed to survive their flight—or fall—and were now rushing toward me.

I inched the car forward as far as I could, but I was still a good way from the house when I had to stop with the truck's front bumper actually touching the larger of the two alpha peacocks. He made it clear he wasn't going to budge. I killed the engine and prepared to wait for rescue.

I glanced over at the farmhouse. I was a little surprised that no one had emerged already—if our peacocks had been making this much noise, I'd have at least peered out to see what was happening. And Mr. Fremont knew I was coming—I'd texted him with my approximate ETA when I left Amanda and Jared's.

Suddenly one of the two larger males launched himself

into the air, wings flapping madly. He landed on the hood of the truck with a loud thump. Then he spread his tail, completely obscuring my view of the house.

I heard more thuds from behind me. I twisted so I could look through the cab's rear window and saw three cross-looking peacocks sitting atop the cage, staring down at me. One of them started pecking on the roof of the truck cab. The other two decided this was a great idea and followed suit. I could hear other beaks tapping at the doors on both sides of the cab. The peacock on the hood didn't condescend to tap—he merely spread his tail and began shaking it at me, as if he thought iridescence alone would be enough to vanquish me.

I felt a sudden, uncharacteristic spurt of anger toward Mother.

"She wants peacocks strolling on the lawn," I muttered. "To add a note of grace and elegance to the occasion." I pulled out my phone and took a little video. The peacock on the hood looked splendid. You couldn't see the ones on the roof but you could hear them scratching and pecking. And one peacock—probably the smallest of the males—began jumping up to peck at the driver's side window. His head kept popping up and then disappearing again, rather like a small dog trying to see out a tall window.

But after a minute or so I decided I had enough video. Besides, it was probably a good idea to keep my phone free to call 911 if it came to that.

I decided to sit tight as long as the windows and doors remained intact. At the first sight of a crack in the glass—or sound of metal tearing on the roof or one of the doors—I was going to rescue myself. I'd start the engine and begin executing a three-point turn. From what I could see of my surroundings, there was plenty of room. I'd do it slowly, so any peacock whose enraged little pea brain still held a shred of self-preservation would have plenty of time to get out of the way. But I wasn't going to let them stop me. It was them or me.

And maybe I shouldn't wait to start turning around. I peered at the side mirror, trying to gauge whether there were any peafowl behind me.

Just then I heard another loud thump from the hood. I turned and saw that an enormous white goose had landed on the hood. He gave an angry honk and glared at me through the windshield before turning and attacking the peacock. At first I was optimistic that the goose had, for some unknown reason, leaped into the fray to defend me, but I soon figured out he was more interested in defending his right to be the one to finish me off. And apparently he was the leader of a small flock of belligerent geese. All around me geese and peacocks were alternating between fighting each other and joining forces to peck at my truck.

I remembered that the sign at the entrance mentioned not only goose eggs but also local honey. Should I be worrying about a swarm of overprotective bees joining the fracas?

"I give up," I said. "If Mother can't live without peacocks for the reception, I will make her some nice wrought iron ones."

I was reaching to start the engine when I heard a human voice shouting to be heard over all the honking and shrieking.

"Stupid birds! Get away from there! Confound every one of you!"

I peered past the avian melee on the hood to see a tall man in jeans and a t-shirt, waving an old-fashioned wooden pitchfork. He began using it to break up the bird fights, occasionally fending off a goose or peacock that tried to lash out at him. Luckily the pitchfork's tines weren't very sharp, so there didn't appear to be any serious danger that he'd skewer them.

The peacocks gave up first. They retreated back toward the house, still shrieking, and regrouped on the roof—although it took some of them three or four tries to make their way up to it. Once the geese realized they were in possession of the field, they milled about briefly, honking loudly, as if celebrating their victory, and then allowed the farmer to encourage them in the direction of the empty pasture.

"You should be ashamed of yourselves," I heard him say to the geese as he prodded them in the right direction. "You, too," he added over his shoulder at the peacocks.

When the last of them was safely waddling off into the distance, he exhaled loudly, as if in relief. Then he turned and strode toward the truck.

I decided it was safe to roll down the window.

"You must be the lady who came to borrow some of my peacocks." He was still panting slightly, and leaned on the pitchfork as if to rest.

"I was," I said. "But give me a moment. I might be rethinking that idea."

"I'm so sorry," he said. "They're not as bad when it's just one peacock and a few of the hens. But here, with the whole flock around—and of course they're territorial. But you probably know all that. Dr. Langslow said you had peacocks yourselves."

"Only two," I said. "I think it's a mistake to let them outnumber you."

"Probably." He shook his head. "Especially the males. I should have given one of those featherbrains away when they were chicks. If you still want to borrow some, how about if you back your truck closer to the yard. Then you can stay inside while I throw down some feed to lure the peacocks over so I can load them up."

"Sounds good," I said. He seemed suspiciously eager to get rid of his peafowl. Was he hoping they'd find a permanent home with Dad? I had my doubts about the wisdom of turning any of his peacocks loose anywhere near the reception—unless we decided to equip our guests with plate armor and cattle prods. But I didn't think I'd have any luck convincing Mother of this unless she met them.

"I'll let you have McCoy," he said. "Get him away from Hatfield and give him a few peahens to lord over and he should behave pretty well."

He strode back toward the house.

I felt a sudden wave of tiredness. I'd gotten up way too early, driven all the way to Charlottesville, endured over an hour of the most hellish noise I'd ever heard masquerading as music, had my excitement at possibly solving a cold case crushed by cold reality, and survived what had begun to look like a remake of Alfred Hitchcock's *The Birds*. Now I had to make the long drive back home with a flock of bloodthirsty peafowl bouncing along on the back of the truck.

I reminded myself that all I had to do was deliver the wretched birds. After that they were Dad's headache. And he could probably enlist a whole regiment of visiting relatives to help.

Mr. Fremont was quick and efficient at loading the birds. And I could tell he really did feel bad about their antics. As I was thanking him, and telling him Dad would be in touch to keep him posted on how they were doing, he shoved something onto the passenger seat—on top of the hams. A cardboard box only slightly smaller than a copier paper box.

"A little something by way of apology."

"You don't have to—" I began.

"No, I insist," he said. "You shouldn't have had to go through that."

I agreed, actually. So I thanked him and I drove off, eyeing the box. It wasn't large enough for a goose or an additional peafowl, but it was definitely large enough for, say, a hen.

When I got to the road, I stopped long enough to flip open the box lid. It contained four jars of honey, a dozen large brown eggs, and several large greasy paper parcels containing what smelled like homemade cheese.

I breathed a sigh of relief, and made a mental note to thank Mr. Fremont when I brought back the peafowl. Better yet, to write a note of thanks to send with whatever naïve friend or relative I could talk into returning the peafowl.

Chapter 27

The trip home was largely uneventful. At first the four pea-cocks seemed to enjoy shrieking at pedestrians or other ve-hicles whenever we came to a stop sign or traffic light, but once I got on the highway, they grew bored and went to sleep. Once they did, I listened to my collection of Maddy duPlaine songs. Only twice—I resisted the temptation to play them all the way home. Instead, I played a few more of Kevin and Casey's podcasts. They were kind of growing on me. If I hadn't known Casey was a history student, I could have guessed from the precision with which he laid out his facts. And for the older crimes, in particular, he did a good job of putting them in historical context. I couldn't wait to see what he did with the murder at Jamestown.

Although the trip home wasn't tedious, I was still glad when I hit Caerphilly. But then the closer I got to home, the more I found myself slowing down. I finally pulled over and texted Michael.

"Are you guys still at Ragnar's?" I asked.

"Yes. Kids having a blast. Won't be home till late. Join us?"

I was tempted. But maybe Kevin and I should go ahead with our attempt to look at the B-school donor cards. The sooner we did it, the better. Of course, if there was anything fishy there, sooner or later Chief Burke would figure it out and get a search warrant, wouldn't he?

Not unless I could bring him some kind of smoking gun. And right now the B-school was the only place I knew of that might be hiding one. And what if the sudden talk about the cheating scandal alarmed them enough to dispose of the evidence? If they changed or destroyed the cards . . . ?

"I will if I can," I texted back. "But I might have to go on an errand with Kevin. One that could keep me out really, really late. If I'm not there when you get back, I'll try not to wake you."

"Roger."

I was relieved that he didn't try to talk me out of it. I suspected he might if he knew what the errand really was. I planned to tell him all about it after it was safely over. Or, if we didn't pull it off, after it was over and I'd already made my one phone call from jail to my brilliant lawyer cousin Festus Hollingsworth.

He texted me a few photos of what the kids were up to. Josh feeding a baby goat. Jamie playing chords on a beautiful guitar, with a figure that might be Cassie, Ragnar's elusive guest, in the background. The boys and their friend Adam Burke eating what I suspected were large bowls of trollkrem, to judge from the shreds of pink froth clinging to their upper lips. For a moment I seriously considered making a detour to Ragnar's, even if it meant taking the peacocks with me.

Michael promised to keep sending me pictures. And ordered me to tell Kevin not to rope me into anything stupid or dangerous. If he talked to Kevin, he might tell him to take good care of me. Odd. I'd been pulling Kevin out of jams since he was in diapers, and the idea that he was now well over six feet and might be useful to have around in a pinch was still a little hard to grasp.

When I got to the house I backed Dad's truck into the driveway and then called him to let him know the peacocks were here. Which was probably unnecessary. The backyard was filled with relatives, some performing what I assumed were wedding tasks, while others were cooking on our fleet of grills and hauling bowls and plates of food out of the kitchen to get ready for the evening meal.

"Wonderful!" Dad exclaimed. "I'm already on my way."

In fact, I could already see him trotting across the backyard. A minute later, he was gazing at the new peacocks with evident delight.

"You might want to put them in one of the sheds for a while," I said. "They're pretty feisty, even for peacocks, and they're probably unsettled from the trip."

"Of course," he said. "Don't worry. We'll treat them with kid gloves."

"I'd recommend chain-mail gauntlets, actually," I said.

He laughed. Well, he couldn't say he wasn't warned.

Then again . . .

"Seriously," I said. "I don't think they're as used to being around people as our peacocks are. Don't let them loose in the yard until we see how they react in their new surroundings. Drive the truck over to the pasture behind Rose Noire's herb garden, and turn them loose in there. Let them settle in with as little stress as possible."

"Of course," he said. "My—they're very handsome, aren't they?"

I wanted to say that our peacocks had once been just as handsome, and would be again when they'd finished molting, but he'd already dashed off. I left the peacocks to him and recruited a few cousins to carry the hams and the box of food from Mr. Fremont into the kitchen.

I was planning to make a quick visit to the basement to tell Kevin that the burgling trip was on, but it took a few minutes to explain that no, the hams weren't for tonight's dinner but for the wedding reception. And then I figured out that there was only room for about half the hams in the refrigerator—we'd need to take the rest out to the overflow refrigerator in the barn. Rose Noire picked up one and dashed outside with it. I was just deciding whether I'd rather make two trips or carry two of the huge hams at once when I heard shrieks coming from the backyard.

"What's going on?" an aunt said, looking up from the piecrust she was rolling.

I had my suspicions, but I peered out the kitchen window to make sure.

The peacocks were running amok. The four of them had gotten loose—or more likely had been turned loose by family members who didn't heed my warnings—and were rampaging around the backyard. Our normally ubiquitous Welsummer hens had all made themselves scarce. I caught sight of two hens who had hidden under one of the picnic tables, and several more had taken shelter in the llamas' pen.

The llamas were all standing guard along the inside of their fence, spitting gobs of smelly green spit at any peacock that came within range. As I watched, one of the Pomeranians began chasing a peahen, barking furiously, but the peahen turned on him viciously, and he scooted underneath the picnic table with the hens and huddled against them as if for protection.

But mostly the peacocks were chasing visiting relatives, chivvying them up and down the yard and pecking at them. And instead of just taking shelter until the birds wore themselves out, the relatives were either running around in a panic or, worse, trying to approach the birds. To catch them, presumably, and the peacocks were having none of that.

And above all the yelling and shrieking I heard Mother's voice.

"Stop those birds! Stop them, I say! *Where is Meg?*"

"Oh, dear," I muttered. Maybe I should have just thanked Mr. Fremont and told him we no longer needed any peacocks.

I pulled out my phone and made a quick phone call to enlist some help. Then I looked into the closet just inside the back door, where we kept whatever bits of the boys' sports equipment were in season. I put on a catcher's mask and chest protector. I considered the matching shin guards and decided mobility was more important. Then I grabbed a baseball bat and a five-foot lacrosse stick that had somehow escaped being put away for the summer. My efforts were a bit hampered by the fact that stray people kept dashing in through the back door, but I was pleased that at least they were being sensible and rescuing themselves. I bucked the tide and strode out the back door.

By now most of the relatives who hadn't rushed into the kitchen had made at least some attempt to evade the peacocks. Some had sheltered in the barn, pulling the barn door nearly closed behind them. I could see half a dozen of them peeking out through the six-inch opening that remained, sliding the door shut whenever a peacock drew near, and then carefully easing it open again. A few people had jumped up on picnic tables, but two of the peahens were enthusiastically demonstrating that since their wings were not merely decorative, this wasn't a particularly safe refuge. Many relatives were looking on from the llama pen. It wasn't beyond the peacocks' ability to flap their way over the four-foot fence, but the llamas were still mounting a very fierce defense, so with luck the peacocks would ignore them and concentrate on the easier prey still available.

"Is the peacock cage still on the truck?" I called out. But I didn't wait for an answer. I marched over to where Holly McKenna was standing on one of the picnic tables, attempting to fend off one of the peahens with a large serving tray. I waited until the peahen was fluttering up onto the table, then gave her a sound shove with the lacrosse stick. She fell down with a squawk that sounded more like fury than pain. Still, I was starting to feel a little guilty about hurting an animal, until I caught sight of the scratches on Holly's shins.

"Run for the kitchen," I said. "I'll cover you."

By this time a few of the more enterprising relatives began to follow my example. Two cousins in helmets—one baseball, the other motorcycle—emerged from the barn carrying pitchforks, accompanied by Dad, who had donned his beekeeper's outfit and was wielding the long-handled tool we used for changing light bulbs in high ceilings. We surrounded the peahen who had been attacking Holly and began figuring out how to herd her in the direction of the truck without actually hurting her.

I heard sudden screaming from near the llama pen, and glanced over to see that the peacock and the remaining peahens had cornered Rose Noire near the fence. She had backed up against the fence and was holding the ham up as a shield against the peacocks, but they were edging closer and closer.

I turned and ran toward her. I wasn't sure my armor would be enough to protect me against three peafowl, but at least I had some kind of protection. If they slipped past Rose Noire's guard, her light, gauzy summer dress would provide none.

But before I reached her, help arrived from another quarter. The llamas leaped the fence—first Groucho, who was particularly fond of Rose Noire, and then all the others. They raced into the fray, screaming in a way I'd never heard before. They managed to get between Rose Noire and the peacocks, but I could tell they were taking a beating. So were the peacocks, of course, and I wondered how decorative they'd look after this was over.

And then Seth Early, our across-the-street neighbor, arrived with Lad, his border collie.

Seth stopped dead. When I'd called him, I hadn't explained what was going on—just told him to bring Lad over ASAP.

Lad didn't need to be told what to do. He bore down upon the closest peahen and began to herd her. She clearly had no desire to be herded, but you don't argue with a border collie. Dad and the cousins with pitchforks provided minor assistance, mainly by waving their weapons whenever the hen seemed to be even thinking about evading Lad's herding. And, of course, Lad would not have been able to close the latch of the cage once he'd herded the peahen up the ramp.

Once the first hen had been captured, Lad ignored the loud cheers from the barn, the house, and the llama pen. He trotted briskly over to where the llamas and the remaining peafowl were still thrashing about and began nipping heels and uttering short, sharp barks to get the combatants' attention.

Just then a large furry body raced by—someone had let

Tinkerbell, Rob's Irish wolfhound, out of the house. Tink barked and wagged her tail when she saw Lad, who was an old friend, but did not seem offended when he proved too focused on his work to reply. Instead, she seemed to be figuring out what she could do to help him.

The llamas withdrew from combat but were still clustering protectively around Rose Noire. Lad had the peafowl on the move. He was driving them toward the back fence. Good idea. I raced ahead of him to open the gate that divided our yard from the field in which Rose Noire grew her organic herbs. And once I got there, I kept going until I got to the other side of the herb garden, where a gate led into the field in which Dad's heritage sheep and cows grazed.

Lad got the idea immediately. He herded the peafowl through the first gate, with Tink loping along to the side, as if along for the ride, though occasionally, if one of the peafowl tried to make a break for it, she'd utter one of her fiercest growls, less sound than ominous vibration. The peafowl tried to scatter when they got into the herb garden, but Lad discouraged them and got them moving toward the other gate. I waited at a safe distance, then ran over to shut and latch the gate once they were safely in the farther field.

Lad and Tinkerbell settled down companionably in the field. Well, it was probably companionable on Tinkerbell's part. Lad seemed focused on watching the birds every second so he could keep them cornered where they were, in the small part of the field that lay between the herb garden and the surrounding woods. Luckily at this time of night the sheep and cows would all be at the other end of the field, out of sight—at least as long as the peafowl stayed put.

I leaned on the fence and watched, still breathing a little harder than usual.

Seth Early came up and leaned on the fence beside me.

"Lad's got the right idea," he said. "You don't want those hell birds finding their way to your daddy's poor sheep."

No, and I didn't think Dad's cows would be very happy either if they met the peacocks. But Seth's life revolved around his sheep, and although he remained fiercely loyal to his own sturdy Lincoln sheep, he took a great interest in Dad's flock of Romeldales and Valais Blacknoses.

"I tell you what," he went on. "I've got some of that black plastic temporary fencing I used when the tornado went through my pastures and blew away such a lot of the fences. If you think you can get some workers to put it up, I can bring it over."

"Sounds like a great idea."

I left Seth to keep an eye on Lad and the peacocks, and returned to the yard to recruit a fence-building team. Dad wouldn't be available, since he was busy performing first aid on the various humans and animals who'd been wounded in the fight. None of the humans appeared seriously injured, though at least a dozen of the women had received enough nasty scratches on arms, legs, or faces that they were interrogating Dad about how soon their wounds would heal, and planning last-minute revisions to their wedding day finery, like lowering hems and adding long sleeves. The llamas' thick wool had mostly kept them safe, except for Gummo, who had received a rather deep gouge on the tip of his nose. Rose Noire seemed more shaken than hurt, and had climbed into the pen to hug the llamas and hum with them.

I found half a dozen relatives who were willing and able to put up the temporary fence—at least as long as Lad and Seth would be watching over them while they did it.

I noticed Mother standing nearby, but she waited until I'd sent the fencing party on its way before speaking to me.

"Where did those . . . rude peacocks come from?" Her voice clearly showed that she was not in a good mood.

"Crozet," I said. I could as easily have said Charlottesville, but as a UVa alumna, I didn't want her to blame the town where I'd spent four happy years.

She didn't seem to find my answer satisfactory.

"And what are they doing here?" Her tone was icy. "And where are *our* lovely peacocks?"

"All our peafowl are molting. Dad borrowed these from

a friend of his so we'd have some presentable peacocks to stroll about during the reception, adding a note of grace and elegance to the occasion."

Did she realize whom I was quoting?

"Those creatures couldn't add a note of grace and elegance to . . . to a garbage scow," Mother said. "We can't have them here during the reception."

"I can take them back if you like," I said. "But they should be fine as long as we keep them away from the guests. They should be reasonably decorative at a safe distance. Let's see how they're doing in the morning."

"Thank you, dear," she said. "I know it wasn't your fault."

Uh-oh.

"And it wasn't Dad's, either," I said quickly. "I don't think Mr. Fremont, who owns these peacocks, really told him what to expect." Which was probably unfair to Mr. Fremont, but he wasn't here, so it was better to have Mother irked with him than with Dad. "I'll just go make sure the peacocks are secure."

Mother nodded, and headed for the kitchen—no doubt so she didn't have to see what the rampaging peacocks and llamas had done to the previously pristine backyard. The peacocks had knocked over a lot of the potted plants, and broken some of the pots to boot. The lush green turf that Mother and the garden club had been cosseting for months was now missing large divots. Many of the ribbon and silk flower garlands had been ripped away from whatever they were decorating.

We could worry about that tomorrow, when it was light again.

I kept an eye on Lad and the peacocks while Seth fetched the plastic fencing. At my suggestion, Dad drove the truck into the pasture and unloaded the cage containing the third peahen, and without even being told, Lad deftly herded the rest of the flock inside. Actually, I got the idea the peacocks didn't mind that much. They'd clearly had a long, tiring day, filled with enough random violence to gladden even their bloodthirsty little hearts.

"Magnificent animals." I looked up to see that my grandfather had arrived. He leaned against the fence beside me and studied the peafowl with satisfaction. If you asked me, they no longer looked magnificent at close range. The peahens looked scruffy, and a couple of the peacock's tail feathers were bent. But then Grandfather wasn't talking about their looks. In theory, as a distinguished naturalist and environmentalist, he loved all living creatures—but he would be the first to admit that he had a soft spot for anything fierce and dangerous.

"And unusually large for *Pavo cristatus*," he added.

"Also unusually combative," I said.

"No, not really," he said.

"Seriously?" I said. "Were you here just now when they went berserk?"

"No, unfortunately," he said. "But from what I heard, it sounds as if they were displaying the kind of behavior they'd need to survive in the wild. A good idea, if you ask me, breeding some more vigor into the family flocks."

"They won't be staying long enough to breed," I said. "And we're not letting them anywhere near our poor peacocks."

He shook his head as if sadly disappointed in me.

When Seth got back, I thanked him and left him to supervise the fence building. And warned Dad to keep an eye on Grandfather, who might be sufficiently disappointed at missing all the excitement to turn the peafowl loose to repeat their misdeeds.

When I got back to our yard, I turned and studied the peacocks for a minute. Yes, at this distance they would still be reasonably decorative. And if Mother thought otherwise, we could get Lad to herd them a little farther and pen them someplace where they'd be out of sight until after the wedding, when we'd all be less busy and someone would have time to haul them back.

At the moment, I barely had enough time before dinner to touch base with Kevin.

Although it helped that dinner appeared to be running

late. The peacocks had overturned the grills on which the brats, burgers, mushrooms, and chicken tenders had been cooking. Rather a lot of the meat had disappeared, and all the dogs—the five Pomeranians on-site today, and half a dozen dogs belonging to visiting relatives—were lying around looking stuffed and stuporous. I didn't see Spike, but he'd probably slunk away to sleep off his banquet in peace and quiet. New brats, burgers, mushrooms, and chicken tenders were now grilling.

I passed through the kitchen and down into the basement. Kevin was, as usual, sitting in front of one of his monitors. He turned around in his chair when he heard me come in.

"About time," he said. "What took you so long?"

Chapter 28

Clearly Kevin hadn't been out of the basement recently. But surely he'd heard some of the screaming.

"Long story," I said. "I spent the whole day trudging around Charlottesville trying to solve the disappearance of Madeleine duPlaine, and then had to do combat with a gang of feral peacocks. Twice. You should be glad I got here at all."

"We need to make our burglary plan." Kevin waved his hand as he said it, and I wondered what he'd done to himself that required putting bandages on three of his fingers. Had I missed seeing him in the Battle of the Peacocks?

"So did you find duPlaine?" he asked. "To hear Grandpa talk, he wouldn't be surprised if you'd already found her and were bringing her home for dinner."

"Not yet," I said. "But I have found someone who can send you a recording of one of her performances. A guy named Duane who does tech stuff at UVa—watch for an email from him."

"Cool," Kevin said. "We can use that when we do a follow-up. Which we're not going to do until we figure out who tried to off Casey, of course," he added hastily. "Meanwhile, since you weren't around to help, I've come up with a good plan for our invasion of the B-school."

"Invasion's a little over the top, isn't it?" I asked. "Can't we just think of it as a friendly surprise visit?"

"First of all, we need to go in separate vehicles," Kevin said, ignoring my comment. "And we'll park in different lots. That way if one of us is seen, or worse, captured, the other one has a much better chance of escaping."

"The college is patrolled by university security officers, you know. Not Imperial stormtroopers."

"And I think I've figured out a plausible reason for our presence."

"A reason that explains our climbing into the B-school building through an open window, picking the lock of the dean's door, and rummaging through his files?"

"Well, no, but at least it's a reason to be there in the building," he said. "Voilà!"

He stepped aside and pointed to a dog carrier sitting on the basement floor. Spike was staring balefully out of the mesh-covered window in the front. He curled his lip and gave an almost inaudible growl.

Now I could guess the reason for the bandages. Spike was wearing the harness we used to keep him from choking when he tried to drag us along behind him, and Kevin had even managed to attach the leash—I could see the end sticking out of the carrier door, so we could grab it before freeing the Small Evil One.

"So your plan is to enroll Spike as a business school student?" I said. "And pretend we're helping him find his way to class?"

"We pretend that you were walking him," Kevin said. "And he slipped his leash and ran into the bushes and then into the building through a window that someone had carelessly left open."

Okay, I'd give him points for coming up with a plan. And it would be better to have some kind of cover story in case we got caught. Of course, plan A was to avoid getting caught in the first place, but we probably ought to have a plan B.

I'd have preferred a more plausible plan B. But nothing immediately came to mind, and Kevin was visibly impatient for my reaction.

"It'll have to do," I said. "Although it might be a good idea to figure out some logical reason why I would have driven all the way to town in the middle of the night to walk Spike on campus, instead of just strolling out my back door."

"Oh." Kevin looked crestfallen. "I didn't think of that."

"He seemed ill," I improvised. "Choking, and having a hard time breathing. I was rushing him to the veterinary clinic to have Clarence take a look at him, and then just as I got to town he puked up a chicken bone and seemed to be fine. And I was going to take him in anyway, but I realized he needed to pee, so I pulled over and got out with him and only then realized that the leash wasn't fastened to his collar. Correction: I lost my grip on the leash. If we need to turn him loose to add verisimilitude to our cover story, we'll have a better chance of catching him again if the leash is still trailing after him.

"And I was making a late pizza run before Luigi's closed, and saw you chasing Spike, and stopped to help," Kevin said. "I like it."

I wasn't thrilled with the story, but I couldn't think of anything more plausible. And it did have one thing going for it—the idea that someone would deliberately bring a yappy, bad-tempered furball along on a burglary would be pretty hard to believe.

"And Casey's going to stay online here and stand by in case we need any help," he said. "Like information that needs to be hunted down or things that need to be hacked into," he added, probably guessing from my expression that I was about to ask what help Casey could possibly provide from fifteen miles away. "By the way, he's staying here for the time being. I gave him that closet you pretend is a guest room—the one no one in the family wants to sleep in anyway. He was kind of freaking out in his dorm—there's always like a million people coming and going there, and he hardly knows any of them and he keeps worrying that they could be whoever tried to run him over."

"There are about a million people coming and going

here," I pointed out. "And I bet he knows even fewer of them. Not that he isn't welcome to stay, but it's not as if the place is a fortress or something."

"Yeah, but I'm making sure everyone knows who he is and what happened," Kevin said. "He'll stay pretty safe here. It'll be like having dozens of bodyguards."

It probably would. I hoped Casey wasn't fond of solitude, because he wasn't likely to get any in the near future. He'd probably have to fight to keep his self-appointed bodyguards from following him into the bathroom.

"I'll mostly just stay down here," came an unfamiliar voice from behind me. I started and whirled to Casey sitting in front of a computer in the farthest corner of the room.

"Sorry," Casey said. "Didn't mean to startle you."

"See?" Kevin said. "No one will even notice he's around. He'll be perfectly safe."

"Speaking of safe," I said. "In the unlikely event that either you or Casey ventures outside in the fresh air, give the new peacocks a wide berth. They're about as friendly as a pack of wolverines."

"Yeah, right."

Did he not believe me? Or did he not care because he had no intention of approaching the peacocks?

"You need to get out more," I said.

Dinner was probably ready. And it might be a good idea to make sure that neither Mother nor the new peacocks were on the rampage again.

"See you at eleven," I said.

Dinner was being served when I emerged from the basement, and I joined the buffet line. For the first half hour or so, the peacock Armageddon was nearly all anyone talked about. Those who had arrived after it was all over were boasting loudly about what they would have done if they'd been around. Those who had been around were explaining just as loudly why they hadn't gone head-to-head with the peafowl.

Apparently Mother was getting as tired of the subject as I was—especially after listening to one particularly long-winded uncle bloviate about what he would have done.

"I'm sure you would have handled everything wonderfully, Ronald, dear," she said in tone that was obviously intended to carry to the far corners of the yard. "But in your absence, I think it was quite sensible of everyone to leave the situation to those who had some experience dealing with peacocks. Like Meg." She nodded graciously at me, and then at Dad and the two young cousins who were still wearing their helmets—although they'd been persuaded to return the pitchforks to the barn.

Dad beamed with pleasure. I wasn't sure I liked being pegged as a seasoned peacock wrangler, but I smiled anyway.

"But Ronald, dear," Mother went on, her voice carrying even better thanks to all the suddenly abandoned conversations. "Do remember how traumatic the whole incident was for so many people. Perhaps we shouldn't be discussing such a painful subject."

Conversations throughout the yard resumed slowly as people gradually found topics that would meet with Mother's approval. When I'd finished my meal, I begged off helping with the various projects people tried to recruit me for, like beginning to repair the damage the peacocks had done to the yard or helping Rose Noire mix and bag an industrial-sized batch of special wedding potpourri.

"I have to compose a stern but diplomatic email to the owner of those peacocks." I said this while scowling in the direction of the peacock prison. Mother beamed her approval, and everyone else left me alone.

Once I was safely holed up in my office, I did compose a draft email to Mr. Fremont—though I wouldn't have called it stern. Diplomatic, yes. I warned him about McCoy's broken tail feathers, but I also made it clear exactly how he'd acquired them. I asked if he thought his peacocks would behave better once they got over the stress of travel, and whether he could suggest anything that would have a calming effect on them.

Then I saved the draft to look at in the morning, in case any of the stress and anger I still felt had leaked into my words, and focused on what I'd really come out here for.

I relistened to the cheating scandal podcast. I reviewed every shred of paper in Kevin's file. And every page of information Charlie had given me. And my maps, both of the campus and of the B-school building. Who knew what bit of information might suddenly prove useful? I wanted to make sure that if our mission went awry, it wouldn't be from any lack of preparation on my part.

I knocked off around nine thirty to join the small crew of relatives sitting around the campfire making s'mores. A very small crew indeed. Mother's obsession with the wedding preparations seemed to have infected nearly everyone. Most of the visitors were indoors, helping out with various wedding chores. A few were flitting about the yard doing nameless tasks, wearing some of the LED headlights we kept around to use during power outages. And had Mother assigned someone to stand sentry over the visiting peacocks all night, or had someone taken on that mission on his own?

I didn't really want to know.

I was almost the only slacker left by a quarter to eleven, when I texted Kevin.

"Takeoff minus fifteen minutes," I said.

"I'll bring Spike up," he replied.

I returned to my office to grab my tote, which was packed full of objects I thought we'd need. Kevin met me by my car and loaded Spike's carrier into the passenger seat.

"See you inside," he said, and flitted off into the night. He was dressed entirely in black, just as Dad would have been if I'd recruited him for the expedition. But since, unlike Dad, Kevin nearly always dressed entirely in black, it probably wouldn't raise as much suspicion.

As I backed out of the driveway, it suddenly occurred to me that our burgling mission would take us very close to the intersection of Bland and West, where someone had tried to run over Casey. Probably a good thing we hadn't brought Casey along. He might not relish returning to such a dangerous spot.

Of course, it wasn't that particular intersection that was dangerous—that was only where his attacker had caught up with Casey. Anywhere he and Kevin went right now could be equally dangerous if that attacker was stalking the two of them. And Kevin, like most young men, was so often oblivious to danger.

So before taking off for town, I texted him.

"You go first," I said. "And keep your eyes open. If you spot anyone following you, don't go wandering around alone. Drive home. Or to the police station. Or—"

"Got it," he texted back.

I waited till I caught sight of his car pulling away from its usual spot. And then I rolled down my window and waited a little bit longer, peering through the moonlit night and straining for the sound of a car starting.

Nothing. So I took off for town. I spotted Kevin's car ahead of me from time to time, but no others. Either no one was following him or they were a lot sneakier than I was.

Chapter 29

When I reached the campus I parked in the small, conveniently empty lot in front of the Admin Services building—since unlike the corresponding B-school lot, it was one I often used when visiting the campus. No one would be surprised to see me there. I made sure I had a stash of treats in my pocket—Spike's favorite bacon treats. It wasn't as if you could get him to behave or do tricks by waving bacon in front of his face—he wasn't wired that way. But in a pinch you could toss a treat as far from yourself as possible and distract him long enough to avoid getting stitches.

I gazed at him through the wire window of the carrier. I was already wishing I'd brought Tinkerbell instead. Or a borrowed Pomeranian.

"Just play along with this," I told him. "It won't take long, and then I promise I'll feed you as much bacon as you want."

He didn't react. Of course, I wasn't expecting him to. Maybe it was a good thing he had no idea what I wanted him to do. If he did, he'd probably do the opposite, just to be contrary.

I grabbed the trailing end of the leash and made sure I had a good hold on it before opening the carrier door. But Spike didn't rush out—he just sat there, glaring at me.

"Okay, we'll do this the hard way," I said.

I hoisted my bulging tote bag over my shoulder. Then I closed the carrier, picked it up, hauled it out of the car, set it on the ground, and opened the door again.

Spike continued to sulk. Fine. I had the creepy feeling—well, not that someone was watching me right now. More

that I would have no way of knowing whether or not someone was watching me at any given moment. Just in case, I decided to put on a show. I started and looked at my pocket, as
if my phone had just surprised me by vibrating. I pretended
to answer it and began carrying on a conversation with my
imaginary caller.

"What's up? . . . No, over by the campus. We were nearly
at Clarence's when he coughed up a piece of chicken bone.
I think that was the problem. . . . Yeah, I'm still taking him
over so Clarence can check him out, but he gave that bark
that means he needs to go to the bathroom ASAP, so I
pulled over to let him do his thing. . . . Not yet. He's just sitting there in the carrier. Maybe he was just tired of riding in
the car. I'll give it a few more minutes, just in case, and then
head over to the clinic. . . . Okay. I'll keep you posted."

I pretended to end the call. Then I made sure my phone's
ringer was off, so it wouldn't ring at an inconvenient time,
and put it back in my pocket.

"You're still going to the vet, whether or not you pee." I
projected my voice for the benefit of the watchers I hoped
weren't actually there.

No response.

"Okay, let's see if I can shake it out of you." I tugged on
the leash. "Let's do a lap around the Quadrangle."

For a few seconds he just braced himself, so I ended up
dragging him out of the carrier and onto the sidewalk, still sitting on his furry bottom. He sat there for a minute or so, and
we stared at each other. Then his ears perked up. He growled
softly, and took off so fast that he was almost dragging me.
And luckily he was headed in the right direction—toward
the gap between the Admin building and its neighboring
building—the gap that would lead into the Quadrangle.

As I dashed along behind him I worried a little about
what had inspired his sudden enthusiasm. Normally he only
acted like this when he'd detected something that needed
chasing, like a squirrel or a person he disliked—which meant

just about any person who wasn't either Josh or Jamie. As far as I knew, the squirrels would be fast asleep at this hour, so he was more likely to be going after a person—and if even one person was lurking in the Quadrangle we'd have to postpone our burglary.

Unless he'd scented something that resembled a squirrel. Like a mouse. Or even a rat. I hadn't heard that the campus was having rodent problems, but then they wouldn't exactly publicize that.

"Let it be mice," I muttered as I stumbled into the Quadrangle.

Spike raced ahead, doing his best to drag me through some of the rose bushes, then stopped dead and stood, looking around and occasionally sniffing as if trying to recapture a scent trail that had suddenly gone cold.

Then he trotted over to a bush—one that featured particularly large white roses that were luminous and beautiful in the moonlight—and lifted his leg on it.

"Nice move," I muttered.

He finished peeing, turned his back on the bush, and began kicking dirt and grass at it. I ignored him and gazed around until I spotted the large holly bush. There were actually several relatively large holly bushes scattered at intervals along the perimeter of the Quadrangle, but only one had Kevin peeking out from behind it, waving at me and beckoning for me to join him. So much for fooling anyone who happened to be watching.

But then he actually did something clever—he made a noise that instantly got Spike's attention: the siren sound of a plastic food bag being crinkled. Spike, like many dogs, believed that such bags invariably contained foodstuffs that were salty, cheesy, or otherwise delectable to the canine palate. He almost pulled the leash out of my hand in his haste to investigate the source of the sound.

Spike and I joined Kevin behind the holly bush. Kevin placated Spike by letting him have the enticing though nearly empty Utz potato chip bag while I tried to find a hiding place relatively free of holly leaves, whose sharp little spines hurt when they poked through my clothes.

"Window's unlocked, as promised," he murmured. "Ready?"

"Put these on first." I reached into my overstuffed tote and handed him a pair of surgical gloves I'd liberated from the elaborate first aid station Dad had set up in our pantry.

"Good thinking," he said. "Now?"

I nodded. Spike had his head and shoulders all the way in the potato chip bag, so I decided to risk picking him up and carrying him in. Kevin followed. Inside I set Spike down, pulled out my phone, turned on the flashlight app, and scanned our surroundings. Kevin followed suit. He was glancing around with curiosity—presumably he hadn't seen the inside of many ladies' rooms. We stood there for a minute or so and listened for any sounds outside, although it was hard to hear anything over the crackling noises produced by Spike's energetic attempts to lick every grain of salt off the inside of the chip bag.

"The coast may or may not be clear, but we'll never find out this way," I said in an undertone. "Your job is to hang on to Spike and keep a lookout."

He nodded and took the end of the leash. I set Spike down and whisked the potato chip bag off of his head. He snapped but his heart wasn't in it—he'd probably already licked it clean. We took a few minutes to pluck off all the holly leaves that had attached themselves to our clothes, hair, and skin, and throw them out the bathroom window. No sense leaving a trail of leaves behind to show not only that unwanted guests had invaded the building but also how they'd managed it. Then I pulled out the map Ingrid had sent me and led the way out of the ladies' room and into the corridor.

I was silently improvising what I'd say if anyone caught us. "We chased Spike in through the window, but were hoping to find a way out that would let us avoid the holly bush."

Yeah, that might work. Or should we go with "We're doing a kind of modern scavenger hunt where we have to take selfies in a bunch of crazy places, like on top of the town hall and sitting behind the B-school dean's desk." That might be a plausible story once we penetrated farther into the building.

Or maybe we should just focus on not getting caught.

I cast a slightly anxious glance at the first door we passed—the one leading to Professor Vansittart's office. But it was closed, and no light shone through the crack between the door and the sill. And I reminded myself that while he was definitely on our suspect list, with luck any number of other middle-aged former B-school students would soon be joining him.

We made our way along the hall to the stairway, and then up to the second floor, in what would have been perfect silence if it hadn't been for Spike's claws clicking softly on the polished wooden floors. We came to a halt outside the sturdy oak door to the dean's office.

I pulled my burgling tools and an actual flashlight out of my tote.

"Shine this on the lock." I handed the flashlight to Kevin and went to work on the lock.

The dean's door had an impressively large antique cast bronze doorknob and strike plate, but the lock itself was an old-fashioned kind I found relatively easy to pick. In a minute or so I heard the telltale click and eased the door open.

Dad would be proud—assuming we ever told him.

"Wow," Kevin whispered. "You weren't kidding. You actually do know how to do this."

I decided to ignore the obvious surprise in his tone.

The dean's office was actually a suite. A large outer office held his secretary's desk and the usual office accoutrements, like a copier and several wooden filing cabinets. It also contained a sofa and chairs where guests could sit in comfort and read the latest issues of *Forbes, Fortune, Businessweek, The Economist, The Wall Street Journal,* and several other business magazines. Although it would take a bold guest to disturb the military precision with which these periodicals were arranged on the coffee table. But I didn't spot any repurposed oak card catalog cabinets.

The dean had an even larger and more pretentiously furnished office, but the card cabinets weren't there, either.

They were in the conference room—three graceful oak cabinets on tapered legs, their brass metal hardware mellowed by age. They covered the better part of one of the room's end walls.

I did a quick count. There were ninety drawers. And none of them labeled. All the little brass label holders were intact—but empty. I pulled out a drawer at random. It was chock full of index cards.

"Holy smoke," Kevin said. "There must be a million of them."

He sounded a little daunted. I could understand—I felt a little daunted myself. But I squared my shoulders and tried to project a confidence I didn't feel.

"Let's get started," I said.

"I brought a camera," he said. "I figure we could take pictures of them."

"I have a better idea." I reached into my tote and pulled out a ream of copier paper. "There's a copier machine in the outer office. With luck I can figure out how to send the cards through the automatic feed."

"Awesome." Kevin looked a little less discouraged.

And we soon found that all ninety drawers didn't contain cards. In fact, only fourteen of them did, and many of them were only half-full. Most of the others held random assortments of office kibble. Paper clips. Binder clips. Several thousand pink and purple staples. Three small ashtrays that looked as if they'd recently been used, even though smoking had been banned in all college buildings for over a decade.

I took the first drawer of index cards—*A* to *Bl*—out of the cabinet and hauled it over to the copier. I removed the dean's paper and inserted a ream of the paper I'd brought, being careful to put the wrapper back in my tote instead of the trash can.

"They probably wouldn't notice a few missing sheets of copier paper," Kevin said.

"Yeah, but they'd definitely notice as much paper as it's going to take to copy all of this stuff," I said. "Go keep watch by the door."

The copier was an admirably new and advanced one, which meant I had to fiddle around with the controls a bit to figure out how to operate it. But on the plus side, it had all the latest bells and whistles, including the ability to adjust the automatic feeder to handle the three-by-five-inch index cards on which the B-school kept its donor records. Before long I had the machine humming away.

As copy machines went, this one was pretty quiet. But still, if there were anyone lurking in the nearby offices or halls, they probably figured out almost immediately that someone was at work in the dean's office. Kevin kept his ear to the door and cast a great many anxious glances over at the copier while I worked away, feeding batches of cards into the machine, carrying drawers of cards back and forth from the conference room, stashing batches of finished copies in my purse, and refilling the paper supply from the packages I'd brought along.

Once I got started, it moved quickly, and yet at the same time it seemed never-ending. I began to mark milestones. Five drawers done—more than a third finished. Seven drawers done—the halfway mark. The last couple of drawers seemed to take longer than all the rest combined, but I knew that was subjective. And I also realized that I had picked the better job. I'd have been a lot more anxious if I'd been doing Kevin's job instead—standing by the door, restraining Spike when the urge to ramble struck him, and straining to hear any noises outside over the steady whirr and clack of the copier.

He breathed a loud sigh of relief when I took the fourteenth drawer back into the conference room and emerged empty-handed.

"We did it," he said.

"Don't celebrate just yet," I said. "We still have to make it out of here undetected."

We retraced our steps back to the first-floor ladies' room and climbed out of the window. We stopped to take off our surgical gloves and I tucked them into my tote. I closed the window behind us.

Just then Spike spotted—or smelled—something that excited him. He gave a couple of short barks and dashed away, jerking the leash out of Kevin's hand.

"Damn!" Kevin exclaimed, a little more loudly than was prudent. Then again, Spike's incessant barking would probably cover any little noises we made.

It would probably attract the attention of a college security officer before too long.

Chapter 30

I made sure my car keys were in my pocket, then shoved my tote into Kevin's hands.

"Take this and get it home safely," I said. "It's got all the incriminating evidence in it. Let me worry about Spike."

He started to protest, then stopped and nodded. He grabbed the tote and headed across the Quadrangle. I started to call out that he was heading the wrong way, then remembered that he would have parked in a different lot, and had probably entered the Quadrangle through another of the gaps.

I set out after Spike. He raced up and down the Quadrangle for a few minutes, barking his fool head off. Then he made a break for one of the gaps—I was pretty sure it was the same gap we'd come in by. Damn. He'd have so much more scope for escaping when he reached the great outside.

Perhaps I should take pride in the fact that although Spike was no longer young, he was clearly still in fine physical shape. He certainly had more speed than me, and I was starting to worry that he might also have more endurance. At least for the time being he seemed to enjoy running back and forth across the Admin building's front lawn, swinging in fairly close to me from time to time and then darting away if I made a lunge at the trailing leash. I even tried tossing him a couple of treats and then holding one out in my hand, trying to tempt him.

He ignored my blandishments. Tonight was not a night to give in to his baser appetites and stuff himself full of treats, his body language seemed to say. Tonight was made for gamboling in the moonlight and singing the song of his people at the top of his evil little lungs.

I went over to the Twinmobile. The carrier was still there on the grass right beside where I'd parked. I sat down beside it and watched Spike racing up and down the lawn. He seemed to be deliberately staying close enough that I could see him, yet far enough away that I couldn't grab his leash. Maybe he'd wear himself out doing that.

Just as I had that thought, he seemed to spot something that interested him and took off across the street. I groaned, leaped to my feet, and gave chase at a steady jog.

Thank goodness it was now nearly two in the morning, so cars were few and far between. He had run into the Annex, a warren of buildings that were old enough to be uncomfortable and inconvenient, but without having any particular aesthetic, architectural, or historic distinction. Adjunct faculty members and teaching assistants were exiled here, along with junior bureaucrats who had not been as successful as Charlie in climbing through the ranks of Admin Services or Facilities. Michael had shared an office there with two other junior faculty members his first year at the college, and according to him both the air-conditioning and the heat were not up to their job, and thanks to its proximity to the main cafeteria, the whole building invariably stank of cabbage and insecticide.

I'd actually been planning to visit the benighted Annex eventually, since the lost souls condemned to dwell in it included J. Morton Fairweather, the one B-school student from the 1990s, apart from Professor Vansittart, who was still here at the college. Well, maybe this would give me an excuse. I could pretend to have dropped something outside while catching Spike.

I decided I should focus on actually catching Spike first.

Up ahead somewhere I could hear him barking. And not barking in the same carefree, taunting manner as a few minutes ago. There was a note of—what? Fear? Pain?

I broke into a run.

I found him near a set of steps that led up into one of the buildings. He'd managed to get his leash caught up in the wrought iron railing on the right side of the steps.

"Aha," I said. "Gotcha."

He had stopped barking and calmed down a bit. In fact, he was looking at me with the peeved expression that clearly suggested he was impatient for me to release him from his annoying predicament. Which was, obviously, all my fault.

When I got close, I reached down to grab the end of the leash and then stopped.

The leash hadn't just caught on the railing. It was wrapped around it. How had Spike managed that?

What if it wasn't Spike who had managed it?

My skin prickled again. What if some human hand had done it? And what if they were still here, watching me? Instead of bending over to untangle the leash, I mounted the steps, sat down on the top one, and pretended to breathe heavily while scowling down at Spike. Actually I was watching for motion in my peripheral vision, and listening for any nearby noises.

Spike growled softly.

"Yeah, I'll let you loose as soon as I catch my breath," I said.

I thought I detected a rustling noise in the bushes to my left. Spike stirred. I willed him to be quiet so I could hear. Yes, there was definitely a rustling noise.

I should pull out my phone and call for help.

And look like an idiot? A wimp?

Better an idiotic but live wimp than a dead person. I was reaching for my phone when—

"Meg?"

I jumped. I'd been focused on the bushes to my left. The voice came from my right.

My friend Aida strode into sight, still in her khaki deputy's uniform.

"I'm glad to see you," I said. "Even if you did scare the dickens out of me."

"So I noticed," she said. "What are you and the Scourge of Caerphilly doing out here in the middle of the night?" Spike wagged his tail slightly as if he rather approved of her pet nickname for him.

Aida was a friend, but she was also a police officer. I fell back on the story of Spike, the chicken bone, and his daring escape when I took him out of the crate so he could pee.

"And I've been chasing him around campus forever," I said. "And when I finally found him—take a look at that leash. Does that look like something he could have managed all by himself?"

She studied the leash for a minute, and then shook her head.

"Someone caught him for you?" she suggested.

"And tied him up here and ran away in the very short time he was out of my sight? Which can't have been more than two minutes, tops."

She nodded absently. She was slowly scanning our surroundings. Her hand was resting on her service weapon.

"Whoever did it's probably long gone by now," she said. "Why don't I see you and the Scourge safely to your car. And then over to Clarence's if you like. He's probably wondering what happened to you."

"Not really," I said. "I thought I'd just surprise him. If—oh, bother. I guess he's not sleeping there over the office very often, now that he's got Lucas Plunkett on night duty. Maybe I should just take Spike home and bring him back in the morning."

"Drop him off and let Lucas keep watch over him tonight," Aida suggested. "If he shows any alarming symptoms, Lucas can get Clarence to dash over quicker than you can bring Spike back into town. And do you really want to stay up and keep watch over him?"

Since I was obliged to keep up the pretense of being worried about Spike, I agreed that this was a good idea. So we caravanned over to the Caerphilly Animal Hospital. Lucas Plunkett answered the night bell. He was in the middle of bottle-feeding a white kitten so young its eyes weren't open yet. My story about Spike and the chicken bone sounded a little sillier each time I tried it, but he listened to it calmly.

"Let's take him back where I can keep an eye on him," he said. "I'll be up all night, between feeding these kittens and keeping an eye on a beagle who had surgery a couple of hours ago."

Of course, since Caerphilly was very far from being an impersonal metropolis, Aida and I guessed almost immediately that the beagle in question belonged to our friend Maudie Morton. And because HIPAA rules didn't cover canines, Lucas readily gave us what details he knew about the beagle's unfortunate encounter with a tourist's Toyota. He seemed to warm to us once he realized we were genuinely interested in his patient's welfare. The beagle was clearly still feeling very uncomfortable, but she seemed happy to see him when he took us over to show us how she was doing, and thumped her tail weakly when he scratched her behind the ear.

"Don't try that with Spike," I said, glancing over at the adjacent cage, where we'd stowed the Small Evil One. "He may look harmless, but—"

"Don't worry," Lucas said. "I've done time. I know a stone-cold killer when I see one."

He and Spike studied each other for a few seconds. Spike eventually snorted, and curled up with his back to us. Lucas seemed to be holding back a smile.

By the time we left, I had no qualms about leaving Spike in the care of an ex-con who might or might not be a murderer. Whatever else he was, Lucas was clearly an animal lover.

And I felt safe enough to decline Aida's offer of an escort home. That prickly feeling of being watched had disappeared when we left the campus.

"Don't worry about me," I said. "We've got a full house, this close to the wedding. Odds are some of them will still be up."

By the time I got home it was nearly 3:00 a.m., and only Kevin was still up. Which I knew already, since he'd texted me the instant he arrived at the house and kept pestering me every few minutes for updates on where I was.

"I've been sticking all those pages through the scanner," he announced as he opened the front door for me. "You want to start taking a look at them?"

"Morning will be fine. Can you lock them up in my office when you're finished?" I slipped the office key off my key ring and held it out.

"Can do," he said.

"And then go to bed," I said.

"I'm too wired," he said. "You want me to do anything with the copies?"

Well, if he was staying up anyway . . .

"Look through them," I said. "We're looking for anyone who gave money from, say, 1995 to 2000. Flag those records for me."

"Roger."

He dashed off toward the kitchen, where the door to his basement lair was. I crept upstairs. I must have made my message about being out very, very late pretty convincing, since Michael was fast asleep.

I had slipped into my nightgown and was sliding between the covers when I noticed that Kevin had texted me. Again.

"WHAT DID YOU DO WITH SPIKE???"

"At the vet," I texted back.

Did he really think I'd have left one of our party behind? Actually, he had probably forgotten all about Spike until he went back down into the basement, saw Widget, his Pomeranian, sleeping on his desk, and realized the house was one short of its usual quorum of dogs. But at least he hadn't completely forgotten about Spike. Widget was definitely having a civilizing effect on Kevin.

With that comforting thought I dropped off to sleep.

Chapter 31

Thursday, May 12

Not surprisingly, Michael woke up before I was ready to. But neither he nor the boys had mastered the art of creeping around so as not to wake a sleeping family member. I opened one eye and wished him good morning.

"Was your late errand successful?" he asked.

Probably not a good idea to keep him completely in the dark.

"Yes," I said. "By the way, in case anyone wonders where Spike is—"

"Clarence already called to say he's fine," Michael said. "He wants to keep an eye on him for a few more hours, but we can pick him up whenever we happen to be in town. What idiot let him get his paws on a chicken bone?"

"The chicken bone story was actually cover for what I was really doing," I said. "Paying a late-night visit to scout out one of the college buildings."

"All by yourself?"

"I made Kevin come along as bodyguard and leash holder," I said.

"Good," he said. "About time he did some work on this project of his, instead of dumping it all on you. Find out anything interesting?"

"Too soon to tell," I said. "Wake me if anyone really, really needs me. Preferably for something other than wedding tasks."

"I think your mother has written you off as permanently AWOL," he said. "Want me to pick up Spike?"

I thought about it for a second.

"No," I said. "Let me do it. It will give me a chance—"

"To duck out, if your mother tries to dump any particularly awful wedding chores on you," he said. "Roger. Go back to sleep."

Actually, I was thinking it would give me another chance to scope out Lucas Plunkett under safe circumstances. Maybe even ask him a few questions if I could think of any useful ones. But Michael was gone before I could articulate that.

And I tried to go back to sleep. I really did. But the thought that the stack of illicit photocopies was waiting for me in my office wouldn't leave my mind. I dozed off a time or two, but slept fitfully and dreamed that I was being pursued through an endless maze of corridors by a swarm of papers swirling about and stabbing at me with their corners like so many wasps.

Or holly leaves. Apparently I'd carried a couple of them home in my clothes. At around nine I got up, tossed the holly leaves out the back window, and studied the activity going on in the backyard.

Demetria, the sidewalk painter, was supervising half a dozen volunteers who were decorating the picnic tables and benches with roses and lilies. Another team of volunteers were festooning the fence around the llama pen with more ribbons and silk flower garlands, and turning the llama shed into a flower-decked bower. Except for Chico, who caught on to things more slowly than the rest, the llamas all seemed to have figured out that the flowers and ribbons weren't particularly tasty, but they had yet to tire of sneaking up behind the volunteers and sticking their long necks over the humans' shoulders to get a closer view of what they were working on.

A crew of younger cousins were using wheelbarrows to haul more large potted plants into the backyard. Garden club members were performing lawn surgery, fitting little bits of new sod into the spots where last night's combatants had gouged holes. Nimble-fingered cousins were repairing the garlands the peafowl had so gleefully shredded and weaving new ones to deck whatever small corners of the yard were not already tarted up like a Rose Bowl float.

I spotted McCoy and the three visiting peahens. Evidently Seth Early had provided enough black plastic fencing to not only section off the small part of the pasture they were in but also to reinforce the fence between the pasture and Rose Noire's herb garden and raise its height to six feet. The peacocks could probably still get over it, of course—they'd managed to flutter up a good ten feet to roost on Mr. Fremont's roof. But they weren't all that good at flying, so with luck it would at least slow them down. Tink and three of the Pomeranians were by the back fence of the herb garden, watching the peacocks, and I had a feeling Lad would be dropping by regularly, in the hope of finding something that needed to be herded or organized. Maybe I should let Dad and the dogs worry about the peacocks.

I should find someplace quiet where I could spend some time with my donor card copies. Someplace quiet and out of the way, so Mother wouldn't try to rope me into the frenzy of decorating.

I got dressed and ventured downstairs to acquire breakfast and scout out the lay of the land.

Rose Noire and several other cousins were in the kitchen, cleaning up after the morning's breakfast service.

"There you are," she said. "I saved you a plate—I hear you were out really late with poor Spike. But Clarence called this morning, and he's fine."

"Great." I think I managed to look as if the news relieved me.

The plate she slid in front of me contained a large helping of scrambled eggs, a mound of fresh fruit salad, and what seemed like half a pig's worth of bacon and sausage.

"Toast?" She hovered by the toaster.

"This should be fine," I said.

"It goes better with toast." She poked down the lever on the toaster. "But could you take it into the dining room? We're going to start on lunch in here."

"Actually, I was going to take it to my office," I said.

"Er . . . actually, your mother and Holly are using your office," she said. "They needed to print something. They shouldn't be that much longer, and of course it's your office so—"

"I'll be in the dining room." If I went out to the office, I might get drafted to help with whatever they were printing.

She trailed after me with a glass of cranberry juice and a cup of hot tea, ducked back in a minute later with two slices of buttered toast, and then left me in solitary splendor.

I texted Kevin.

"Did you take the photocopies to my office?"

While waiting for his answer I pulled out my notebook and ate a slice of bacon while crossing off things I'd already done—two activities that always improved my mood.

"No," he finally texted back. "By the time I woke up, your mother and Mrs. McKenna were already in there. I brought them back to the basement."

"Good thinking," I told him. "Can you bring them to me in the dining room?"

He didn't answer. Which probably meant that he would bring the photocopies, provided nothing more interesting captured his attention first. I started on the scrambled eggs and scanned my notebook.

A few minutes later, Kevin showed up with a copier paper box. And my tote.

"Here are those papers you wanted me to print for you," he said in an overloud voice.

Aha. Dad was trailing after him.

"So what did you find out in Charlottesville?" Dad asked.

"Apart from the fact that our peacocks are actually pretty well-behaved for their species?" I said.

Dad winced and I took pity on him.

"Maddy duPlaine's drummer confessed that after witnessing her murder, he killed her killer, and he named the lake where both bodies could be found," I began.

"Fabulous!" Dad exclaimed.

"But he's been confessing this for years, and the Charlottesville police long ago got tired of draining all the lakes he's been naming," I said. "Besides, we now have evidence that she couldn't have been killed then." I explained about the Mary Chapin Carpenter song that almost certainly hadn't been written back when duPlaine disappeared.

"Fascinating," he said. "So she's still alive."

"Was still alive ten or twelve years ago," I said. "No telling now. But it certainly complicates the case."

"Perhaps your podcast alarmed her," Dad said. "And what happened to Casey wasn't so much an attempt on his life as a warning to back away."

"Or maybe she's sick and tired of people raking up her case," Kevin said. "And our podcast was the last straw, and she lost it, and is going to turn into a serial killer and knock off every blogger or podcaster who covers it."

"Well," Dad said. "I don't think that's very plausible."

"Kidding." Kevin rolled his eyes. "And I hate to say it, but I can't figure out why our podcast would have alarmed her. It wasn't our most original episode, you know. I think we did a good job of telling the story, but it was mostly local color and speculation. We didn't have a single fact in it that hadn't been out there for years on a couple dozen blogs and websites."

He reached into my tote and pulled out some of his case files. He opened the one on the duPlaine case and we all stared down at her photo for a few minutes.

Was she still alive? The song Jared had found—correction, the song someone had sent to Jared—what if she'd sent it? As a message, maybe. What if it was her way of saying "I wasn't murdered twenty years ago. I disappeared. I made a new life—please leave me alone to live it."

I scribbled a task into my notebook—to look up the lyrics

of the three songs someone had sent to Jared. Maybe there was a message there. Maybe—

"Ooh! Your burgling tools!" Dad was holding up the little kit, which seemed to have fallen out of my tote when Kevin had pulled out the files. "Were you planning on using them anytime soon?"

He sounded eager. Way too eager.

"They're lockpicking tools," I said. "Not burgling tools. And no, I'm not planning on using them anytime soon." It wasn't actually a lie. I thought of adding that Kevin had wanted to borrow them, but decided to quit while I was ahead.

"Oh, you're no fun," Kevin said. "Grandpa, help me out. I made Meg get out her lockpicking stuff to show me. I'm trying to talk her into competing in locksport."

"Locksport?" Dad's curiosity was aroused. It was almost like seeing one of the Pomeranians spotting a treat. "What's that?"

I was glad he asked so I didn't have to.

"The sport or hobby of defeating locking systems," Kevin said. "There are organizations for people who want to do it, and conventions with classes and contests and stuff. I heard about it because some of the conventions include computer security challenges as a part of their program. I've been thinking of going, just to check it out. And locksport gets a bad rep, like white hat hacking, because people don't understand that the enthusiasts have a strict ethical code—and they're doing their part to help improve physical security, the way ethical hackers improve cybersecurity through penetration testing."

I doubted that the lockpicking I'd done last night would pass muster under the strict ethical code of locksport enthusiasts. And I certainly had no intention of helping the B-school improve their physical security.

"So this really is a thing?" Dad asked. "You're not pulling my leg?"

"Come on," Kevin said. "I'll show you the website."

They disappeared into the basement. I tucked the little case containing my lockpicking tools back in my tote. Although I feared the damage had been done. I sighed. Things were so much more peaceful when Dad wasn't in the grip of one of his obsessions.

Chapter 32

I went back to work. I opened up the copier paper box and began studying the B-school's donor cards. They were very informative. They covered not just donors but also targets, including all of their alumni—and many of them had more than one card. A few really dedicated donors had whole packs. The person's name was at the top of each card, and in the first card it was often accompanied by an *A* for alumni or *F* for family. I soon figured out that a big green dot in the top right corner of the first card meant an active donor and a black dot meant the person was deceased. Although anyone who thought they could get out of donating by kicking the bucket was mistaken. Cards with black dots often contained detailed information about the B-school's efforts to determine whether the dear departed had remembered his alma mater in his will, along with a history of the dean's efforts to cajole the heirs into establishing scholarships, endowing chairs, or making other memorial donations.

The cards also had detailed contact information. Home and office addresses. Phone numbers. Email addresses. Employment histories. Boards the targets served on. Charities they were affiliated with. Family members, with particular attention to spouses, parents, siblings, or children who were also alumni or donors. Some cards included neatly sketched family trees showing up to four generations of alumni. Most cards featured at least a few of the kind of telling personal details that would help a glad-handing dean create the impression that he took a profound personal interest in whomever he was talking to. Nicknames. Pets. Honorary awards. Favorite alcoholic beverages. Golf handicaps. Medical issues.

And long, detailed lists of donations, including restrictions on how the donations could be used. Some of the older cards came right out and stated which minorities or causes the donors didn't want their money to support. By the twenty-first century they'd given that up, but I suspected the notation "supports traditional values" served much the same purpose.

Sorting through the donor cards was not giving me a warm, fuzzy feeling about the B-school.

And I was pretty sure I'd figured out how the cards kept track of donations that were really payment for the B-school's leniency toward erring students. Back in the 1800s, they just came right out and said things like "in gratitude for the leniency shown toward Mr. Falthorpe's many disciplinary infractions" or "to thank the faculty for their assistance in helping Mr. Braintree with the more difficult aspects of his course of studies." More modern notes spoke of "outstanding support from the faculty toward helping Mr. Smith realize his full academic potential" or the dean's "wise tolerance for the foibles of youth."

By matching the donor cards to Charlie's list of students attending B-school classes the year of the cheating scandal, I identified six parents who had either donated for the first time that year or significantly increased the amount they'd donated. Claude Vansittart's parents were among them, and their one-time donation was larger than any of the others. But perhaps that was because Claude's younger brother, Vincent, was also attending the B-school at the time. Both Claude and his brother had their own donor cards. The size of Claude's donations suggested he probably had a source of income other than his college salary. Vincent was the principal in an investment firm, and the way his donations ebbed and flowed suggested that VVS Holdings was finding the road to success somewhat rocky.

And I took a close look at the other five big donors who

just happened to have children attending the B-school that year. Four of children—three sons and one daughter—had donor cards of their own. Actually the fifth did, too, but his donor card sported a black dot and the date of his death was only three years after he'd graduated. It was always possible that his parents were sensitive about the possibility that the podcast would besmirch their son's posthumous reputation, but I figured they were pretty low on my suspect list.

Claude Vansittart was the only one of the remaining five still in academia. Which didn't let the others off the hook—it just made them less interesting as suspects.

Just then Kevin appeared in the kitchen.

"I've got my top suspects." I handed him a sheet of paper on which I'd written the names. "On top of the Vansittarts that you already know about. Can we start finding out what these people were up to Saturday night?"

"Roger," he said.

"By the way, nice save on the lockpicking thing," I added.

"I may have created a monster," Kevin said. "Grandpa's down there trying to pick the lock on my file cabinet. Are file cabinet locks fiendishly difficult?"

"Not with those inexpensive file cabinets you've got," I said. "I could do it with a paper clip. Your grandfather's not exactly a quick study on this lockpicking thing."

"That's kind of what I suspected." Kevin glanced at the basement door as if to make sure Dad wasn't sneaking up behind him. "I figure sooner or later he's going to give up and start trying to talk you into going to one of those locksport conventions with him."

"You're probably right," I said. "See if you can get him fired up about watching you compete in the hacking division, will you?"

"I'll try," he said. "But you know Grandpa."

Yes, I did.

Kevin disappeared into the basement again.

I went back to poring over the donation records, focusing on the cards for the ones I suspected of being involved in the cheating scandal. And their parents, and in two cases, grandparents. It was a glimpse into a rarefied world of privilege and the old-boy network, of summer houses and trust funds.

Rose Noire poked her head in.

"The mothers have finished with your office," she said.

"Great." I didn't look up. I was reading a concise note on the thirty or so letters of recommendation a previous B-school dean had written in an attempt to help a large donor's son get accepted by a reputable law school, and taking my hat off to the perspicacity of the law schools' admissions officers. I'd never heard of the law school that finally accepted the kid.

"And we're going to need the dining room when we start cooking," she said. "Otherwise we won't have enough space for the prep work."

I glanced at my phone. It was only three. I wondered, briefly, what elaborate culinary plans Mother and Holly McKenna had come up with for tonight. But at least Rose Noire was giving me a chance to escape before the madness began.

"By the way," I said as I shoveled files back into my tote. "Mother and Holly do know about Ragnar's party tonight, don't they?"

"Oh, yes," she said. "That's what we're going to start working on—some Scandinavian delicacies to take to Ragnar's."

Great. Mother was instigating a culinary competition with Alice. I definitely needed to make myself scarce. I slung my tote over my shoulder. Then I piled the papers in the copier paper box Kevin had brought them up from the basement in. He hadn't brought the lid, and I was a little paranoid about walking around with the box open so anyone could see the fruits of our burglary. So, on my way through the kitchen, I grabbed a dish towel, covered the box with it, and headed for my office.

The backyard was looking . . . well, I had to admit it looked nice. But a little too nice. Like the sort of yard that was off-limits for Frisbee throwing and pickup games of Wiffle ball. Where you'd feel guilty about spitting watermelon seeds on the ground. And where you'd never think of throwing out feed for a flock of chickens. Where had all of ours gone? I stopped to scan my surroundings and finally spotted them. They were out in the same pasture as the wayward peacocks, although at least someone had erected a nice little temporary fence to keep the two flocks apart.

I felt a sudden surge of impatience. I wanted our yard back. And our house. And our lives.

"Three more days," I muttered. Well, more or less. Today was Thursday. The rehearsal and rehearsal dinner would be tomorrow. Saturday would be the wedding itself, and the enormous reception. And rather a lot of the out-of-town guests would stay around to eat up any leftover food, clean up the house and yard, and give themselves plenty of time to dissect any juicy bits of gossip that arose from the weekend's events. But Monday would be mostly waving goodbye. I just had to get through today, Friday, Saturday, and Sunday.

And a lot of it would be fun, I reminded myself. And thanks to Kevin, I had a reprieve from a lot of the un-fun things I'd have been dragged into helping with.

I squared my shoulders and marched into my office.

I dumped the copier paper box on the floor beside my desk and pulled the stack of case files out of my tote. I opened up the file on the cheating scandal. My plan was to read through it again while all the info from the B-school donor cards was still swimming around in my brain. Of the three cases I'd been focusing on, it had the fattest file. The Madeleine duPlaine file was still pretty sparse. The papers the chief had given me definitely added to the bulk of the Lucas Plunkett file, although they hadn't given me any exciting new ideas about that case. But the file on the cheating scandal had started out thicker than the others, mainly thanks to the information Kevin had collected on Professor David Bradshaw. A copy of his dissertation, badly photocopied and shrunk down so each sheet of paper contained two pages side by side. A wad of articles from the college paper and the *Caerphilly Clarion*. A copy of the file from the Caerphilly Police Department's brief investigation of his suicide. And now we had a whole box full of additional paper. I hoped it wouldn't turn out that we'd killed several trees in vain.

I pulled out the copy of the dissertation, thinking it might give me some idea of his personality. I was still reading the thesis statement when Dad burst in.

"Your mother is organizing an assembly line to put together the party favors for the reception," he said.

"Can you tell her I'm busy trying to keep Kevin alive?" I asked.

"I already told her you were busy." He looked sheepish. "And I'm afraid I also told her you needed me to help you. If I'd be in the way—"

"Pull up a chair," I said. "Or at least a box." My office only had the one chair, and I was too comfortable to move, but I had plenty of sturdy boxes.

"Thank you. And if there's—ooh, you've got the files on Kevin's cold cases! May I look?"

"Help yourself." I spent a few seconds trying to think if there was anything useful I could ask him and drew a blank. I made sure the dish towel was still covering up the box of photocopies and I went back to reading. Dad began digging into the files.

"I thought you said you had a suicide case," he said after a few minutes. "Where is it?"

I glanced up.

"The cheating case," I said. "Professor Bradshaw. You're holding it."

"This one?" He held up the file and I nodded. "Impossible. This is no suicide. It's murder!"

Chapter 33

"What makes you think that?" He had my attention now. I set down the dissertation and scooted a little closer.

"Take a look at these autopsy photos." He slid several glossy black-and-white photos in front of me. I took a moment to brace myself before looking, but as autopsy photos went—and thanks to Dad's avid obsession with crime, I'd seen a few—these weren't all that bad. They were front, back, and side photos of Professor Bradshaw's neck, all clearly showing the dark line of bruising where the rope had been.

"Okay, what are you seeing that I'm not?" I asked.

"It's simple. Okay, I'm going to hang myself." He glanced around the room and grabbed the dish towel I'd used to cover up the box of photocopies. He twisted it into a rope and then looped it around his own neck. "Here I go." Holding the ends of the towel at the back of his neck he pulled up, simultaneously making a grotesque face and sticking out his tongue.

But I saw what he was trying to show me.

"Of course," I said. "The rope marks are all wrong. The marks in front should be right under his chin, and the ones from the knot at the back should be higher, and the sides should slant up from front to back. These marks just go round in a level circle."

"Which means he was strangled." Dad stopped pretending to hang himself, to my immense relief. "Not hanged. It's remotely possible that he could have found a way to strangle himself and still leave a mark like that, of course."

"But then he'd have been found wherever he'd done it."

I reclaimed the dish towel from where Dad had tossed it and covered the box again. "Not hanging from the rafters. Someone had to have moved him there."

"Exactly."

We both stared down at the autopsy photos for a few seconds.

"How long ago did you say this happened?" he asked.

"Twenty-six years."

"A very cold case," he said. "But there's no statute of limitations on murder."

I nodded. I thought of adding the tidbit I'd learned from Vern—that in Virginia, there was no statute of limitations on any felony. But I decided not to step on the drama of his statement.

"Top marks to Kevin and Casey for spotting this," Dad said.

"Actually I'm pretty sure they didn't," I said. "They were just spinning an intriguing theory. What are the odds that they'd actually turn out to be right?"

"True." Dad sighed and shook his head, no doubt feeling another pang of regret that none of his descendants had followed in his medical and forensic footsteps.

"Who did the autopsy?" I asked. "Not Dr. Smoot, I hope?" I rather liked Dad's immediate predecessor in the medical examiner's post, although I could see why Chief Burke was just as happy that he'd resigned. Having the medical examiner show up at crime scenes and autopsies wearing an all-black Dracula costume, complete with fake fangs, tended to unsettle people who didn't really know him.

"Heavens, no," Dad said. "Smoot might be weird, but he's capable. This was before his time." He opened the file. "A Dr. C. F. Pruitt."

"It would be a Pruitt," I muttered. The Pruitts had been Caerphilly's leading citizens, at least in their own minds, for decades—until they'd all fled the county after being revealed as a pack of grifters and crooks. These days there were more Pruitts in the state penal system than in Caerphilly.

"And before the chief's time, too," Dad said. "He'd have noticed this even if an incompetent medical examiner missed it."

"You think we should tell the chief about this?" I asked.

"Probably." He gazed down at the photographs. "But let me do it. Since I can do so from a professional standpoint."

More likely, he wanted to do a little snooping on his own before turning it over to the chief. Which would be great if we were completely sure it was a cold case. But given the attack on Casey . . .

"Let's go tell him together, then," I said. "You can break the news about the death being murder, and I'll be handy in case he needs any of the information I've learned about the case."

"Good idea," Dad said, and went back to studying the file. "Assuming he's in."

I called the chief's cell phone.

"Can Dad and I come down to see you?" I asked. "We may have found something interesting on one of those cold cases."

"I'll be here all afternoon," he said.

I took the lid off of the box of copier paper by my printer and put it on the box full of card copies. Then I shoved the box into the back corner of my office and camouflaged it by putting a box of file folders and a stack of printer cartridges on top of it. Someone doing a determined search of my office would find it, but then why would anyone be doing that? And at least anyone who just wandered in would be unlikely to find the fruits of our burglary. Dad was so busy studying the autopsy that he didn't seem to notice my fussing with the box.

"Come on, Dad," I said. "The chief's waiting for us."

Dad wanted to talk about the autopsy all the way to town, but I steered him away from that by bringing up the subject of the upcoming party at Ragnar's—a subject about which we could both be equally enthusiastic.

When we walked into Chief Burke's office, he looked up,

and the irritated expression on his face was quickly replaced by a smile.

"Don't tell me," I said. "We're interrupting you at a bad time."

"More like a good time." He waved at his guest chairs. "For being interrupted, that is. Feels like I've spent the whole day dealing with paperwork and bureaucracy. What seems to be the trouble?"

Dad and I sat down, and he looked at me expectantly. Didn't he want to explain his find himself? Of course he did. But clearly he wanted me to do the introduction. Set the stage properly for his dramatic revelation.

"I was reviewing some of the files Kevin gave me," I began. "The ones about the cold cases he and Casey featured in their podcasts. The file about the college cheating scandal actually included a copy of the police report on the professor who allegedly committed suicide because of his involvement."

The chief smiled slightly, and I suspected he was amused by my amateur's use of the word allegedly.

"In fact, it even included a copy of the professor's autopsy report," I went on. "Which I hadn't really looked at, because autopsies aren't my thing. But they're definitely Dad's thing, so when he came into my office and saw the contents of the file spread out on my desk, he made a beeline for the autopsy report."

I looked over at Dad to continue. The chief raised an expectant eyebrow.

Dad reached into the folder he was holding, pulled out three autopsy photos, and spread them out on the chief's desk.

The chief glanced down, his expression puzzled. Then he frowned and his mouth tightened. He looked up at us.

"It wasn't suicide," he said. "It was murder."

Dad nodded. He slid the rest of the brief autopsy report and the even briefer police report onto the chief's desk.

The chief glanced at the first page of the autopsy report and sighed.

"Dr. Pruitt, of course. Thank goodness he was gone by the time I came to town, but I've heard stories. Nothing quite this bad, though. And back in the nineties the chief of police was a Pruitt, too."

He was scanning the rest of the reports—not that there was much of them to scan. Then he raised his eyes to me.

"You've been looking into this one, right?"

"It was the most accessible," I said. "In spite of being the oldest. I've actually talked to the two people who found the body."

"Excellent." He pulled out his notebook and flipped it open. "Tell me about it."

So I told him all about it. Well, almost all. I figured I'd keep the burglary to myself if possible. But I told him about the list I'd gotten from Charlie Gardner. The widely shared theory that some students had escaped being expelled because their parents bribed the school with huge donations. And Ingrid and Professor Forstner being the ones to find the body.

"This kind of upends the theory I've been working on," I said when I'd gotten that far. "I've had Kevin looking to see which people on that list are working in academia or some other job where being caught cheating even a quarter of a century ago would still matter. But if someone killed Professor Bradshaw to cover up the cheating scandal, where they're working now is pretty irrelevant. I can absolutely see a murderer trying to kill Casey and Kevin to cover it up."

"Yes." He was shaking his head slightly. "Damn them."

Dad and I both started. The chief rarely used language stronger than blast or tarnation.

"Dr. Pruitt and Chief Pruitt," the chief explained. "Were they merely incompetent, do you think? Or actually corrupt? Either way, they let a murderer go free. And it's going to be an uphill battle trying to figure out who did it."

An uphill battle. But not a lost cause. I liked his attitude.

"Tell me to butt out if you like," I began.

"If you're asking whether I want you to stop investigating

this case, the answer is yes," the chief said. "Absolutely. Immediately."

"I figured as much," I said. "What I meant was that I may know where you can find some useful evidence."

He nodded for me to continue.

"Charlie Gardner says the B-school keeps its donor records separate from the central college ones," I said. "I've got Kevin searching for them online, but Ingrid Bjornstrom doesn't think he's going to find anything. She thinks they only keep them on paper."

"You're suggesting that if I could get access to the business school's donor records I might narrow down this list considerably." He gestured at the copy of Charlie Gardner's printout.

"Yes," I said. "Because their records would show who suddenly gave a big donation right after the cheating scandal broke."

"Seems like a reach, but I'll get the county attorney thinking about it," he said. "Thank you."

"It's a sore spot with the alumni office that the B-school keeps its own separate records," I said. "It's possible that I might be able to find someone who was nosy enough to have found a way to snoop in those records. If I do, or if Kevin finds anything online, I'll let you know."

"Good."

If the county attorney gave a thumbs-down to giving him a search warrant for the B-school's donor records, I could always feed him the names I'd identified. First I should come up with a plan on how to do it without getting myself and Kevin in trouble. Would the chief accept it if I told him I had gotten this information from someone, but couldn't reveal my sources? Better yet—did Kevin and Casey count as journalists? Maybe they could pretend they'd found it and refuse to reveal their sources.

One way or another, I'd figure it out. Because I couldn't sit on the information.

"We'll let you get on with it, then." I stood, and while I could tell Dad was reluctant, he followed my example.

The chief was picking up his phone as we left the office, but he paused for a moment to call after us.

"Clay County's still off-limits, too," he said. "Just because this Bradshaw case suddenly looks more suspicious doesn't mean I'm not keeping my eye on the Clay County case."

"Aye, aye, Captain." I saluted as I said it.

The chief smiled and started dialing.

Dad was beaming as we headed back for the car.

"Kevin and Casey will be overjoyed," he said. "To think, their podcast solving a cold case!"

"Don't celebrate prematurely," I said. "It's not solved yet."

Dad nodded and pursed his lips as if trying his best to avoid saying anything else that might jinx the case. I thought of pointing out that, so far, all their podcast had done was almost get Casey killed. Solving the case would be thanks to my hard work, his expertise, and what promised to be an enormous effort by the chief and his officers.

Probably better just to distract him.

Chapter 34

"Do you mind if we stop by Clarence's to pick up Spike?" I asked.

Of course, now that I'd reminded him of the reason I'd taken Spike to the vet, Dad was full of questions about what had happened. Fortunately, Spike had swallowed chicken bones before—chicken bones, fish bones, and any number of other things the canine digestive system wasn't designed to handle. I was able to describe the fictitious incident with sufficient detail and accuracy to satisfy Dad's professional curiosity.

"And I'm sure no one actually gave him a chicken bone or whatever it was," I added, in the hope he'd refrain from trying to find the culprit. "Someone probably dropped it by accident."

"Or left a plate around where he could reach it," Dad agreed.

Spike didn't look particularly glad to see us, but Clarence did.

"I think he's fine," Clarence said, restraining an impulse to pat his patient on the head, because he knew how badly that could end. "But he might still have a bit of a sore throat. Feed him canned food for a few days, and thin it out with water so it goes down easily."

I nodded. Actually, Spike very well might have a sore throat, although not because of the nonexistent chicken bone. As usual, he seemed to have spent his entire time at the animal hospital barking nonstop at all his fellow patients, and was now sounding a little hoarse. He was probably ready to go home and rest from his vocal exertions.

For that matter, Clarence was probably pretty happy to see Spike leave, no matter how much of an animal lover he was.

"I felt bad dumping him on the new guy," I said. "No vet tech should have to cope with Spike in his first month on the job."

"Oh, Lucas did just fine," Clarence said. "You can't imagine how much easier my life is, with someone reliable to cover nights here. I'm half tempted to ask him if he can come in tonight, so I can go to that party of Ragnar's, but there'll be another party soon, and he's overdue for a night off. He gave up his last one this past Saturday night to help me with the surgery on Maudie's poor beagle."

Which had been lucky for Lucas, I realized. The surgery had given him an alibi for the time when Casey was attacked.

Dad promised to bring Clarence a very large doggie bag of Scandinavian food from Ragnar's party, and we took our leave.

Spike slept all the way home.

When I got home, I went down to the basement to confer with Kevin. He swung his chair around and nodded at me when I got to the bottom of the stairs, which was the Kevin-esque equivalent of a wildly enthusiastic greeting.

"You want the good news or the bad news?" I asked.

"Surprise me."

"Your grandpa just figured out from the autopsy photos that Professor Bradshaw's death was murder, not suicide, and Chief Burke's going to investigate it."

"Whoa." His eyes grew wide. "This is going to make for an awesome follow-up."

"But not until I give you the go-ahead," I said. "Because if it was someone connected with that case who went after Casey the other night, imagine how much more eager they're going to be to shut you guys up now."

"Good point. Is that the bad news part?"

"No." I sighed. "The bad part is that Chief Burke could really use that information we got last night."

"Rats," he said. "And I bet you're going to say we have to confess about the burglary."

"I told him the theory about large donations being connected to the cheating scandal," I said. "He's going to try to get a search warrant for the B-school files. But there's no guarantee he will."

Kevin grimaced and nodded.

"So, just in case we need to give him the data, can you disguise it somehow? Like maybe turn it from photocopies into a data file?"

"Yeah, that would work," he said. "Good thinking."

He sounded surprised. I decided not to take that personally.

"And then we send him the data file from an untraceable email address," he went on. "The way someone sent those songs to Jared."

"You're getting the idea," I said. "Now, how long have you and Casey been doing the podcast—about three months?"

"Give or take."

"Delete any data that's newer than, say, six months old."

"So it looks like someone got hold of the data before we even heard about the cheating scandal," he said. "Awesome. I'm on it."

He swiveled his chair and began typing on his keyboard. In spite of those misadventures in typing class, I'd eventually worked up a pretty decent speed, but I couldn't hold a candle to Kevin. I found myself irrationally encouraged by how fast his fingers were flying to produce the deception I'd suggested.

A deception that shouldn't be necessary. I felt a sudden wave of guilt.

"One more thing," I said.

He swiveled to face me again.

"I'm sorry," I said. "Burgling the B-school was a bad idea.

It could backfire. I shouldn't have gotten you involved. In fact, I shouldn't have done it at all."

"Seems to me it worked pretty well," Kevin said. "Look at all the useful information we got."

"Information we can't really do anything with," I said. "We can't give it to the chief without getting in trouble. Or use it on your podcast. So how useful is it, really?"

He frowned for a few seconds, then nodded.

"Yeah," he said. "So next time we try harder to find a legit way to get the data."

He turned back to his computer and resumed his rapid typing.

I went back upstairs.

The kitchen was full of people cooking Scandinavian cookies and smelled divine, but I managed to escape without being put to work. In the backyard several dozen people were making sachets. No, the elegant little lace-trimmed trinkets seemed to be little packets of birdseed for pelting Rob and Delaney when they left the church. But there would probably be sachets later—Rose Noire and several of her herbalist accomplices were harvesting vegetation in the herb garden. In the back pasture Lad appeared to be teaching four of the Pomeranians how to herd things. Thank goodness he appeared to have started with our Welsummer hens rather than the peacocks, so the Pomeranians would probably survive. Several teenage cousins wearing catchers' masks and holding leaf rakes were keeping watch over the peacocks.

I ended up in the library, where for several hours I helped the cousins who wanted to do last-minute alterations to one or more of their weekend outfits, to cover up their peacock wounds. Even though I'd warned Dad about letting the peacocks loose, I still felt some guilt about not having stayed to see them safely unloaded. But only a little guilt, and I figured I could let go of that after a few hours of sewing.

And it gave me time to think. Not all the time—sometimes I was able to lose myself in the friendly chatter of the visiting aunts and cousins. But my mind kept circling back to the cold cases.

Ironically, the Madeleine duPlaine case—the one most interesting to me, and the only one Chief Burke hadn't warned me off—was the one that seemed the biggest dead end. At least I knew—what? Not that she was alive, but that she had survived ten years or so after disappearing. And very well could be still alive.

If she hadn't been murdered twenty years ago, the odds were she disappeared on her own. I'd spent enough time helping out at the Caerphilly women's shelter to know that there were plenty of reasons why a woman might want to disappear and start a new life someplace else. If that was what had happened to Maddy, I should back away and leave her in whatever peace and safety she'd found.

I was fine with that, as long as the mystery of who'd attacked Casey didn't remain unsolved. As long as we could figure out that it had been someone connected with one of the local cases. Well, not we. The chief.

I should let Maddy's case go, at least for the moment. Content myself with knowing that, wherever she was, it wasn't at the bottom of Beaver Creek Lake. Listen to the four songs I had and hope that maybe eventually Kevin or Jared or Tad would find others.

Maybe I should focus on solving the dilemma of how to get the chief the information he needed to work on Professor Bradshaw's murder without confessing to our burglary. Which technically wasn't burglary, I reminded myself, since nobody lived in the B-school building. But what was it? Trespassing seemed too mild. Breaking and entering? Maybe I could figure out a hypothetical case and run it by Vern Shiffley. He'd know.

Better yet, maybe I should run the whole thing by a brilliant lawyer. My cousin Festus Hollingsworth would be attending all the wedding festivities. He'd probably be at Ragnar's tonight. I could ask him. He might even have a suggestion on how to get the information to the chief without getting in trouble.

That idea cheered me immensely. Of course, being able to do something about a problem always cheered me. Maybe I could think of something else to do.

Maybe Ingrid Bjornstrom or Professor Forstner would give me some useful information. Correction: maybe they could give the chief some useful information.

But I could help. Talk to one or both of them. Make sure they realized that the chief needed probable cause to get a search warrant for the B-school files.

Professor Forstner, I decided. I had the feeling Ingrid would already be nervous enough about her part in helping us get into the B-school building. I didn't want to stress her any more. But Forstner struck me as the kind of cool customer who could pull it off—answering the chief's questions with the truth, but shaping his answers in a way the chief could use them to get access to the greater truth hiding in the B-school files.

And if I went to see Professor Forstner I could also break the news about his friend's death being murder. Unless the chief had already talked to him, but even in that case, I could apologize that I had to drop the case, but reassure him that the chief wouldn't. And hint, as strongly as I could, that if the chief could just get into those files . . .

I finished off the sewing project I was working on—adding a pair of flowing three-quarter-length sleeves in gauzy flowered silk to a cousin's formerly sleeveless dress. Then I extricated myself from the sewing circle and went in search of Michael. He and the boys were loading bakery boxes full of Scandinavian cookies into the Twinmobile. There didn't appear to be room for another person.

"If you want to come with us, we can take some of these back to the kitchen," Michael said. "We'll have to make a couple of runs anyway, unless I can find someone else to help with it."

"I can go separately, and take another load," I said. "I have an errand I want to run on the way anyway. And with two cars, we'll have options if one of us gets tired sooner than the other."

Michael nodded, gave me a quick kiss, and drove off with Josh riding shotgun and Jamie in the middle row, nearly invisible beneath the many boxes marked with what I assumed were the names of their contents: Smultringer. Hjortetakk. Sandkaker. Krumkaker. Sirupsnipper. Fattigmann. Berlinerkranser. Bordstabler. Pepperkaker. Serinakaker. Spritz. Pleskener. Why was my mouth watering already when I had no idea what any of this was?

I went back into the house and borrowed a couple of cousins to help me load the back seat of my car with some of the remaining boxes. And then on an impulse I grabbed an extra box, fished two or three different cookies out of half a dozen of the boxes, and arranged them in the empty box. I carried that box out to the car myself and set it on the passenger seat.

"If anyone needs me, I'm hauling food over to Ragnar's," I said to Rose Noire and the rest of the crew in the kitchen. And then I ducked out before anyone could think of any other wedding-related errands I could run along the way.

As I was about to get into my car I noticed that in their pasture across the way, Seth Early's sheep were on the move. Which struck me as slightly odd, because it wasn't anywhere near lambing time or shearing time or State Fair time or any of the other times when Seth's sheep were supposed to be doing anything other than grazing in the field. Of course, since they were all woolly Houdinis with a bad case of wanderlust, they frequently managed to escape the field to visit Seth's neighbors—only last week I'd found one in the basement, chewing its cud and gazing thoughtfully at Kevin's row of computers. But this didn't look like an ovine escape attempt in progress. It looked more like what you'd see if Lad were herding them—except that Lad was standing just inside the fence, watching what was going on. I strolled over to take a closer look.

The Pomeranians were herding sheep. Under Lad's watchful eye. Occasionally he'd utter a short, sharp bark, or lope over to demonstrate the proper technique before retiring to the edge of the field to supervise.

"I see you've taken on some apprentices," I said to Lad. He wagged his tail as if acknowledging my presence, but didn't take his eyes off the herding.

So was teaching the Pomeranians to herd a good thing or a bad thing? I should probably figure that out, because it was definitely a thing. On the plus side, maybe it would bleed off some of the Pomeranians' seemingly infinite supply of energy, and if they took up herding the sheep who showed up in our yard back to Seth's pasture, it would certainly be helpful. On the minus side, when bored Lad tended to herd anything that moved. I could easily see the Pomeranians running our chickens ragged, not to mention our visiting friends and relatives.

Maybe the Pomeranians would be less single-minded than Lad. Time would tell. I tore myself away from the interesting spectacle—the pups had now learned that if they vaulted onto the backs of the sheep they could herd while riding around with a better view—and got into my cookie-laden car.

Evidently I'd spent longer watching the sheep than I thought. I waved in passing at Michael, who was already heading back to fetch another load of cookies. And the shadows were getting long. I set out for town.

Chapter 35

I had every intention of going straight to Professor Forstner's house, but the way there led past the New Life Baptist Church. It was lit up, and I caught the deep notes of the organ playing a series of notes. Familiar notes, although I couldn't immediately identify them. Not a hymn I knew.

This wasn't the regular choir practice night, was it? I didn't think so. What if the choir was having a rehearsal of the songs they'd sing at Delaney and Rob's wedding? The songs they'd been so secretive about?

I pulled into the New Life Baptist parking lot, found a spot that was already half obscured by the usefully long shadows of the surrounding oak trees, and made my way across the gravel expanse. I felt very exposed and had to remind myself to just walk normally. No slinking or sneaking.

I found an open window—a small one, that only gave a view of a couple of polished oak pews, all empty. But I could hear just fine. Rustling papers. A few muted chuckles or scraps of conversation. Then a sharp rapping noise.

"Okay, everybody got it?" Minerva Burke, the chief's wife, who directed the choir. "Let's take it from the top."

The choir launched into a rendition of U2's "I Still Haven't Found What I'm Looking For." Which I knew was Rob's favorite song from one of his favorite albums ever, but still—didn't the lyrics make it a rather problematic song for a wedding?

Then I pushed those thoughts aside and just listened to the glorious, full-throated splendor of all those voices raised in song. And just when I thought it couldn't get any better, a soloist joined in—Aida's daughter Kayla, I was positive— and the melody flowed back and forth between her and the rest of the choir, sometimes in harmony, sometimes in a kind of call-and-response fashion. And as if they'd heard my quibble about the lyrics, they'd changed them so in the last verse they were singing "in you, I have found what I'm looking for."

It was all I could do to keep from applauding or shouting "Brava!" when the song ended. I could tell from the contented hum coming from the choir that they were rather pleased with themselves. As they should be.

"We're getting there," Minerva said. I knew from her that counted as high praise. "Kayla, you want to do your other song?"

The organ gave a few introductory notes, and then Kayla sang "Somewhere" from *West Side Story*. I had tears in my eyes by the time she'd finished.

And I decided it was time to leave. I suspected they were planning at least one more song, but suddenly I wanted to be surprised by it. So while the choir was still rustling and murmuring, I sprinted back to my car and hopped inside before I could hear anything.

I wound my way through the side streets that let me avoid the tourist traffic around the town square until I came to Professor Forstner's house. I could see light behind the curtains in one of his front windows, so I parked in front, picked up the box of cookies I'd packed for him, and went up to ring his doorbell.

The door opened. Forstner's face didn't look hostile or unwelcoming. Just surprised, and maybe a little anxious.

"Sorry," I said. "I hate to bother you again, and so soon, but I learned something I thought you'd want to know."

He stepped aside wordlessly so I could enter, and when he'd closed the door he led the way into the living room. He sat, as before, on the rather formal Victorian armchair, and I took my previous place on the sofa. I realized I was still holding the box of cookies. I set it on the coffee table.

"By way of apology for bothering you so soon," I said. "It's krumkaker and sirupsnipper and a whole lot of other Scandinavian cookies whose names I couldn't pronounce if I knew them."

"I assume you wouldn't be bothering me again if it wasn't something reasonably important." His slight smile was a little brittle, but his tone was civil. "And urgent."

"I have news," I said. "Actually, it shouldn't be news, but it is."

"And you wanted to watch my reaction?"

"If you like. Then there's also the fact that my mother has always drummed it into me that it's the height of inconsiderateness to break any kind of upsetting news to anyone over the phone."

"Probably a holdover from the days when ladies were supposed to have the vapors at the mere mention of bad news," Forstner said. "Whatever the vapors are. Well, go ahead."

"Okay." I took a deep breath. "Professor Bradshaw didn't kill himself. He was murdered."

His mouth fell open and he didn't speak for a couple of seconds. Then he visibly pulled himself together.

"If this is some harebrained idea of your nephew's—" he began, in an angry tone.

"No," I said. "It's what my dad thinks. And while he has a lot of harebrained ideas at times, when it comes to medicine he's rock solid."

"And he thinks it's murder." The anger had drained out of his voice. Replaced by a flat tone of shock.

"I was reviewing all the case documents Kevin gave me," I said. "Including the ones about the cheating scandal. Dad strolled in and of course he picked up the autopsy report. Which had photos—including several of Professor Bradshaw's neck. Dad saw immediately that it couldn't possibly be hanging. Or any kind of suicide. If you want the details—"

"No." He shook his head firmly. "I would rather not know the details. Your father's judgment is enough for me. Ingrid was right. They killed him."

"Ingrid thought that?"

"That was her first thought when we found him, yes. I'm afraid I discouraged that idea. It seemed all too obvious to me why it was suicide. Only now you say it wasn't. But of course when the medical examiner ruled it suicide, we thought he knew. Before your father's time, obviously. Was the former medical examiner incompetent or corrupt?"

"No idea," I said. "But I'm betting Chief Burke will do his best to find out. It was before his time, too—he's no doctor, but the instant Dad showed him the photographs the chief could see for himself it was murder. The chief takes a dim view of anyone getting away with murder on his turf. Even if it did happen long before he got here."

"He's a good man." Forstner's smile was bleak. "But he's going to have a pretty tough time solving this, isn't he?"

"He's also a seasoned homicide investigator," I said. "And there's no statute of limitations on murder."

"No, but so much of the information he would need to solve the case will have just disappeared. Evidence, witnesses, alibis—everything."

I nodded.

"He'll want to look at me, of course," Forstner said. "And Ingrid. Don't they often suspect the person who finds the body? And while I vividly remember where I was at the time David died, it could be difficult to prove."

"Why?" I asked.

"What is my alibi?" He smiled slightly. "I was in Atlanta, giving a paper at a meeting of the American Historical Association. First time I'd ever done that, and believe me, it was a big deal, especially for someone who was then still relatively young. The days leading up to the convention were crazy, because the whole cheating thing had just broken, and on top of putting the finishing touches to my paper and practicing my delivery I was trying to keep David from despairing.

If I hadn't been presenting, I think I would have canceled going. In fact, I tried to talk him into getting a plane ticket and coming along with me. Doing some sightseeing in Atlanta, or just getting away from the craziness here. He told me not to be silly, that he'd be fine. Afterward, of course, I assumed he was, well, sending me off so he'd have the privacy to do away with himself. I didn't really enjoy the conference that much. I kept calling to talk to him, and then Saturday night I called and he didn't answer. I kept calling all day Sunday—except when I was presenting my paper. I had one of those dreaded Sunday morning time slots, when most of the attendees were either tired of going to panels or hungover from the Saturday night celebrations. Or both. I got through my paper somehow. And when I got back to Caerphilly, I didn't even go home. I went straight to his house. While I was arguing with his landlady, Ingrid showed up, and had the presence of mind to pretend that the dean of the business school had sent her to check on David."

"Good thinking," I said.

"Of course, in retrospect, it might have been less traumatic for her if she hadn't managed that," Forstner said. "I'd have gone to the police and asked for a welfare check. I could probably have browbeat them into it eventually. Especially after he'd missed a class or two. Ingrid would still have been upset, of course, but she'd have been spared the trauma of walking in and seeing him hanging there."

I nodded.

"I expect Chief Burke will be reopening the case," I said.

"Good. I assume he knows where to find me."

"Yes," I said. "I told him you might have some information. And frankly—you know that theory I mentioned, that the B-school donation records might help us find out who was involved in the cheating scandal?"

"Yes," he said. "And thus who might have a motive for murder. Shall I suggest as much to the chief?"

"I already did," I said. "And he sees the point. He's just not positive he's going to be able to get a search warrant for the records. So if there's anything you can tell him that he can use for probable cause—"

"Understood," he said. "This is no time to hold back and protect the honor of the college. I think if I share enough of what David told me about how his department worked, the chief should have plenty of fodder for his search warrant."

"Excellent." I stood up, and he followed me to the door.

"Thank you," he said. "For telling me. And for the cookies. Tell me, do they go well with a good, stiff drink? Because I think I need one."

"I'm sure they will."

He stood in the doorway looking after me as I walked back to my car and got in. I had the impulse to go back and keep him company for a while. Or invite him to Ragnar's. But common sense told me he probably wasn't in the mood for either. I decided maybe I would wait till morning to get in touch with Ingrid. Maybe by that time the chief would have broken the news to her—and he'd had lots of experience doing that kind of notification, right?

As I drove off, I looked in the rearview mirror and could still see Forstner standing there, looking forlorn in the small rectangle of light.

And it was because I was staring at Forstner in the rearview that I noticed when the gray pickup truck started its engine and began following me.

I had a bad feeling about this. I normally refrain from texting while driving, but I picked up my phone. Should I call 911? All the pickup was doing was following me. Still. I texted Aida.

"Remember that gray pickup that was following me?" I asked. "I think it's back."

I decided to head for a more populous part of town. Maybe if—

"Head for the station," Aida texted back.

I texted back "OK" and took a right turn at the next intersection. The station was about a dozen blocks away.

Just then the gray pickup sped up and passed me. I breathed a sigh of relief when I saw its taillights ahead of me.

Then the taillights brightened to show that the pickup had braked right in front of me. I had to slam on the brakes to keep from hitting it, sending boxes of cookies flying from the back seat onto the floor. A red pickup zoomed up behind me and stopped, almost touching my bumper.

A man got out of the gray pickup and began walking back toward me. He was about my height, on the pudgy side, wearing jeans and a bright orange t-shirt.

"Ambushed," I texted.

Chapter 36

Before I could text anything else, the man came up to my window and held up something. A Clay County deputy's badge. Though he wasn't in uniform, so he was either off duty or working undercover. Or maybe the Clay County Sheriff's Department had declared Thursday Rude T-shirt Day. His read "Sex Instructor. First Lesson Free."

I rolled my window down a couple of inches.

"What seems to be the problem, Deputy?" I asked.

"Sheriff Dingle would like to talk to you."

"Okay," I said. "I'll call him in the morning and make an appointment to see him." I was about to roll the window up, but he stuck a lug wrench in the opening.

"Didn't you hear what I said?" the deputy asked. "Sheriff Dingle would like to talk to you. Out of the car."

"I'll drive over to Clay County and—"

He pulled the wrench out of my window opening, then casually broke the window glass with it. He reached in and grabbed my arm.

"Out of the car," he repeated. Behind me I could see another, shorter man had gotten out of the red pickup. He was also in civvies.

I needed to stall them long enough for Aida to send the cavalry my way. So I unfastened my seat belt as slowly as possible. I reached for my phone.

"Just leave that phone of yours on the seat," he said.

"I'm not leaving it behind," I said. I stuck it in my pocket. That seemed to satisfy him.

I opened the door and stepped out of the car.

"Am I under arrest?" I projected my voice as much as possible. We were in a quiet residential neighborhood—surely someone would call 911 if I could stall the two guys long enough, and that would let the Caerphilly police know exactly where I was.

"Now why do you have to get all hostile on us?" the shorter one said. "We just want to—"

"If you're planning to arrest me, do it, and let me call my lawyer," I said. "If you're not arresting me, then I'd like to go home. Please get out of my way."

"Okay, I guess we have to do this the hard way," the taller one said. They moved forward, and each of them grabbed one of my arms. I could tell from the loose, casual way that they did it that they weren't expecting any kind of fight. And I could have given them one. I had to tamp down my instinct to resist. Use the self-defense techniques I knew. Stomp on the instep. Knee the crotch. Slam an elbow into the solar plexus. Jerk my head back into the face and break the nose. Even if I didn't win the fight I could do some damage. Make them pay. My old martial arts teacher would have been proud of me. Not only that I remembered so much of my training but also because I was wise enough not to use it. Because these guys were cops. And they had guns. And for all I knew, they could be the kind of bad guys who wouldn't hesitate to use their fists—or even their guns—on an uncooperative civilian. Especially one who was also an uppity woman.

I resigned myself to the idea that I'd be making an involuntary trip to Clay County if the help I was hoping for didn't arrive soon.

They half dragged me to the gray pickup, and the shorter man let go of my arm long enough to open the back door. But just as they were shoving me into the back seat of the truck cab, I heard another voice.

"Excuse me, gentlemen. What's going on here?"

Chief Burke stepped out of the shadows. He wasn't holding his gun, but his coat was pulled back and his hand was hovering not that far from it.

A cruiser pulled up, and screeched to a halt. Vern hopped out.

Two more cruisers arrived. Aida and Horace.

"We were just taking the little lady over to talk to Sheriff Dingle." The taller man held up his badge. "He just has a few questions he wants to ask her."

"Is Ms. Langslow under arrest?" the chief asked.

"Not exactly," the shorter man said. "We just—"

"Ms. Langslow, are you accompanying these men of your own free will?" the chief asked, turning to me.

"I am not," I said. "I already told them that I would contact Sheriff Dingle tomorrow to make an appointment to talk with him. And that's when they started forcing me into the truck."

"And I don't recall that window of yours being broken when I saw you this afternoon," the chief said. Since the broken glass from my window littered the pavement on the left side of my car, it was pretty obvious what had happened.

"Now look here," the taller man said.

"I suggest you step aside so Ms. Langslow can return to her own vehicle," the chief said.

The shorter one took a step back. Evidently he was the brains of the duo. The taller one stayed where he was, and when I slid down from the back seat of the truck cab, he reached out and grabbed my arm.

"Take your hands off me." I jerked my arm, but he had a tight grip on my biceps.

"I suggest you do as Ms. Langslow asks," the chief said.

I looked up to find that Vern, Aida, and Horace had all three drawn their weapons. The taller deputy pulled his hand away as if my arm was a hot burner. The shorter one stepped back another yard or so. He looked nervous. As well he should. He might have heard the rumor that Horace was always stressed to the max for a week before taking his twice-annual firearms qualification test, but he should also know that Horace always passed. And surely he knew that

Vern and Aida both invariably placed well in the annual state police marksmanship contest.

The taller man looked mad, and I could see he was fighting the impulse to draw his own gun.

"You're under arrest," the chief said. "Horace, why don't you pat them down and cuff them?"

"You can't arrest us," the taller man said. "We're—"

"Out of your jurisdiction," the chief said. "And you just committed kidnapping and assault and battery on one of my citizens."

"And destruction of property," Aida added.

"And impersonating police officers," Vern added. "Duane Dingle, I happen to know your cousin the sheriff fired you three months ago for not giving him his percentage on the kickbacks. And Jimmy Parrish, since when have you ever been on the force?"

The shorter man, who I figured out must be Jimmy, hung his head and looked sheepish. Duane just looked mad. Horace had probably been wise to disarm and cuff him before the more cooperative Jimmy.

"We'll take these two down to the station and start processing the charges," the chief said. Vern was ushering Duane into the back of his cruiser. Aida had taken Jimmy. Horace had already pulled out his camera and was taking pictures of my broken window and the little pile of glass beads on the pavement. "You can come on down when Horace is finished documenting the damage to your car."

"Great," I said. I hoped I didn't sound as shaky as I felt. "So you think maybe these are the same guys who tried to attack Casey?"

"Almost certainly," he said. "At least according to my sources over in Clay County."

"You actually have sources there?" I tried not to sound surprised.

"Things are changing in Clay County," he said. "Not fast enough, but yes, the honest folks there are getting a little more willing to speak up. And they tell me Lucas Plunkett wasn't anywhere near the filling station the night someone robbed it and killed the attendant. The real culprit was a cousin of the sheriff and married to Lucas's sister. He was a two-time loser, out on parole from his second armed robbery conviction. And Virginia has a three-strikes law on violent felonies. He'd have been facing mandatory life if they convicted him."

"So Lucas took the rap to keep his brother-in-law out of prison?"

"Not exactly," the chief said. "I think it was more a case that the brother-in-law's buddies suggested to Lucas that it would be better for his sister's health if he took the rap. But last year Lucas talked his sister into going into the Caerphilly women's shelter and getting relocated, so she's safe now. I think the brother-in-law and his buddies were afraid with her out of their reach, Lucas might talk. And one of those buddies is Sheriff Dingle."

"Ooh," I said. "Is Clay County about to lose another sheriff?" The last two had both been convicted of various corruption charges, thanks to Chief Burke and the Virginia State Police, and were now serving lengthy prison sentences.

"Could be," the chief said. "Of course, odds are the Clay County voters will find themselves another crook to replace him, but there's nothing we can do about that."

"I think we've got enough," Horace said. He was holding an evidence bag in which he'd scraped up a generous portion of the little glass beads that had once been my side window.

"Whoever invented safety glass should get a Nobel Prize," I said. "Thank goodness it's not winter. I assume I should follow you over to the station."

"If you would be so kind," the chief said.

"I dropped by to see Professor Forstner," I said. "I wanted to break the news about his friend's murder and urge him to come down to talk to you. Maybe I should have let you talk to him first, but I wanted to break it to him gently."

"It's okay," he said.

"What about Ingrid Bjornstrom?" I asked.

"We talked to her this afternoon," the chief said. "The information she gave us about the business school records may be enough to get the search warrant we need. I thought I'd wait to see how that went before interviewing Professor Forstner."

"Charles Gardner in Administrative Services might also be helpful," I said. "He's done battle with the B-school over access to their donor records. He might have gathered intel on what's in them."

"Good." He pulled out his notebook and flipped it open. I repeated Charlie's name, and pulled out my phone to give the chief his number.

"See you down at the station," he said.

"I'll be on my way as soon as I let Michael know I won't make it to Ragnar's party for a bit."

He nodded, and took off. I texted Michael that I'd be delayed. I was just reaching to start the car when I got a call.

Michael, probably, calling to ask if anything was wrong.

But the caller ID was for Ingrid Bjornstrom.

"Meg? It's Ingrid."

"Are you okay?" She sounded shaky.

"I'm fine," she said. "Just a bit upset. The police dropped by a little while ago and told me about . . . about Professor Bradshaw."

"I'm so sorry." I felt guilty. Although maybe it was a good thing the police had told her, since the Clay County stalkers might have distracted me from my good intentions.

"Can you drop by to see me?" she asked. "I want to ask you something. But I have to show you something first."

"Sure," I said. "When would you like to meet?"

"Could you do it now?" There was a sharp note of anxiety in her voice. Or was it fear? "I mean, of course, if you're busy—"

"No, I can drop by now," I said. "As it happens, I'm already in town. I can't stay long—I'm expected someplace else. But—"

"This won't take long," she said. "And thank you." She rattled off her address.

It wasn't all that far away. I could drop by, see what she wanted to show me—and maybe if it was something she ought to be showing to the police, I could take her there with me.

So I drove over to Ingrid's neighborhood. It was nice. Not quite as fancy as Professor Forstner's—the yards and houses were all a little smaller. But still—a nice neighborhood. She lived in a neat little bungalow with a neat little yard in front. I couldn't tell in the dark, but I suspected her landscaping would be pleasing, though less elaborate than Professor Forstner's. To the right of the front door was a picture window. The blinds were closed for the night, but the light leaked out around the sides of the blinds and between the slats, giving an impression that the inside would be cozy and welcoming.

I rang her doorbell and studied the shrubbery beside her front stoop while I waited. Azaleas. And blooming, though in the dark I couldn't tell the color.

The door opened.

"You came!" Ingrid was definitely under some kind of stress. Her eyebrows were twitching.

"Of course," I said as I stepped inside. "It wasn't—"

An arm appeared and snatched her out of sight. The door slammed behind me, and I whirled around to find myself facing a man with a gun.

Chapter 37

"Into the living room." The man gestured with the gun.

I recognized the distinctive nasal voice of Claude Vansittart's brother Vincent.

"You picked a bad time to do this," I said.

"Now," he said.

I turned and went into the living room. I wanted to make sure Ingrid was okay. And there wasn't much I could do with an armed Vincent between me and the front door.

In the living room Ingrid was perched nervously on the edge of a beige camelback sofa. Across the coffee table from her Claude was perched in much the same manner on a matching wingback chair. He was holding a gun that looked identical to his brother's. I got the feeling he wasn't very comfortable with firearms, and would prefer to put it down.

Vincent looked as if he'd rather enjoy using his.

"Sit," Vincent said.

I sat beside Ingrid on the sofa.

"I'm sorry," she whispered.

"As I was trying to tell you, your timing's lousy," I said to Vincent. "If you listened in on my phone conversation with Ingrid, you'll remember that I said I was expected someplace else. That would be the police station. If I don't show up soon, they'll be looking for me. Just let us go and we'll call it quits."

"I told you this was a bad idea," Claude said.

"Shut up," Vincent said. "We won't be here much longer."

They would if I had anything to do with it. If they wanted to leave, I'd work on staying put.

"I don't see why we need her," Claude said. "I don't see that we need either of them."

"They're trying to get at the donation records," Vincent said. "And they're probably trying to get the police interested in them."

"I'm sorry," Ingrid said to me. "I'm afraid I told them that I was going to let you into the business school tomorrow night."

Tomorrow night? So they didn't know we already had the records. I wasn't sure how that would come in useful, but I liked that she wasn't just caving.

"I could let us into the building," Claude said.

"You could," Vincent said. "But when they find the bodies in the morning, do you really want your card to be the last one used?" From his expression, I could tell he was exasperated at finding his brother such an incompetent co-conspirator.

"Oh." Claude frowned. "But what do we need *her* for?" He pointed at me.

"According to Ingrid, she's a locksmith," Vincent said.

"So?" Claude looked both puzzled and annoyed.

"Ingrid can't get us into the dean's office, but she can."

I thought of pointing out that I was a blacksmith, not a locksmith, but I didn't want to cast any doubt on my usefulness.

"But won't it look suspicious if our donation cards are missing?"

"They won't be missing." Vincent was clearly running out of patience. "Once we're in, we get her to make new cards for us." He was indicating Ingrid. "You said yourself that they sometimes had her work on updating the cards or replacing damaged ones. We just have her leave out the donations the old man made to keep us from being expelled over the grade fixing. It will be in the same handwriting as a bunch of other cards. They won't suspect a thing."

"We can't just leave out those amounts," Claude said. "What if they do an audit?"

"Why would they audit a bunch of twenty-five-year-old records?"

"Twenty-six-year-old records," Claude corrected. "And why wouldn't they? They're investigating a twenty-six-year-old murder."

"So we add the same amount to someone else's record," Vincent said. "Think of a classmate you dislike. Didn't I explain all of this to you yesterday?"

"I wasn't really listening," Claude said. "I thought you were just blowing off steam. Brainstorming. I didn't realize you actually intended to do any of it."

"Typical." Vincent rolled his eyes. "Time we headed over to Pruitt Hall."

"We don't call it that anymore," Ingrid said. "They haven't decided on a new name yet, so we just call it the business school building."

"Like I said, time we headed over to Pruitt Hall."

Clearly Vincent wasn't in sympathy with the forces of progress that were sweeping away all vestiges of the Pruitts' association with Caerphilly College. Maybe his father had been a buddy of the Pruitts. Could that have something to do with why a Pruitt police chief and a Pruitt medical examiner had called Professor Bradshaw's death a suicide?

"Get up." Vincent gestured with the gun.

Ingrid and I rose.

"If we get out of this," she began.

"When we get out of this," I corrected.

"Yeah, right," Vincent muttered. "Move."

"I want you to hold me to a promise," Ingrid went on, ignoring Vincent. "I am going to quit my job at the business school. I don't care if I never find another one. I'm not working any more for those ungrateful, soulless wretches."

"I'll help you find another job," I said. "You'll be fine."

"You'll both be dead if you don't get a move on," Vincent said.

"And how will that be different from what you're planning to do when you get us over to the B-school?" I said.

"Except for the fact that you'll be on the wrong side of the dean's office door."

"Can't we just let them go?" Claude said. "Once we've destroyed the evidence—"

"Just shut up and let me take care of it," Vincent said. "You'd have let Bradshaw go, too, wouldn't you?"

"I had him under control. He knew I'd tell the administration about his secret life if he told anyone."

"Then why did he have an appointment with the college treasurer and the internal auditor for the day after we went to see him?"

"He didn't," Claude said. "Even if he did, how could you possibly know?"

"I saw it on his calendar while I was searching his house."

"I don't remember you searching his house."

"Of course not." Vincent sounded impatient. "You were curled up in a fetal position, moaning about how mean I was for making you help string up the body. Take it from me—if I hadn't dealt with him, he was going to tell on us. The same way they will if we let them go. And we don't have time for this now—move!"

He probably meant the command for Ingrid and me, but Claude was the one who jumped. Ingrid and I just headed for the front door.

I was keyed up and on high alert. Here in the house we were trapped. But once we got outside, our chance to free ourselves would come. Well, probably my chance to free us. I didn't doubt Ingrid would do whatever she could to help, but neither of us was psychic, so I shouldn't come up with a plan that required careful coordination.

"You two go first," Vincent said. "Claude, you follow them, and see that they don't make a break for it. I'll bring up the rear."

Ingrid's hand was trembling as she opened the door. She took a few steps out and then stopped on her front stoop, so abruptly that I almost ran into her. Apart from a little intake of breath, she didn't react. But I could see why she stopped.

To our left, out of sight of anyone still in the house, Professor Forstner was standing. He put his forefinger to his lips.

Lucas Plunkett, on our right, just tightened his grip on the tire iron he was holding.

"Move!" Vincent snapped.

Ingrid and I stepped forward briskly, and the two Vansittarts followed. Professor Forstner launched himself at Claude with a flying tackle that carried them both off the stoop and onto the lawn to our right. Lucas brought the tire iron down on Vincent's right arm. Vincent bellowed in pain and dropped the gun. Lucas grappled with him, and the two fell off the stoop and into the azalea bushes on the left.

"Call 911!" I shouted to Ingrid as I hurried to recover Vincent's gun. She nodded and ran inside—I deduced that either she didn't have a cell phone or she hadn't had it on her when they captured her.

Professor Forstner was still grappling with Claude. And while Claude didn't seem to be holding his gun any longer, I couldn't see where it was, either. So once I recovered Vincent's gun, I maneuvered around until I was behind Claude and pressed the barrel of the gun to the back of his neck.

"Freeze." I needn't have said it—he froze as soon as the metal touched his skin.

"And that goes for you two clowns in the bushes," another voice added. I looked up to see Aida striding up the front walk toward where Lucas and Vincent were still struggling.

Ingrid stepped outside.

"They were already on their way," she said. "Oh, my goodness."

I turned to see that the street was filling up with Caerphilly police cruisers—lights flashing, but sirens off.

"We didn't hear you coming," I told Aida.

"We like to sneak up on a possible hostage situation," she said. "You want to give me that thing?"

I handed her the gun.

"There's another one just like it lying around here some-where," I said.

She nodded. Vern Shiffley arrived and he and Aida strode over to extract Vincent and Lucas from the shrubbery.

"Lucas is on our side," I called, just in case.

I went up onto the stoop to stand beside Ingrid as we watched the police round up the two Vansittarts and haul them off to jail.

Professor Forstner and Lucas joined us.

"How did you two happen to show up in the nick of time?" I asked.

"I saw that gray truck following you when you left my house," Forstner said. "So I got in my car and followed them. Called 911 when I saw them box you in. And even though it looked as if it was over when they hauled those two ruffians off, I was still worried. You were going to be driving around without any way to keep assailants out of your car. I thought I'd follow you to safety."

"And I'd been following Duane Dingle and his buddy around to see what they were up to," Lucas said. "Called 911 myself when I saw them stop you. And I had no idea if maybe they had more friends sneaking around after you, so when you took off again, I tagged along."

"We introduced ourselves outside Ingrid's house," Forstner said.

"And I snuck around to her backyard and did a little eavesdropping through an open window," Lucas said. "Figured we could get the drop on those two when they went out of the house."

"It was wonderful," Ingrid said. "I can't thank you enough."

"I expect we'll be down at the police station all night giving our statements," Forstner said.

"Not how I planned to spend my night off," Lucas said with a sigh. "But it'll be worth it, seeing two sets of bad guys locked up."

An idea came to me. I sent a quick text to the chief. "You'll be pretty busy for a while. Okay if we witnesses drop by Ragnar's for a bit to recharge our energy?" A few seconds later he texted back "LOL. Fine. I know where to find you when I need you."

I turned to the other three.

"I think the chief will be fine if we don't go down to the station right away," I said. "In fact, I bet he can wait till morning to get our detailed statements. You all need cheering up. Come with me."

"Come with you where?" Lucas said.

"Are you sure?" Forstner said.

But I noticed that they were following me to the car. Ingrid didn't even try to argue.

"It's a surprise," I said as I calculated the best way to reach the road to Ragnar's farm.

Chapter 38

"More trollkrem?"

I tried not to even look at the platter Ragnar was holding, full of those enticing little bowls of frothy pink goodness. I'd had a lot of trollkrem. Also a lot of smultringer—which turned out to be Norwegian doughnuts—sirupsnapper—a lot like ginger snaps—and krumkaker—cookies shaped like miniature ice cream cones and filled with something rather like clotted cream.

Ingrid and Professor Forstner also shook their heads. But Kevin and Lucas both helped themselves to trollkrem. Only one each, though. I glanced around Ragnar's library, where we and a dozen or so other party guests were sitting, sunk so deep in the comfortable and well-cushioned black velvet chairs and sofas that eventually standing up was going to be a real challenge. Several of Ragnar's long-standing house-guests, acting as volunteer waitstaff, were also passing around platters and getting very few takers, not because the Scandi-navian delicacies weren't delicious but because most of us were long past hungry and only a few were still, as the hobbits say, filling in the corners.

"We need to do updates on both of these cases as soon as the chief gives us the okay." Kevin was nibbling rather than inhaling his trollkrem.

"Do them first," Lucas said, pointing his trollkrem spoon at Ingrid and Forstner. "And even when you get to my case, don't count on interviewing me anytime soon. It's one thing if someone like Chief Burke wants to speculate on what he thinks really happened five years ago. But it's probably better for my health if I keep my mouth shut for the time being. Those two creeps he has locked up aren't the only people who might get upset if I tell my version of what happened."

"Understandable," Forstner said. "I, on the other hand, can't wait to set the record straight on what really happened to my friend David. As soon as the chief gives the word, I'm in."

"Yes. It's been too long already." Ingrid glanced at the trollkrem tray that Ragnar was holding out. "*Nei, takk skal du ha,*" she said with a smile, patting her stomach apologetically. I assumed this must be something like "No, thank you" in Norwegian. Ragnar beamed with delight.

"*Alt i orden!*" he exclaimed, and dashed off to dispense lingonberry-flavored goodness to guests who hadn't yet had their fill.

"There you are!" Dad bounced in. The entire front of his clothes was flecked with powdered sugar. Of course, a lot of us were in the same boat. Scandinavian desserts, at least as interpreted by Alice and Mother, seemed to involve a delightful amount of powdered sugar.

"The man of the hour!" I said. "This is my dad," I added to Ingrid—everyone else already knew him. "He's the one who figured out that Professor Bradshaw's death was murder rather than suicide."

"But you're the ones who caught the killers!" Dad beamed around at Forstner, Lucas, Ingrid, and me.

"We wouldn't even have known there were killers to catch if it hadn't been for you," I countered.

"It was a team success." Dad sat down in an open spot on one of the couches. He was holding a plate of something. Rosette cookies, heavily dusted with powdered sugar. He held the plate out in case anyone wanted some, but we all closed our eyes and shook our heads.

Well, except for Kevin and Lucas. And even they only took one each.

Just then the band started up again in the ballroom, and several people raced over to shut the library door. Not that we had anything against Rancid Dread, our local heavy metal band. They'd improved a lot over the years—as I could testify, since I'd been hearing them play since they'd been in middle school. These days, as long as you didn't actually hate heavy metal music, they were reasonably enjoyable to listen to. Especially since when playing at parties like this they let down their hair and played cover versions of a fair number of rock-and-roll oldies. But while they'd gotten better, they hadn't gotten any quieter. I preferred to listen to them from at least one room away.

"We can do some taping tomorrow," Kevin said, raising his voice a little to be heard over what was still a lot of volume. "I'll start with Dad, and—"

Just then the volume of the music jumped up, signaling that someone had opened the library door. We all turned to look—and to make sure the new arrival shut the door behind him—and spotted Chief Burke.

He headed over to where we were sitting.

"They told me I could find you all here," he said.

"Don't tell me," I said. "You want us to come down to the station so you can take our statements."

"No, tomorrow will be fine." He reached into his pocket and pulled out his notebook. "I just wanted to get you all on my schedule." He took a seat and leaned back, pencil poised at the ready.

"Then we can rest assured that you have enough to hold those wretched Vansittart brothers for tonight?" Forstner asked.

"If I hadn't when we arrested them, I certainly would by now." The chief chuckled and shook his head slightly. "They've both been implicating each other nonstop even before we got them down to the station. I could barely get them to shut up long enough to Mirandize them. Of course, they could go back on any or all of that once they talk to their lawyers, but we've got what they said to Meg and Ms. Bjornstrom."

"And what I overheard through Ms. Bjornstrom's window," Lucas put in. "What about Duane Dingle and Jimmy Parrish?"

"They're also proving very eager to assist in our investigations," the chief said, taking a rosette from the plate Dad held out. "They've confessed to the attempted attack on Casey Murakami, by the way. And we'll be turning them over to the state police, who have a keen interest in pursuing their allegations that Mr. Plunkett was framed."

"Not that I'm ungrateful," Lucas said. "But I wish they'd developed a keen interest five years ago."

"Amen," the chief said. "There's no guarantee—you know how witnesses who have something bad to say about the Clay County Sheriff's Department tend to clam up when they get on the stand."

"If they even make it to the stand." Lucas looked glum.

"But we're going to try."

They looked each other in the eye for a few long seconds. Then Lucas held out his hand and the chief shook it firmly.

After that, we sorted out the times when each of us would drop by the police department to give our statements. The chief rose to go, carefully brushing the traces of powdered sugar off of his uniform.

"Ragnar tells me that if I go down to the kitchen, Alice can heat up some kjøttkaker, raspeball, and grovbrød," he said. "Am I going to like that?"

"Meatballs, potato dumplings, and freshly baked brown bread," Dad, an enthusiastic convert to Scandinavian cuisine, had become good at translation.

"And have you ever eaten anything here at Ragnar's that you didn't like?" I asked.

"Good point," the chief said. "I'll see you all tomorrow."

He strolled away and, after a brief burst of noise when he opened the library door, he was gone.

"I hear you're thinking of leaving the business school," Forstner said to Ingrid. "If you're serious, let me know. One of our senior admins is leaving, and you'd be perfect for the job."

"And if their job doesn't suit, call Charlie Gardner," I said. "He says several departments have been trying to lure you away for years."

"Thank you." Ingrid looked flustered. "I am most definitely leaving the business school. Of course, I'll need to give proper notice."

"Whenever you're ready, let us know," Forstner said. And then, as if sensing that Ingrid wasn't keen to discuss her job future this publicly, he turned to Dad. "Did Meg tell you about the cold case I suggested for Kevin and Casey," he asked. "You might like it—it has a medical aspect."

The two of them began discussing the colonial Jamestown murder case. Ingrid listened in with an expression of genuine interest. I turned to Lucas.

"Speaking of jobs," I said. "I may have a one for you."

"I'm pretty happy working for Clarence," he said.

"This would just be a one-time weekend house-sitting gig," I said. "Actually, house- and dog-sitting, with the emphasis on the latter. You can run it by Clarence, but I'm sure he'll approve."

"If he approves." Lucas still looked wary. "If it was for you, I assume you'd have said dog-, chicken-, peacock-, and llama-sitting. So for one of your friends?"

"Yes," I said. "Although she has other animals, too. A couple of middle-aged horses and a flock of chickens on top of about three dozen assorted dogs. Mostly hunting dogs of some kind. Some of them elderly, with special medical needs. She needs someone to take care of them the weekend after next while she goes to an out-of-town family wedding— kind of a problem because all of the nieces and nephews she usually hires for the job are going to the same wedding. She'd expect you to sleep out at the farm, so you could take care of the morning and evening feedings and medications, plus giving them some human company."

"Sounds doable," he said. "I like hunting dogs."

"And if you did a good job taking care of them," I said, "you could probably win over Judge Jane Shiffley's heart.

Which would go a long way toward convincing her to write a recommendation saying that you possess the requisite good character and fitness to qualify for admission to law school and eventually the bar. Even if it takes a long time to overturn your conviction and clear your name."

His jaw fell open, and he just stared at me for a second or two.

"Um . . . yeah," he said. "That would be great."

"She considers dogs better judges of character than most humans," I said. "So if you do right by the dogs, you'll be fine."

"Okay." His face broke into a smile. "Thanks."

Another burst of noise and Kevin dashed in.

"Lucas, come on," he said. "That guy I told you about is here."

Lucas stood up.

"Thanks again," he said, and strode off after Kevin.

I wondered, briefly, what guy Kevin was introducing Lucas to.

I'd worry about it later. Lucas could do worse than hang out with Kevin.

And vice versa.

Suddenly a long arm, clad in a dress shirt rolled up to the elbow, reached across my field of vision and grabbed a rosette.

"Is that the aspiring law school student you want me to mentor?" I looked up to see Festus Hollingsworth at my elbow.

"That's him," I said.

"I notice you didn't tell him Judge Jane might be looking for a permanent critter sitter," he said through a mouthful of rosette. "That furnished apartment over her garage would be quite an improvement over the Armpits."

"I figured we'd take it slow," I said. "Judge Jane knows his situation. If she approves of him—"

"Good idea," Festus said. "But I think it looks promising. And he's got Clarence's endorsement. If he does okay with Judge Jane, you can send him over to talk with me. I can probably find him some work on one of my cases—one of the wrongful conviction appeals. It'll only be legal scut work, but it'll still look good on his law school application."

With that he nodded, grabbed another two rosettes, lifted them as if in a salute, and strolled away.

I sat back and contemplated how things were turning out. Ingrid was almost certainly headed for a happier job situation. Lucas was probably on track for the legal career he wanted. Kevin and Casey were safe, and provided with ample fodder for their next few podcasts. And while the chief might complain that his jail was so full there would be no room for the weekend's DUIs, I knew he was proud of how rapidly he'd cleaned up all the cases that had landed on his plate.

I was probably even entitled to call the Madeleine duPlaine case a modified success. I hadn't solved her murder . . . because she hadn't been murdered. At least not twenty years ago in Charlottesville. Thanks to Jared's connections to the local music world, I'd found that out. And for that matter, thanks to Faulk's suggestion that I enlist Jared and Amanda's help in the first place.

And it occurred to me that I hadn't yet had a chance to tell Faulk what I'd learned about Maddy and share with him the new files of her music that Jared had uncovered.

I pulled out my phone and texted him.

"You here at Ragnar's?"

I sat back and watched a couple of the volunteer waiters circulate with trays of trollkrem and kjøttkaker. A few minutes later Faulk texted back.

"Going deaf here in the ballroom. Where are you?"

"Library."

"Stay put," he said. "I'll be right over."

I leaned back and relaxed, listening to the music and enjoying the knowledge that I didn't have to go anywhere or do anything until tomorrow. Tomorrow would be busy—the interview with the chief, followed by the final wedding rehearsal, and then the rehearsal dinner. But that was tomorrow.

Chapter 39

A blast of louder music announced that someone had arrived. I had closed my eyes and was enjoying the band's cover of Led Zeppelin's "Ramble On." Before I could work up the energy to lift my eyelids, I heard a voice close at hand.

"Diet Coke or daiquiri?

I pondered for a moment

"Frozen?" I asked.

"The daiquiri is. The Coke's just really, really cold."

"Both," I said. "Unless I'd be depriving you."

"I'm fine."

I opened my eyes to see Faulk settled on the sofa opposite me, with his feet up on the coffee table and a beer can in his hand. Not a beer I'd ever heard of, but Faulk was fond of obscure craft beers. Just then another blast of loud music hit us, and I saw one of the volunteer waiters slipping out of the library. The woman with the trollkrem. Just as well.

"How did Charlottesville go?"

I took a sip of the daiquiri and sat up straighter.

"Jared's gotten his hands on three more recordings by Maddy duPlaine," I said. "And yes, I'll send you copies. One was a cover of a Mary Chapin Carpenter song. 'I Was a Bird.'"

"Don't know it offhand, but I look forward to hearing it."

"Which was written in 2010."

Faulk's eyes widened.

"She's alive?"

"She was in 2010," I said. "A lot could have happened since then."

"True." His face fell a little. "But still—she didn't die back then."

"I bet she disappeared of her own free will," I said. "Maybe she thought it was the only way to get rid of her stalker. Or the only way to get rid of her two clueless band members. Or maybe she just didn't want to sign a record contract and get into the rat race of the music industry."

"We'll never know," he said. "But at least she didn't die on my watch. I've always wondered if it was somehow my fault—if there was something I should have noticed or done. This eases my mind a lot."

I nodded and we were both silent for a few minutes. Although it didn't feel like silence, because just then the band began a very creditable cover of "Don't Stop Believin'" and I'd have closed my eyes to listen anyway.

When the song came to its close, I opened my eyes and saw Faulk getting up.

"Band's taking requests," he said. "And Tad wants to dance."

"I'll go with you," I said.

The last time I'd checked, Michael and the boys were giving small children moonlight rides on Ragnar's ponies, but surely it was getting pretty late for the children, if not the ponies. If the band was taking requests, maybe I could lure Michael up to the ballroom and ask for something we knew how to dance to.

I ended up on the terrace, where I could see and hear the band, but once the noise made it through the French doors the open air and landscaping damped it down to a pleasant level. Michael and the boys were stabling the ponies, but promised to join me soon. I sat on the low stone wall that surrounded the terrace and enjoyed the scent of the potted gardenias. About ten feet farther along the wall Cassie, the guitar maker, appeared to be doing the same thing. A serving tray with a few small bowls of trollkrem sat beside her on the wall. I realized that she'd been helping out tonight as part of the waitstaff, although evidently she was very good at being self-effacing, because I hadn't recognized her.

And the band had definitely drifted into a mellow mood. They were doing a series of covers of rock ballads and folk-rock songs, including some that were actually suitable for slow dancing. They were still loud, but it was a normal loud rather than a heavy metal loud, and listening to them here on the terrace was enjoyable.

"He's doing great, isn't he?"

I looked up to see Ragnar standing beside me, beaming at the French doors that led into the ballroom.

"Who?" I asked.

"Willie." Ragnar frowned at me. "I thought you knew Willie."

"The bass player from Charlottesville?"

Ragnar nodded. I got up and strolled over to one of the doors. Yes, Willie was playing with Rancid Dread, giving their usual bass player a chance to grab some trollkrem and krumkaker. And I was astonished at the change in Willie. He still looked happy—I wasn't sure his face was capable of more than a passing frown—but now instead of zoned out, the way he'd looked when playing with Rock's horrible band, he looked tuned in. Energized. Fully engaged.

I strolled back to the edge of the terrace. Ragnar had seated himself beside Cassie on the low stone wall.

"He looks happy," I said. I wanted to say that watching him made me happy, but I decided I didn't need to. Their expressions showed that they already knew that.

"How do you know Willie?" I asked Ragnar.

"We musicians get around," he said.

We all leaned back and listened for a few more minutes.

"He needs a better band," Ragnar said finally.

"Maybe," Cassie said. "Or maybe he just needs a place where he can be happy and make music. Some people don't care all that much about fame and fortune. Not everyone dreams of performing in front of cheering crowds, you know—some people couldn't care less, and a few actually hate the idea."

"I shouldn't try to find him a gig?" Ragnar looked puzzled.

"Why not just let him exist for a while?" she said. "If he stays here he'll probably jam with other musicians. Maybe he'll find some he wants to play with. Maybe after a while he'll start saying he wants to find a new band and you can help him. Or maybe he'll just stay here indefinitely, tending the sheep or pruning the roses or doing whatever other useful work he finds to do when he's not making music for his own enjoyment."

"I don't insist that my guests work," Ragnar said. "They can if they want to—"

"And most of them eventually decide that if they want to stay they should find a way to contribute," Cassie said. "Not because you insist. Because their self-respect does."

"That's true," Ragnar said. "That's usually how it happens. A guest seems to find something they like doing—something that makes them happy. And it makes me happy, too, because then I know they're probably going to stay around for a while."

"What if it's someone you don't really want staying around?" I asked.

"I don't get many of those," Ragnar said. "Somehow people seem to know when Ragnarsholm is right for them."

I nodded.

"Lars took off this morning," Ragnar said in what was probably not a non sequitur. "I think he found it a little quiet out here. But isn't it nice that having him here led to so much good eating?"

Cassie smiled, and lifted up the tray of trollkrem. Ragnar frowned slightly and studied the little glass cups as if it mattered deeply which of them he chose. Someone who'd been standing in one of the French doors moved, and a shaft of light illuminated Cassie's face and the long, graceful hands holding the tray.

Something clicked in my brain and suddenly I wasn't on Ragnar's gardenia-scented terrace but in the Prism's stuffy, un-air-conditioned basement, sipping a watery Coke and gazing across a sea of heads at a tiny stage. Gazing at that smile and those hands—holding a guitar instead of a tray.

I tried to hide my reaction, but Cassie glanced over and spotted it. Just for a moment, she looked alarmed and frowned slightly. But when I didn't say anything and tried to keep my expression normal, she relaxed and smiled again.

Ragnar appeared to have been thinking about something.

"You'll tell me if you think Willie's ready to find a band and I don't notice?" he asked. "Because this sounds like something very subtle, and I'm not good at subtle."

"I promise," she said.

"Good!" Ragnar beamed. "I like Willie. He can stay as long as he wants. He's a good bass player, and people like having him around. He doesn't have to do anything else unless he really wants to. Sometimes making people happy is the most important work."

With that he ambled off, looking cheerful.

Cassie—it was probably better to keep thinking of her as Cassie—gazed at me as if expecting me to say something. I thought about it for a while and decided maybe I would. But I'd keep it low-key.

"Won't it be inconvenient if Willie stays?" I asked finally. "You're already dodging Faulk."

She smiled.

"I don't think Willie would recognize me unless he heard me singing," she said. "Musically, he's amazing—he has perfect pitch, and can play anything if he's heard it even once. But he doesn't pay much attention to anything else. And seems to like everybody, but I actually think he has that condition where you can't recognize people's faces."

"Prosopagnosia." It made sense, remembering how warmly he'd greeted me at Amanda and Jared's house. "You're probably right. Faulk's another matter. You slipped out of the library when he came in."

She nodded.

"He can keep a secret," I said.

"Yes. And I might tell him. Because I'd like to stay. At least for the time being."

"I hope you do," I said. "The boys like you. Speak of the devil."

Josh and Jamie came running over, and I could see Michael striding along behind them.

"Mom, you know Miss Cassie?" Josh asked.

"She says I might have a talent for the guitar," Jamie said. "That maybe I could take lessons."

"I could give him a few, if you like," Cassie said. "See how it goes."

"Does that mean you're staying around?" Jamie asked.

"For now, yes," she said.

"Can we do acoustic *and* electric?" Jamie asked.

"Of course." Cassie smiled at him.

"What about you?" I asked Josh. "Not interested in learning the guitar?"

"Guitar's okay," Josh said. "But I'd rather learn the drums. Ragnar says he can teach me. Can I?"

We could probably find a rehearsal space for drums and electric guitar. In the barn, maybe. Or in whichever shed was farthest from the house.

"You can badger your mother about music lessons tomorrow," Michael said. "The band's finally playing something I recognize." He gave a low, sweeping, theatrical bow. "May I have this dance?"

Chapter 40

Saturday, May 14

"Wasn't it a beautiful wedding?" the aunt said, dabbing at her eyes with a handkerchief.

I agreed that it had indeed been a beautiful wedding, and sipped my lemonade. She proceeded to give me a detailed recap of all the most beautiful parts, as if she'd forgotten I'd been there, front and center, as the matron of honor. I half listened while trying to figure out if she was Aunt Jane or Aunt June. If I were one of a set of identical twins, I'd have given up dressing to match my sister as soon as I had control over my own wardrobe, but here they were, well into their seventies and still looking like bookends. As long as it made them happy, who was I to complain?

Clearly the wedding was having a mellowing effect on me. The wedding, or possibly the fact that we'd now gotten through the rehearsal, the rehearsal dinner, and the wedding itself without any particular mishaps.

Quite a few close calls, but none that couldn't be handled. And Mother hadn't even heard about most of them. Strangely, the several days I'd spent investigating Kevin's cold cases had restored my ability—or was it my motivation?—to perform the combination of crisis management and cat-herding needed to pull off a successful family event.

"They looked so happy there at the altar," Aunt June-or-Jane enthused. Yes, they really had. Just as happy as they had a few months ago when they'd gotten secretly married with only Michael and me as witnesses. Clearly they enjoyed getting married. I wondered if they'd already started making plans for another ceremony. Just after Christmas, perhaps, to celebrate their first anniversary. Maybe they could make it a semiannual event.

And the fact that none of five people in the know had spilled the beans was nothing short of a miracle.

"And that choir!" Aunt Jane-or-June exclaimed.

Yes, the choir had been amazing. And the decorations in the church. And the Reverend Robyn's joyful sermon. I felt a sudden surge of fondness for Aunt June-or-Jane, who wasn't going to ask any of the nosy questions so popular with some other family members. Like how much had this thing cost, and who was paying for it? Did the newlyweds have any plans of finding a place of their own anytime soon? And wasn't the bride's dress looking just a teeny bit tight about the tummy? Both Aunt Jane and Aunt June were perfectly capable of talking a good hour without saying anything original—but also without saying anything mean or catty. And since she demanded nothing from me other than agreement with her enthusiasm, right now talking to her was very restful.

Suddenly a metallic jangling noise rang out. I glanced over at the back stoop to see Rob energetically banging on the triangle dinner bell that hung just outside the back door.

"Attention, everyone!" he shouted. Delaney was standing by his side, and the two of them had that look. The one that suggested they were up to something.

"Everyone," Delaney said. "Rob and I wanted to say a thank-you to the people who made this possible. The people who planned every second of it—our mothers!"

A round of cheers and applause greeted this announcement. When it died down, Rob spoke up.

"And in addition to the mothers, all the friends and relations who helped carry out all those very detailed plans." Rob raised the champagne flute he was holding.

"We owe you." Delaney lifted her champagne. "Big time."

More cheers.

"Seriously," Rob said. "I have second cousins once removed

who did a lot more to make this day possible than I did. By a long shot."

A chorus of more raucous cheers, mingled with a few raspberries, met this statement.

"So Rob and I decided to give you a sneak peek at what you escaped," Delaney said. "What this wedding might have looked like if our mothers and all of the rest of you hadn't pitched in to help and we'd had to do it all ourselves."

"Take it away, guys!" Rob shouted.

From the speakers we'd set up to play music for dancing later on came a string of familiar notes—the first few bars of "Here Comes the Bride"—but played on a solo electric guitar. Soon drums and a bass chimed in. Beyond the crowd I could see Ragnar, Willie, and the woman I was working on thinking of as Cassie rocking out in an inspired—if slightly warped—version of the traditional wedding song.

Jamie appeared around the corner of the house, still wearing the suit he'd worn to the church. He was walking at a slow, stately pace, and most people probably couldn't tell from his solemn expression that he was in serious danger of bursting out laughing.

And was that a bouquet he was holding? No, actually it was a tuft of flowers and ribbons on the end of a braided ribbon lead rope. The other end of the rope was attached to Groucho, the largest of the llamas, who was dressed in an uncanny imitation of the lavender dresses and flowered headpieces that the bridesmaids had worn. And Groucho carried it off splendidly—a lot better than a couple of the less self-assured bridesmaids. Not surprising, actually—Rob and the boys frequently took the llamas to compete in costume contests, and all five llamas had grown very fond of wearing costumes, partly because they loved being the center of attention, and partly because they knew they'd be bribed with many treats both before and after any costume-related activity. Groucho marched along in time to the music, with an expression of great dignity on his face, stepping proudly and gracefully—then suddenly squealed and leaped straight up in the air.

Harpo, who had been following him at the same stately pace, had suddenly dashed forward, lowered his head, and goosed Groucho. It was the llamas' favorite game.

Chico, Gummo, and Zeppo followed behind Harpo. Jamie led them around the circumference of the yard in a slow, stately procession, interrupted every thirty seconds or so by one or more llamas leaping up as if their legs were springs. Even Zeppo, who brought up the rear and wasn't in danger of being goosed, occasionally leaped into the air out of sheer exuberance.

At a safe distance behind Zeppo I spotted Josh. He was leading Tinkerbell, who also wore a flowered wreath on her head. They'd spared her a bridesmaid's dress, though—she only had a ruffle of lavender around her neck. And sitting in a contraption they'd strapped to her back—something like the howdah you'd see atop a camel or elephant—sat Spike. His lavender ruffle had a few toothmarks in it, and he'd knocked his flowered wreath askew so that it had fallen over one eye. He gazed over the crowd with an expression of dignified contempt, as if daring them to laugh at him.

But laugh they did. The laughter almost drowned out "Here Comes the Bride," which was a pity, because Cassie and Ragnar were throwing in wonderful impromptu guitar and drum solos at random intervals.

"But where are the Pomeranians?" I heard someone ask.

I was wondering myself.

Just then the answer turned the corner. Half a dozen peafowl came strutting into the yard—our two, plus a peacock and three peahens from Mother and Dad's farm. Clearly they were still in the middle of molting. The peahens, who were less brightly colored and lacked the dramatic tails, merely looked disheveled and scruffy, as if someone had stuck portions of their plumage in a blender. The two peacocks looked downright disreputable. Hard to say which was more unprepossessing—our poor bird, who'd lost about half the feathers in his tail, making it look thin and faded, or Mother and Dad's bird, who had completely lost all his tailfeathers, leaving him with a tail that looked as if it was made up of only long off-white sticks. But neither peacock seemed to realize that anything was amiss—they continued to preen and shake their mutant tails as if onlookers should still be impressed.

I was surprised at how well-behaved they were, until I realized that they were being herded by all seven of the Pomeranians. Some of the Pom bunch clearly showed that they'd been paying attention to Lad's lessons, while others were still trying to figure it all out, but even the newcomers were obviously learning fast.

I was opening my mouth to say that at least they'd left Mr. Fremont's peacocks out of the procession when a gasp ran through the crowd. McCoy and his three peahens had appeared around the corner of the house. People began backing away and looking around for cover, until they realized that Lad was right behind them, herding them with great efficiency.

And behind Lad, Seth Early and Rose Noire were walking. They were both holding baskets, so at first I thought they were serving as flowerpersons. But the rabble of chickens following them—both our copper-brown Welsummers and our black Sumatrans—revealed that they were actually chucking small amounts of feed on the ground to keep the chickens motivated to follow.

"Thank goodness." Michael appeared at my side. "I thought they were going to make an announcement about you-know-what."

"With luck we'll all manage to keep that to ourselves for the rest of our lives," I said. "Although I'm working on a way of placating Mother if she ever finds out."

"Good luck," Michael said. "And speaking of placating your mother, the boys and I are going to take the borrowed peacocks back to Crozet tomorrow. Want to come along and make it a family expedition?"

"Tomorrow?" I asked. "It sounds lovely, but what's the hurry? Isn't Mother rather expecting us to pitch in with cleaning up and entertaining the visiting relatives?"

"I think she'll give us a pass on cleaning and entertaining if we whisk the peacocks away. She's worried that your father is becoming attached to them. Or that your grandfather is going to requisition them for his zoo. So Seth and Lad are going to come over early to help us get them into the cage, and they'll be halfway across the state before your dad and grandfather notice they're gone."

"And then we'll be back to just our usual peacocks," I said. "Count me in."

Acknowledgments

Thanks once again to everyone at St. Martin's/Minotaur, including (but not limited to) Joe Brosnan, Lily Cronig, Hector DeJean, Nicola Ferguson, Meryl Gross, Paul Hochman, Kayla Janas, Andrew Martin, Sarah Melnyk, and especially my editor, Pete Wolverton. And thanks also to Rowen Davis, David Rotstein, and the Art Department for yet another glorious cover.

More thanks to my agent, Ellen Geiger, and to Matt McGowan and the staff at the Frances Goldin Literary Agency— they take care of the practical stuff so I can focus on the writing.

If I hadn't discovered true crime podcasts as a way to stay sane during quarantine, Meg's nephew Kevin would never have founded Virginia Crime Time, and this book would not exist. Thanks particularly to Nic and the Captain of *True Crime Garage* and James Renner of *The Philosophy of Crime* and *True Crime This Week*.

Many thanks to Per Erik Manne and David C. Niemi for correcting the bits of Norwegian that appear in the book— and if there are any mistakes still remaining, it's on me.

Also thanks to Mark Bergin, retired police officer turned fellow crime writer, who is always ready with good advice on police procedure. If Chief Burke and his department ever get anything wrong, it was probably something I should have asked Mark about.

Many thanks to the friends who brainstorm and critique with me, give me good ideas, or help keep me sane while I'm writing: Stuart, Aidan, and Liam Andrews; Deborah Blake;

Chris Cowan; Ellen Crosby; Kathy Deligianis; Margery Flax; Suzanne Frisbee; John Gilstrap; Barb Goffman; Greg Herren; Joni Langevoort; Alan Orloff; Art Taylor; Robin Templeton; and Dina Willner. And thanks to all the TeaBuds for two decades of friendship.

Above all, thanks to all the readers who make Meg's adventures possible.